FORBIDDEN

Blood Ties Series

A.K. ROSE

ATLAS ROSE

STOP!

Before you take a steep dive off a cliff and down into the darkness I need to make sure you're aware how dark it is. This one is *dark*. Dubcon/noncon, forced proximity, captive, forced O's, insertion, revenge plot, drugging, mind control, degradation/praise ki.nk, forced exhibition, violence....so much violence and touch her and...well, you know what.

Take a breath.
Then another.
You good?
Okay, let's do this.

When hate fucking takes on a whole new meaning.

ONE

Helene

Blinding beams from the oncoming traffic bounced off the heavy downpour, making the headlights a piercing kaleidoscope. I winced and looked away, shaking the rain from my eyes as I stood on the side of the street.

Red, blue, and white sedans were blurs as the traffic flew past. A black sports car splashed through a puddle the downpour had left behind, the deluge instantly soaking my heels. But none were the car I waited for. Not...yet.

Still, he was coming.

The *monster* my sisters were afraid of.

A cold wash of rage ripped through me. Flickers of torture surfaced. Memories of when London St. James had held The Priest captive, beating him bloody to find the Devil himself, Haelstrom Hale.

But The Priest had given us nothing, nor did his brother, the bastard my sisters called The Teacher, Kane Cruz. It was The

Principal we needed. The ruthless sonofabitch who did Hale's sick bidding. He was the one who'd lead us to Hale.

Tonight, he would know who I was.

Because I'd introduce myself in a way he'd remember.

Thunder snarled overhead, pulling my focus back to the plan. I searched the line of traffic. It hadn't been meant to rain tonight...yet, here it was. Almost like fate deemed this would happen, whether I was ready or not.

But what if I couldn't do this?

What if I...failed?

Panic rose. *Think of who this is for.*

Think of Vivienne and Ryth.

Their faces stayed with me. Wide brown eyes that were quick to show anger; blue-green ones, etched deep with fear. I clung to the memories. Real ones this time, not from photos I'd hoarded over the years. But from days ago when my two sisters stood in front of me and I'd told them the truth. A truth I'd waited my entire life to tell them. A truth they'd both taken hard.

I steeled my spine and lifted my hand to stare at my cell.

Even if they hated me right now, they were worth fighting for.

A tiny red marker flickered along the street where I stood. I watched that marker inch toward me until it grew close. Ending that view was more terrifying than what I was about to do. Still, I pressed the button and turned my focus to the dazzling lights. Sparks danced in my eyes as I searched for the steel gray Audi I was here for. The sleek, dark blur hurtled toward me, almost prowling between the lanes of traffic to merge back into the lane closest to the curb.

There. There he is.

My dress flapped as I took a step, fixing my gaze on the street ahead. I knew what I had to do. Rain fell into my eyes, blurring my view. Only I hadn't planned for rain. My heels hit the asphalt and my feet slipped in the sodden shoes. There was no terror now, just a numbness that plunged deep as I tried to resurrect my plan and lunged.

It all felt so *distant.*

The rain.

The traffic.

None of it was real.

Until I fell sideways instead of forward and that hulking blur of steel bore down on me

I turned my head to the dark outline behind the wheel, to the white flash of bared teeth and the wide, unflinching eyes. Tires skidded as the driver hit the brakes, swerving to head straight for me.

But it was too late. Too late to get out of the car's way, too late to stop what was about to happen. I was in fate's hands now... and a monster's.

THUMP!

The impact was brutal.

My feet were snatched out from under me as I was tossed like a feather, my head landing with a *crack* against steel. But I had no time for pain before I pitched forward once more, coming to a stop against the rain-soaked asphalt. A scream sounded, muffled at first before it turned shrill and deafening. I didn't know if it was mine or someone else's. But it never ended, even as the pungent scent of rubber and grease invaded my lungs.

Rain fell into my eyes, forcing me to close them.

Please...

The plea filled me.

The heavy *thud* of footsteps sounded and a dark shadow descended, blocking the headlights. I blinked and tried to lift my head, until agony split my skull.

"Jesus fucking CHRIST!" The deep male roar came above me. *"What the fuck were you thinking?"*

"Oh, my God!" a woman howled, ending that godawful scream. "You just hit her! You just *hit that poor woman.*"

A moan ripped free. That one was mine, deep and choking, until I tasted blood. *Shit, that was hard...fucking rain.* This was no feigning being hit anymore. This was *real.*

"You were speeding." The woman's voice grew in octaves. "I saw you flying around those cars! *Someone call the police!*"

"No," that voice boomed. Then silence. Silence while darkness rose inside my mind to greet me. Silence while the world seemed to slow to a crawl. Silence...until he spoke again. "I'll take her to the hospital myself."

What?

Terror rose.

This wasn't the plan.

This wasn't...

I tried to open my eyes and agony drilled through my skull.

"Just call an amb—" My breath caught as the pain split my head in two.

Strong arms slid under my back and my hips. My head dropped backwards, sending a stabbing wave through my temple.

"Wait," I mumbled as that desolate emptiness grew bolder and darker in my head. *"I said...wait."*

He said nothing, nor did he wait.

Just lifted me from the street and carried me through the night.

Pieces of my memory were snatched away by that rising tide of darkness inside me. My eyes stopped twitching as the rain suddenly slackened. The muffled *thud* of a car door followed, before a dark, masculine scent pushed in with every draw of my breath.

And I couldn't stay awake anymore.

I was falling, slipping into that emptiness, but I fought it.

I shifted in the back seat, pushing against the rich black leather, knowing deep down the car was turning. This wasn't supposed to happen. I was just supposed to glance off the car with barely more than a scratch. An ambulance would be called. Riven Cruz would demand my details, and just like that, I'd have an in.

But not like this.

This was too close.

This was...terrifying.

That pulsing wave pushed deeper. I moaned, fighting to stay awake.

Tires squealed against concrete. We turned again and again and again.

Until we stopped. I forced my eyes open, wincing as that unbearable wave slammed forward time and time again. The engine died. A car door opened and closed. Cold air washed in, stealing that masculine scent away. There was nothing for a second. He was a dark blur to my squinting eyes, standing in the open car door, staring down at me.

Then he bent forward, slid his hands under me once more, and lifted me from the car.

No.

I wanted to demand he put me down and let me go. But my mouth refused to work and the words wouldn't come. Warmth pressed against me. A soft *thud* came from the car door before we moved.

The motion of his body rocked me.

The heavy thud of his steps was the only sound.

He didn't speak, not that I thought he would.

Riven Cruz was a cold, vile sonofabitch.

Hospital.

The word surfaced.

He was taking me to the hospital.

I kept my eyes closed, my mind fading in and out. I faintly became aware of the rush of steel doors, then we were rising, floor after floor, until a faint jolt brought me back once more. I opened my eyes as the elevator doors opened, to see him staring straight ahead.

He looked straight through, not straight ahead.

Through the hallway.

Through everything.

As though he was a ghost.

He didn't even adjust my weight as he stepped along. Gray ate at the edges of my world, forcing me to close my eyes again. Only this time I didn't really surface. That hollowness held me under, holding me captive as only faint sounds registered. Footsteps moved away, then the scrape of a chair.

I breathed in the tang of antiseptic. A sting came in my arm, sharp and cruel. *WAIT!* Panic moved in, unleashing one... single...deafening beat of my heart for only a second, until everything dropped away completely.

There was no fading, no flickers, no...nothing.

Darkness.

That's all that existed.

Until that darkness gently brightened.

My head swam. Sounds were dull and blurred. I moaned and tried to open my eyes, but my lids were so heavy...so *very... heavy*. I blinked and tried again. Colors were fuzzy. White. Gray. Black. The *clink* of a glass sharpened my attention. I inhaled hard, slowly focusing on the man in front of me.

A man I knew.

His head was canted down, staring at me as he lifted a tumbler half full of some kind of Scotch. I could smell the scent of it from here. The room sharpened and colors stayed where they were supposed to be. Especially the dark gray of those eyes fixed on me.

Terror pushed in, snatching away the washed out blur and plunging me into blinding clarity. *Shit...shit.* My mind raced a million miles an hour. I wasn't supposed to be here, not in his apartment. Not *with him, on a* plush, oversized white leather sofa. Silver and black furnishings drew my gaze as I searched for an escape. Outside the floor to ceiling windows, the city sparkled.

Think.

I swallowed, my mind so slow and foggy as I desperately searched for a backup plan...a plan C, now that Plan B had gone to hell. My knees were bent uncomfortably. I shifted, lifting my hands from my side, until a tether snapped, jerking them to a stop. Something pulled on my ankles, biting hard.

I looked down. The room spun when I did that. The view of my bare thighs turned hazy, swimming harder. *Whoa. Easy. Easy.*

But as my vision cleared and the room sharpened, I saw just how much trouble I was in. My hands were tethered on each side of me, strapped to my ankles, in such a way, I could neither lift my arms nor straighten my legs. People didn't do that, not normal people anyway. They *don't do th—*

"Your name."

It wasn't a question, but a demand.

I lifted my gaze. The room shimmered again, then my squint sharpened *on him.*

*My name...my...name...*my stomach rolled as I tried to remember what the hell had just happened. The car...the rain... the *goddamn rain.* I opened my mouth to speak but my tongue was slow to work.

"Helene," I slurred. "Helene." *King.* "Montgomery."

"Helene Montgomery." He rolled the name around on the tip of his tongue and took a swallow, watching me with that stare that looked right through me.

He was waiting.

Waiting for me to panic.

To start screaming and pulling at the tethers around my wrists.

My dress was hitched up around my waist, my knees open and my panties on full display.

He looked at them...no, not looked. *He stared.* My body recoiled and muscles inside clenched tight.

"You stepped out in front of my car." He lifted his gaze to mine. "Where were you going?"

Lies blended with reality. I licked my lips. "On a date."

"A date." His gaze returned to my panties. "They say if a man takes a woman home and she's wearing matching underwear, it was she who decided to have sex that night."

He moved to the side of where I sat and reached out, slid his finger under the strap of my black dress, and dragged it down, revealing my mocha brown lace bra, the one that matched my panties.

I lifted my gaze to his. He was still waiting for me to crack, wasn't he? Pushing me to find out just how much terror I'd endure. I held that stare defiantly. He tugged harder, exposing the tops of my full breasts and the raised pink slash of a scar.

My scars.

I swallowed hard. My milky white thighs parted, the scars on them still hidden from view. But all it'd take would be one tug of my dress and he'd see.

Please, God.

Don't let him see.

There was a tiny scowl, a pinching between his brows.

I wasn't reacting like he expected me to react.

"On a date," he said carefully. "With whom?"

Whom?

I licked my arid lips. My mind raced, pulling a name from thin air. "Michael DiAngelo."

A twitch came at the corner of his eye. He fixed that cold stare on mine. "Michael Di Angelo," he repeated, his voice deepening. "And what does Michael DiAngelo do for a living?"

My breaths raced. "He's a...he's an elementary school teacher."

He looked down at the tops of my breasts. "And was this your first date?"

I swallowed hard. *No. No more twenty fucking questions.*

"Was this your first date?" he growled, baring his teeth.

Memories of that second before the accident came rushing back. He was a dark blur...a dark blur that curled his lips like an animal.

A monster. That's how my sisters had described him.

They were right.

Riven Cruz was a predator and right now I was his prey.

My pulse skipped and sped. The tethers jerked tight as I yanked. "Undo my hands."

He turned and walked away, disappearing behind me. I twisted on the seat, desperately trying to look behind me, until that agony roared back to life. I let out a moan and closed my eyes. Still, panic thundered, blending with the muffled sound of his steps.

I opened them once more, finding him next to me. Only, in his hand was a syringe. He met my gaze as he pressed the tip of the needle to my arm.

"No...NO!" I bucked.

But it was useless.

The sting came.

The plunger pushed all the way to the end.

I stared helplessly as that darkness moved in.

"I'm afraid you won't be making your date, Helene Montgomery." The Principal murmured. "Tonight, or any night for that matter."

TWO

Riven

SHE DIDN'T SCREAM. I LOOKED DOWN AS HER EYES fluttered closed and a slow, soft exhale came from her parted lips.

My hand clenched around the syringe, my finger still poised over the plunger, like the trigger of a gun. I watched her for a second before I turned and walked into the kitchen, placing it down on the cloth next to the sedative.

She didn't scream.

That nagging thought made me turn my head.

Thick brown curls spilled down the arm of the sofa she lay on. My pulse gave a heavy *thud*. I wanted to tell myself it was fear that triggered the response. But it wasn't. It was more than that.

Trouble.

I inhaled.

That's what she was.

One I needed to get rid of.

Only...that fucking woman. A twitch came at the corner of my eye. *I saw you flying around those cars! Someone call the police!* My breaths deepened as that fucking bitch's screams came back to me. I could kill her. My focus sharpened on the woman lying on my sofa, Helene Montgomery, and the one from the accident. I could kill them both and get rid of this *problem*.

My mind raced, trying to remember who else was around us. But I couldn't quite piece it together. Was there a crowd? I stilled, scowling. Maybe? *Fuck*. If there was a crowd, I couldn't very well take them out. One missing report on the goddamn six o'clock news would bring too much heat.

Heat I didn't need.

Not right now.

I glanced back at her.

She was trouble. No matter how I looked at it.

Still, she didn't scream.

I moved before I knew it, leaving the needle behind to return to her. The strap of her dress was pulled down, the tops of her creamy breasts exposed. I stared at them before forcing myself to look away.

Memories slammed into me.

Breasts.

Mouths.

The Daughters' bodies on full display.

Revulsion filled me, but still I turned back to her, to that raised pink line that cut across the soft white flesh. She was...*imperfect* and nothing like the women I'd tortured. But she could be, couldn't she? She could very well be. An eerie feeling came to life as I stared at her. She was familiar, like somehow I'd seen her before. But I couldn't have, because I *never* forgot a face.

My breaths deepened as my focus fixed on that jagged line. One that reached all the way down to...

I leaned over and tugged the dress down until her breast spilled out. Her dusky pink nipple was smooth. So damn enticing. Without thinking, I reached out, grazing my thumb across the satin flesh. Her body reacted, tightening under my touch. I flicked my gaze to her closed eyes.

There was no twitch behind her lids and no change in her breaths. She was still under, still...

I shifted my focus to that tiny pebbled thing and leaned over. Helene Montgomery was out cold and vulnerable. So I could do anything I wanted. But it wasn't her nipple I licked. It was that tight, raised pink line. The one that excited me for some sinister reason.

She was ruined anyway, wasn't she? I closed my eyes as my tongue hit her skin; the tip tracing the line that dipped into the valley between her breasts before I pulled backwards and licked her nipple. So what was a little more destruction?

Soft.

Warm.

Unconscious.

Not screaming or wailing or fighting me every inch of the way. This one was all...*mine*. Mine to do anything I wanted. My own private *plaything*. A surge of excitement slowly rose.

I gripped her breast and clenched, driving that warmth deeper into my mouth. My tongue circled, teeth grazed hard. I sucked and licked, incensed with this sick depravity when her peak grew tight. Warmth flooded me. My body tightened and my cock grew hard, stiffening until I jerked my head away.

I wrenched my hand away and stumbled backwards, wiping my mouth as though she was poison.

I swallowed hard and stared at her.

Poison...I liked.

What the fuck was I doing? My mind raced as it all hit home. A woman I'd abducted and now drugged was in my living room, leaving behind who knew how many bystanders who'd watched it all. Not to mention I didn't know who the fuck was missing her.

I raked my fingers through my hair. All I'd need would be one fucking text from Hale and my world would come crashing down.

If he was alive.

No. I shook my head. Not *if*.

He *was*.

I knew it...and so did that sonofabitch, London St. James.

It was the only reason we were still alive. If he'd believed otherwise, St. James would've put a bullet in my brother's head and mine in that goddamn warehouse.

A warehouse I'd gone to just to save my brother. A shiver ripped through me. A trip where I'd almost met my fate...and left my sister's in the hands of a fucking monster. If I died, if *any* of us died, it'd be all for nothing.

Beep.

I wrenched my gaze to the phone on the counter, then moved. My heart was pounding as I snatched it and looked at the screen.

Kane: He's awake. We need you at the rectory in 30 minutes.

It wasn't Hale. I slowly exhaled. No communication was just as fucking terrifying as him reaching out from beyond the grave.

I typed back. *Confirmed.*

Then I slowly turned my head to the unconscious woman in my apartment. I needed to do something about her. But what?

Beep.

I looked down.

Kane: Bring more drugs and guns.

War was coming, one I wasn't prepared for because we didn't have a side we stood on. *No.* We stood on our own. I turned and headed for my bedroom, then flicked on the light in the bathroom.

Sparse.

Empty.

Stark white tiles made me wince as I strode to the vanity and yanked open the mirrored cabinet door. Bottles and bottles of drugs lined the shelves, enough to start a small clinic. I turned to glance over my shoulder—or knock out a woman I had in my home.

Right now, my brother needed them. I grabbed what I could, as well as fresh needles and more bandages and antiseptic, gathering it all in my arms. Glass bottles clinked as I tossed them on the bed before I went to my closet and grabbed a black pack and loaded them all inside. Guns were next, some of the ones hidden behind the wall in my bedroom. Just one of the many stashes I had throughout the apartment.

I grabbed as many as I could, securing them and a lot of loaded magazines into the bag, and headed out. I never looked back when I pulled the door closed, just headed for the elevator, glancing at the locked stairwell door that I held the only key for. I pressed the code into the keypad and waited for the elevator. The penthouse was as secure as any locked room at The Order. One way in and *no way out.*

The doors opened with a swoosh, so I stepped in and headed for the garage.

Why hadn't she screamed?

The thought nagged at me as the elevator jolted to a stop and the doors opened. I stepped out and headed to my Audi parked just outside the access door. Lights flashed as I pressed the key fob, opened the door, and stowed the bag inside. But I didn't climb behind the wheel, not yet. I moved around to the front to check the grill and the bumper. There was barely a scratch... almost like it'd never happened.

My gaze went to the elevator. I fought the need to go back up there, to make sure she wasn't some figment of my sick imagination. I licked my lips and could still taste the faint trace of her perfume. No, she was no illusion. She was very...very real.

The heavy thud of my pulse came louder before I turned, pulled open the driver's door, and climbed in behind the wheel. She would have to wait. I started the car and pulled out of the almost empty garage, heading back onto the city streets.

The rectory.

I'd told them not to go there.

But did they listen?

No.

They didn't.

Just like I'd told them to clear out and lie low until we got confirmation about Hale's whereabouts. Because we *needed* that confirmation. One fucking message. That's all it'd take. One more lead. One more opportunity.

Because he was still out there.

I drove the back streets, watching the rear-view mirror the whole way, and turned at the towering sandstone structure of St. Augustine's Church. My brother's black Mercedes was parked across the driveway to the rectory out back. I clenched my jaw, then pulled in behind it and killed the engine.

"Idiots," I muttered as I climbed out, grabbed the bag, and headed for the door. One hard *thud* while I snapped. "It's me."

The heavy locks opened with a *clunk* before the door cracked open. I pushed inside, not giving a fuck when the door smacked into Kane's arm. He fucking deserved that and a lot more. "Where is he?"

"In the back," my brother snarled, pissed.

Good.

That made two of us.

The place was barely big enough to swing a damn cat. I headed along the cramped hallway to the single bedroom in the back. Muted yellow lights barely made a dent in the darkness, but it was enough to see the curled figure on the bed. If it hadn't been, the wet, labored breathing sounds were enough to draw my gaze.

"Has he woken up?" Glass clattered as I dropped the bag to the bed.

"Once or twice."

"Has he said anything?" I yanked open the bag and rifled through the bottles.

"You mean apart from *he's sorry?*"

I said nothing. What good was fucking sorry? That wouldn't get us what we wanted. A gurgling moan came from the hunched over form in front of me. Slowly my brother turned his head, his blood-shot gaze finding me.

"You look like shit." I pulled out a vial of antibiotics and a syringe.

"Thanks," he moaned. "Motherfucker St. James."

"No, *motherfucker you,*" I snapped as I plunged the needle into the vial and pulled the plunger back.

I was always cleaning up their goddamn messes, one way or another.

Her face rose instantly. Wide brown eyes fixed on mine.

Creamy skin.

The pink scar line.

Knocked out cold in my apartment.

I froze, my focus on the filled syringe.

"What is it?" Kane asked.

"Nothing." I pulled out the needle and turned to Thomas, yanked down the sheet and stabbed my brother in the thigh.

He hissed as I plunged it deep and shot him full of antibiotics. The painkiller was next before I tugged down the dressing on his other thigh and checked the bullet wound that motherfucker St. James had left behind.

"Any word?" Kane asked.

"From who?"

"Both."

I shook my head, tugged the dressing back in place, and lifted my gaze. "No." I straightened. "But you need to get this shit cleaned up. We need to be ready. If he's gone to ground, then that means there's another facility we don't know about."

"There isn't," Kane muttered, looking down as Thomas' eyes fluttered closed from the drug. "There can't be."

"He's gone somewhere, hasn't he?"

Kane scowled, thinking.

But there wasn't a damn scenario I hadn't considered.

"The bodies."

"Being disposed of."

He looked at me. "You're back there?"

"I don't really have a choice now, do I?"

I was still playing the part, still a fucking lackey for Hale's games, and while I fulfilled my role of pretense, I scoured every inch of that place for a lead I could use. A lead the Hunter was waiting for. A lead we *all* were waiting for.

"You'll keep us updated if anything happens."

That didn't sound like a question. *He means like drugging a woman and keeping her in my home, because that happened.* I swallowed, my pulse kicking in my chest as the memory of her came to life. I gave a nod. "Yes. There are guns and drugs in the bag. Make sure he keeps up the fluids. I'll check in tomorrow, right now..." *I have a plaything to attend to.* "I need to sleep."

"Got it."

I glanced at sleeping Thomas one last time before heading for the door. I couldn't get out of there fast enough, leaving the door open as I headed for my car. The door thudded closed before the engine growled to life and I was pulling out of there.

You didn't tell them.

Why didn't you tell them?

That nagging voice demanded.

I spun the wheel and accelerated, heading back the way I'd come. Because...because she wasn't real, was she?

No.

She wasn't.

I pushed the car harder, speeding through the streets until the towering apartment building rose in sight. A surge of adrenaline hit me hard as I tapped the brakes and pulled up to the boom barrier. I stabbed the button, all but slamming the car against the scanner as I pulled up.

"Come *on*," I snapped as the gate gave a shudder, then a jerk, and finally rose.

I'd fucking told them to fix the damn thing. I punched the accelerator and surged through. Thoughts of the woman surfaced. Was she gone? Was she awake and tearing apart my goddamn apartment? I glanced at the clock. I hadn't been gone that long.

An hour.

I spun the wheel and raced for the parking space. I was out in an instant, slamming the door closed behind me and throwing out my hand to hit the button as I headed for the doors, my long stride eating the distance.

"Mr. Cruz!" Vernon called, stepping out from around the front desk.

My cheeks burned. Was this about *her?* The woman in my apartment? The elevator doors opened. "Not now," I answered over my shoulder, stepped inside, and hit the button, ending his view as the doors closed between us.

My heart was pounding as I rose.

A hard inhale sent a rush of cool air into my lungs. I focused on my breaths, slowing them down as the lights above the door counted to the penthouse. It fucking took forever. My jaw clenched when the damn thing shuddered to a stop.

I was already moving, banging my shoulder against the door to get out. My front door was in my sights. I stabbed in the code, threw the door open wide, and stepped inside.

She was still there.

Her knees bent.

Head dropped backwards.

I slowly closed the door behind me and moved in, drawn to her like a moth to the flame. Only I wasn't a moth, was I? I was a monster. A cold. Cruel. Monster. Who liked the idea of having her—I moved closer, stopped in front of the sofa, and looked down at her—maybe a little too much.

Her lips were parted, her breast still exposed. I could almost taste her skin. Almost feel that warmth under my tongue. I lowered my gaze to her brown lace panties and her wrists tethered to her ankles. It was a cruel position.

An *exposed* position.

One I very much enjoyed.

I reached out, brushed my hand against her knee, and gave a jerk, opening her thighs wider. I wanted in there. In the warmth. Invading her like the bastard I truly was. My pulse thudded louder. I wanted to spread her open. Lay her bare. My focus shifted to an imperfection...to a cruel silver slash.

"What the fuck?" I bent down, pushing her legs wider, to the criss-cross pattern high on her thigh.

The cuts were so fine. Razor fine.

I jerked my gaze to her closed eyes. She'd cut herself. There was no other reason for that. I returned my eyes to the thin, straight line. With a razor, no doubt. I lifted my gaze to her dress, hugging the outline of her body. A dress she'd worn for him.

Jealousy tore through me.

I was jealous of that man I didn't know. Of that...*Michael DiAngelo.*

He didn't deserve a woman like her. Her scars called me. Ruined. Tortured. I reached out, brushing her crumpled dress higher until the tops of her panties were exposed. Then without thinking, I grabbed the gathered dress, yanked it up with one hand, and lifted her thigh with the other, tearing it until I slid it over her breasts, before I tossed it.

Her body was savaged.

I searched for the injuries sustained in the accident but they were minor, a scrape, the redness that'd no doubt become a bruise. It seemed her concussion had been the worst of it. But it was her previous wounds which held me transfixed. A deep, freshly healed wound on her side that was more savage than a razor could leave behind. Then another scar under that. The neat hole was one I knew all too well...a bullet.

I stared at them as the floor seemed to drop out from under me.

This was no woman.

This was...*fate.*

THREE

Helene

Cold plunged deep inside, unleashing a trail of goosebumps that raced down my spine.

"Don't fight it," a command followed. "You don't want to tear this beautiful cunt apart now, do you?"

That icy sensation pushed wider and wider and wider until a ratcheting sound came.

"So...fucking ruined." His voice sharpened in my ear. "Unlike anything I've ever seen before."

A voice I knew.

A voice I feared.

My lids fluttered open.

"I can't stop thinking about you, Helene Montgomery. Can't seem to get you out of my head," he murmured. "And that is a *very* dangerous place to be."

Pressure came between my legs. Cold pushed in...cold where there shouldn't be any.

"You shouldn't have stepped out in front of my car. Shouldn't have...*let me see you.*"

Wake up now, Helene...wake all the fuck up! That faint voice in my head grew louder.

I sucked in a breath, fighting that blanket of emptiness that weighed me down.

Thick strands of russet brown hair were all I saw. His head was bent. Warmth licked my nipple, drawing it in sharply. A pinch followed, tearing a moan from the back of my throat. It wasn't until he moved that I understood.

He was fucking me.

No...he was...

He froze, released my peak from his mouth, and slowly lifted his head. "No one knows you're here, only me."

Terror roared to the surface. I bucked, yanking the binding around my ankles, desperately driving my hips into the air. But my thighs were splayed wide and something was wedged inside me. Something he pushed in deep, gaping me open even more. I inhaled a breath and parted my lips to scream.

He moved fast, smothering the sound with his hand. "You want to scream?" Those cruel eyes bored into mine. "Go ahead. I like the sound muffled against my hand."

I tried to fight. Tried to *think.*

Had he raped me?

It was the only thing that surfaced.

Had he?

I pushed the question away, trying to slow my out-of-control breaths. The last thing I needed was to faint. I fixed on him instead as he turned his head and looked down. My dress was gone, my bra and panties along with it. My knees were splayed wide, and I was completely bare. He saw it all—a hitch came in my breath—he saw *everything*.

"Your scars." He shifted his hand, turning it to grip both sides of my mouth. "Tell me about them."

"Let me go," I roared, but my words were brittle and broken.

Please.

That's what I really wanted to say.

Please, let me go. Please, don't do this.

It took all my strength not to beg.

"You don't want to tell me?" He trailed his fingers over my breast, then down my body. "That's fine. I'll trace them with my tongue, let them tell me themselves. How about that?"

My body clenched with the words. I looked down at my thighs splayed wide. "Get that *thing* out of me."

His hand moved lower, to the top of my pussy and slid down.

I closed my eyes as a shiver tore through my core. Reflex made me fight, desperately yanking the tethers around my wrists as his thumb found my clit.

My pussy clenched. That cold inside me was so raw.

"That man...Michael DiAngelo. Were you planning on having sex with him?"

Who?

My mind struggled to catch up, taking far too long to resurrect the lie. What else had I said? I tried to remember, but I was dragged back to how that voice, so devoid of emotion, made my pulse quicken.

Desire rose. Sick, corrupt desire. I tried to yank my knees together and dislodge his sickening touch. "Get *the fuck off me!*" I screamed, wrenching my head away.

His cruel grip smashed my lips against my teeth, forcing my gaze back to his. Those dark gray eyes twinkled, incensed with madness. "Were *YOU planning on having sex with him?*"

"*YES!*" I screamed, tasting blood. "*YES, I WAS GOING TO HAVE SEX WITH HIM!*"

His jaw flexed, his lips curled. His breaths were far too fast for him to be in control. He was violent at that moment. Violent, terrifying...and mesmerizing all at the same time.

For some terrifying reason, I couldn't look away.

"Then let it be me instead."

What?

He lowered his hand, grasped my throat, and clenched as he rubbed my clit, pinching the nub until I bucked and twisted, unleashing a scream. One that set the back of my throat on fire.

"Scream all you want." His grip slammed me against the back of the sofa. "No one can hear you."

Heat and power radiated from his touch. He circled gently now, slowly sliding both fingers to either side. The more I fought…the more I felt him. The way he pressed his body against me. The way his hand never squeezed too hard.

Just enough.

Enough for him to thrust his hips against me, still fully clothed.

Enough for him to slide his fingers lower until they slipped over that *thing* inside me.

"Need to get you out of my head, Helene Montgomery." He plunged his fingers inside. "And back in the game."

White stars ignited behind my eyes. *"No!"* I howled. But it was more than a moan. A moan that came once more. *"No…."*

"You're *trouble*," he groaned against my ear, thrusting his hips against me. His hold around my neck was more of a caress. "Trouble I need out of my system."

I bucked harder, driving his fingers deep.

My body betrayed me, sending an ache deep.

"Fight all you want, but you're fucking wet. You want to be owned. You want to be used. You're just a *thing* for me. A tight cunt I splay wide. I could force the toe of my shoe inside and you'd fucking come. Wouldn't you?"

He pushed two fingers over that thing. His thumb flicked my clit.

I closed my eyes, shaking my head and unleashed a tortured sound.

"Go on. Beg."

Tilted hips made him *rub*.

I squeezed my eyes closed and the grinding of my hips slowed.

"Eyes on me," he commanded.

That voice.

That fucking voice.

"Now."

I forced my eyes open, meeting his.

His lips curled, the smile bitter.

"Good girl."

My body clenched with the words, and he felt it. That callous smile grew wider. He looked away, slid his fingers out, and that ratcheting sound released, letting my body tighten.

"Now come for me, Helene Montgomery," he demanded, thrusting his fingers back in.

I shook my head, my body clenching around his fingers.

"Obedient fucking slut." He pulled away, leaving his grip around my throat until the last possible moment as he rose.

Then he released me, letting a rush of air plunge deep. I shook my head as he stepped in front of me, then sank to his knees.

He lowered his gaze to between my legs. "Elementary school teacher." He spat the words as though he was offended. "Fuck that."

I slammed my heels down, driving my body back against the sofa arm to get away. But he grabbed my thighs, dragging me back down.

"No...NO!"

He forced my knees apart and lowered his head, licking my scars before he closed his mouth over my pussy.

The fight was snatched away from me.

His tongue pushed in.

He was so gentle.

And so fucking good.

He lifted those eyes to mine and opened his mouth wider, eating me out.

Elementary school teacher.

Tears blurred his face as my knees dropped wider. But it wasn't under his control anymore. *It was mine.*

That ache rose, making me tug on those bonds. He circled my clit with his thumb and sucked, drawing that terrifying hunger closer. Throat muscles worked as he swallowed.

His lips glistened as he lifted his head, that relentless thumb making me moan and meet his thrust. "That's a good fucking girl," he said, splaying my pussy wide before thrusting two fingers in deep. "You want to be wined and dined, or you want to be grabbed around the throat and fucked within an inch of your life?"

My core clenched as he thrust harder.

Using me brutally.

I arched my spine.

Hating him.

Hating him...

"Just a nobody," he grunted. "A nobody who likes to come all over my fucking sofa. Go on, nobody. Make a mess all over me."

"*Pl-*" I whimpered, my head twisting frantically under those merciless thrusts. "*Please!*"

"Come *for ME!*" he bellowed.

White sparks exploded behind my eyes as my hips slammed upwards. He met those thrusts with his mouth, his tongue pushing in, making me clamp my thighs around his head.

My clit pulsed and my core clenched. I grasped the tethers, driving my breasts upwards.

A lick came along my slit before he lifted his head.

I sucked in panting breaths, coming back to reality.

Monster.

My sisters' words rose.

He's a monster.

He gave his mouth a swipe of his hand and rose, looking down at me with a possessive stare, before he reached down and gently pulled the speculum from inside me. "Michael DiAngelo wouldn't have a clue what to do with a thing like you."

I winced as my body clamped down. "Fuck *you.*"

He scowled, sucking in a hard breath. My gaze lowered to the tented, thick bulge in his pants. The sight of that slammed into me, making my body tighten once more. I forced my gaze away, clinging to that hate.

Thump!

The blow came from the door.

I wrenched my gaze toward the sound a second before he did.

Beep.

Came from a phone somewhere behind me.

He moved fast, striding around the sofa.

Thump. Thump.

The insistent blows came at the door. Terror plunged into me. I yanked the bindings as soon as his head turned away from me. As he strode around the sofa arm, the screen of his cell was still alight. I caught the message as he headed toward the door.

Unknown: Answer it. H.

H.

H?

It had to be Hale.

It had to be.

I shook my head. "No."

But it was too late as he reached for the handle and opened the door.

It was pushed inward. Two men dressed in white plastic coveralls moved in without saying a word. They didn't notice me, not at first. One placed a bag down onto the floor, then straightened.

He froze when he saw me. Then Riven turned his head, following that stare to me.

"What the fuck?" the cleaner muttered, glancing back at the man called The Principal. But it wasn't terror or confusion in his gaze. It was anger.

There was a curl of his lips and a flare of satisfaction in his eyes. He grabbed his cell and lifted it, his fingers moving across the screen.

"What are you doing?" Riven demanded.

The cleaner never answered.

Seconds slowed. The *thud* of my heartbeat was suspended as everything moved in slow motion. Riven turned, finding me still naked and tied up. There was a flicker of rage in his eyes, an explosion that seemed to gather momentum as he turned back to the cleaner that was typing on his cell.

A roar came.

Savage and terrifying.

Riven dropped his cell and lunged, slamming into the man sent to wipe any trace of him from this place. The cell was knocked from the cleaner's hand and sent flying, clattered to the floor, and hit against the sofa I was tethered on.

Thud.

Thud.

Screams followed, But not Riven's as he pushed his thumbs into the cleaner's eyes.

The other man with him stood frozen.

"Untie me!" I screamed. *"NOW!"*

But he didn't. He just stumbled backwards, then turned for the open door.

Thump.

Thump.

CRACK!

I slowly turned my head, aware of the thunder of footsteps out in the hallway. Riven straightened. His fingers, that seconds ago had been coated with my come, were now covered with blood. A scream of desperation came from outside the door.

Riven just turned and strode toward the door, stopping to reach behind a cabinet and pull a gun free before striding out of the apartment. The booming of my pulse smothered the sounds...

Until. *"No...No! NO!"*

Crack!

A shot sounded, leaving nothing but emptiness behind. Terrifying emptiness.

Slowly, Riven walked back inside. He never looked at me as he walked to where I lay, just bent in front of me and grabbed the cell from the floor. Flecks of blood covered his face, macabre and breathtaking. He pressed the button on the phone, scowled, then lifted the gun.

No!

I waited for the muzzle to aim at my head. But it didn't. He just turned and hurled the phone across the room.

"Shit!" he roared. *"SHIT!"*

I jumped at the sound. He retrieved his own cell, his frantic fingers moving over the screen until he lifted it to his ear. "It's me. We have a problem. I received a message. Yes...yes and no."

Only then did he lower his gaze, those cruel eyes meeting mine. "Cleaners were sent here. No, because I killed them. Yes...yes, that's right. I don't know. I'll make some calls, find out what I can. You need to get ready to move. Yes, *now*."

He lowered the cell and ended the call.

His silence was more terrifying than his screams.

"I said you were trouble," he said finally as he stepped back around the sofa, disappearing from view.

Only when he stepped back around, he carried a syringe and a vial.

One I'd felt the sting of too many times.

"No!" I bucked as he lifted the vial, piercing it with the tip of the needle. "*NO!*"

He gripped my arm, holding me as he leaned down.

I reacted on instinct, drew my head backwards, and with a scream, threw my head forward, slamming into his.

He stumbled backwards, his eyes widening as his knees buckled. I flung myself sideways to fall from the sofa onto the floor.

A low moan came from him as I jerked my gaze to the bag sitting on the floor, then inched toward it. My ass skidded against the tiles before I yanked the bag, toppling it on its side. A knife spilled free, clattering to rest near my hand.

"Get the fuck back here," Riven warned.

I didn't stop, just grabbed the knife and yanked it against the tether on my right side, slicing it in two. My left side was next. I scanned the contents of the bag as I yanked the tethers loose. But there was no gun. Just the knife, tape, and some tools. I gripped the knife and shoved against the floor, lunging for the open door.

"*No!*" Riven roared.

Panic filled me as I stumbled, my feet slow to move.

Blood splattered the closed elevator doors. The dead cleaner lay on his back, arms out wide. I jerked my gaze to the keypad outside the elevator, a keypad that needed a code for me to access.

Fuck!

I spun, scanning the rest of the empty hall that ended on the other side of the building, then narrowed in on the fire exit... one that had a lock. *SHIT!* I lunged, my mind racing.

Red.

Red against white.

I jerked my gaze to the fire extinguisher hanging on the wall as a low, deafening roar came.

Move! I lunged forward, slowing just enough to grasp the heavy metal canister and yanked it from the wall.

An ache tore through my side. The wounds from the bomb blast were still healing. But I didn't care about that now, just lifted the heavy steel canister over my head as I raced for the door.

I could hear his steps and his jagged breathing bearing down on me.

A mewl ripped free, my elbows trembling, still weak with the drugs as I smashed the extinguisher down with all my weight... snapping the lock.

Boom!

The canister hit the floor as I yanked the now busted lock, tearing it free, and the door swung open. Darkness waited, darkness and an empty stairwell.

I didn't look back, just plunged inside.

And prayed.

FOUR

Riven

A ROAR RIPPED FREE AS I SURFACED. BLOODY, SEARING...
and terrifying.

Crack!

The hollow sound ripped through my head like the blow of a
fist kissed with steel. I shoved against the floor, the white tiles
blurring before they sharpened. Blood. Bodies. *Her.*

Reality slammed into me hard.

I rose to my feet, looking past the dead cleaner splayed out on
my floor, then I moved, snatching my cell from the end table
before stumbling to the doorway. At the far end of the hallway,
she dropped the extinguisher with a deafening *CLANG* and
tore the broken lock from the stairwell door. Then she was
gone, hurtling into the darkness, leaving me behind.

No...

NO!

I stumbled, slamming my hand against the doorframe of my apartment, and charged after her. There was no room for thinking anymore. Now some other sick need was in control.

All I saw was that open stairwell door as I ran past the dead body of the second cleaner. Still, reality pushed in...and with it came the text from an unknown number. One initialed with an H.

It was Hale.

It had to be.

Calling me to heel.

But there were never just two guys sent to wipe someone and their records from existence, were there? No. There were *never* just two.

There were more coming.

I flinched as the rage brought blinding clarity.

No...there were more here.

They'll kill her.

They'll kill...*Helene Montgomery.*

I threw the door wider and plunged into the gloom, throwing my hand out to grasp the railing. The faint, frantic slaps of her bare feet only seemed to incite that strange hunger. I plunged down the stairs as below me the spill of light followed the howl of hinges.

She was escaping.

She was—

I didn't run. I hurled myself downward, taking the stairs three and four at a time until I slammed my shoulder against the cracked open door.

She was there in front of the elevator, her arms wrapped around her naked body.

Ding.

The sound of the elevator followed. I lunged as the door opened and she leaped inside.

"Come on!" she howled as she frantically stabbed the button. *Tap...tap...tap...TAP.*

My boots slammed into the floor as I ran, and in the distance the elevator doors closed.

I was going to lose her...

I was *going to lose her!* I lunged, desperately driving my hand out for it to be crushed. Agony came, shooting through my knuckles as the doors slowly opened.

"No...NO!" she shrieked, stumbling backwards until she slammed against the wall.

I sucked in hard breaths and slowly stepped inside, turning my head to press the button and close the doors. "Now..." my breaths were an inferno. "How is that any way to treat your host?"

"You *bastard!*" She lunged, swinging her fist in a perfect damn hook...*if it had landed.*

But there was no room to move. Not for her, at least. I grabbed her wrist and stepped forward, driving her against the cold steel wall as we descended. "I *am* a bastard, Helene. I am *the* bastard. The one you'll cower from. The one you'll scream for."

Faintly, I realized just how fast we were moving...and how warm her body was against mine. I reached between us, her breasts brushing my arm. Fuck if my cock didn't twitch with the touch. Still, I worked the buttons of my shirt, then yanked. "You *will* put this on."

She worked her mouth, then threw her head forward and spit in my face.

Spittle dribbled down my cheek as I clenched my jaw. My hard breaths were savage. But I kept control, driving her hand over her head and forced myself against her.

"You want to spit on me, Helene?"

She writhed, trying to get away as I lowered my head. "I could fuck you right now. You do realize that, don't you? I'm hard enough. I bet you're still wet, too. I could drive into your soft cunt, bury myself deep. I bet you wouldn't even fight me...after a while."

She stiffened with the words, then lifted her gaze to mine. "Go ahead and I'll cut that cock off and shove it down your throat."

Boom.

Boom.

BOOM!

My heart pounded with the threat. I grew hard at the rage in her eyes. She wasn't just any woman. No, Helene Montgomery was a survivor. I licked my lips. That need bellowed inside me. I wanted her. I wanted her more than I'd ever wanted any other woman before.

But the elevator thudded to a stop.

I stepped backwards, yanking her with me, and shoved her hand into the sleeve of my shirt. "There are more coming. Do you understand what I'm saying? There are more men, just like the ones in my apartment, coming. You want them to find you?"

I worked fast, driving her other hand into the other sleeve, pulling my shirt closed as the doors opened. I spun, making sure I was in front of her and reached behind, grasping her wrist.

"No," she answered.

"Good." I stepped out into the apartment foyer. "Then do exactly as I say and we might just get out of here alive."

The muffled sounds of the city traffic grew louder as I dragged her with me. The moment I turned my head to the night desk and the pain in the ass behind it, Vernon Bridges, he turned his head toward me, his eyes widening as the sounds of night traffic died away once more.

"Mr. Cruz!" he called as two men stepped into view.

One of them was still tugging the last closure of his plastic overalls. Vernon looked at them, then back to me. "Your cleaners, sir. Your—"

Thwack!

Vernon jerked as the back of his head exploded, dropping him instantly to the floor. I turned to the two men as the one with the gun looked at me.

Helene desperately yanked her hand from mine. But there was no getting out of this. Not for her and not for me. Not anymore.

The cleaner scowled as his partner tugged his overalls up and moved to the body, dragging Vernon out of view from the tinted windows.

"The garage," I muttered, stepping backwards. "Get to the goddamn garage."

I spun, panic filling my head. My keys were still in my pocket. I'd been so desperate to get back to her, so goddamn desperate to *play*, I hadn't bothered to pull them free.

Now, I was thankful.

I dragged them free as the automatic doors opened, leading into the empty parking lot...and my car waiting in front. I stabbed the button to unlock the car as I gripped her arm shoved her toward it, and opened the passenger side door.

"Let go!" She fought, twisting around and clenching her fist.

I had to be careful...this woman was *dangerous*.

One hard jerk and I snapped her head forward. "*Listen* to me!"

She had no choice but to meet my stare. Rage waited. Not glinting or sparking like an explosion in her eyes. No, like a predator waiting. My stomach tightened. *What the fuck?*

I swallowed, wetting my throat enough to speak. "Those men in there are dangerous. They work for a powerful man. A man I—"

I searched her gaze, trying to explain the corrupt, lethal world I lived in. But how could I? How could I explain my life to someone who had no idea of the things I'd done...*and who I'd done them for?*

"You mean the dead men in your apartment?"

I scowled. "Yes."

"The men you killed."

"Yes."

"Why?"

I shook my head. Fully aware every second was a ticking time bomb, I didn't have time to answer to some random woman... some woman I'd just hit with my fucking car.

"Why did you kill them?"

My scowl grew deeper. I fixed on her as my mind raced. I hadn't thought. That was the truth. I'd just...acted. But why? Why kill men I *knew* were sent from Hale?

That split second came rushing back to me.

The moment the cleaner had turned his head.

The moment he'd...*looked at her.*

"Because...because he looked at you."

Naked. Spread. Still glistening from my mouth. *Mine.* That violent hunger slammed into me. One that now had a name, *possession.* I jerked back to reality, gripping her arm tighter as I leaned close. "Because he fucking looked at you. No one is allowed to do that. Not them...and not Michael *fucking* DiAngelo. Now—" I reached, grasped her head, and shoved her down. "Get into the goddamn car."

She buckled, falling inside. I slammed the door closed and stepped away, turning to pin her against the seat with my stare. If she ran now, I'd be fucked. If she ran now, I'd be—*desperate.*

But she didn't run, leaving me to yank open the driver's door and slide behind the wheel. The automatic doors to the apartment building opened as I stabbed the button to start the engine. Helene stared straight ahead as I threw the car into reverse and pulled out of the parking space.

Shit.

SHIT!

What the fuck was I thinking?

Beep.

My cell chimed in my pocket. I ignored it, turned the wheel, and flew out of the garage. There were dead bodies everywhere, in the hall and in my apartment. The *wrong* dead bodies. How the fuck was I going to explain that to Hale? I jerked my gaze to her as Helene grasped the seatbelt and yanked it down, clasping it in place.

My mind raced as I braked at the boom gate, watching the rear-view mirror. They never followed as the gate rose. I yanked the wheel, flying out of the garage and into the street.

I pushed the car hard, turning the wheel to head toward the quiet, residential streets. I needed a place to think...to figure out what the fuck had happened and how to get us back on board. Because we needed to be.

We were so damn close.

Close to finding the information we'd waited ten fucking years for.

The information that had brought us to Hale.

I clenched my fists around the steering wheel and stared straight ahead.

Until she moved, pulling my shirt in front of her and worked the buttons. She drew my focus. I glanced her way, watching her shift against the door in an effort to get as far away from me as she could.

I'm sorry.

The words were stuck in my head. Because there was no way they'd ever reach my lips. The Principal was *never* sorry.

Towering apartment blocks faded into the endless dark. I turned the wheel and accelerated, heading toward a safe house I owned in Brentville...until my damn cell vibrated.

With a snarl, I adjusted, reached into my pocket, and pulled out my phone.

Unknown.

The screen was alight with the ID. I glanced at the road, then back again, my thumb moving to answer the call, but it ended. *It ended.* The repercussions of that were unfathomable. Just like the situation I was now in.

Three missed calls.

Two from my brother, Kane, and one from Hale.

My cell vibrated in my hand again, making me jump. I turned the wheel and stabbed the button, answering the call. "I'm here."

"What the fuck is going on?" Kane barked, then grunted into the phone.

"I can't explain. Not yet. Not until I—"

She came at me in a rush, slamming my head into the window. The wheel jerked, tearing from my hands. The car skidded sideways. I dropped my phone, scrambling to correct the spin. But she came again, screaming and punching, driving her knuckles into my cheek.

Agony roared.

Blinding me with tears.

Thud.

The car mounted the curb before I flew forward with a *grunt,* slamming against the wheel as we came to a stop. The world slowed. A door cracked open.

"No," I slurred, shaking my head to stop the world from spinning.

She didn't stop to listen, just thrust the passenger door open and tore away.

NO!

I jerked my head upwards, to see her fly around the front of the car and race along the headlights. I stabbed my seatbelt.

"Riven!" My brother roared from the phone.

I bent, snatched it up, and shoved the driver's door open. *Don't let her escape. Don't...let her escape.*

I pressed the button to end the call and shoved my cell into my pocket, leaving my goddamn Audi and the now busted streetlight behind.

"Helene!" I roared. *"Helene!"*

I stumbled, then ran, chasing her. With every sudden breath, I grew clearer, watching my white shirt flapping as she veered into someone's driveway and raced along the side of their house.

She was going to get away.

The hell she was.

I lengthened my stride, leaning into the hunt. My breath was steady, that damned hunger rising to the surface, overtaking everything else. She was fast, even if she stumbled slightly no doubt from her concussion...vaulting over a fence until the tail of my shirt caught.

Rip.

The sound of tearing fabric only triggered that need further. I pushed harder, grasped the top of the fence, and leaped over it, landing with a *thud.*

She stumbled, her arms windmilling as she found her balance and raced ahead.

A damn dog came from out of nowhere, slamming its massive body against the fence. Panic punched through me. I jerked my gaze toward the beast as it barked savagely, lunging over and over again.

When I turned back, she was gone.

"Fuck!"

I left the goddamn dog behind, racing forward, hunting her between darkened cars and quiet houses. I dragged my tongue across my lip, still tasting her. My heart boomed. My senses were on fire. I could almost sense her. Almost...

There.

The house in the distance was vacant, no cars in the driveway and a *For Sale* sign out front. I raced toward it, tearing along the driveway to reach the back. The rear door was open. The closer I came, I saw it was kicked in.

A surge of pride made me smile. I stepped up, pushing the door wider.

The air almost *trembled* with anticipation.

I was going to make her pay for slamming my head against the goddamn window. I probed the wretched throb at the side of my head and pulled my fingers away. Blood shone almost black as I made my way into the kitchen.

The place was sparsely furnished, staged perfectly for a showing. I scanned the living room over the breakfast bar and turned along the hall...heading for the bedrooms. *I could feel her hiding, waiting.*

The door at the end of the hallway was closed. Every other one was open. My smile grew wider as I neared. I wanted her...I *ached* for her.

I reached out, grasped the handle, and turned it. The moment I stepped inside, something hurtled toward me. I threw myself backwards just in time.

Crash!

A lamp shattered against the wall. I wrenched my gaze to her as she bared her teeth and stepped sideways, my shirt just reaching the tops of those perfect milky thighs. My heart clenched at the sight. Fuck, she looked beautiful. The terrifying, dark things I'd do to her.

Fight me, I urged in my head as I took a step toward her. I wanted her to. I wanted her to give me all she had. I wanted her to—

With a primal scream, she lunged.

And my heart came with her, slamming against my chest as she barged into me.

I could barely fight her, she was so mesmerizing.

Her white teeth shone in the gloom.

I grabbed her, wrestling her as she drove her fist upwards, right into my stomach.

Oof.

I doubled over as she swung again, only this time her blow was too wide.

"Missed m—" I started as something wrapped around my neck and pulled tight.

What the fuck?

She howled, turning around to grasp the ends of the cord around my neck tighter. I threw my hands out, trying desperately to grasp her from behind. But all I grabbed was my shirt...

Rip.

Panic ignited inside me.

Wait.

WAIT!

I tried to breathe and fight...the reality was that I could do neither.

The pressure around my neck faded.

And took everything with it.

My knees buckled.

I felt the fall.

Mel...my sister's face lingered faintly in the dark.

The dark that rushed into me.

I'm sorry.

FIVE

Helene

HE DROPPED TO THE FLOOR IN FRONT OF ME WITH A brutal *thud,* his head hitting the floor hard. I sucked in a breath as my own knees wobbled.

"Fuck." I collapsed onto the bed, staring at the man on the rug.

My mind was spinning. I tried to think. What the fuck...*what the fuck?* I clenched the bedding, trying to still the shakes. But it was useless, my teeth gnashed as they chattered.

What are you waiting for?

Run.

Call someone.

Who?

My father?

My team?

Hell, London, for that matter.

And say what?

I swallowed, my throat closed and dry. The remnants of the drug were still in my system, making my belly clench, driving the urge to retch into the back of my throat. Still, I stared at him, at the way his head was turned toward me, his lips parted, His eyes closed. Not such a big man now, are you? my mind snarled.

Michael DiAngelo wouldn't have a clue what to do with a thing like you.

Those words resounded in my head, and my pussy clenched.

I hated that, how I'd come against his mouth, those sparks so goddamn blinding.

I'd never felt like that before. Never been used...wanted, the sole object of someone's hunger, even if it was fucking sick. He'd put a goddamn speculum inside me, for Christ's sake! Still, I wondered if he fucked like that? Like he was in complete control over my body, commanding every tremor and orgasm with those cruel fucking hands.

Michael DiAngelo wouldn't know what to do...

But would *he?*

"Fuck you." My words were a choked hiss.

I shoved upwards, my knees trembling with the effort. I needed water...and to think. Still, it didn't stop me from kicking him in the stomach with my bare foot as I stepped over him.

I headed out of the bedroom and along the hall back to the kitchen. The place was staged for an open house, three neat tumblers filling an otherwise empty open shelf. I grabbed one, praying to God the water was still switched on.

One turn of the handle and I whispered *thank fucking God,* watching the water fill the glass. I drank, letting dribbles trickle down my chin as I drained the glass, then refilled it once more. Only I didn't lift the glass to my lips. Not yet.

Instead, I stared out into the night. He was out cold. Now was my chance to run.

So why wasn't I running?

You know why.

I clenched my grip around the edge of the sink. My sisters' faces came rushing back.

No! Ryth's voice was first. *You're not him...you're NOT KING!*

I flinched now, just as I'd flinched then. To hear that your own father didn't just have two other daughters was tough, but to know he'd started all of this, all the Daughters...and the Sons before it was corrupted by Haelstrom Hale. It was too much. Especially in her condition.

She was almost due to have the baby...and Vivienne.

I winced.

Vivienne hated me.

An ache tore through my chest, making me bow my head. *No, she fucking loathes me.* I didn't blame her. It wasn't as though I'd been there when she needed me. Not when I was old enough to know the truth. She was in The Order by then, locked in those fucking cells...trained by the monster now lying on the floor in that bedroom.

I needed to remember that. *He* had hurt her. *He* had hurt them all.

Vivienne.

Ryth.

All the Daughters.

I closed my eyes as the images of that cellar slammed into me. My knees trembled, forcing me to buckle to the floor. I dropped, curling my feet underneath me. *He* had them killed. Even if he didn't, he'd known it was happening.

He's a monster.

Vivienne's words rose.

He *was* a monster.

A sick, disgusting monster.

Why did you kill him? My scream rushed back...

I shook my head, desperate to rid myself of the memory of his answer. But I couldn't. I couldn't...and there wasn't a damn thing I could do to stop it. I closed my eyes and leaned my head back against the cupboard.

Because...because he looked at you.

Because he'd looked at me.

It wasn't just his words, though, was it?

No. It was that possessive gleam in his eyes, the one that matched the curl of his lips as he bared his teeth.

Because he looked at you.

He'd fucked all this up over some guy staring at me naked, my legs spread, my pussy exposed for him?

The Principal didn't act like that...not one bit.

Not the one I knew, at least.

I shook my head. *No, don't start this. Don't let him get under your skin.*

But he was already...under my skin and inside my head. I needed to get him out, or at least in the box where I could control him, use him even. I narrowed my gaze on the wall, picturing him still lying on the floor. If I ran now, I'd lose him and the only way to find Hale.

I shoved against the floor, grabbing onto the sink to help me up. My knees still trembled, but I held on and drained the glass, then washed it under the water, wiping my prints from the glass with a staged kitchen towel and carefully returning it to the shelf.

My steps were slow returning to that bedroom, fighting every instinct I had to run. I was giving up everything. My sanity. My freedom, even my life. All for my blood. They'd never know about this. They'd never know what I did to keep them safe.

Maybe this was how it was meant to be? Maybe this was...the balance? A kind of sick justice. They suffered then and this was me suffering now...like a deep, fresh cut. Maybe then that gaping, festering wound inside me might finally heal.

A moan tore from him, croaking and rough, but loud enough to send a shiver down my back.

Now or never.

Make the call.

Now...or never.

Standing at his back, I watched his eyelids flutter open.

Beep.

The screen of his cell lit up inside his pocket, making him snap his eyes open. I backed away quietly. My bare feet made no sound as I headed for the doorway. My pulse was booming as he slowly shoved upwards and looked around, leaving the last moment for me to turn.

I was headed for the living room when he unleashed a grunt and pushed to stand. That water sloshed in my belly as I frantically searched for something to occupy my focus...just long enough for him to find me.

It was like waiting for my death.

Seconds...seconds while I opened the cupboards in the living room, searching the empty cupboards while I tracked the heavy thud of his steps. I made my legs wobble a little as I clutched the edge of the cupboard. Making myself...*weak.*

"There you are," he growled as his hand descended, covering my mouth.

I bucked, trying to control the instinct to fight.

"You fucking choked me?" He sounded surprised.

I'd done worse...a lot worse.

His hand muffled my roar as he dragged me backwards, slamming me against his body, leaving him to tower over me. I hadn't realized how tall he was...and how strong. He grabbed my hands and wrenched them behind me.

"I'll just make sure you don't get to do it again," he grunted, wrapping the same cord I'd choked him with around my wrists.

"Get the *fuck off me!*" I howled as he let my mouth go.

"I don't fucking think so."

He jerked the cord hard, securing the knot, then bent, grabbed me around my knees, and hauled me over his shoulder.

"*No!*" I bucked and kicked, driving my head toward his.

He snapped his gaze to mine. Those dangerous eyes held a warning.

Still, I defied him, thrashing as he carried me from that house and out into the night once more. I didn't stop, even as he growled, swinging me left and right, searching for a way back to the car he'd crashed.

He swore under his breath, then I caught his mumbled words. *"What the fuck am I doing?"*

I smiled. "Fucking up your entire life," I answered.

Slap!

I bucked as the blow landed on my ass and the searing sting followed, tearing through the soft flesh.

"One more word," he warned, turning right on the street in the dead of the night, carrying a barely clothed woman over his shoulder. "One more fucking word and I'm going to use that mouth for more than giving lip, got it?"

I swallowed, falling silent.

"That's what I fucking thought."

A twitch came at the corner of my eye. If any other man had spoken to me like that, I would've laid him clean out. So why the fuck wasn't I fighting? I knew why.

Hale...*right?*

I stared at the road under his feet as I bounced. Yeah, Hale.

He carried me down some tiny lane, coming out on the street where we'd crashed. I stared at the darkened houses, bouncing with every step. Cold moved in, the night air reaching under the bottom of his shirt.

My damn teeth wouldn't stay still, chattering together. He adjusted his hold, wrapping his arm further around me to give me more of his warmth.

I clenched my fists, not liking the way he responded. Maybe he just wanted a better hold? Yeah, that was it. Because the reality was far more disturbing. I'd rather he hurt me. At least that I understood.

But this?

This...*kindness.*

I didn't like it.

Not. One. Bit.

He walked for what felt like ages until the crunch of glass sounded under his feet. I turned my head, glimpsing the front of his Audi against the streetlight pole and thrashed, desperate to be out of his hold. "Let me the fuck down."

"No."

I jerked my gaze to his. That icy stare was fixed straight ahead as he reached into his pocket and rounded the car.

Click.

I froze at the sound.

"No." I jerked against his shoulders, fighting him as he grabbed my thighs, yanking me down. *"No!"*

My hair flew into my face with the fall. But I didn't land, he caught me under my arms at the last moment and eased me down against soft carpet.

"Can't trust you, trouble." He pushed me down and straightened, reaching up to grab the lid of the trunk. "And yet, I can't seem to let you go."

"No!" I shoved upwards. *"Wait!"*

But the trunk lid slammed down with a *thud.*

Blackness swallowed my world once more, only this time I was conscious.

"No!" I drove my heel against the side of his trunk. *"Fuck YOU! Fuck you, you goddamn hateful MOTHERFUCKER!"*

Thud!

The sound of the door followed.

I could hear him muttering and snarling before the growl of the engine covered the sound. *Crunch.* Metal groaned, shrieking as we reversed. That sound shouldn't have brought me so much joy...but it did.

"Good," I said. "There's a lot more where that came from...a whole lot more."

Just enough, though, right?

Just enough fight to make it real.

I jolted as the car came to a stop, then surged forward.

But that smile didn't last, slowly fading under the roar of the engine.

I didn't know where he was taking me...more than that, I didn't know why he cared.

But he did.

Enough not to kill me.

And to kill another just because he looked at me.

The Principal was not the man I'd thought he was...

Which was *terrifying*.

SIX

Riven

THE BLACK STEEL GATE ROLLED OPEN AS I PULLED INTO the drive of my Darkwood estate. This place was my escape, my reprieve from the madness, and not a place I brought someone home to...not like her, at least. I pulled the now ruined Audi inside the gate and hit the button for the garage door, listening to the silence in the trunk.

Was she asleep?

Dead?

Gone? Was she gone?

Jesus.

I clenched my jaw, wincing at the blinding glare as the headlights bounced off the white walls before I killed them. I moved fast, driving my shoulder into the door and left it open as I rounded the car before I stopped.

What if she wasn't in there?

What if this was all...*over?*

The idea of that hit me. I could see it now. One press of the button and the trunk was empty. I lifted my gaze to the garage door as it closed. She could be anywhere...I'd never find her. That savage need inside me would hunt. I knew that...even if I hated it. I'd spend the rest of the night driving darkened streets until the morning.

Then I'd search her name...and track her down.

I might even find her holed up with Michael DiAngelo, how about that?

Find her in his arms.

The pathetic bastard smoothing her fucking hair and crooning of love and protection.

Fuck that.

Thump!

I flinched with the blow.

"I know you're there." Her muffled snarl made the corner of my lips curl. "Let me the fuck out or I'll piss all over your brand new carpet. Try getting that stench out."

My smirk died instantly as I stabbed the button. "Do that and I'll..."

She shoved upwards, hate burning in her eyes. "You'll *what?*" She stilled. "Tie me up? Strip me naked? Rape me? How about that, Mr. *Cruz?*"

Shit, that's right...she knew my name.

I said nothing, just stepped forward, grabbed her hands and her waist in one move, and lifted her out. She gave a grunt when her feet touched down. But it wasn't one of anger...it was of pain. She gave a hiss of agony, lifted one foot, and looked down.

The overhead lights glinted off a shard of glass embedded in her foot.

Fuck.

I thought I'd carried her over the glass from the crash? Looked like I was wrong. Only it wasn't just the glass, was it? She bent sideways a little and there was fresh blood on my shirt...

Her wounds filled my head. Had she hurt herself trying to escape? Had she hurt something? Maybe it was when she'd almost fucking killed me? Yeah, maybe then. I narrowed in on her, *very* aware of the sting around my goddamn neck, reminding me just how close I'd come to the end.

Only she hadn't finished the job...why, I wasn't sure.

Not yet at least.

I stepped closer, watching her snarl and take a limping step backwards, leaving smears of blood behind.

Her DNA was going to be all over this goddamn place.

Just like it was back at the apartment.

My cock came alive at the memory of her come all over my sofa.

I wanted more.

Over my mouth.

My cock.

Any way I could get it.

I wanted in that cunt…so fucking bad. Balls deep, coming all over her and down that pretty throat. My pulse sped. *Jesus, what the fuck was I doing?* I swallowed hard as she stumbled backwards. "You're getting blood all over my floor."

She looked down and winced. "Good." Her tone was spiteful as she met my gaze. "Come near me and I'll pull out the shard and stab you in the eye."

"It's about all you could do with it," I muttered and strode forward to grab her around the waist.

"Wait!" She kicked.

But I didn't lift her over my shoulder this time. Instead, I carried her across my chest in my arms as I strode to the interior door into the house. She fought for a second, then stilled, lifting those brown eyes to mine. They weren't honey or mahogany, or even amber for that matter. They were burned coffee, almost black. The eyes of a survivor. She scowled, then turned away, breaking the connection.

I carried her along the hall and past the expansive foyer that encircled the rainforest I had growing half inside. The place was crafted around the look. Lush greens of the tropical gardens softened the harsh steel and cold glass. Paired with polished timber floors this place was…perfection.

My perfection.

My private paradise.

One I'd brought no one to…not until now.

She turned her head, mesmerized by the hiss of the mist and the lush gardens as I carried her past the kitchen and along the hallway to the main bedroom.

"Lights," I commanded, and the room lit up with a soft amber glow.

"What do you know?" she muttered, scanning my bedroom. "A monster with taste."

I jerked my gaze to hers, stopping long enough to snarl. "Bathroom lights *on*."

Her feet dropped, maybe a little too hard, before I drove her against the cupboard.

"Better watch that pretty mouth of yours, Helene Montgomery." I pushed harder. "Before I fuck it."

The lines at the corner of her eyes creased as she scowled. Jesus, she was cute when she was mad. I fought the need to prod her anger a little deeper. But I lifted her instead, placing her on the edge of the vanity. A quick yank of the drawer and I pulled a pair of tweezers free and reached for her leg.

She pulled away, causing me to glare at her. Then she stilled, allowing me to grasp her leg and gently lift it upwards.

Look at that...

Trouble could play nice after all.

My gaze went to the hemline of my shirt as it rose on those creamy thighs, ones criss-crossed with razor fine scars. I exhaled slow and hard and bit my lower lip.

"What?" she croaked.

I met those scorched-earth-colored eyes and answered. "Nothing."

But it wasn't nothing as I searched her foot for the glass, but my other goddamn senses were on her body and the way she shoved my shirt between her thighs. I wanted to yank it out, to tear the buttons off and the ripped fabric free. I wanted...I wanted her spread out on my bed so I could look at her.

No.

So I could look at what was mine.

My gaze flicked between her thighs as I dropped her leg.

I had to shake myself out of this. She wasn't mine. She wasn't anyone's...she was dangerous.

Not dangerous because I was scared—dangerous because I was desperate.

I glanced at the blood on the shirt. "Your side."

"It's fine."

I gave a shrug as my cell vibrated, then jerked my head toward the toilet. "You wanted to use it so bad, then use it."

She seethed. "You've got to be kidding me."

My smile was cruel and fast.

Resignation met humiliation in her eyes as she glanced at the toilet, then back to me. "At least turn around."

I stayed right where I was.

"Sick motherfucker," she muttered under her breath.

I let it slide because she was right. I *was* sick. I watched every twitch in her body as she limped to the toilet, then turned, pulled the ripped bottom of my shirt upwards, and sat.

The rush of liquid came barely a heartbeat later. Her cheeks reddened as she grabbed a wad of paper, then reached between her legs.

"See," I murmured, my focus fixed on the glimpse of her snatch before the shirt fell. "That wasn't so bad now, was it?"

"Not for you, you creepy old perv."

A twitch came at the corner of my eye...*old?*

"At the foot of the bed," I snapped.

"Or else?"

Anger rose. "Want to find out?"

She held my stare while the phone in my pocket buzzed and jittered, before she gave a slow shake of her head and turned. Christ, she was a pain in my ass.

My cell fell silent as she limped into the bedroom, leaving bloody smears behind, then sank to the floor at the foot of my bed.

I moved to the dresser, pulled it open, and punched in the code. I kept weapons and armor in every damn house I owned, but particularly in this one. Steel glinted in the light. I plucked a set of cuffs free and turned, finding her glaring up at me. Her knees were bent, the shirt slowly falling down around her hips.

The sight made me freeze.

She was playing me.

And I was falling for it.

I stole a heavy breath and forced myself to step forward. "Hands."

"Should be around your goddamn throat."

I lunged, grabbed hers, and forced them above her head, pushing her back against the bed until her spine bowed. Her eyes widened, her hands trapped between mine as I clenched my grip. "Keep pushing me."

Her neck was stretched, tendons tight. My breaths came hard and fast as I dropped my head, breathing in the scent of her, that fucking intoxicating scent. Jesus, I needed to fuck her. It wasn't a want anymore, but a damn compulsion.

I licked her throat, tasting the tremble of her pulse. "I'm two seconds away from tying you to that bed, Helene Montgomery. Two fucking seconds from strapping your arms and legs on either side and tearing what's left of my shirt from your body. I'll take my time, but by Christ, know this, by the time I'm done with you, you won't remember a *single fuck* when my cock wasn't buried inside you."

She unleashed a sound.

A suffering, tormented thing.

One that tore an ache across my chest.

I eased my hold and pulled away, finding her eyes closed.

"Look at me."

There was a shake of her head.

I tightened my grip. *"I said look at me."*

She did, meeting my stare. Her dark eyes were so fucking empty it made me ache. I lowered my head, my lips parting, swallowing her breath as I almost—

"Don't," she whispered. "Don't."

I pulled away, searching for that longing.

It wasn't just me she battled now, was it? It was her own need… her own infernal goddamn monster. The one she felt like a slow, possessive lick between her thighs.

I released my hold and slowly rose, standing over her. She looked good down there, almost on her knees. "Hands," I croaked.

This time, she lifted them without so much as a whimper.

"Good girl." I held her stare, plucking the knot in the cord I'd used to bind her.

The cord she'd used to almost end me.

There was something about that which didn't sit right. But I didn't linger, just tugged the cord free and replaced it with the handcuffs, ones I made sure weren't too tight.

"Now stay," I murmured.

My cell was already vibrating as I strode back to the dresser and pulled out a black t-shirt. My guest needed clothes and a shower in case there were more shards, but that would have to wait.

"Yeah," I answered my brother's call.

"What the fuck happened?"

I tugged on my shirt and strode from the bedroom. "I crashed the car."

"You crashed the car?" he repeated in *that* tone. "Are you okay?"

I headed into the kitchen and pulled a glass from the overhead cupboard. "I'm fine. I..."

"Are you having problems? You know you can talk to me."

I stilled, my hand hanging in the air as anger moved through me. "You going to fucking diagnose me now, brother?"

"No, you know this isn't like that."

"No?" I placed the glass on the counter. "Then what is it like?"

His voice was steady, cool. The same distant fucking tone he took with his clients. I yanked open the refrigerator and grabbed cheese and tomatoes, then pulled two steaks from the freezer.

"This isn't you," he said carefully, finally remembering who he was damn well talking to. "The killing, the crash. Maybe all this is too much. I warned you of this when we started. I said getting this close to Hale would influence us, that it'd *change us*."

I threw the steaks into the microwave and hit defrost. "Yeah, well, we didn't really have a choice then, did we? Just like we don't have a choice now."

"We *always* have a choice, brother."

I shook my head and lowered it, clenching the edge of the counter. "No. We don't. Not unless you're prepared to throw away years of planning, years of...*terror...and of degradation*. Christ, the things I've done, the things we've *all* done."

"We don't even know if she's still alive."

I snapped my head upwards, rage searing the back of my throat, until in an instant the choking avalanche of emotion just died away.

"We just don't," Kane urged. "We've had no response for over five years. That's a long time, Riven. A long time."

"I won't give up on her."

"No one's asking you to. But we need to be realistic here."

Beep.

The microwave beeped, pulling me back into reality. "The reality is this. *She* is our sister. *She* is our blood. If Hale still has her, then I will find her and save her, with or without your help. If this is too much for you, brother, then say now. No hard feelings."

He gave a hard bark of laughter. "Riven, *everything* about you is a hard feeling. There isn't a damn soft spot in your entire existence. I doubt you even know what being soft means."

"It's kept us alive, hasn't it?"

"Yes...yes, it has."

I stabbed the button, pulled out the now defrosted steak, and grabbed the skillet from the hook overhead, placing it on the stove. "Then we stick with the plan," I replied, turning on the heat and moving to the cupboard to grab the olive oil. "We keep going until we get confirmation either way."

"Then we pull the pin."

I lifted my gaze. "We pull the pin...and watch the entire fucking thing explode."

"And finally, bring our brother home."

Our brother.

That ache in my chest moved deeper. "Yes. But for now, leave him out there. He's better in the dark."

"Will do, and Riven."

"Yeah?"

"We couldn't do this without you."

My breath caught in the back of my throat. I couldn't speak. I couldn't even breathe. Instead, I forced that torment all the way down, back into the abyss. When I spoke, my voice was cold and steady. "I'll contact you with further information."

"Until then."

I lowered my hand, pressed the button, and ended the call. My pulse was booming, carried away by my brother's words. I forced myself to focus on the steaks, swirling the oil in the skillet before I placed them down on the heat. This is what I needed. Focus. Tasks. And a plan that would pull this all back together.

I took my time, cooking the steaks to perfection and sliced tomatoes and hard cheese, laying them expertly on both plates, then froze.

What was I doing?

Feeding her. That's what.

I was feeding the woman I'd abducted, assaulted, and allowed to hear my fucking name. Because...because she had to eat. I wiped the edge of the plate and looked down. The meat was sliced to perfection, worthy of a five-star restaurant. I grabbed a set of utensils and buffed the fork before I took the plate and a bottle of water from the refrigerator and headed for the bedroom.

The moment I saw her, that compulsion roared to the surface. She sat exactly where I'd left her. Her knees bent, her hands still cuffed. There was a flicker of satisfaction as I neared, watching her flinch and placed the plate on the end of the bed before I uncuffed her.

"Eat." I commanded, giving a jerk of my head toward the food.

She jerked that smoldering stare my way, took one look at the plate, and turned away. "I don't eat meat."

The smugness died. "What?"

She looked my way. "I...don't eat meat."

Motherfucker.

I looked from her to the plate, then turned around and strode away. *Goddamn woman. GODDAMN WOMAN!* She was pushing me. *Testing my limits.* I strode back into the kitchen and scraped the entire meal into the garbage.

My breaths were savage.

My pulse was out of control.

And there was a tic in the corner of my eye again.

"I don't eat meat," I muttered. *"I don't eat goddamn meat."*

I turned around, eyed the small basket of fresh fruit my housecleaner had left for me, then snatched the bright red apple from the top of the pile. I strode back, my fist gripping it tight and stepped into the bedroom.

"Here." I tossed the damn thing toward her. "Unless you don't eat apples as well?"

She grabbed it with both hands, glaring at me. Then she pulled it toward her, bared her teeth, and bit down hard.

Spiteful fucking thing.

I wanted to let her starve.

To let her—

Juice dribbled down her lips and down her chin. She never even wiped it, just took another bite. Those brown eyes filled with poison as she chewed in wounding gnashes of her teeth.

I'd never seen anything so fucking sexy in all my goddamn life.

The rage.

The *promise*.

Fuck, this woman was devastating.

Beep.

I jolted at the sound and wrenched my gaze down to my hand. I still held my cell...and the bottle of water. I swapped it over, scanning the caller ID. *Julius Harmon.*

"What the fuck?" I answered the call. "Yes?"

"Our mutual acquaintance isn't happy," Harmon warned. "And he wants you gone. You *and* your brothers."

My jaw clenched.

Sweat rose along the top of my brow as his words hit home. Hale wanted me gone?

He wanted me gone...

"But I've convinced him otherwise," Harmon added carefully, his tone crooning. "I still believe you're an asset, Riven. Please don't cause me to think otherwise. I told him from now on you would be a team player. Are you, Riven? *Are* you a team player?"

My lips curled. "Yes." I stared at the woman on the floor in front of me. "Yes, I'm a team player."

"Good. I was hoping you were going to say that. Very glad. I'm taking over operations from here on out. We have other... shipments coming. I will need you and your brothers to oversee their arrival. You'll house them...clothe them...get them ready as you've done in the past. I will contact you with further instructions. Until then, get your fucking shit together. *Do you hear me?* Get it *together.*"

"Yes." I forced the word through clenched teeth. "I...*get it.*"

"Good." He exhaled hard into the phone. "Lie low. Make no further rash decisions. I'll be in contact."

"Fin—" I started, but he was already gone.

Leaving me to unravel.

"YOU GODDAMN BASTARD!" I roared, hurling the bottle of water across the room. *"I'LL FUCKING KILL YOU! I'LL... FUCKING KILL YOUUU."*

I stilled, sucking in hard breaths, and came back into myself...to lower my gaze to hers.

"You'll eat what I give you. Do I make myself clear? You'll eat, shower...do *everything* I tell you to do," I warned, my rage simmering under the surface. "You call me a monster now, but you haven't seen the things I'm capable of. You don't want that, Helene Montgomery. Trust me."

SEVEN

Helene

Fear moved through me as he turned and strode from the room. Real fear, not the fleeting feeling I'd had while I'd fought for my life. No, this was...deeper than that. This was *dangerous.*

I'LL FUCKING KILL YOUU!

Those words still lingered in the air.

But who had he been talking to?

I tried to piece it all together.

Yes, I'm a team player.

But whose team was he playing on? Hale's, that I knew. But this wasn't him, was it? So, was there someone else in charge? I tried to think. Not Macoy Daniels, thanks to London, or Ophelia, thanks to his damn son. So, who then? Who was taking over and forcing Riven Cruz to his damn knees...I tried to think, but there was no answer.

Not yet, at least.

His heavy steps resounded over and over. He was out there pacing, thinking...and planning. That made him vulnerable... and me. I jerked my gaze toward the doorway as those steps grew louder. When he stepped back into the room, he didn't look at me, not at first.

"Shower," he snarled, lifting those unflinching eyes to mine. "And don't fight me."

I pushed my hands against the floor and slowly rose. *My sisters. Remember my sisters.* I clung to the memory of their faces as I lifted my hands. "The cuffs," I said carefully. "I can't very well wash with them on, can I?"

The twitch came from the corner of his eye.

He didn't trust me. If I was going to survive this, I needed to change that. "Please." The word was a whisper, but he heard.

His eyes widened. His chest rose. Maybe a little harder than I'd seen before. *He likes it when I beg.* That aching tension surged inside me at the thought.

He stepped forward, reached into his pocket, and pulled out a set of keys, finding the small cuff key.

"Cruz." I watched his face as he pushed the key into the locks one at a time. "That's your last name, right? May as well tell me your first. We're already in this deep, aren't we? What's a little deeper?"

I tried to make him a little more comfortable, playing to his needs as the cuffs fell free and he tossed them to the bed.

"Riven," he answered, meeting my stare.

"Riven," I repeated, praying to God I sounded like I didn't know a damn thing about this man already...and his two brothers.

He watched me carefully, then gave a jerk of his head toward the bathroom. I moved without so much as a whisper, limping a little as I headed inside. He was going to watch me. I knew that. Still, I couldn't seem to push that out of my head as I fumbled with the buttons of his shirt. The weight of his stare sent a shiver through me as I shrugged out of the sleeves and let the damn thing fall.

I didn't look back, just stepped into the shower and reached for the faucet, switched on the spray, and waited for the hot water. A shiver took hold, pebbling my skin and my damn nipples. I crossed my arms, relieved when the faint steam rose before I stepped in.

Turn around. Make him look at you. You need him, remember?

That nagging voice again, and I wanted to strangle it.

But it was right. No matter how terrified I was.

I needed him.

And this was the only way.

I eased my head backwards under the warmth and turned around, meeting that ravenous gaze. He never looked away, seizing my stare, then slowly looked down. My pulse was booming as he found the scars on my breasts, then the wound at my side, the one that made me look like I'd been chewed up and spat out.

I had.

If only he knew *how*.

The bomb that had torn apart the Order had been rushed and sloppy. The call from my father, being held captive in those walls, had set me on a downward spiral. It had made me reckless...and mistakes had happened, one of which I was still healing from. He stared at that wound, no doubt trying to work out what exactly had happened.

My mind raced, trying to create the lie. A car accident? A gas explosion? An innocent bystander in a car bombing? What one would he believe?

None of them.

My hand slowed, trailing the soap in my hands along my stomach and lower. He wouldn't believe a thing I said. That's why he wouldn't ask and I needed him not to. I continued the slide, slipping my hand between my thighs.

The muscles of his throat flexed as he swallowed. My cheeks burned as I reached up and grabbed the shampoo from the shelf. One good squeeze and I lathered and rinsed my hair before I conditioned it. He watched my every move, searching my eyes more than my body.

Those eyes.

Those hard as steel eyes bored into mine, desperate to peel layer after layer from me.

I looked away, breaking the connection. My pulse was thready and panicked, forcing me to turn and switch off the water. I squeezed my hair, leaving it to slowly drip down my shoulders as I stepped out.

He never made a move to hand me a towel, only stood in the way as I glanced at the neat pile of towels folded at the edge of the vanity. I had no choice but to lean around and press my body against him as I snagged one from the top and yanked it free.

Bastard.

My cheeks burned as I lurched backwards. I swiped the towel down my body and under my arms before drying my hair and wrapping it around my head. He turned around, grabbed another, and advanced.

Panic pushed in, forcing me backwards. "What are you doing?"

He knelt and dropped to one knee as he slid the towel along my legs, catching the trail of water without saying a word. I froze, looking down at him. He took his time, rubbing the plush cotton over the grazes of the accident, then the scars between my thighs and softly dabbed the mess at my side.

"This looks infected," he murmured.

"I...I ran out of antibiotics."

He gave a *humph,* then rose and placed the towel on the vanity before opening the mirrored cabinet and pulling out a small container.

"What's that?"

He turned around. "Antiseptic powder. Military grade. Don't worry, I'm not about to inject you again." *Why not? He'd done it before.* I'd be more compliant that way. He knew that. So what'd changed? What in the last few hours had changed that he'd not only decide I was better conscious but that I was...*taken care of.* I flinched, wrestling with the only possible reason, my cheeks burning as I muttered. "I wouldn't put anything past you."

He just hinted a smile. "Smart girl." Then he unscrewed the top and stepped closer. "Now, don't move."

I wanted to do anything but stand there while he came closer. But his hands were careful, gentle almost, as they pressed against the top of the wound and squirted the powder between the weeping edges.

I hissed at the sting before grinding my teeth and swallowing the pain.

He straightened instantly, then reached up to tug the towel from my head and fisted my wet hair. "You want to moan? Then moan. Don't hold it in for me."

That vicious hold yanked my head backwards. Anger roared, stealing away the bite of pain. "I don't want to *moan*," I forced through clenched teeth.

He searched my eyes, my spine bowing under his brutal strength. But as I held that stare, I didn't see cruelty, not like I'd seen before. No...there was something else. Some flicker of sadness hit me in the chest, and he knew it.

He might still be a monster.

But he was in pain.

Deep, soul-wounding pain.

Who the fuck are *you?*

He opened his mouth to speak, his breaths coming hard and fast, until he snapped back to reality, let my hair go, and stepped away. "Don't move." He turned, placed the powder on the counter, and yanked off his shirt.

Where the fuck was I going to run to?

I stared at his hard chest as he dropped his t-shirt to the floor and unbuckled his belt. I looked away at the sound of his zipper. Still, I saw enough in the corner of my eye to draw my eyes back to him.

His body was lean and muscular, flexing as he stepped into the shower and hit the faucets before he turned. He never looked away as my gaze lowered, taking in his strong chest and the soft ridges of his stomach before I froze.

Blood hummed in my veins, thudding in my chest as I stared at his cock. It was flaccid, but still it slapped the inside of his thigh. Jesus, if he was that big now...he would be fucking massive hard. He grabbed the soap and ran it over his chest and under his arms before reaching between his legs.

He didn't just wash, he *stroked,* sliding his hand under his balls, then along the length of his cock. My cheeks burned and my mouth was dry, breathtakingly aware of his unmerciful stare.

The dark hairs on his abdomen stuck against his skin as he tilted his head back and let the water run down his throat and chest. My brain wouldn't focus. I was stuck, not in fight or flight...but in infatuation, in that rush that hit me right between my thighs.

This was wrong.

Especially with him.

The man who'd drugged and raped me.

The man who'd had his head between my thighs.

I moaned, turning my head away as that desperate, sick sound escaped.

He switched off the water and stepped out, watching me as he grabbed the same towel he'd used to dry my legs and ran it over his body. "I like that sound from you, Helene," he muttered as he dried. "I hope to hear more of it."

"Fuck you," I whispered, without a hint of rage.

He smiled, dropped the towel to the floor, and closed the distance. "That's very much the plan."

I flinched, jerking my gaze to his. Anger rose to engulf my cheeks, but he didn't linger long enough to see, just strode into the bedroom and yanked open a drawer.

"Clothes." He tossed a pair of black boxers onto the bed, followed by a black t-shirt.

I approached hesitantly, then reached out, grabbed the shorts, and pulled them on. The t-shirt was next, slipped over my head. But the moment I'd tugged it down, he grabbed my arm and yanked me forward.

Snap.

One of the cuffs closed around my wrist. The bastard almost smirked when he closed the other around his own. "Just in case you get any ideas."

"What the fuck?" I yanked my hand until the steel clanked tight.

He glanced toward the bed. "I'm tired and I'm sure you are, too."

"Oh, no...there's no fucking way in *hell* I'm sharing a bed with you."

He gave a shrug. "Suit yourself." Then he strode to the bedside, jerking me forward as he tugged down the bedding. He was stronger and taller than me, forcing my body to go exactly where he wanted it to as he dropped to the bed and slid toward the middle.

My arm yanked forward, stretched out across the clean sheets.

That motherfucker...

That—

"Lights," he commanded.

And the room plunged into darkness.

Leaving me to stumble, fall...and land right beside him.

I hit the mattress, then scooted toward the edge...as far as I could away from him.

This wasn't happening.

This was so not—

I swore I heard him chuckle as he leaned forward, pressed his naked body against mine, and wrapped an arm around my waist. "Sleep, Trouble. I have a feeling you're going to need it."

EIGHT

Riven

YOU WILL TELL ME WHERE HALE IS!

I jerked awake with London St. James roaring in my goddamn ears. But he wasn't here, was he? No gun pressed against my brother's head. No men waiting for me in the dark. Just the softness of the mattress underneath me...and the sudden, delicate draw of breath at my side.

Warmth.

Warmth pressed against me.

A soft, seductive scent washed in, unfamiliar and strange. The memory of the last twenty-four hours rushed back. The accident. The cleaners...and her. *Helene Montgomery.* The way she'd bucked and fought me every step of the way, almost fucking killing me in the process, and the way she'd hid her scars.

Jagged, cruel gashes of fate.

She was ruined.

But it was more than that. She intrigued me, and that was a very dangerous situation...for her and for me. Still, I found myself drawn to her, to the fighter in her eyes and the faint silver marks on her body. Marks which urged me closer, to know her story, to understand what had driven her to do the things she'd done, to cut and slice and bleed. I wanted to know the thoughts of all that blood and all that pain, to feel such hatred for yourself, to know such unbearable agony.

My pulse sped, until she let out a soft, sudden snore.

She snored.

She...

The more I thought about her, the deeper I slipped.

This shouldn't be happening.

She *shouldn't be happening*. Not now when everything was at stake.

Murmured words I couldn't quite hear slipped from her lips. I held my breath and leaned closer.

"But you're...you're my sister."

Sister?

Seemed like I wasn't the only one with family trouble. Maybe she would tell me about them. Maybe they'd caused her pain. I clenched my jaw. I didn't like that. No, I didn't like that one bit.

What the fuck are you doing? Reality pushed in. I lifted my gaze to the glint of steel around my wrist. She was a captive...a goddamn captive, and I was fucking playing house?

Get your fucking shit together. Do you hear me? Get it together.

Harmon's words pushed in.

I shook my head, then gently rolled over and stretched out until my tendons pulled taut and my muscles howled in protest. Still, she never moved and those tiny, gasping snores never quieted as I grasped the key from the nightstand. One tiny *click* and the cuff fell before I undid hers. She barely moved. The deep draw of her breaths told me she was still asleep. Good.

I rolled and climbed out of bed before padding to the walk-in closet. A surge of awareness came, stopping me. I swiveled around, flicking my gaze to hers. But her eyes were closed.

In and out.

In...and out.

Her breaths never changed.

Hmm.

I pulled jeans from the drawer and strode toward the kitchen. It was still early, only a few hours after I'd fallen asleep. But my mind was racing and my heart...it needed a reason, a reason for all of this, a reason for hope. I slid a cup under the coffee machine and pressed the button before heading upstairs to my study.

I grabbed the laptop and the charger before heading back down. A splash of creamer and I set myself on the edge of the bench, turned on the computer, and logged in. That nagging feeling of being watched washed over me once more.

I glanced toward the hallway, seeing nothing but gloom, then scowled and turned back to the blinking green lights on the server. I scratched the prickly hair on my jaw. My head was a goddamn mess. I needed to get back in the game. I needed to get control.

The bitter tang of coffee made me wince. Still, I swallowed and typed out the commands.

RC: *I have another name*

...

...

...

...

...

The lights blinked and blinked. I waited, drinking my coffee, and watched for a response. A response that may never come. Maybe he was hunting? Maybe he was—

SC: *Give it to me.*

My heart leaped at the command. I typed:

RC: *Julius Harmon*

...

...

I waited, but there was no response. Not that I'd really expected there to be. Not anymore. I logged off the server and closed the laptop down. Sitting back, I lifted my gaze to the brightening sunlight in the window.

She only had an apple.

My brows pinched.

She only had an apple, so she must be hungry.

I shook my head. No, that wasn't something I cared about. If she didn't eat what I'd made her, then it was her own goddamn fault.

Chomp.

The memory of her consuming the apple filled me. Before I knew it, I'd risen from the bench. I was hungry myself, wasn't I? I turned my focus inward...but my belly was quiet.

"Fuck it," I snarled and yanked open the cupboard, pulling out the glass container of oats.

She didn't eat meat. So, what the hell *did* she eat?

Was she vegan?

Was she sick?

I stilled, standing over the stove. What if meat made her ill? What if any animal products did that?

Shit.

I snatched my cell from the counter and started typing a list. Fruits, vegetables, dairy-free butter and spreads. By the time I was done, my housekeeper had a message a mile long. I lowered the cell, then turned my attention to the oatmeal, searching the cupboards and the refrigerator for anything I could use.

I cooked the oats and added nutmeg, then spooned it into a bowl and topped it with sliced fruit. Soft slaps of bare feet snagged my attention. I jerked my gaze upwards and terror moved in, watching her step closer. "I smelled food," she said carefully, her gaze flicking to the bowl.

"I..." I started. "I hope you're hungry."

Her belly gave a howl. The sound was loud and constant, causing me to push the bowl toward her. She glanced at the laptop as she slid onto the stool and pulled the oatmeal toward her. But if she cared about the MacBook, she hid it well, turning her attention to annihilating the food in front of her.

"*Ooo...hot,*" she hissed.

"*Careful,*" I snapped, striding closer. "The milk isn't cold. It's long-life, and all I had."

Between gaping mouthfuls, she muttered. "These are the *best* oats I've ever had in my damn life." She attacked again, scooping up the fresh peaches I'd sliced and shoving them in her mouth.

She ate like she was starving.

I'd never seen anything so goddamn mesmerizing.

Beautiful even.

I'd done that. I'd fed her like that. The best oats, that's what she'd said. The best oats she'd *ever* had. "I can...I can cook you more if you'd like?"

I heard myself say the words, and yet it wasn't me. I didn't care, not about others and certainly not about her.

She gave a hint of a smile. It was just a flicker. Still, those dark brown eyes seemed to *shine.* "Sure, that'd be good."

I slid my cell from the counter and tucked it into my pocket as she unleashed a deep, guttural moan and rubbed her belly. "Jesus, I don't think I've ever eaten anything so damn fast in my life. I feel like I'm about to explode."

The motion drew my gaze as she tugged the black t-shirt higher, revealing her soft belly underneath. She stiffened, then lifted her gaze and tugged the shirt into place.

"Don't." I met her gaze. "Don't do that."

"Don't do *what?*"

I rounded the counter, yanked the shirt, and tugged the damn thing upward until it not only revealed the swell of her belly, but the scars under her breasts as well. I froze, staring at them. One looked like a...like a knife wound, another a burn.

She shoved backwards. "Get the *fuck off me.*"

I let her go, unable to do anything else.

She almost slipped as she scurried off the stool and stumbled away from me. "Don't you fucking touch me. Do you *hear me?* Don't you fucking dare."

Oh hell no. This wasn't happening.

I would not let her hide and cower and hate.

She could direct that at me...

But not herself.

Not anymore.

I strode forward, closing the distance. She couldn't get away fast enough, stumbling until she slammed against the wall. One slap of my hand on the wall beside her and I blocked her in. "You *will* show me all of you."

She jutted her chin higher. "Over my dead body."

Dead?

No.

I don't think so.

A different scenario came to mind. One that would suit me a helluva lot better and would thoroughly piss her off. I flicked my gaze to the bedroom. "I suggest you use the bathroom."

"Why?"

"Because I'm handcuffing you to the bed."

Her mouth dropped open before she murmured. "You wouldn't."

I lowered my hand and leaned down. "Try me."

There was a twitch in the corner of her eye before she slowly stepped sideways, sliding along the wall away from me. I liked the sensation of stalking her, allowing her just enough space to turn and run. She was smart, doing exactly as I'd told her and made for the toilet.

Her lips curled as I stepped into the doorway, watching her as she peed, then wiped. My breaths moved deeper, invading her privacy like that. I wanted more. I wanted *everything.*

She yanked up the boxers before turning to flush, those cheeks blazing as she moved to the sink. I saw the hesitation. The moment her brain screamed to fight. But she pushed that voice inside her head down, focused on washing her hands, and grabbed the towel.

"What did I do wrong?"

My breath caught. "What?"

She turned and met my stare. "I said, what did I do wrong?" She moved closer. "This is a punishment, right? I pulled my shirt down and now you're going to punish me for it."

I scowled. "This isn't a punishment, Helene."

"No?" She stepped past me and went toward the bedroom.

I followed, grabbing the cuffs. "No."

She fought me, just like I knew she would. But she wasn't strong enough to win...and in the end, I cuffed her wrist to the steel headboard before sucking in a hard breath. She jerked away when I brushed the hair from her eyes.

"Touch me again and I'll bite."

I smiled and nodded. "Just like I thought."

I didn't want to leave her. But I had to. As much as I enjoyed seeing her in my clothes, she couldn't wear them forever. So I pulled on a shirt and sneakers, grabbed my cell and the keys, then headed for my car.

An emptiness washed over me as I backed out of the driveway. My hands clenched around the wheel, desperate to reach for the gears and drive back inside. But she wasn't going anywhere. Not without me or the key in my pocket.

I forced myself to move, leaving her behind, and headed for a luxury shopping mall two suburbs away. I pulled in and parked near the entrance. If she wanted to hide from me, then I'd give her no option. I killed the engine and climbed out, locking the busted Audi behind me.

A glance over my shoulder and I winced at the dented grill and smashed headlight. That was another thing I needed to fix. But first...clothes. I headed for a clothing store I'd been in only once to purchase a top for a date. One she'd refused to wear, throwing it back in my face.

But that was different.

That was then.

And she wasn't Helene Montgomery.

I stepped in and cast my gaze across the store. Heads turned my way. Even unshaven and in sneakers, they gravitated toward me, all smiles and shy glances. Until they came closer, close enough to stop in their tracks.

I didn't know how they sensed it, but they did, making a sharp turn away from me...and hurried out of my way.

They smelled it.

All the horrific things I'd done.

Get on your fucking knees.

Don't look at me.

Wider.

WIDER.

You're nothing but a cunt. Do you hear me? Something warm for men like me to use.

You will wear red. Do you hear me, DAUGHTER?

YOU...WILL...WEAR...RED.

My own callous screams resounded in my head. It was as though they heard me, casting terrified glances my way as they scrambled out of my path. Until I reached the counter and the blonde behind it had no choice but to meet my cold, unflinching eyes and smile.

"How may I help you, sir?"

"I require clothes for a woman."

Her shoulders curled as I cast my gaze downwards. Hate rolled through me, making my lip tremble. She invoked the same savage rage the others did. They were a means to an end, right? A *thing* for me to train. Not a person. Not someone like — "About two sizes larger than yourself."

Her brow furrowed as she recoiled. "A size twelve?" she questioned, her voice shaky.

I gave a nod, then watched her hurry around the end of the counter and head to the racks of dresses, ladies' suits, and leisure wear.

"Is there anything in particular she likes?"

I searched my memory. She'd worn black the night I met her, black and brown, the same color as her eyes. "Black. I'd like to see clothes in black."

She pulled several sheer blouses and slacks free. I nodded and chose a few. "Shoes, as well," I said, casting a glance along the display. Only I didn't know her size.

Smears of blood rose, marking her damn territory all the way through my house from the shard of glass in her foot.

Come near me and I'll pull out the shard and stab you in the eye.

"Sir?"

I jerked my gaze upward.

"Is there something funny?"

The curl at the corner of my mouth fell, leaving me to shake my head. "No." I glanced at the heels and the flats in her hand. "I'll take them both."

The attendant gave a nod. "Is there anything else?"

I glanced around the store. "Yes, in fact, there is. Lingerie, I'd like something specific."

NINE

Helene

____

"*You fucking BASTARD!*" I yanked at the cuff against the headboard, driving my foot against the pillows. But the steel refused to budge, grinding against my wrist until I had to stop. Agony ripped through my hand. I collapsed and grabbed my hand, massaging the bone under the cuff. "Motherfucker," I moaned as I sucked in hard breaths and searched the room for something I could destroy.

But there was nothing.

There was nothing.

I unleashed a roar and kicked a pillow, sending it flying across the room.

I was going to kill him.

No.

I *should have* killed him when I'd had the chance. I clenched my teeth, turning my gaze to the doorway. I wouldn't make that mistake again. Sisters or no sisters, this motherfucker was going down.

The soft *click* of a lock froze me. I held my breath as the sound of footsteps moved in...only they weren't his. I shook my head. *They're not heavy enough.*

Some soft humming came. A woman?

"Hello?" I called out, and the humming stopped. *"Hello, can you hear me?"*

The steps came closer along the hallway. I scrambled over the covers, straining as she stepped into the doorway. She was a small, older woman carrying a bag full of groceries.

"Hi there." I smiled, forced a chuckle, and lifted my cuffed wrist. "So, funny story."

She was nervous, looking over her shoulder.

"My name's Helene and I was playing around with Riven's handcuffs and accidentally handcuffed myself to the bed. The only thing is, I left my cell in his car. So, I was hoping I might use yours?"

She gave a small shake of her head, as though the mere sight of this was terrifying.

"It's my fault," I said carefully. "And I know Riven will be upset when he sees what I did. But I'm sure he'll be relieved to know you helped me."

She scowled.

"What's your name?" I urged, my heart thundering.

"Maria."

"It's just a call, Maria," I urged desperately. "I'm sure Mr. Cruz will be so very grateful you helped me out."

Please...come on...PLEASE.

She took a slow step, reaching into her pocket to pull out a scuffed Nokia.

"Thank you." I tried not to stare at the cell as she came closer.

She carefully handed it over. I smiled at her. "I'm so grateful for this." I glanced at the groceries in her arms. "I won't be long."

She gave a nod and stepped backwards without saying a word. The moment she turned, I opened the flip phone, closed my eyes, and drew up the number I'd committed to memory in the hopes we might one day have a connection.

I stared at the worn keypad and entered the number.

It rang once, twice.

Come on...answer.

"Hello?"

"Viv."

Silence, then a hiss. "Helene?"

"It's me," I whispered as relief hit hard.

"Where the *hell* have you been? We've been looking for you!"

She was pissed...*really* pissed. I smiled. That only meant one thing. *She cared.* "I need you to listen to me, V, okay?"

Silence. "Okayyy."

"You know that Plan B? Yeah, well, that went sideways." I glanced at the doorway, listening to Riven's housekeeper putting away groceries. "So I'm now making it up as I go along. But I need you to take this number down, okay? If you don't hear from me or if..." *I turn up dead.* "Anything else happens, I'll need you to follow it."

I pressed the button to access Maria's contacts, then her messages, finding Riven's caller ID. It wasn't the Unknown number I wanted, but it was something. But there was something about the message...it looked like a damn grocery list. Made sense. Still...what he'd asked for nagged at me. I closed the message down and read her back the number.

"Now, repeat it back to me."

She did, reciting it perfectly. I exhaled hard.

"Helene?"

"Yeah?"

"Are you safe?"

I opened my eyes, listening to the movement in the distance. If I told her the truth, what then? I knew Vivienne, maybe a little more than she wanted me to. She was stronger now. *Protective.* Even if it was me. "I am for now. I just need you to take care of yourself, okay? Stay with London and the sons. Tell Ryth...tell Ryth I'll be back as soon as I can." *And with Hale's head on a fucking spike.*

"Okay, but if you need me to come and get you, all you have to do is tell me and I'll be there."

Pride swelled in my heart. There might be hope for us yet. "I will."

"Be safe, Helene." Her voice deepened. "Don't piss me off."

My smile widened. "I'll try not to do that," I finished, ended the call, and quickly deleted the number I'd called from the list of calls made.

But it was the message that stopped me from calling out to Riven's housekeeper. I opened it back up and found Riven's text, scrolling down the list he'd sent her:

Vegan butter.

Nut butter.

Is Nutella vegan? If so, get that as well.

Vegan crisps.

Oat milk.

Fresh vegetables...a lot of them, and fruits as well. Everything in season from that fresh fruit market on Maddison.

Also, wine. The usual.

Spare no expense.

Spare no expense?

My pulse was booming as I reread the instructions. This wasn't just any list, this was...

You'll eat what I give you. Do I make myself clear? You'll eat, shower...do everything I tell you to do. You call me a monster now, but you haven't seen the things I'm capable of. You don't want that, Helene Montgomery. Trust me.

He'd been a monster at that moment. Terrifying me. But that...

That message wasn't from someone who liked to be cruel.

My hand went to my belly and I was remembering the way he'd yanked the shirt from my hold, exposing my belly, when Maria's footsteps came in the hallway. She stepped into the doorway, forcing me to give her a lie of a smile. "Thank you." I held out her cell. "He didn't answer."

She took the cell, scowling as she looked at it.

Then she turned and almost ran out of the room.

But it didn't matter. I'd called the person I needed to call. My sister.

The housekeeper left, and in the silence...fear moved in.

I couldn't trust Riven and I sure as hell couldn't feel anything for him. He was *The Principal,* the sick bastard who'd not only hurt my sisters, but so many women. The memory of that cellar pushed in. Bodies piled on top of bodies. I'd *never* trust a man who'd done that. Not even if my life was on the line.

He could shove his fucking nut butter.

The deep snarl of an engine rose before it suddenly ended. Not the purr of the Audi...someone else.

I shifted on the bed, one hand tethered by steel, and looked for something I could use as a weapon.

Heavy steps approached in the hallway.

My pulse kicked.

They came closer.

Closer.

A shadow spilled along the hallway...

Before Riven stepped in.

I exhaled hard. "You scared the *shit* out of me."

"Really?" He held my stare. "Why?"

Why?

WHY?

Because that's not the sound of the Audi...and because your housekeeper was just here. If it wasn't you, then it could've been...*it could've been worse. So much fucking worse.* I needed to get it together. I needed to keep my cool.

I shook my head. "Because your housekeeper was just here and I...and I..."

He scowled at that, turning with his hands full of bags, and snarled. "Shit. I forgot, I..." He stiffened, then swung back to me. "You could've screamed. You could've had the cops here in ten minutes. But you didn't." He dropped the bags and came closer to the crumpled bed. "Why?"

My eyes widened.

I shook my head.

"I...I don't know."

It wasn't the truth. But it wasn't a lie either.

He came close and reached into his pocket, pulled out the handcuff key, and released my wrist. "Take a shower, Helene. I brought you clothes."

He stared down at me, those dark eyes watching my every reaction. Did he think I was turning soft? Did he think he scared me? I ground my teeth and held that stare, letting him know exactly the fight he'd get if he tried anything.

He didn't, but neither did he move as I slid from the bed and hurried into the bathroom. Only this time, I closed the door and shut him out. *Boom...boom...boom.* My pulse filled my ears as I waited for him to barge in. But he didn't. Instead, the heavy thud of his steps moved around before the rustle of the bags came.

I yanked off the boxers and t-shirt, then used the toilet before stepping into the shower. There'd been a change between us, a blurring of the lines. I didn't like it. He wanted control, and I wanted information. The moment I got what I needed, I was done...and so was he.

Really?

The word rose.

Are you really going to end him? I just can't see you doing it, can you?

Fantasy mingled with reality. Him kneeling in front of me, my gun pressed against his head, finger on the trigger. Could I squeeze it? Could I blow his brains out over the wall? But it wasn't the violence that pulled my focus. It was him...*on his damn knees.*

The sound of his deep voice slipped under the door to reach me. I closed my eyes, my breaths deepening as I fixed on that sound. The water pummeled my body. All I needed to do was angle the showerhead to hit my nipples...*Oh God.* That urgent longing hit me right between my thighs. Desperation forced my eyes open, to find the bathroom door still closed.

I closed my eyes again and turned away from the door, curled my shoulders to hide my body, and let my hand trail down. It was nothing, right? Just release. Just a sick, desperate release.

Then I could get my head back in the game. And I needed that. I pushed my finger in.

Just a nobody.

I squeezed my eyes closed. Shame and humiliation burned in my cheeks.

A nobody who likes to come all over my fucking sofa.

My finger slipped out, then joined with another before I pushed both inside.

Go on, nobody.

I braced one hand against the tiles, curling my fingers as I stroked.

Make a mess all over me.

A tremor raced, making me catch my breath.

"Go on."

My body clenched.

"Fucking *come.*"

I yanked my eyes open as a cruel hand clasped around my throat. I was yanked backwards and slammed hard against the wall.

Stars, that's all I saw...then there was him.

Those dark, hateful eyes were narrowed in on me. "You want to fuck, Helene?"

Water fell into my eyes, blurring him. Still, he was there...*and so was my desire.*

"*Well?*" He pushed closer.

I shook my head. *"No!"*

"Liar!" he spat the word.

Water stuck his shirt to his chest, that expanded with every consuming breath.

"Tell me." Those words were a warning. "Tell me you weren't thinking about *him*."

Him?

My mind was slow to catch up, still captured by the fading white bursts behind my eyes.

"Michael DiAngelo," he forced through clenched teeth.

I shook my head, but my mind was racing as I was shoved out of the stall.

"Get dried," he commanded, switching off the water.

I just stood there, frozen. What the fuck happened? What the fuck was I supposed to do?

*I'm just making it up as I go along...*those same words I'd said to Vivienne came back to me now. Make it up, right? He stepped out of the stall, his clothes stuck hard against his chest.

"You want to think about riding another man's cock in my presence?" Riven snarled, tearing his sodden shirt over his head. "I know you called someone. It was him, wasn't it? Well?"

My knees trembled as I stumbled forward and grasped the vanity. It wasn't another man. That was the most terrifying thing. It'd be easy if it was. If my *stupid, sick mind* would learn to cooperate.

Movement came from the corner of my eye. His bruising fingers gripped the back of my neck, pulling me hard against his chest as he growled in my ear. "Did you give him my name? Did he promise to track me down? Hurt me, kill me, even? That's who you were thinking of, right? Your white fucking knight, DiAngelo, driving into your wet cunt. Tell me, Helene, does he at least have a big cock?"

I thrashed, fighting him. *"Let me go!"*

"I bet he does." That low, reverberating tone hit between my legs. "I bet you fucking rode it well, didn't you? I bet you bounced on that fucking thing all day, then climbed onto his face. Or does he not like that? Is that it, Helene? Does your *school teacher* not like to eat cunt?"

My scream bounced off the walls. He was fucking crazy. A sick, degrading bastard I wanted dead. Still, that hunger wouldn't go away. Revulsion filled me as I met his stare and he searched my eyes.

He saw.

I don't know how much.

But it was enough...

"From now on, you shower in front of me." His voice was husky. "You do *everything* in front of me...and the next time you decide to make your one rescue call, Helene...make sure it's to someone who'll be alive long enough to save you."

"What?"

Those beautiful lips were chilling as he smiled. "I have his address and his phone number. Believe me, he won't last the day."

Terror slammed into me. No, this wasn't happening. This couldn't be...

"Now." He strode forward, snatched a towel from the counter, and shoved it against my chest. *"Now move."*

I couldn't move...and I couldn't think. There *was* no Michael DiAngelo...

I stumbled forward, still dripping.

"Hand."

I shook my head. "No..." He lunged forward, grabbed it himself and yanked me closer to the bed. *"No!"* I pulled away. "You don't *understand!"*

He descended like an avalanche, driving me backwards until I hit the bed...and fell.

"I don't understand?" he snarled, lunging to slam his hands on either side of me on the bed. "Let me tell you what I *do* understand, Helene. While I was out, you tricked my housekeeper into giving you her cell phone. You told her you were calling me, which you didn't. Then I find you fingering your wet cunt and panting like a dog in heat. So, the only reasonable explanation is that you're thinking about him, waiting for him...craving him."

His body pressed against mine, his muscular thighs forcing mine apart.

I couldn't speak, couldn't say a word.

Because the truth was far too terrifying.

"There *is* no Michael DiAngelo," I finally whispered bleakly. "There never was."

He was beautiful when he smiled.

Chilling and breathtaking.

One slow nod and he rose. Reaching up, he clasped the cuff around my wrist, then the headboard once more. "When I come back, you'll be punished." He turned his head and met my gaze. "But don't worry, I won't hurt you...not this time at least."

He lifted his hand, his fingers outstretched as though he wanted to touch me. But then he curled his fingers and pulled away.

"Wait!" I called as he stepped away from the bed and turned toward the doorway. *"WAIT!"*

He was gone from the room in an instant, only the thud of his sneakers left behind.

"He's not real!" I screamed. *"He's NOT REAL!"*

But my pleas were useless. The deep snarl of an engine came seconds later. He was gone...and I was still naked trying to understand...who the fuck was he going to kill?

TEN

Riven

____

Michael DiAngelo.

Michael DiAngelo.

MICHAEL DIANGELO!

I climbed back in behind the wheel of the Range Rover and pressed the button to start the engine. But I didn't put the vehicle into gear, not yet. Instead, I lifted my gaze to the doorway and clenched my fists around the wheel. Rage pumped through my veins and pulsed at my temple.

She'd almost escaped.

I shook my head.

She'd almost...

I reached forward, shoved the four-wheel drive into reverse, and backed out of the driveway. It didn't matter. Not anymore. She wasn't going anywhere, now or ever. I pulled up the name on my cell. It didn't take long to find him. Michael DiAngelo, who worked as a teacher for St. Augustine Elementary in Preston, was about as fucking boring as watching paint dry... and was also married.

I sucked in a hard breath and turned the vehicle toward the middle-income suburb.

He's not real!

Lie.

Did he really mean that much to her? Enough that she'd risk her own goddamn life to save him?

Did she really mean that much to me?

I winced, avoiding my own gaze in the mirror and left my suburb behind. Cars on the road blurred into one. Those hunched behind the wheels were meaningless. All I saw was him. Forty-three, overweight, soft brown eyes and a beard that looked like it hadn't seen the inside of a barber shop in years.

That's the man she wanted?

The man she preferred...over me.

I pulled the address up on my phone and punched it into the car's GPS. It wasn't my usual ride, but thanks to Trouble, I didn't have that option anymore. I followed the streets, scanning front yards littered with children's bikes and abandoned balls, pulling up at one of the few houses that actually looked *neat*.

Too neat.

I scowled, eyeing the beaten ten-year-old blue Mazda sitting in the driveway, and grabbed my cell. It was the same car I'd found on his social media profile. The same one he stood in front of with his wife as they started their fourteen-mile hike in the Rockies. The same car I stared at now.

I reached forward and stabbed the button on the glove compartment. As the door dropped open, I reached inside and pulled out my gun.

She called someone, Mr. Cruz. Maria's words rose. *I think it was a man...but I cannot be certain.*

I shoved the glove compartment closed and opened the car door, stepping out.

Was it Michael? My own desperate tone followed.

I closed the door behind me, slipped the gun into my waistband at the small of my back, and inhaled hard. I was fucking desperate...and dangerous. The sun beamed down as I walked around the four-wheel drive and headed for the front door of the house. As soon as I neared, I heard the soft sound of music, blues by the sounds of it. I pressed the doorbell and stepped backwards, pasting a smile on my face.

The music dulled and footsteps followed. Then the door opened and the most boring looking man in fucking existence greeted me. "Michael?" I muttered. "Michael DiAngelo?"

He smiled and scowled, opening the security door. "Yes, do I know you?"

"Riven," I answered. "Cruz. I'm here for the Alpha Banks Newspaper. We're doing a piece on influential alumni and I was hoping I might take up a few moments of your time?"

The grin was instant. "Me?"

It didn't take a goddamn genius to see he was petitioning for the ten-year Alpha Banks fundraiser to return. To him, this was his big shot. "Only if you have the time?"

"Of course." He couldn't get me inside fast enough, holding open the door and stepping back inside. "I'm just blown away, that's all. *Influential Alumni?*"

I looked around the bland as fuck house and stepped just inside, turning to keep the gun out of view. "Absolutely," I answered numbly. "You were at the top of our list."

"I was?"

I didn't answer, because I sure as hell wasn't here to stroke his damn ego. He motioned toward the kitchen. "Can I get you a drink?"

"Sure." I glanced at the photos of him and his fucking wife.

The happy couple, right? So happy he fucked another woman...*my woman.*

"Will your wife be joining us?" I asked.

"She's away for the weekend." He yanked open the refrigerator and bent for the bottles of water on the bottom shelf. "At some spa retreat. So, it's just us."

Just us, huh? "And your mistress?" I said coldly. "She won't be here as well?"

He froze, then slowly straightened. I reached around, grasped my gun and pulled it free, already taking aim. "Just so I know who else you might be expecting."

"My mistress?" he repeated carefully as he turned around.

He stiffened when he saw the gun. His eyes widened before they shot to mine. "What...what is this?"

I stepped closer. "*This* is me making sure you stay away from her and killing any idea you have of a rescue mission."

"A *rescue mission?*" he parroted.

What was he, fucking stupid? I lifted the gun, taking aim.

"*Wait!*" He threw his hands into the air, dropping the bottle of water.

It hit the floor with a *thud* and rolled.

"I don't *have* any mistress and I have *no idea about any rescue mission.*"

"Liar." My lips curled.

"I promise. Please, I promise you. You have the *wrong g—*"

Crack!

He jerked backward, then fell. A tiny trickle of blood on his forehead was barely noticeable. Pity about the refrigerator door behind him.

You have the wrong...

You have the wrong.

Wrong.

Wrong...

WRONG.

He was a liar. And by the looks of him, a shit fucking boyfriend as well. If *I* was her lover, I'd make sure she wasn't trying to cross a goddamn street in the middle of a downpour on her own...not dressed like that.

No.

If she was mine, she'd be right where she was.

At home.

With me...

Always with me.

I walked up to the dead body of Michael DiAngelo and looked down at those wide unflinching eyes and the spider veins across his cheeks before I let my gaze drift down. He was fatter than his photos, thick around the middle. I fought the wave of revulsion. A man like him with a woman like Helene?

It didn't make sense.

You have the wrong g—

Those words nagged at me. Something didn't feel right. Still, I pushed it down as the image of her face rose. She was still handcuffed and naked in my bed. It was time for me to fix that.

I stepped over the splayed body, making sure I didn't touch a thing and walked out, shouldering open the door as I went. I tucked the gun against my back and climbed into the car. *Get back to her...get back to her...*

Christ, I'd never felt this *fucking desperate.* I started the engine, peeled out of the street, and floored it to get home.

Streets blurred.

Cars I didn't give a shit about.

I didn't see them.

I didn't see anything.

Only her.

I stabbed the gate button, pulled into the driveway hard, and then the garage. The bitter smell of the new engine filled my nose as I climbed out and closed the door behind me. My footsteps echoed as I entered the house. I couldn't hear her...I couldn't...

"MOTHERFUCKER!" she screamed. The sound bloody, violent, and raw.

I stopped at the end of the hallway. My breaths were out of control, as was my pulse. *You have the wrong...you have the wrong...*

I took a step, then another, stopping in the doorway. She was kneeling on the bed, her arm stretched as far as the cuffs would allow.

"I *hate you*," she spat, her eyes wild with fury. "I *fucking hate you*."

"I know," I answered. Just seeing her was the calm to my storm. Just knowing she was *here*. "I also know there's no rescue mission, Helene. There's no one to save you. No one knows you're here."

She flinched, drawing in gulps of air.

I moved closer, glancing at the clothes I'd brought, now strewn across the room. It was almost like fate that the piece I wanted was closest to the bed. "So, this is how this will go. You will wear the clothes I provide you, or you will wear none at all." She never flinched when I lifted my hand and fisted her beautiful hair. "Do I make myself clear?"

"Eat a fucking dick."

The corner of my lips quirked as desperation roared inside me. I was a madman...consumed by lust. I lunged, yanking her head backward until she toppled and fell back onto the bed. "I think you have that mistaken. That role is specifically for *you*."

There was no stopping this...even if I'd tried.

I reached down, unbuttoned my jeans, and shoved down my zipper, then released her hair to grasp her jaw. "You bite me and I'll make it so you never bite a fucking thing ever again, got it?"

I was so fucking hard. The tip pulsed as I knelt on the bed and squeezed my fingers into the flesh of her cheeks. "Now fucking open wide."

She thrashed, whipping her head from side to side. But I held on, angling my hips as I reached for my cock and looked down. I didn't want to miss this. I didn't want to miss a goddamn thing where she was concerned. "Open."

She glared up at me, her cheeks squished against her teeth.

"I said, open."

She did, parting those reddened lips.

"Wider." I choked on the word.

She did, her gaze riveted to mine as her mouth widened. I tore my focus from her eyes to that mouth and the darkness of her throat. My grip eased, my thumb sliding down to stroke that perfect channel. "I'm going to fuck you, Helene. I'm going to fuck you hard." I lifted my gaze. "Believe me when I tell you this isn't a punishment...it's a claiming."

I slid the tip of my cock along the smooth skin of her lips, my other hand stroking, urging...*hoping*.

She opened her mouth, letting me push in.

Warmth closed around me.

Warmth...and her.

"I can't stop..." I bucked my hips, driving all the way inside. "Not even if I wanted to."

Memories slammed into me. But not a memory of here, or of *her*.

Them.

All of them.

Gagging, fighting. Some of them had already given up. *Open wider, wider. Sucking cock will be the only thing you'll be good at. They'll pay for this mouth, do you understand that? Your mouth, your cunt. That's all you'll be to them. That's all you'll be to anyone. I'm here to make sure you're perfection.*

She thrashed, her free arm went from the bed to claw my arm, drawing back my focus. Chills tore along my spine as a wave of revulsion hit me. But I didn't ease, not yet...not until I'd touched perfection. She kicked, her heels driving into the bedding until I suddenly pulled out, leaving her gasping.

Spittle trailed from her mouth to the end of my cock.

"Again."

She shook her head.

"*No?*"

"No." She curled her lips, baring her teeth.

Butterflies roamed the inside of my rib cage at the sight. She was fucking perfection...utter...fucking...*perfection* and this... this was so far from the things I'd done at The Order. I knew that. I *felt* that. For the first time I wanted it to be different... with her. I gripped her jaw, easing her mouth open. She didn't fight me, not like she should. I pushed in, softer this time.

"That's it." I groaned as my cock slid into her mouth. "Now suck."

Those lips closed around me. Her breath was a blast against the base as I lifted my other hand to the mattress over her head. "Fuck, that's it..." I thrust, watching her cheeks move with the impact. "Jesus fucking Christ."

Her feet stopped thrashing.

Now she looked scared.

My gaze was fixed on hers.

Not scared of me. The words hit me: *No. She was scared of herself.*

"My mouth to fuck. You got me? My pretty potty-mouth to fuck. You make me mindless, Helene. You make me so fucking mindless." I clenched my ass, driving all the way in until my balls rubbed her chin. "And me being mindless is a very dangerous thing..." Those wide, panicked eyes shimmered with tears as I stroked her cheek. "For everyone else but you."

She blinked, and that shimmer was gone. I pulled out, only this time her head lifted, her tongue chasing the ridge of my cock. "That's it," I urged, closing my eyes. "Fuck, I knew you were trouble."

I waited for the sharp bite, almost tempting fate now that I wasn't looking. But it never came...*it never came.* I pulled out, my cock shining with slick from her mouth.

Chills danced down my spine as I stared into her eyes. There was something changing between us. Some shift of power I couldn't quite pinpoint, one that made me feel...cautious. My focus was fixed on her mouth, on those soft lips. I wanted to kiss her, to taste her mouth, then her cunt as she came into my mouth.

My heart thundered, driving me to shift my knees backwards.

"Where are you going?" she asked breathlessly.

I didn't answer, just lowered my head, my teeth grazing her tight nipple. I wanted her...but for some sick reason, I wanted her to want me. If she didn't...if she didn't, I'd soon find out.

"No." She yanked at the cuffs as I moved lower.

Her legs wrapped around my back, stilling me. My lips curled as I reached around and grasped one ankle, gently pulling her away. I didn't want to hurt her, not one fucking hair on her head. But fucking her? Forcing myself inside any goddamn hole? That was all I wanted. The only question was, *did she want me to?*

Her foot slammed against the bed as I grasped the other. She shoved her hips upwards, desperate to buck me off. Which only did the opposite. Her pussy pushed against me, the slick she'd left behind cooling on my skin.

"You're fucking wet," I murmured, meeting her panicked stare. "You're so fucking wet, you're almost panting. Are you panting, Helene?"

"Fuck *you*," she moaned, whipping her head from side to side.

My smile grew wider as she shot upward and fisted my hair. "You want to control me, Trouble?" I murmured, lowering my head to the apex of her legs. I gripped the inside of her thighs and squeezed until she winced in pain. "Want to use me?"

She liked that.

I understood it now.

My fingers slid along her swollen pink lips and gently pinched her clit. Her breath caught as a low, primal growl reverberated in the back of her throat.

"Go on, tell me you don't like this."

She shook her head as I slid my fingers down and spread them wide. "Look at that, you're practically dripping. I warned you, trouble, warned you what would happen." I licked that tiny hood and felt it tremble against my tongue. "I told you there wouldn't be a time you wouldn't remember being fucked by me. I think it's about time I made good on that promise. What do you say?"

I plunged my tongue deep inside her, licking that silky, sweet flesh until she bucked and yanked my hair. My hands went under her legs and gripped her ass, lifting her hips so I could get all I wanted.

"Oh, *God...Oh...my...God.*"

He wasn't going to help her.

And neither was Michael DiAngelo.

Not now...

Not ever.

*Mine...*that word filled me as I dipped, forcing my tongue deeper inside. She clamped her knees against my head, but still she rode me. Fuck, she rode, her clenched fist in my hair driving me harder and harder, until there was no coming up for air. I drove my hips against the begging, that desperate need to come overwhelming.

Only, I wanted to come *inside* her.

I lifted my head and moved upwards.

She unleashed a snarl that caught in the back of her throat when I grabbed her knees and forced them to her chest. "Hold still now." Two fingers plunged deep inside, coming away creamy. "Another fucking mess, Helene. Christ, you're a messy slut. You're just going to come all over everything I own, aren't you?"

She closed her eyes as I thrust deep, spreading her pussy.

How many times had he fucked her?

I fisted my cock with one hand and fingered her hard with the other. It didn't matter. She had me now. She whimpered as her jaw clenched, desperation creasing her brow. "That's it. That's my girl." Two hard thrusts of my fist and my cock twitched in my hand. Her pussy clenched around my fingers, her greedy fucking pussy so desperate for what I wanted to give. Fingers plunged inside her as come coated her slit, driving my seed inside.

"Oh...Ohhh...Godddd..." She bucked as much as she could with her knees so fucking wide. I stroked both fingers inside her.

"I will fuck the memory of him out of you if it's the last thing I do," I croaked, watching as she opened her eyes.

That stare was a shotgun blast to my chest. One I knew there was no coming back from. This was bigger than an abduction. More violent than rape. This was an obsession.

"Fuck," I muttered, sucking in hard breaths.

Stunned. Silent.

There was only one reason for that, and it was undeniable.

She felt it too.

ELEVEN

Helene

No...

No...

No!

My heart fluttered, like a bird trapped inside my empty chest. Betrayal surged inside me, fluttering, racing. That surge of desire coaxed me to abandon everything I'd fought for and loved.

Monster.

I needed to remember his name. His *true* name. This...this—I searched those stony eyes, watching his amused mouth quirk at the corner—this wasn't him. Not the real him. This man was a murderer, a rapist. Jesus, he'd raped me, hadn't he? He'd raped me before and again now. My pussy clenched, the throb in my clit ticking like a bomb inside me.

I was going to kill him.

I knew that.

I was going to put a bullet through his brain for all the things he'd done. *For the Daughters.*

He sucked in a hard breath and looked down at his come-drenched fingers. Ones he'd thrust inside me seconds ago. My body shivered as though I was sick.

"You will not shower," he said, pushing his fingers back inside me.

My pussy clenched.

"You will wear the clothes I instruct."

Boom.

Boom.

Boom.

My pulse raced as he withdrew his fingers.

"I see you so much as hide a single fucking hair from me, Helene, and so help me God, I will fuck you raw."

He pushed backwards, slowly climbing from the bed, and I had no choice but to watch him. Because he would. He would keep good on his promise. Taut muscles stretched as he adjusted his shirt, corded and well-used now that he'd taken out his anger on my body.

Stupid...

STUPID.

I flinched, hating the roar in my head. I'd thought I knew this guy. I'd had him all figured out. He stepped backwards, tugged up his zipper, and buttoned his slacks before he bent down to snag something from the floor. But had I? Had I really figured this guy out? The thunder in my chest said otherwise.

Chills raced and my pulse suddenly slowed.

No, that tiny voice whispered inside my head. I hadn't figured him out at all. Because if I had, I'd never have stepped in front of his goddamn car. I would never have *allowed this.*

He tossed the rose-gold-colored bodysuit my way and moved closer. One twist of the key and my wrist fell to the bed before he looked down at me. "Give me a reason to punish you, Helene Montgomery, *please.*"

I stared down at the thing he expected me to wear, then met his stare. Hard breaths punched into my lungs. I opened my mouth...the words screaming in the back of my throat *FUCK YOU!*

But I didn't say them.

I didn't *dare* say them.

One look down to the t-shirt that hugged his stomach and the hard ridge of his still semi-hard cock and I knew he wasn't done with me...not in the slightest. That ravenous hunger still glinted in his eyes.

He looked down at the bodysuit, the command clear as fucking day.

I hated him.

I snatched up the *thing* he'd chosen for me to wear. There wasn't anything there, just thin goddamn straps crossing a sheer, soft chemise front and cups. It'd show everything, every scar, every dimple. I jerked my gaze upward and bared my teeth, hoping like hell he saw his death over and over in my eyes.

Those lips quirked higher. "Well?" he prodded. "I'm waiting."

With a snarl, I yanked the thing over my feet and slid the satin up my thighs. Christ, this was beautiful. I wanted to ruin it because of him, but as I adjusted it on my hips, I became attached to it.

I'd *never* wear something like this.

Not something so revealing.

Or expensive, for that matter.

Not even with my father's money.

No, that was used to buy guns and mercenaries and anything else we needed to find my sisters and keep them safe. There was no room for anything else. No room for beautiful things... no room for me. Only what I had to do to survive and for my blood.

I swallowed hard as I slid the straps along my arms to my shoulders and adjusted the cups of the bra. My nipples rubbed the soft fabric, which only made them harder. He looked. Of course he looked. Those ravenous eyes missed nothing where my body was concerned, and that's how I needed it to stay.

But the moment the bodysuit was in place, he stepped away and headed around the bed to pick up the bags of clothes he'd brought with him. I sat at the top of the bed, watching him as he pulled the clothes out one by one, removed the tags, and walked toward the closet.

Fear cut through me the moment he turned on the light. *What the fuck was he doing?* I shook my head and opened my mouth to speak as he returned, grabbed more clothes, and headed back to where he was placing them on the hangers...right next to his.

Must be serious if he makes space in his closet for you.

I shook my head as he walked back out, only this time meeting my gaze.

But I couldn't speak. Because, what if he hadn't thought of the implications?

"If you make a list of the bathroom items you like, I'll have those delivered."

He was *moving me in?* "I'd rather choke."

He closed the distance instantly, stopping to brace one hand on the headboard and lean down. "And I'd rather choke you, Helene...with my cock. But for now, I'll take the goddamn list."

My body trembled, then ached. I winced and glanced behind him, desperate to get away. "I need to pee."

He straightened. "By all means."

I didn't care anymore, scooting my ass forward to push past and made for the toilet. It'd been hours since he'd left me and right now my bladder was screaming. Movement came from the corner of my eye. The moment I stepped into the bathroom, he followed, causing me to spin around. "I'm just peeing, for Christ's sake."

He glanced at the toilet. "Then pee."

I sopped, glaring at him, then thought about the logistics and looked down to the sheer fabric of the bodysuit. I'd never worn something like this, never had to worry about how this *happened.*

"Pull it aside," he murmured.

The heat of his stare was like a brand on my skin. Still, I had no other choice as my bladder sent out a spear of agony. I winced, reached down, and yanked the fabric of the crotch aside before I sat. Heat flooded from me and the bastard never moved. I kept the fabric out of the way and turned for the toilet paper...but I only had one damn hand.

Fuck.

"Here." He stepped closer and folded the tissue before tugging it free. "Let me."

"What?" I jerked my gaze upward.

But he was already kneeling to reach between my body and the seat to wipe along my crease. Those sickening fucking fingers were so firm and tender, making my body clench and heat. I looked away as humiliation crawled into my cheeks.

"There." He rose carefully and moved to the sink to hit the faucet, then the soap. "I'll meet you out in the kitchen."

I eased the fabric back and slowly rose as he walked out. So that was it? Not that he didn't trust me. He just wanted to...*humiliate me.*

A nerve twitched at the corner of my cheek as I turned and pressed the button to flush the toilet, then moved to the sink. That was it. I met my gaze. He not only liked to control, he liked to humiliate, as well, make me uncomfortable, make me beg.

I swallowed hard as a surge of excitement hummed deep inside me when I lowered my gaze to the bodysuit he'd made me wear. Rose gold...it looked almost nice against my naturally tanned skin, until I turned and the ugly silver scars were revealed. I turned back and grabbed his hairbrush, dragging it through my hair.

I'd been through an accident, a drugging, a chase, murders...*and him.*

I looked like a damn mess.

The more I brushed, the softer my hair became, until it shone, letting me make my way out of the bedroom, deciding to obey him and head to the kitchen.

Is Nutella vegan?

The words rose in my mind as the clatter of a pan came through the air. I stopped at the end of the hallway, watching him as he swirled hot butter in the frying pan. I glanced at the freshly open tub of vegan butter. I didn't like this. Not that he'd made room in his fucking closet for the clothes he'd bought me or the fact he was standing there, cooking me...oat-flour pancakes?

I said nothing, just watched him while my mind raced. I needed to push this along, find out what he knows about Hale, find out what he knows about everything. I took a step closer, nearing the other side of the breakfast bar. "Seeing as how we're getting comfortable, Riven, you never told me what you actually do for a living."

He stilled for a second, then kept going, ladling the oat batter into the pan. "You could say I'm in acquisitions."

"For a bank?"

He didn't answer, just focused on making sure the heat was even as the mixture sizzled, filling the house with the most delicious smell.

"Well, it certainly looks like you've done well for yourself."

He turned, carrying the pan over to slide a delicious looking golden pancake onto a plate in front of me. "Better than an elementary school teacher."

I flinched at the words. He'd threatened to kill someone, someone that didn't really exist. I didn't know if he'd used it to manipulate me or if he'd really killed a complete stranger. I tried to find the answer in his stare. A shiver tore through me. Icy and honed. My pulse sped in response.

I was never scared. Not when the repercussions were only mine. But here, standing in front of him...meeting that unfathomable stare, I was fucking terrified. He was a monster. I *knew* that. A predator in every sense of the word.

I might've been the one who'd stepped out in front of his car. But every action and every consequence that came after that moment had been under his controlling hand. Riven Cruz wasn't just a monster, he was a predator, and to catch someone like that, you couldn't remain prey. You had to be his equal.

"You're lying."

He stilled, then turned.

I met that dark stare.

"This isn't acquisitions." I looked around at the sheer opulence of the place. Wood, glass, steel, and the faint trickling of running water from the internal rainforest.

He rounded the end of the counter, sliding a plate in front of me. One, perfectly golden brown pancake took up the entire surface. He said nothing, just pushed a freshly opened tub of vegan butter toward me, then a bottle of expensive maple syrup. "I guess it depends on *what* you're acquiring."

Heat rushed to my cheeks as his stare nailed me to the spot.

Women.

That's what he acquired.

I needed to remember that.

That same sickening wash of rage rose inside me. My jaw tightened. I glanced at a small knife sitting near the stove. One he'd used to slice the butter and place it into the pan. I clenched my teeth, imaging all the things I could do with that knife...and there were plenty. A flicker of confusion filled his stare, a tiny furrow between his eyes. He saw...*He saw.* His lips parted and his mouth opened to speak.

Until the sudden vibration of his phone shattered the moment.

He turned away and snatched the thing up, staring at the screen. But he didn't answer, just turned and looked at me over his shoulder. That scowl deepened before he strode away.

He lifted the cell to his ear. "Yes."

I pulled the plate closer and spread butter across the top before grabbing the syrup, all the while trying to listen in. But the conversation was all one-sided. He barely spoke, gave nothing away.

"Everything is fine. I'll contact you when I know more."

I jerked my gaze away as he ended the call and stabbed the fluffy stack instead, carving into it with the knife. Heavy footsteps sounded as I shoveled it into my mouth.

"What did you say you did for work, Helene?"

I turned my head, chewing loudly and with my mouth open, both things I knew would piss him off. "I didn't."

He held my stare.

Had he already searched my details? I'd be surprised if he hadn't, not with the whole captor/women trafficking vibe he had going on. I also knew exactly what he'd find when he punched my details into the system.

Helene Montgomery.

26 years old.

Worked as a hairdresser for 2 years.

Then went into retail at Walters & Co as a fashion buyer.

Moderate salary.

Saving to buy her own house.

No pets.

No family.

Both parents deceased.

Single child.

No priors apart from a few outstanding parking fines.

No...nothing.

A whole lot of nothing.

Social media accounts go back five years.

Five lonely years.

That's how long I'd been planning this exact moment, the second I came face to face with those who controlled, manipulated, and hunted my blood. Five years as Helene Montgomery. Five years of him finally understanding who he was up against.

No one came after my family.

Not if they wanted to live.

"How are they?" he asked carefully as he glanced at my half-finished plate.

"A little dry, actually."

A nerve twitched in the corner of his eye. It took all my strength not to burst out laughing. If it had been anyone else, I might've. But Riven wasn't anyone else. Instead, I swallowed, making sure to really gulp that mouthful down and pretend to cough...just for emphasis.

Any other man might've turned and walked away.

But Riven wasn't just any man, was he?

He stayed put as I grabbed my orange juice, but then he grabbed my wrist and whispered in my ear. "The living room...*now.*"

I stayed there, my gaze fixed on the counter as he straightened and strode away.

Fuck you!

I jerked my gaze after him. *I HATE YOU!* My breaths came hard and fast, so fast the kitchen brightened and blurred. I tried to slow down, tried to keep control of the situation, one where I needed to allow him to call all the shots.

Just until I get to Hale.

I closed my mouth, inhaling deeply before I dared follow him. The room sharpened again as my bare feet softly padded on the tiled floor. I'd barely glanced at this place last night as he'd carried me inside. But now that I wasn't kicking and screaming and hating myself for allowing the asshole to live, I saw just how stunning this place was.

It wasn't a house.

It was an *oasis*.

"You will kneel."

I jerked my head to where he sat on the plush black leather sofa. The bastard even had his legs crossed, one arm casually lying across the back as he watched me like a damn hawk. A rush flowed through me and a lightheaded, tingling sensation followed.

He lowered his gaze, taking in the barely there fucking thing he'd demanded I wear. Those hateful eyes glittered as he ordered again. "Kneel."

"Don't you mean heel? I'm not a fucking dog."

He met my rage. "No, you're my property."

My mouth twitched. I wanted to say a lot more. *Just think about Ryth. Think about Viv...think about the babies.*

I slowly sank, resting on my heels.

"Good. Now spread your legs."

Motherfucker—

I did, inching my knees apart.

"Wider."

That twitch came again. Heavy breaths followed as I pushed. He didn't even look down. No, the hatred in my stare riveted him. Was he goading me? Pushing me until I cracked, until I said or did something that would give him leverage? I pushed my shoulders back and straightened my spine. Maybe I might make *him* crack instead?

I opened my knees, pushing them as wide as I could. *How's that you...you...fucking gorgeous piece of shit?* I lowered my hand, slipped my finger underneath the lace cup of the bra, and eased it aside.

Anyone else might think he was unmoved. But not me. I saw all the signs. The way his eyes seemed to seize mine, as though he was desperate to look *anywhere else* and the deepening of his breath.

I was under his skin.

His throat muscles worked as he swallowed...then finally gave in.

I lowered my hand, dropping it to my thigh. "I think these are a little too tight, don't you?" I dug under the folded satin bands that dug into the flesh of my hips.

"No." His voice was throaty. "I think..." He met my gaze. "I *know* it's the perfect fit."

"Oh, yeah?" I whispered, almost daring him. "How about here?"

I tugged the elastic at the side of my pussy. *Pull them aside.* His command from moments ago in the bathroom filled my head. He liked to see....so I'd let him see. I slid my fingers in, finding my tender clit. Soft, swollen. *Sensitive.* My breath deepened. It wouldn't take long. A few strokes, a couple of—

He moved fast, launching from the sofa to grab me around the shoulders and drive me backwards. My ass hit the floor, but he held the rest of me suspended.

"No," he snapped, his eyes blazing. "Only *my* fingers belong there. Do you understand me? *My fucking fingers.*"

Anger flared. I was close to coming.

Close to getting exactly what I wanted.

And he saw it.

His lips quirked. "Are you feeling desperate and horny and pissed off?

I curled my lips.

"Good," the bastard answered. "Now you know how I feel every time I look at you."

My pussy throbbed all on its own.

No.

No.

This wasn't happening.

He eased me back, then straightened. The bulge in his pants was right in my direct line of sight.

Oh, God.

"I want to fuck you. I want to lick you. I want to fill you with me over and over and over again until your belly grows with life. How do you feel about that, Helene?"

I lifted my gaze. "Good luck with that, motherfucker. I can't have children."

"Can't?" He grabbed my arm and dragged me upwards until I met his stare. "Then I guess I'll have to find that out on my own, shall I?"

One hard push and I stumbled backwards...toward the bedroom.

TWELVE

Riven

MINE.

Mine.

MINE.

Desperation seared through every nerve in my body until I *throbbed.* She stumbled backwards, her eyes widening. But she never cowered. Oh no, Helene wasn't that kind of woman. It's what triggered me, what made her so real. She wasn't a blur in my head like all the other faces. No, this woman was neon fucking bright.

My steps thudded as I drove her back toward the kitchen. Her eyes darted left. Of course she lunged, trying her best to scurry around me.

I moved fast, grabbing her around the waist. "The hell you do."

"Get off me!" She bucked, kicking and swinging that fist.

Only now I knew her. Now I *expected* her, ducking my head for her blow to hit my shoulder before I carried her down the hall, hissing and spitting, into the bedroom.

"I'll fucking *kill you!*" she howled.

"Oh, I have no doubt about that," I answered, throwing her onto the bed.

She hit and bounced, before she was up and launching herself toward the door. I raced forward and reached for her...before she *roundhouse kicked me in the head.*

Stars.

That's all I saw for a moment.

Bright, detonating stars.

Had there been a bombing?

An explosion of some kind?

The bedroom trembled, bright and blurring as I stumbled. But she was gone. *She was gone.* I shook my head, then cast the hollow thumping aside and turned around.

Go on.

Do your fucking worst.

With a roar, I lunged. Where...where was she? I tracked the sound of her steps, but the woman didn't just fight like a damn cat, she moved like one as well. "Oh, *Hellle-eene!*" I called, racing to the garage and the only transport out of here.

The kitchen was a blur. The living room we were just in was empty...even the foyer was bare. I glanced toward the garage and lunged, shoving the door wide to stare at the Range Rover.

But it was still there. I strode to the driver's door, yanked it open, and grabbed the key from inside, then turned around.

She was still inside.

My mind raced at the possibilities...before the throbbing in my head made me wince.

First, she choked me out.

Then, she almost damn well knocked me out.

The woman was a goddamn force.

And I fucking loved it.

I smiled, striding back into the house. "You realize this is only going to make me fuck you harder, right?" Christ, my cock was hard. My whole being felt alive...*awakened* in a way I hadn't felt for...*ever.*

I lifted my gaze to the floor above. To what was actually the primary suite, if you weren't working for someone like Haelstrom Hale. But I couldn't afford to be cornered...not in my own damn house. But still the upstairs called me. Was she hiding in a cupboard or under a bed?

My smile grew wider.

Fuck, I hoped so.

Stair after stair, I climbed, until I hit the landing. The main bedroom was at one end, the retreat which opened onto its own private balcony at the other. I stilled as it hit me hard. The balcony...*of course, the fucking balcony.* I flew toward the room and the glass door leading outside, tearing through the doorway like a fucking madman.

The door was ajar, letting a cool breeze wash over me as I stepped forward. *"Fuck!"* I roared, my eyes searching for her.

Something sharp pressed against my back. "That's right, motherfucker. Now, let's get one thing straight. Nothing happens unless—"

A knife.

That's what she had.

The damn knife still smeared with her butter that I'd left on the counter

I swiveled around, not even caring if she stabbed me.

Because all that mattered was that she hadn't left.

"Unless?" I urged and stepped closer, so close the knife dug into my abdomen.

Pain flared, sharp and piercing, then a wet sensation followed. There was blood, that I knew. Still, I didn't look down, just leaned into it.

But she did. She looked down as the honed tip of the knife dug deeper into my belly. "Go on," I murmured. "Unless what, Helene? Unless you like it? Unless you come?"

Her eyes widened as her breaths raced. She jerked her focus from the knife to me.

"Unless what?" I whispered. "Unless you say yes? Is that it, Helene? Do you want to say yes to me?"

A tiny shake of her head told me all I wanted to know.

I lashed out and grasped her wrist with the knife as I stepped forward. She had no choice but to stumble back.

"You've had so many chances." I searched for that flicker of panic as she stumbled backwards. "So many times, you could've run. But you didn't...you didn't...now I'm asking myself *why?*"

She swallowed hard, her grip on the knife easing just a little. Was it on purpose? Was she begging me to take charge? I didn't know. I looked down, to where the cup of her bra had slipped below her puckered, dusky pink nipple. All I knew was I was about to come just thinking about it.

She backed up until she hit the wall at the far end of the sunroom, with me crowding her every step. I yanked her hand holding the knife above her head, letting her wrist take the brunt of the impact as I pushed my body against hers.

"Now anyone would think that's saying yes, don't you think, Helene?"

Hate flared in her eyes.

The cut in my belly was throbbing, pulling at my focus, but all I wanted was her. "I bet if I spread your pussy, you'd be glistening. Isn't that right?"

With a snarl, she slammed her hips forward and into mine, driving with full force against my cock.

Fuck!

Agony ripped through me. I grabbed her and hauled her off her feet. Fists and punches followed, but it was all too late as I took both of us to the floor. I clenched my grip, holding her with my other hand at the last minute so she didn't slam her head into the floor

"Is that it, Helene?" I roared. "I *KNOW* you can do better than that!"

She whipped her head from side to side, baring her teeth.

Christ, I loved it when she did that.

My breaths slowed, and my voice turned husky. "I bet if I *dipped right in there, you'd almost fucking come.* Maybe I need to find out for myself?" I moved my hand to grasp her throat. "You fight me and I'll handcuff you to the bed and do it anyway. Your choice."

She bucked. Of course, she bucked. Helene was *never* going to be a woman who didn't go down swinging. Faces filled my mind of all the Daughters I'd hurt in that place. All the spirits I'd broken. Women who could've been exactly like Helene.

But they weren't, were they?

I hadn't had a choice. Not then...or there.

I had a choice now.

I shifted my weight, leaving my hand in place. Blood was smeared along a scar across the front of her body. But it wasn't her blood, it was mine. A sense of relief hit me at that. One I didn't quite understand. I left my hand around her throat and dipped my head down, licking the blood on her skin. "Yes, I will cuff you to my bed and fuck you six ways to Sunday."

She unleashed a moan, causing me to inch lower, until *I* was the one who slid my finger under the satin band of her bodysuit. "Open your legs for me, Helene."

There was barely a fight from her. Her thighs parted, giving me all the access I wanted. Fuck, I wanted it all, *I wanted it all.* "You fight. You kick. You scream." I dragged my gaze to hers as

I slid my finger down her perfect cunt. "Yet, you're fucking dripping."

I curled my fingers, dragging them back up, before pushing into her. She writhed, moaning.

"That's it, fight it." I thrust in slowly, spreading her open before I dipped my head down. "Fight with all you have."

I spread her, tasting her even as I met the rage in her eyes. Panic flared amongst that deep, dark brown. Her shaking head was saying one thing, her body another. Her knees widened. Her hand landed on the back of my head, pushing my mouth harder against her perfect fucking cunt.

I took it all, sliding my fingers along the outside of her clit before I rose. "You'll come to want this, Helene." I licked the taste of her on my lips as I worked the button of my slacks before I shoved the zipper down. "In the end, you'll fucking beg."

She bared her teeth before she worked her mouth and spat. "Fuck you."

Spittle landed on my cheek, dribbling down to my jaw. Anger flared, but was quickly smothered with a smirk of satisfaction. I grabbed both her wrists, pinning them above her head as I settled between her legs. "No..." I grunted, driving all the way inside her. "Fuck *you*."

Jesus fucking Christ.

I sucked in hard breaths and dropped my head. She moaned, arching her back. Her core clenched around me, sending my pulse racing. She felt...*like home.* That's how this woman felt, just like *my future.* I opened my eyes and lifted my head to meet that rage.

But there wasn't rage.

Not anymore.

I thrust, driving into her. "You will want me," I croaked. "You will want me as much as I want you."

There was no spittle this time, no snarl. She just closed her eyes, her breaths racing as I gripped her wrists, took all my weight on my forearms, and caged her in.

Desire flooded me. I focused on the sensation and the pure hunger for her. I'd never felt anything so goddamn blinding, making me clench my ass as she wrapped her legs around my waist and gripped me tight.

"That's it, Trouble," I grunted. "Come for me."

Her eyes squeezed shut as that frenzied race to the end took over. She was close...so...fucking *close.*

A moan ripped free, desperate and aching. I drove my cock deep and turned my head, riveted by her mouth...

Kiss her.

The need was overwhelming.

I leaned in until she turned her head away from me and let out a shuddering whimper. My balls clenched at the sound, before I hauled in a breath and tensed.

The rush was blinding as I unleashed a groan and filled her.

Breaths.

That's all there was.

Heat and power radiated from her.

Still, I wanted more.

I pulled out, looking down between us at the last second. Come coated both of us. But it was just the start, wasn't it? I met her stare as she turned her head. "You belong to me."

The corner of her mouth trembled and *there* was that rage. I couldn't help but enjoy every second as I reached down and slid the satin band of her panties back in place before I fixed my slacks. "Now, seeing as how you can't be trusted..."

"Try it and I'll—" she stared.

But she didn't have time to finish before I yanked her forward, then bent and lifted her over my shoulder. Her blows were instant, slow this time, and not quite as strong. I took a fist to the side of my head, and one on my ear, which made my head ring. Still, I carried her back down the stairs and through the house toward the bedroom.

"Can't have you running away now, can I?" I tossed her gently back onto the bed. "Not until I put a tracker in you."

"Do it, and I'll bite it out."

I lifted her hand and locked the cuff around her wrist to tether her to the bed. "You know? You're the first woman who's said that who I believe would."

She glared at me, that hostile stare spewing as much disgust and hate as one could without saying a word, and for the first time in my life, I was struck by the beauty of her. It was stupid, mortifying, really. In my entire life, I'd *never* found anything perfect. Not by looks, or by attachment.

But she was.

She fucking was.

Her chin jutted up, those perfect lips parting slightly to show her teeth. *I could fall for her.* The thought chilled me to the bone. "Stay there." My voice was a croak. "I'll get you water."

She said nothing.

Just raged.

Christ, she was cute.

I walked out and stopped just outside the bedroom door. My pulse was erratic. But that was *nothing* compared to my mind. *What the fuck are you* doing? *Seriously. What if…what if the others found out?*

Heat ripped through me, jealousy and anger followed. I didn't give a fuck…not anymore.

I raked my fingers through my hair and headed into the kitchen, grabbing two bottles of water from the refrigerator before looking at the mess I'd left behind.

How are they?

Jesus, I'd sounded smug.

A little dry, actually.

The corner of my lips tugged a little higher. If anyone else had said that to me, they'd be dead. But not Helene…*no, not Helene.* I turned, staring at the hallway, hating that seething, savage pull to return to her. I needed to figure this out. I needed time.

Yes, that's what I needed.

Time…with her.

I gripped the bottles and headed back to the bedroom. I couldn't think about anything other than her right now. I licked my lips, my cock hardening at the thought. I couldn't even stay away from her for a second, could I? Not a goddamn second.

Fuck.

Darkness waited as I cracked open my eyes. Darkness followed by the low, throaty moan of a woman beside me. The scent of sex hung heavy in the air. The cloying taste was followed by hunger, hunger like I'd never felt before.

My body came alive, making me search the gloom for the outline of her body. I fucking wanted her so bad it might ruin me. No, so bad, *she* might ruin me.

I shoved the sheet aside. Cool night air swept over my bare legs as my hand found the warmth of her thigh, then the smooth satin band of the bodysuit I'd forced her to wear.

I'd forced a lot of things.

Still, I couldn't seem to stop myself, not where she was concerned.

I rolled over, shoved my boxers down low, and reached for her pussy. She woke the moment I yanked her panties aside and pushed my way between her legs.

Her cry was sharp, ringing as I thrust in. I smothered it with one hand, feeling the heat of her breath as I grasped her shackled wrist.

"Shh..." I pushed in deep. "Easy, now. Go back to sleep."

She bucked, fighting me until my weight pinned her down, letting me drive all the way in. "You fight me...you fight me and it'll be worse."

She unleashed a tortured, carnal sound and stilled, her breaths panting as I fucked her. I turned my head, finding that hateful stare. She wasn't broken. I *knew* broken when I saw it. No, *she was giving in.*

I smiled, curling my spine to drive into her harder. "I warned you before, Helene, I have to have you."

"Fuck you," she gasped, but widened her legs for me.

I didn't even wait for her to come. Just smiled and thrust, holding onto the feral rage in her beautiful eyes. Something shivered inside me. My pulse raced...my heart clenched as I stared at her and in an instant slowed my thrusts.

I fully intended to leave her desperate. But one look...one piercing stare, and I drove upwards, watching her breath catch and her eyelids flutter. Christ, I wanted to hear her moan, wanted to know she wanted what I did to her. "Can't seem to help myself where you're concerned," I murmured. "Why is that?"

"Because..." she panted. "You're a *sick fuck.*"

I *was* a sick fuck.

Especially where she was concerned.

I didn't just fuck her.

I punished her.

Thrust after thrust, until she thrashed her head from side to side, fighting what her body craved. I lowered my head, finding the peak of her nipple. My breath was warm, blowing back on me as I grunted, driving deep. "Come for me, Helene...*come,*" I commanded.

Her body convulsed.

Her core clenched.

I slammed my eyes closed, overwhelmed by the feel of her, and shuddered all the way down to my core. Her hand clutched the sheet, her legs spread wide open under me. But it was her eyes that transfixed me. Wide. Glassy. Like she was stripped raw, exposed, and completely and utterly surrendered.

I eased out of her, brushing her wrist and the metal cuff with my thumb. I'd never wanted to kiss someone so badly in my entire life. This was more than a need to connect...this was a need to belong.

"Sleep, Helene." I searched her eyes, brushing a strand of her hair aside. "I'm the only monster you need to worry about tonight."

She did, closing her eyes, mumbling. "You're bad enough."

I was...only the longer I was around her, the deeper this monster was starting to fall.

She shifted, making me move back from her body. I waited for her breaths to deepen, until I was sure she was under, and rolled over, grabbed the key from the nightstand, and unlocked the cuff around her wrist.

A murderer.

A rapist.

A shell of a fucking man.

That's all I was.

I eased her hand against her body, watching her chest rise, then fall.

She smelled like me.

Like my wants and desires...*and my future.*

The room lit up with a ghostly green glow. I rolled carefully, snatched up my cell, and glanced at the caller ID before answering. "I'm here."

"It's time," Harmon spoke tersely. "New shipments will be there by morning. I want them prepared as quickly as possible, do you understand?"

My pulse spiked, thundering in my ears. "Yes."

"And I expect you'll show my men the same respect you'd show me?"

I forced the words through clenched teeth. "Of course."

"Good. Remember, this is your one and final warning, Cruz. Step out of line and you'll find yourself and your brothers staring down the barrel of a gun."

I swallowed hard, turning my head to stare at the sleeping form in my bed. "Understood."

"By morning," Harmon finished.

But I didn't need to respond, because he was already gone, leaving me staring into the dark once more.

My teeth clenched until my jaw bulged.

I closed my eyes as a wave of hopelessness hit me. I shook my head, my soul in torment as I grasped the drawer of my nightstand and eased it open. The soft glow of the keypad was all I needed to steady me, allowing me to punch the code into the lockbox and pull the gun free.

Stupid.

Stupid!

What the fuck had I *thought* was going to happen? I winced and turned around, finding the slow rhythmic rise of her chest. That I could play happy fucking family with a woman I'd drugged and held prisoner for the rest of my goddamn life?

This wasn't me.

It wasn't anything I deserved.

I stood and stepped toward the foot of the bed. It wasn't what *she* deserved, either.

I lifted my gun and rounded the side of the bed before I froze. Her lips were parted, her eyes closed. I loved her hate...but when she was like this, she looked so peaceful.

One pull of the trigger and it'd be over.

It was better this way.

For me.

For her.

She'd never know.

My hand shook as the gun rose.

She'd never know.

THIRTEEN

Helene

"I NEED YOU TO WAKE UP."

I opened my eyes instantly, to see him at the side of the bed, staring down at me. Heat bloomed, stirring something in the pit of my soul. That reaction alone terrified me, until my gaze sharpened and I saw the gun in his hand.

"What time is it?" I asked, carefully meeting his stare, my mind racing.

"Almost morning."

He was dressed in black slacks and a black open-collared shirt. His hair glistened as though still damp. Had he showered? I inhaled the rich scent of soap on his skin. He had, and I hadn't heard a damn thing. My body hummed as goosebumps raced. Even now I was ready for him, craving his cruel caresses and his devastating devotion. One look in his eyes and I felt the burn of his hunger.

"You need to shower and get dressed."

"Now?" I pushed up, realizing my hand was free.

There was no sign of the cuffs anywhere.

"Yes, now," he answered. "Your clothes are in the bathroom. We need to leave."

"Leave?"

He scowled for a second, anger flaring with his clenched jaw. "Yes, Helene, we're leaving."

I wanted to demand where...but he wasn't in the mood for more questions, and right now, I needed time to think. I gave a slow nod and slipped from the bed, padding into the bathroom, expecting him to follow. But he didn't, leaving me to peel the still come-stained bodysuit free and toss it to the floor.

I smelled of him.

My own scent was smothered by his desire.

I scowled, wrestled the flushed heat of desire that followed, and hit the faucet.

The hot water steamed up the shower as I stepped inside. Black on black shifted in the bedroom as he paced. I grabbed the soap and lathered. Something had changed in the last few hours while I'd been asleep. Something I needed to understand.

Harmon.

It had to be.

Was the new shipment of Daughters finally at The Order? Is that where he was taking me? If that was the case, then Hale could also be there. My thoughts raced, finally shaking off the fog. If only I could get a message to London. I stilled, my hand cupping my tender breast. I looked down, to see the peak reddened from the graze of his teeth. No, London wouldn't wait. He'd descend, all guns and rage, driving every tiny scrap of information we might find underground.

No.

I needed to be careful. I needed to wait. I swallowed hard, quickly washed the rest of my body, and turned off the water, then stepped out. Jeans, underwear, a t-shirt, and a black sweater sat neatly folded on the vanity. I dried and dressed, and stepped into the bedroom.

Socks. Boots...and Riven.

He nodded to the rest of my things. "We need to leave."

I pulled them on, watching him from the corner of my eye. The gun still in his hand made me cautious. I tugged the laces around my boots and rose, meeting his stare. If he was going to kill me, then he wouldn't have cared if I'd showered or not.

Either way, his DNA was all over me.

Teeth marks on my breasts.

The trace of his come, still deep inside.

He wasn't disposing of evidence, that I was sure of.

One motion of his hand and I headed out of the bedroom, past the kitchen and into the garage. The almost black sky waited outside. He hit the button behind me and the lights to the Range Rover flashed and the doors unlocked.

Silence followed as I climbed inside.

I should be fighting.

At least pretending to.

But I didn't.

I climbed in, closed the door behind me, and reached for the seatbelt as he slid in behind the wheel.

"Want to tell me where we're headed?"

He started the engine, then pressed the button for the garage door. "A place I'd hoped you'd never see. But it's this...it's this or..." he wrestled with the words.

I swallowed hard, glancing at the gun still in his hand. It was this or a bullet to the brain. "Then I guess we'd better get going."

His dark eyes barely glinted. There was no excitement now, no desire, no fight even. Just a stony stillness. One I didn't like at all. He put the car into reverse and backed out of the drive, leaving the garage door to close behind us.

It felt strange leaving what should have been my prison, only it hadn't felt like a prison. It'd felt like a battleground, one where I'd held my own. Blood had been spilled there, rage and desire living, throbbing things we'd created. It was *us*—I glanced toward him as he accelerated, leaving the house behind—it was us.

Still, my mind raced as we headed out of the city. What the hell did Riven think he was going to achieve by keeping me locked in a place like that? My pulse raced. I knew those cells, and I'd seen firsthand what they'd done to the Daughters there.

Daughters like Ryth and Vivienne.

But this...this felt different. *He felt different.*

He wasn't the monster I'd been expecting. No, he was a different breed. One cloaked in secrets.

His problems were not my problem.

I needed to remember that.

His hands were clenched around the wheel. His focus was fixed on the road, but still, I could see he was lost in the panicked, racing thoughts inside his head.

I turned back, staring into the faint spill of sunlight in the distance as we came closer to the compound on the outskirts of the city. All I cared about was getting to Hale and anyone who stood in my way of that was dead.

"I'm going to lock you in this place."

I flinched at the sudden sound of his voice.

He glanced my way. "But I need you to know it's not what you think."

"Not what I think," I repeated as we turned the last bend in the road and the steel fence glinted in the distance. "And what is that, exactly?"

The four-wheel drive slowed.

Goosebumps raced over me as I stared at the shrouded outline of hell.

Because that's what this place was...*hell.*

He never answered, just turned the wheel and braked hard. A guard stepped out of nowhere, hidden by the hut at the front of the gates. Gates that'd been rammed by Ryth's stepbrothers to rescue her. I could still see the gouges in the steel.

The window rolled down, and the guard advanced. "There's only me here." Riven met the guard's stare. "Isn't that right, Connor?"

The guard never even looked my way, just gave a careful nod. "Absolutely, Mr. Cruz."

The gates rolled open, letting us take the long drive to this place of nightmares. The closer we came, the colder the car felt. Only no one had touched the temperature. It was all me...and him.

"There are things I need to do here, people I need to take care of. But you won't be part of that. Still, I need you to be quiet and not make a scene." Headlights spilled against the brick as he pulled around to the rear of the building. "Can you do that, Helene? Can you stay quiet, stay safe, until I can deal with these people?"

The structure was perfect and sound...until it wasn't. The glaring lights cut over the blown-out brick wall at the far side, the one closest to the towering trees of the forest. I glanced into the dark gloom, remembering the moment I'd followed Vivienne and the others into that hell.

I was alone.

Alone, stepping into the stench of blood and terror.

Fear chattered my teeth, chilling me to the bone. I turned away from the forest to the blown out far wall of the building as we parked. My pulse was thundering, the *boom...boom...boom* almost smothering his words.

"I just need..." he killed the engine, leaving us staring at the shattered bricks. The remnant from a bomb. *My bomb.*

But it was Riven I focused on as he dragged his fingers through his hair. "I just need to keep you safe. There are others coming. Others who aren't as nice."

I met his stare. "So, you're protecting me?"

How could he...when *he* was the monster?

There was a twitch at the corner of his mouth. His breaths deepened as I stared at those hard lips, those cruel, smothering lips. "Protecting, controlling, call it what you want."

I jerked my gaze to his. At least he called it what it was. "Maybe I'll take my chances. Maybe I might just scream and beg and plead when these other men come."

He leaned closer, that menacing glare detonating with sparks. "Try it and I'll kill every last one of them...right before I drag you from this place and keep you chained for the rest of your goddamn life."

I swallowed hard. He would. I could see that now. "Why?" I whispered. "Why me?"

"Because you, Helene...found me."

He waited for a second before he shoved open the door and climbed out. The headlights stayed on, illuminating the damage I'd caused. I sat there for a second with his words ringing in my ears. *You found me. You...found me.*

My pulse skipped, then raced to catch up. I had no choice but to follow as he turned, waiting for me. The headlights died with the thud of the door. The sunrise cut through the trees, spilling all across the newly installed side door as we stepped inside The Order and closed out the rest of the world.

Our footsteps thudded, echoing in the hallway. Riven's cell vibrated as I glanced at the locked double doors. His deep voice resounded as he answered. "Now is not a good time."

I glanced at him, hurrying to catch up to his long strides.

"No...I'm at The Order. Yes, you could say that."

A chill raced through me as he spoke.

"We have a new shipment coming. No...no, I don't want you here," he said in a rush, finding me in the corner of his eye. "I need to go. I'll talk to you later."

He pulled a small keyring from his pocket, pressed a card that hung from it against the scanner for the doors, and pushed through. My steps slowed. My gaze moved to his. I was putting a lot of trust in him right now. The kind he didn't deserve. But there was something pleading about his careful stare, something that entwined with that desperate need to protect those I loved...

And I stepped through.

Thud.

I flinched as the door closed behind me. He headed along the hallway that looked just like the one we'd left. I glanced over my shoulder, swallowed, then followed as he came to a door at the end of a row, pushed a key into the lock, and bore down on the handle.

But I couldn't force myself to walk through.

Flashbacks detonated like bombs inside my head. *Riven unleashing his rage, hunting me as I'd rigged the explosion in the south side of the building...and hauled my father out of this place.* I needed to remember the kind of man I was dealing with. The monster...who was now back in his lair.

It was all I could do to stop from fleeing this place as fast as I could.

He fought hard not to meet my gaze, but in the end he lost. "This entire wing isn't used anymore. You'll be safe here. You'll be..."

Controlled. Isn't that the term he'd used before?

The air suddenly turned heavy, so heavy I could barely breathe. I looked at that cell, from the heavy lock on the door to the single cot inside.

"You can trust me on this," he said carefully.

Those were words I *never* thought I'd hear from his lips. But these were dangerous times, and I had nieces to protect.

"I doubt that very fucking much," I answered bleakly and stepped into the cell.

The door closed instantly. I watched him through the glass section of the door and for a second, I swore I saw panic in his dark eyes. I hoped it was, anyway. He only held my life in the palm of his hand. I'd felt the cruelty of that hand...and also...tenderness.

Still, I fucking hated that desperate feeling as the door closed and he turned away. "You'd better come back for me, motherfucker," I whispered, wrapping my arms around myself. "You'd better come back."

FOURTEEN

Riven

THE DOUBLE DOORS CLOSED BEHIND ME WITH A *CLACK*. The locks engaged, right before panic descended. I stumbled to the wall, bracing myself as the hallway blurred. My breaths were hard, strangled fucking things that I forced out until the harsh, heaving rasp was all I heard.

What the fuck was I thinking?

She shouldn't be here.

Not in this place.

Not with me.

I closed my eyes. I wasn't me when I was here.

I was...someone else.

Someone dangerous.

Dangerous for her.

Goosebumps raced along my spine, until I remembered the cameras watching. Without lifting my gaze, I dropped my hand and straightened my shoulders, then kept on walking, forcing myself to focus.

I needed to keep her quiet.

Just until I could get this shipment of Daughters done...and out of here.

Because they were the only thing that mattered.

The only thing that'd lead me to Hale.

My cell vibrated. Jaw muscles bulged as I lifted the damn thing and saw the caller ID. *Kane.* "Not now," I snarled, slipping the phone back into my pocket, and headed back along the hall to my office.

White painted doors.

The name *they* called me printed in black block letters.

The Principal.

I hated that fucking name.

Hated this entire business.

Still, I never let that show as I slipped the key into the lock and stepped inside. One quick scan of my office and I moved around my desk and eased into my seat. This room was bugged. That I knew, with hidden cameras and microphones. There were few places here hidden from prying eyes. One of those places had occupied my focus for the last two weeks, from the moment Hale's body had been pulled from that river. A body I now knew wasn't his.

I needed to return to that office, to keep looking for any hint of where he'd disappeared to...later.

Right now, I had a truckload of Daughters headed my way.

I reached forward, clutched the mouse, and logged into my computer, bringing up the tracking information sent to my email.

19 assets en route.

Assets.

I winced at the word. Something living, breathing...created for no purpose other than our whims, reduced to one simple term *asset*. That's all these women were to men like Hale. And I was the one who made them that way.

My hand shook as I grabbed the mouse and clicked the link, opening up the GPS map. A red light blinked, moving closer to the compound not more than an hour away. An hour. That's all I had.

A fucking hour.

I pushed up from my chair and glanced at the map one last time before I turned and walked out.

A fucking hour.

An hour before, the Daughters were here, and Harmon's men with them. Men I couldn't trust. My strides lengthened as I headed for the fucking place in this hell I needed to be, the *only* place I needed to be. Hallways blurred. Rage writhed under my skin like a serpent desperate to shed its skin. Maybe I was aching to reveal my true nature and murder every last one of them.

I slammed my card against the scanner, then pushed through the doors. *How many times have I been here?* Scouring through every fucking scrap of paper and file he'd left behind. I was so desperate to find anything that might lead me to the black site he'd kept hidden.

A black site he was now at...

And the one where he kept our sister hostage.

How many children had he forced her to breed?

How many familiar faces would one day stare back at me.

My steps faltered at the thought. I pressed my card against the scanner on his door, then pushed through. On the outside, the room looked perfect and neat. That's what you were supposed to see. What you weren't was the remnant of the fingerprint dust as I'd scoured every inch of this room.

Still, I'd come up with nothing.

No address.

Nothing I could use to track back to the one fucking person who could put an end to this.

Haelstrom Hale.

I strode around the desk, glancing at my watch as I logged in. There had to have been information sent to his email, a location where this shipment of women was headed...anything. I scanned Hale's inbox, finding a few irrelevant emails about various houses he'd shown an interest in buying, but nothing else. Still, I jotted down the addresses, typing them out in a text message I sent to The Hunter.

If nothing else, it kept him moving, like a shark circling its prey.

We'd find him.

One way or another…then we'd find her.

I logged off and rose, wincing as my cell vibrated again. Kane's name flashed across the screen. I hit the button to send it to voicemail as I pulled the door closed behind me. By the time I strode to the back dock and opened the door, greeting my head of security with a careful nod, thirty minutes had passed.

"Make sure they are secured as fast as possible," I muttered. "I want no incidents."

"Yes, sir," he answered.

I pulled out my cell and texted the doctor on call. He responded instantly, telling me he was already on the way. *19 assets.* That's what we had arriving. Assets that would no doubt require medical care by the time we locked them in their cells.

Beep.

I glanced at the message from the doctor advising he and his medical team were on standby. Fuck, I hated this shit. "Get ready with the trackers," I muttered as the call cracked over the two-way.

They're pulling through the gate now.

My pulse raced as all thoughts turned back to the woman locked in the cell. The woman who had no place being somewhere like this, or with me, for that matter.

As the crunch of tires and the low rumble of the truck's engine sounded, my cell vibrated once more. I didn't even look at it this time, just stared straight ahead, sinking into that cold, empty pit inside me. The truck pulled in, then swung around, back-up lights washing over me.

Two black Explorers pulled up alongside the truck and parked before the engines died. Men with guns climbed out. I focused on the passenger-side door of the first car, on the one who didn't seem to carry a weapon. No, he looked like he *was* the weapon.

He looked at the building as he adjusted his jacket, then turned and spoke to his men. I didn't care about what he said. It was his eyes I focused on and the way he moved. Thick shoulders bunched under a tailored jacket as he turned and nodded.

His men moved instantly, like a SWAT team swarming around the truck as it reversed again and braked to a stop. I expected him to head toward me, to at least give me a goddamn name. But the bastard never even looked my way. His men stepped up to the loading dock, pushing past my men with snarls and savage stares.

Walker cut me a look of rage as he was forced aside. I gave a shake of my head as the head of their outfit climbed the stairs, glancing at the truck as the rear door opened. I cleared my throat and straightened my spine.

"Astor, get them inside as soon as possible," he commanded, staring at the Daughters as they were unloaded one by one.

Their faces blurred into one.

Terrified.

Pale.

Hands clasped, tied in front of them.

19 assets were unloaded by four guards and told to stand in front of us.

I waited for Harmon's man to look my way, to at least give me his attention for a second. But the bastard never even acknowledged I was there, not until he took a step toward the locked external doors and turned, meeting my gaze. "I'll require keys."

I kept my face stony. "Walker will assist you with any access you might need during the checking-in process."

He scowled, then stepped closer. "You're not understanding me. We're not here to offload the cargo and leave. We're here to take over."

What the fuck? Rage plunged all the way inside. "Under whose authority?"

He just gave a chuff. "Mr. Harmon's authority. Would you prefer I call and confirm this with him?"

Harmon's warning rose to the surface. *I still believe you're an asset, Riven...don't cause me to think otherwise.*

So, this was it?

This was him making sure I 'got my shit together.' I stared at the unflinching bastard and felt the ground at my feet tremble. My standing here was fragile indeed...more now than ever. "Walker," I said, staring into the bastard's eyes. "Give—"

"Coulter," he answered.

"Give Coulter here your keys until you can provide him with a set of his own."

"No," Coulter responded, searching my stare before he lifted his hand. "I'll take yours instead."

I clenched my jaw as the Daughters shivered, clinging to each other as they wept. Their whimpers were all I could hear. His lips curled as I reached into my pocket and pulled my set free, handing them over.

He enjoyed this.

Let's see how long that'd last. I watched as he turned and motioned to his men, ushering the Daughters inside. I waited for them to disappear before I spoke to Walker. "I want him watched like a fucking hawk. The moment you sense anything I can exploit, I want to know about it."

"Will do," he answered, leaving me as he followed them inside.

It wasn't just Harmon I needed to be wary of now. It was everyone...everyone who wasn't my blood...or...*her*.

Dark brown eyes filled my mind, until a weight dropped on my chest. *Fuck.* She was here...and now so were Harmon's men.

I strode forward, pressed my card against the scanner, and followed them back into the bleak halls of The Order. Footsteps thudded as doors were opened and locked. Walker strode ahead, catching up to them and motioned to the far east wing of the building.

Their cries echoed.

A chill raced.

It was the same all over again.

All these women.

To be trained and used.

How the fuck had we gotten here?

I hung back, listening to Daughters cry out as one by one they were separated and forced into cells. They should be used to it after coming from the orphanages. But they never were. They still fought and cried, and planned to escape. None of them made it...

Not until that Banks bitch...and London's whore.

Fuck him.

Fuck all of them who weren't blood.

Thud.

Thud.

Thud.

Doors to each cell were closed and locked. I risked a glance at Coulter as he watched his men before I turned and walked away. My head was thundering. My panic was out of control. I needed a tether for this madness...a connection for my tainted soul.

I needed *her*....

I slammed my card against the scanner and pushed through the door. Step by step, desperation grew inside me, until it was all I could do to stop from running. *Boom. Boom. Boom.* My pulse was a beast roaring in my head as I shoved aside the next set of doors, then turned.

The wing where I'd put her rose in the distance. I hurried, driving my card against the scanner and pushed through. *Get to her. Get to her. Just fucking...get to her.*

My hands clenched. My jaw was a fucking vise as I lifted my gaze to the locked door at the end of the hall. *Please be there. Please, I need...I need you.*

I slammed my card against the scanner, then bore down on the handle.

Thud.

I stopped.

Thud.

Staring at her as she rose from the bed and took a tentative step closer before she stopped, then scowled. "Riven?"

In a rush, I went to her, grabbed her around the waist, and pulled her against me. "Fuck…I…" I closed my eyes, breathing in the scent of her hair.

Her hands fluttered against my shoulders. Still, she didn't pull away. That was something.

"What's wrong?" she asked.

I couldn't speak, not for a long while. All I could do was hold her, pulling her all the way down in the filth of this place with me. I was destroying her, risking not just her life but now mine. Fear lifted its head. The kind of fear that made me feel unhinged. Just like I was when I was around her.

I opened my eyes and pulled away. "Nothing."

"It doesn't look like nothing." She searched my gaze. "Something happened, didn't it?"

She saw more than I wanted her to.

More than she should…for her sake.

"There's been a change around here. Those other men I spoke about…they're not leaving."

She jerked her gaze toward the door. "They're staying?"

I gave a careful nod.

"Then you'll need to be careful." She met my gaze. "And ruthless."

Ruthless. Yes, that's exactly what I needed to be. I scowled, searching her eyes. She shouldn't be this calm. She shouldn't be this...controlled. An icy whisper of fate filled me. There was chaos all around me...and in the middle of it all...was her.

I reached out and clasped the back of her neck. My breaths deepened as I fell into her eyes. "Yes," I answered. "Ruthless I can do."

She swallowed hard. "Yes, you can."

I felt steadier around her, more in control. That same hunger burned between us. I knew she felt it too. She grazed her bottom lip with her teeth, pinning the soft flesh in place. If I had more time... "I'll come back tonight," I said carefully.

"I'll be right here." She forced the words through clenched teeth.

I forced myself to turn around, because if I didn't, I'd have her up against the wall...whimpering like the good fucking whore she was.

My cock hardened at the thought.

Fuck, I wasn't doing myself any favors around this woman. My senses screamed, howling for me to turn around as I walked out of her room. I closed the door, listening to the lock click shut. She stood in the room, waiting for me. I met her stare through the glass before I was grabbed...and turned.

Rage.

Dark, barely controlled rage.

"What the *fuck* are you doing?" Kane snarled, shoving me against the wall.

Panic roared through me, turning me dangerous. I swung my brother around, fisting his shirt before I shoved him against the wall. "What the fuck are you doing here?"

He punched my shoulder, pushing me off. "You don't answer your fucking calls?"

No. Not when they weren't important.

"There were men...men who tracked us back to the rectory."

Everything else fell away. "What? Who?"

"I don't know," he snarled. "We didn't hang around to find out."

Realization hit me like a blow. "So you came here?"

"Where the fuck else were we supposed to go?"

He scowled, searching my eyes, then glanced along the hallway. "Why are you here? This wing is closed."

My pulse skipped, then sped. "Nothing."

He scowled even harder. "Don't *nothing* me, Riven. I know you too well." He turned his head, glancing at the closed door.

Heat rushed to my cheeks. "Don't," I warned.

He just shot me a glare before he moved. I lunged, grabbing his arm. "I said *don't.*"

But it was too late as he slammed his card against the scanner and bore down on the handle...shoving the door wide.

"Wait!" I hissed.

He stepped inside. I had no choice but to follow. Helene was there, turned around, her back to us.

"Who the *fuck* is this?" Kane snarled.

Slowly, she turned around and met my brother's stare.

The world stood still. I didn't know what to do. Thoughts of knocking my brother out rose before I pushed them away. "It's not—"

"Helene?" His eyes widened with terror. "What the *hell* are you doing here?"

FIFTEEN

Helene

My breath burned a hole through the center of my chest. All I saw was Riven's dark eyes as they narrowed on me.

"Wait," he jerked a dangerous glare at his brother. "You *know* her?"

Kane stepped closer, brushing a strand of hair from my face, and like all the times when he'd made a move before, I fought the need to flinch. "Know her?" he answered, searching my stare. "You could say that. She's one of my clients."

I swallowed hard, aware of Riven's every move.

"*Your fucking client?*" he snarled.

Jealousy rippled from him as he curled his lip and clenched his fists. I saw the moment that fragile hold cracked, and Kane felt it too. He turned to meet his brother's murderous stare.

Goosebumps rose along my arms, making my hair stand on end. In an instant, Riven lunged, grabbing his brother by the shirt to yank him backwards and drive him against the wall. "You better not fucking lie to me," he barked. "How the *fuck* do you know her?"

But Kane was just as savage, pushing him away with a punch to the shoulder. "Get the fuck *off* me."

They fought, right in front of me, grappling each other with grunts and snarls in attempts to get the upper hand. This was no sibling rivalry, this was cold, barely controlled rage.

"You fucking bastard," Riven growled, punching Kane's shoulder. *"You motherfucking bastard."*

But he was angry at the wrong person. The moment he realized that he froze, staring into his brother's eyes, then turned to me as he sucked in hard breaths.

Beep.

His phone chimed. With a clench of his jaw, he snatched it up and scowled at the screen before muttering, "Fuck."

"What is it?" Kane sucked in a hard breath and tugged down his creased shirt, risking a glance my way before fixing on his brother once more.

"We have a problem." Riven tore his focus from his cell. "Harmon's men are taking over the compound...and right now, his goddamn commander is moving into Hale's office."

"His men?" Kane snapped. "What fucking men?"

But Riven never answered, just glanced my way. "This...this isn't over. Not by a fucking long shot. I'll deal with this...then, Helene Montgomery, I'm coming back to deal with *you*."

I swallowed, watching him turn. "Kane, with me," he commanded as he headed for the door.

But his brother didn't move, confusion and pain etched in his stare as he jerked his focus my way.

"Now, brother," Riven insisted.

They left, closing the door behind them...and taking all the oxygen in the room. My knees trembled the moment the lock clicked, and my pulse raced until all I could hear was the thrashing sound in my ears.

What the fuck have I done?

I closed my eyes.

WHAT THE FUCK HAVE I DONE?

The scream resounded. My knees gave way, buckling under me. I wrenched my eyes open as I hit the floor, bruising my shins before I slammed my palms against the cold tiles. But I didn't get up, I couldn't move. My hair fell in a curtain, hiding my face as a terrified sound escaped my lips.

One shake of my head and panic took hold.

I'd failed.

I'd failed...

Tears blurred my sight. I'd failed them. In one fucking split second, I'd failed them. Why did I step out into the traffic like that? Not when I knew it was goddamn pouring down? I should've stopped it. I should've stopped it...

Would it have made a difference?

I sucked in a breath, trying to quell the fire in my lungs, and slowly lifted my gaze to the door, where the only hope I'd had of finding Hale had disappeared, taking his brother with him.

You fucking know her?

I could still feel the rage in those words.

You could say that. She's one of my clients. I shook my head as all the sessions with Dr. Kane Cruz surfaced.

We've made good progress today, Helene. But I think we could make even more if we went through some of those after-hour sessions I talked about...it could help with the dissociation you feel when you cut.

I could still feel the weight of his stare down my body as he told me just how close I was to exploring how deep my abandonment issues were. He'd made it well known what kind of extra sessions he thought he could provide me, and just how that would benefit both of us.

He could help me feel something more than the release.

And I could help him feel...me.

But it wouldn't help me, would it?

Because he had no idea who I was...

Not then.

But he did now.

I closed my eyes and bowed my head until my forehead touched the cold tiles. Yes, he was beginning to, at least. It wouldn't take long for them to know the rest, and then...then, what? Then they'd kill me?

I tried to search for the answer, tried to let instinct lead the way. What would they do? They couldn't very well let me go, not once they'd figured out I was Ryth and Vivienne's sister. They might kill me, or they might use me.

If they knew my last name was King.

I lifted my head, my breath caught. If they knew I was a King, they might let me go, or use me as bait. That could work...that... could work...*right?*

I sat there, staring at the door, waiting for some voice inside my head to comfort me. But it never came, and as that silence in my head became too much to bear, I rose. It was the only card I had left to deal. The only one of any use...*apart from my body.*

I lowered my gaze, hating how even just the idea of that made my skin feel flushed. I hated him. I hated all of them...but still. I swallowed as my brain admitted I wanted him. I wanted his cruel fucking hands on my skin. I wanted his savage, brutal nature.

There was no hiding with him.

No dark rooms to hide in.

No clothing to cover my skin.

He wanted me bare and raw.

So fucking raw, the mere brush of his fingers made me shudder.

So raw I craved his touch.

I shook my head as my belly howled.

These walls were going to be my undoing. I headed for the closed off section where there was a toilet and a sink and tugged my pants down. This place may as well be a prison, but there was no sentence here, was there? No other inmates I could see to pass the time. I wiped and flushed, then rose and made for the sink, washing my hands and cupping water to drink.

A cold trail dribbled down my chin. I swiped it with the back of my hand and stared at the door. That's all I did, even when I started to pace yet again. I walked and stared, never once taking my eyes from the glass panel and the empty hallway outside.

If I die before I can get to Hale, I'll have failed them.

The only two people who'd ever mattered.

The only two worth sacrificing for.

The cell blurred, even that fucking doorway ceased to exist.

Survive.

That's all I needed to do.

Survive...any way I could.

My legs ached and my mind slowed. Time in here stood still. There was no sun or moon to gauge the time. Still, something inside me said it was late. I'd lost an entire day in this cell, Arrived in the dawn, only to stand here under these fucking lights.

My belly howled once more. I winced, pressed a fist into the ache, and glanced at the cot in the center of the room. I couldn't risk going to sleep, not now, not here. Not when everything hinged on their whims. I made for the far end of the room and slid down the wall until I sat. This was just like Ryth and her stepbrother, Caleb.

They'd sat, just like this, waiting while hell was unleashed in the world outside.

At least she'd had company.

Boom...boom...boom...

The heavy sound of my pulse swallowed the sound. But it was the flash of darkness...followed by the click of the lock that made me flinch.

The door opened.

Riven stepped in.

I slowly pushed to stand as he fixed that terrifying glare on me...then lifted his hand.

A sandwich...

A fucking sandwich.

I lunged, scrambling across the room as my stomach unleashed a tirade of snarls and whimpers. I yanked open the wrapping, my fingers moving too slowly as I tore apart the neatly cut triangles and shoved them into my mouth.

"It was the only non-meat filling I could find."

I stopped chewing and lifted my gaze to his. He gave me nothing, no comfort, no softness. But it didn't matter, as long as he gave me food. I chewed and swallowed, biting down on the thick sliced bread once more.

He watched me eat, then glanced around the room. "You should've told me you knew my brother, Helene."

The hard wad of bread refused to go down. I swallowed again and again and again. "You shouldn't have taken me prisoner."

He searched my eyes. "Your name isn't Helene Montgomery, that I know for sure. You lied about your name, probably lied about many things. Tell me, tell me why you were out in the rain. Tell me you were going on a date with the man I killed. Go on...*TELL ME!*"

I flinched as his roar resounded.

Heavy breaths.

Wild eyes.

He was a man close to the edge.

A man...who reacted.

He moved fast, striding forward. Instinct took over as I stumbled back, still trying to swallow the fucking thick bread at the back of my throat. My boots hit the wall an instant before my head cracked back, impacting with a piercing lash of pain.

His hand was around my throat, his fingers curled as I finally dislodged that wad, feeling it hurt all the way down.

His body pressed against me, his head tilted down until he murmured against my ear. "The only question is...what do we do with you now?"

I knew.

Maybe I'd always known.

Maybe fate was a cruel fucking bitch that wanted to see me fucked.

I closed my eyes.

Maybe fate was me?

SIXTEEN

Riven

THE *CRACK* OF BREAKING CRYSTAL SHATTERED THE silence. I winced, standing in the doorway of Hale's office, watching as the new asshole shoved the top shelf Scotch out of his way. Stacks of files took the decanter's place and a nice array of weaponry.

"He won't like this." I warned as I stared at the once neat office now in ruins.

"Who?" Coulter never even looked up.

"Hale."

Then the bastard stopped, slowly lifting his head. The tight curl of his lips said it all. "And what makes you think he's still alive to give a shit?"

He knew.

They *all* fucking knew.

Hale was more than just alive.

He was probably orchestrating this entire fucking thing.

Still, Coulter went back to destroying Hale's office with a kind of ferocity I almost admired. It wouldn't stop me putting a bullet through his head, but it sure was fucking entertaining.

I took a step backwards. "So, if you don't need me..."

It wasn't a question. We were getting the fuck out of here before all this blew up in our faces.

"Don't *need you?*" Coulter stopped me, his lips curling as he met my stare. "See, that's where you're wrong. We want *you*, Riven. We want you and your blood right here. Where you've always been...to be the face of all this." He splayed out his hand. "To the bitter fucking end."

The world stopped turning.

The floor seemed to drop away beneath my feet.

I scowled, this wasn't damage control, or a cover-up.

This was them flicking the kill switch and hanging us out to dry. I searched that glinting fucking stare as that chill moved deeper.

The *click* of unlocking doors sounded behind me. Heavy footsteps came closer. My shoulder was slammed from behind, forcing me to stumble before I caught myself.

I spun, rage burning inside as the guard smirked my way, casting the large bundle of rolled maps onto the desk. Maps I knew intimately. "What's going on?"

No one answered. No one even fucking twitched, and that icy feeling wormed its way further inside.

This was more than going down with the goddamn ship, that I knew.

This was them burning it to the ground.

"What else do we have?" Coulter muttered.

"This is where we are now." The bastard who'd barged me stabbed the map. "But this entire wing here is free. This is where we move them." Then he moved his finger right over the room where I'd put her.

Fuck.

I stared as Coulter narrowed his gaze and turned the map to get a better view. I glanced at the map as the realization dawned. I was trapped in this place...like a rat in a fucking cage...only now I'd dragged my brothers and a goddamn liar with me.

I turned around and left. I doubted they'd even noticed I left.

Panic drove me along the glaringly bright hallways. I headed to the connecting door that would take me to my personal quarters, the ones I shared with my kin. All I saw was that bastard's finger pointing right at the room where I'd put Helene.

Thoughts of her and Kane rushed into my head. I pressed my card against the scanners and pushed through the doors. It wasn't just how his eyes had widened the moment he saw her, but how quickly that flare of surprise had turned to a look of desire.

He wanted her.

No.

He craved her.

I scanned the dark, woodgrain interior of my apartment as Kane stepped out of the doorway to Thomas' room. He wiped his hands on a towel, his shirt sleeves rolled high. I scanned the darkened room behind him. "Is he asleep?"

"For now," my brother answered in a clipped, pissed tone.

He watched me stride past the kitchen, heading for the fully stocked bar. This place might not be crammed with designer furniture, but it had what we needed, and right now, that was alcohol and a lot of it. I needed to be fucking numb, to forget this entire fucking day...for a second at least. I grabbed a bottle, unscrewed the top, and poured half a glass.

"You want to talk about this?" Kane glanced at the glass as he stepped closer.

"Not really." I lifted the glass to my lips and took a deep swallow.

It burned all the way down. Still, it wasn't enough.

"I didn't know."

I took another hard swallow.

"If she means that much, I can—"

I moved fast, holding onto the glass with one hand as I grasped his neck. "You can *what, brother? Leave? Forget her? You really think you can do that?*"

I drove him back against the wall with a *thud*, catching the wince of pain as his head hit. Still, he never fought. Not this time. Not like he had before in front of her. I searched his eyes, watching his calculating mind search for a way inside my head.

Not this time.

Not...this time.

I shoved him hard and dropped my hand.

"I had no idea you were involved with her," he started. "If I'd known, I wouldn't have—"

Wouldn't have...wouldn't have what? Fucked her?

Is that what had happened?

Is my brother...is he Michael DiAngelo?

"Was it you?" I asked, my tone dangerous. "Was it you she was going to meet?"

"Meet?" He scowled. "No, we don't have another appointment for at least another two weeks. We were meeting monthly."

"Meeting." I answered. So he wasn't the asshole she'd been going to see the night I struck her with my car.

"Yes." He pushed off the wall, stepping closer. "She's a client."

I knew my brother, knew the way his mind worked. "Have you fucked her?"

He licked his lips, and there it was. That need. That hunger. He might not've fucked her...but he'd wanted to. Or at least, he'd tried.

I wanted to think about that. I bet she hadn't cowered under his touch. I bet she'd looked him right in the eye and told him to keep his damn hands to himself, just like she'd tried to tell me... for a while at least, until that sick need inside her caught a taste of the hunger she'd been born craving.

Now she couldn't get enough.

"It doesn't matter," I answered, remembering how that bastard guard had stabbed at the maps in front of me. "None of it does. Not her. Not this. Not even us. They plan on filling this place with as many Daughters as possible...then setting it alight and us along with it."

He froze, scowling. "What does that mean?"

Some part of me was relieved to share the burden. "It means we can't leave. We even try and we'll be locked in those fucking cells along with all the women we shoved there."

The blood drained from his face. "Why?"

"Why the fuck do you think?" I lifted my glass.

His eyes searched mine as it slowly dawned. "They're going to use us."

"Yes. They are...and right now, until we get the location of the black site, there's not a goddamn thing we can do about it. We leave now and we're out. We leave now and—"

"Our sister is lost for good."

I slowly nodded. "Yeah, she is. Which is why right now we need to let them think they have the upper hand. We need to play the game while they truck in as many shipments as they need, and we need to, but we can neither leave nor have any involvement here. They want us around by reputation alone. A reputation we built on the backs of all the cruel things we've done here. They'll kill them all, every Daughter, every guard, and then they'll come for us."

"No." He shook his head.

I didn't have the heart to watch him journey through all the fucking stages until he slammed into acceptance. But that's where he needed to be, if we had any chance of making it out of this alive. I turned from him and walked back to the Scotch, as I drained my glass.

Only this time I didn't pour for me.

Amber splashed against the bottom of a fresh glass sitting beside the bottles. I screwed the cap on and carried it back, holding it out. "Here, it'll help the rancid taste of what you just swallowed."

"I banked on greed," he said slowly, raising that stunned gaze to me. "I never thought they'd—"

"Yeah, well, you were wrong."

His hand shook when he lifted the glass. Ripples of the liquid caught the light. He swallowed, swiping his mouth before he glanced toward the darkened bedroom. "Maybe we can get him out?"

"We try to leave and we'll be gunned down. I know that for a fact."

"Fuck," my brother whispered, and glanced at Thomas' room.

Hell, five seconds in a room with Coulter and anyone could see that. We were here for one reason and there was no way they'd let their fall guys escape.

Beep.

I looked at my cell.

Coulter: You're required in the meeting room. Immediately.

"Speak of the devil," I snarled and turned, striding toward the connecting door before I stopped. "They'll be taking over the rooms where I left her. If they find her—"

"They won't," Kane answered instantly. "I'll make sure of it."

I gave a slow nod. A few hours ago, I wouldn't have trusted him at all with the knowledge of her, but now I didn't have much of a choice. I left my brother, making my way back through the interconnecting doors...to face my goddamn replacement.

SEVENTEEN

Kane

I COULDN'T WAIT TO LEAVE, HEADING OUT OF OUR quarters the moment my brother left. My steps were quiet, barely more than a whisper against the hard, tiled floor. I pressed my card against the scanners, then pushed through, slowing the moment I saw her door.

He had her.

The woman who'd evaded my every single attempt at seduction.

Now she was here.

I lifted my card, pressed it against the lock of her room, and opened the door. But I didn't enter, just stood in the doorway watching her turn around.

"Kane," she murmured, her pupils widening in fear.

I fought the urge to smile. Instead, I crossed my arms and leaned against the doorjamb. "What kind of game are you playing at here, Helene?"

Her brows narrowed before she shook her head. I pushed off the doorjamb and stepped inside, rounding her side before I stopped at her back. I never touched her, never even brushed a strand of her hair. Not this time. She'd caught me off guard before, made me forget who I really was. It was so easy to slip into the promise of someone else. The falseness. The mask. The doctor.

But no more.

Helene would get the real me now. The man I'd tried to hide.

"If there's one thing I know, it's the fact that there's no such thing as coincidence. So, let me ask you one more time. What kind of game are you playing at?"

This time she didn't shake her head.

"I..." she started. "I was crossing the road."

"Lie."

She froze.

"It was fate, wasn't it?"

Her head bowed.

There.

That's it.

I brushed her hair aside, staring at her neck. "Tell me, are you in that pit of desperation right now, Helene? Do you feel that blackness, that uncontrollable urge to cut and burn?"

Her head dipped lower. "Yes."

I stared at the perfect line of her throat and fought the need to lick my lips. I could almost feel how soft she was, how fucking sweet she'd taste, all broken and ruined. "I told you before, I can give you a better form of release. The rush of surrender. The power of using your body as a weapon." I lowered my gaze along her curled shoulders to the rise of her breasts. "By letting your mind go and just feeling."

She turned around and met my stare. Still she said nothing as she searched my stare. I saw that same hunger now that I'd seen in our sessions. Her breaths deepened, her eyes shifted to my mouth. She wanted this...she wanted *me*.

All she had to do was *give in*.

No wonder my brother was obsessed. One look into his eyes and it had been obvious.

Now, Helene Montgomery was trapped...and under our complete control.

The thought of that made my pulse race. I leaned closer, whispering against her ear. "You should've said yes out there. You could've seen me in a much better light."

"A false one," she whispered back. "So, who's the liar now?"

I just smiled.

Beep.

I lifted my cell and glanced at the screen.

Riven: Get the fuck out of there NOW. They're on the way.

I jerked my gaze up, scanned the room for any evidence she'd been here, and grabbed her arm. "We're leaving."

She resisted, pulling her arm out of my grasp. "Where?"

I stopped, seeing the panic in her eyes. "There're men coming who you don't want to meet. Understand?"

She swallowed, glanced at the door, then nodded.

I dragged her out of the unlocked door and glanced back along the way I'd come. Movement came through the glass section of the doors. There were men headed our way, and fast.

"This way." I pulled her with me, heading to the opposite side of the hall and toward an exit we rarely used. The door had barely closed with a *clunk* behind us before the sound of doors opening on the other side came. I held the door, leaned close, and strained to hear.

Deep voices murmured, never missing a beat.

They hadn't heard us.

I turned, grabbed her, and pushed her past the cleaning closet to the exit door. My pulse was booming by the time we stepped out into the howling winds of the night. She stumbled backwards, wrapping her arms around herself.

Cold wormed its way under the rolled sleeves of my shirt. I glanced at her t-shirt and jeans, knowing she must be freezing.

"Come on," I murmured, motioning her forward.

She glanced at the trees. I could almost see her weighing up her chance. Should she make a run for it? Would she make it? Would I let her go? I was intrigued, even more so when she turned away from the hope of escape and instead started walking, heading along the outside of the building.

She didn't run.

I scowled, listening to the bark of hounds in the distance. Maybe she'd heard them before I had. Yeah, that could be it. She didn't want to take the risk. Instead, she'd taken the biggest risk of all...putting her life in our hands.

We walked around the far corner of the building and stopped at the external entrance to our private wing. I stepped up, pressed my card against the scanner, and opened the door, gesturing for her to slip inside. Warmth hit us instantly.

I shivered, quietly closing the door behind us as she looked around. "What is this place?"

"Our private living quarters."

She turned around. "Yours and Riven's?"

I glanced toward the darkened doorway where our brother slept. "And our brother, Thomas."

She followed my focus, scowling. I took a step toward her and she moved instantly, shifting her gaze back to me and taking a step backwards until she hit the door.

"Do you want to survive this?" I murmured, lifting my hand to brace against the wall beside her. I searched those dark eyes.

"Yes."

It was the answer I needed, the one which provoked me to move. I reached up and cupped her breast in a cruel grip. She winced for a second before her breath caught. "How far are you willing to go?"

Her chin lifted as I lowered my head and nuzzled the side of her neck, her warmth so perfect against the palm of my hand.

She unleashed a moan, and that sound was like every dark thought I'd ever had, all wrapped up in the flesh of this woman as she finally answered. "As far as I have to."

Hard breaths consumed me, and that insidious hunger slammed into me. Her pulse spiked, the vein jumping under the brush of my lips. "I was hoping you were going to say that."

All the sessions we'd had came rushing back in my mind. Her teeth grazed soft flesh as she bit her lip, looking at me with that ravenous stare. She hadn't given into me before. Maybe she would now?

Heavy breaths pressed my chest against hers. "You *need* this. You *want* this. You want the surrender and sweet rush of release. So the choice is yours, get on your goddamn knees, or don't...and I stop this now."

She stiffened, then turned her head.

She understood all too well right now.

Her life was in the palm of my hand...as was her breast.

I watched that realization dawn. Then slowly, like silk falling, she dropped to her knees. I never moved, just held her stare all the way down. My cock hardened as she hit the floor in front of the doorway of my brother's room until it felt like I was going to fucking explode.

"Please," she whispered.

Fuck, the way she begged. I grasped her mouth, slid my thumb inside and grasped her chin. Pink waited, soft and wet. "Do you think you are nothing more than a toy for me to use any way I see fit?"

Her breath blew across the back of my thumb. Sparks ignited. She liked this. The degradation...and the praise. I gripped her mouth, dragging her closer to my aching fucking cock until her lips pressed against the bulging outline.

Warmth spread from her gasps until those lips pressed against the thick ridge.

Jesus fucking Christ.

"Your mouth is mine. Your pussy is mine." I opened my eyes and looked down. "You should've taken the better version of me, Helene. But you didn't, you left me hungry...you left me fucking starved, and now...now all that changes. I am going to fuck you, do you understand that? I'm going to use and use and use. I'm going to force myself inside that pussy, just like I'm going to force myself inside your head. I'll bury myself so deep there will be no escape from me."

She let out a whimper, a strangled, tortured sound.

"Take it out," I demanded. "Take it out and put it into your mouth."

Her body trembled, shaking and shuddering as she reached for the zipper of my slacks and pulled her mouth away.

I did not love.

I did not fall.

I did not obey.

But when that zipper inched down and she reached inside, I thought for a blinding, terrifying second that I could. I could experience...perfection. Her fingers reached through the gap of my boxers, pulling the length free. My cock sprang out, hitting her cheek.

Those dark eyes were endless as she met mine. Hollow, empty pits that always looked so desperate. How many times had she sat across from my desk, staring at me with that same stare? She opened her mouth as her fingers gripped the length of my desire, and a shudder tore through me.

"Wider." The word was a choked hiss.

She did, parting those lips until they stretched wide. I slammed my hand against the doorjamb as the head slipped along her lips and into her mouth. My hips rocked forward, desperate to gain one more inch.

"That's it. That's so it." She sucked, sliding me all the way in until I felt her throat constrict, gripping me like a fist. "All the goddamn way, Helene...all...*the...*

goddamn." I punched my hips forward, driving her head against the edge of the doorway.

I couldn't control myself, not this irresistible hunger to have her, or that violent, uncontrollable lust. My hand slid around to grip the back of her head as I fucked her.

"*Breathe,*" I grunted, staring down at her. Her eyes wide in fear, those lips stretched so fucking thin.

So. Fucking. Thin.

I slammed my eyes closed as that thick vein that ran underneath spasmed.

No.

I tried to stop it.

But I couldn't...not with her. One hard thrust and I pushed all the way in until she beat her hands against my thighs and thrashed her head, desperate for air.

Almost...there.

A guttural grunt and I unleashed a moan. My body jerked, spasming as I filled her mouth and pulled away.

She gasped and spluttered, swallowing my seed all the way down. Hard breaths consumed me as I watched the spittle dribble from her mouth.

"Unh-uh." I dragged my thumb through the beautiful mess, pushing it in. "Every fucking drop, Helene. Every. Drop."

Anger seethed in her stare. Her cheeks heaved with consuming, engulfing breaths. Still, she had no option but to yield to me and open once more.

Beep.

My cell vibrated in my pocket. But I didn't turn away from her. Not yet. Not until I was done. That thought rose as she sucked the last trace from my thumb and yanked her head away.

"Good." I brushed the backs of my curled fingers along her cheek. "Very good."

"Fuck you," she hissed.

I smiled. All in good time.

Beep.

I winced, hating the intrusion, and tucked myself back into my slacks as I stepped away. One glance into my brother's darkened room and I reached for my cell, scanning the message.

Riven: You're needed here now.

"Fantastic," I muttered, and the last traces of excitement turned cold.

One glance her way and I stopped. "Stay here and stay quiet. You're a smart woman, Helene. I don't need to tell you what will happen if those men find out you're here, do I?"

She gave a small shake of her head.

One nod was all I gave before I headed for the door.

EIGHTEEN

Helene

____

My body trembled watching Dr. Kane Cruz walk casually out the door as though he hadn't almost choked me a second before. My knees were weak, barely holding as I pushed up to stand, swiping my mouth, desperate to rid myself of the taste of him.

As the *click* of the door sounded, rage exploded inside me.

"You motherfucker." I stumbled backwards, holding onto that doorway, and sucked in hard breaths. "You goddamn *motherfucker.*"

The dark edges of the apartment narrowed in. My head spun, deprived of enough oxygen. The deep gulps of air did little to help me. It was that sick, fucking desire that nailed me to the spot. That aching throbbing between my legs that held me prisoner. I couldn't move, couldn't risk *rubbing myself.*

I was wet, soaked. Each shift of my weight only increased the need to finish what his depravity had started.

Tell me, are you in that pit of desperation right now, Helene? I closed my eyes as those words surfaced. *Do you feel that blackness, that uncontrollable urge to cut and burn?*

Cut and burn? I shook my head, feeling it drop.

No. I didn't feel the urge to cut and burn. Not anymore.

A new sickness controlled me, making me lower my trembling fingers down until I rubbed between my thighs. Wet. That's what I was. Revulsion rolled as I rubbed again, digging my fingers in deeper, finding that aching center of me.

How far are you willing to go?

I shook my head as my clit pulsed and quivered as my orgasm drew close. With the taste of his seed in my mouth, I rubbed harder, inching my thighs apart. Until with a moan, I tore at the button and the zipper of my jeans and drove my fingers all the way inside.

How far?

How far are you willing to go?

White sparks detonated behind my eyes as my answer followed. *As far as I have to.*

My body quivered. I slammed my eyes closed, biting down on my cry of release as that wave of euphoria slammed into me. *Oh, God...oh, GOD.* Warmth and wetness followed. I opened my eyes, staring through the apartment of my tormentors. I hated them. So. Fucking. Much.

Then why the fuck did you just come harder than you ever have in your entire life?

A moan ripped from my lips. I hung my head in shame. This wasn't happening. Not now...not to me.

No.

It was *happening...but it was for a reason.*

It was for those I loved.

I lifted my head, pushed the white hot burn of revulsion aside, and turned around. Purpose moved through me. I needed to get my head together and *both of them out of it.* A glance toward the door and I forced myself to move. They'd be back any second and right now I was alone.

I scanned the apartment I'd only seen on maps before and took a step forward. It was smaller than I'd expected, and warmer, too. The complete opposite of the penthouse apartment where Riven had held me prisoner. My gaze fixed on the shelf of decanters filled with alcohol and the used glass sitting beside what had to be Scotch.

I grabbed the crystal and poured, splashed just enough in the bottom of the tumbler to rid myself of the taste of him, and drank. The heady burn hit me hard, making me cough and splutter. I wasn't used to straight alcohol. But right now, I'd take anything.

The masculine scent of them was overwhelming, hitting me hard. I swallowed the rest of the swill and placed the glass back down. The kitchen held no secrets, leaving me to turn to the other two doors. Their bedrooms, had to be.

That same tremble found me as I stepped closer. I had to hurry. I knew that. Still, it was like stepping in front of that car all over again. Only this time I knew what I was in for.

How far are you willing to go?

His voice echoed inside my head, deep and hypnotic, crawling under my skin. I shook my head, desperate to rid myself of his hold, and took a step forward, grasping the handle and opening the door.

Darkness waited for me.

And the seductive, crisp scent Dr. Cruz wore.

Just get it done. I forced myself to step inside and flick on the light. The room was sparse. But it was exactly as I'd expected. Unfeeling. Empty. Not a photo or personal item in place. "You are one cold bastard, aren't you?"

I moved deeper, rounding the neatly made bed in the middle of the room to stop at the bare nightstand. I yanked the drawer, opening it to find a gun and some papers, nothing that held any interest for me. The black steel glinted, drawing my focus. I could take it, put a bullet in all three of them, and be out of here by morning.

But would that get me closer to Hale?

And who the fuck was taking over The Order?

I needed answers. More than that, I needed time.

Time to get under their skin and turn them against everyone and everything.

You want them.

I stilled as those words took hold. One shake of my head and I knew the movement was a lie. My pulse thundered as my throat still ached from the brutality that had happened only minutes before. Still, they'd never hurt me. Not really. If anything, they'd risked their own lives to save mine.

The only question was...

Why?

I lowered my gaze to that gun as that hunger to understand took hold once more. Without them, I was just as lost as I'd always been. I pushed the drawer closed and took a step backwards. My gaze moved to the bed one last time before I turned toward the door.

I couldn't make myself enter the second room. I froze with my hand on the handle, fear gripping me tight. Riven's controlling fist was still wrapped around my throat, his sick need still roaring through my blood. I shouldn't want him. I shouldn't crave him.

But I did and I hated myself more now than ever. I clenched my grip around the handle and forced myself to turn it before I stepped inside. The light from outside refused to enter, leaving the murky gloom to control the space.

"Okay, you sonofabitch," I whispered as I rounded the side of the bed and headed for his nightstand.

Only his gun was on the top, and so was a single photo in a brushed steel frame. I picked it up, staring at two older kids, a boy and a girl who looked like his younger sister. He had his arm around her protectively and those same dark eyes which haunted me looked almost *normal.*

The room seemed to tremble, or maybe it was just me. This... this was important. In the space of a breath, it felt like I'd stepped outside my body and was now looking in.

His sister.

Somehow, she was involved with all this.

I needed to understand how.

Maybe, just maybe, if she was somehow tied up with Hale, Riven might be willing to work together with me.

Then what?

Are you going to become friends?

Have you forgotten what he did to your sisters?

Have you forgotten what he did to you?

I placed the photo back down on the dresser. No, I hadn't forgotten at all. I couldn't forget. Not *ever*. I'd carry that knowledge like a festering wound for the rest of my life. But pain didn't give me the answers I needed. Pain only weighed me down, until I was so heavy I couldn't move.

I needed to move now and turned my attention to the dresser. I yanked open the top drawer to find another gun sitting on a stack of papers. But it was the three burner cells that drew my attention. Now, that was something I could use.

Excitement hummed in my veins as I grabbed one and lifted it out. One press of the button and the screen came alive. It had service...I glanced over my shoulder, then pressed the number I'd memorized, the same one I'd called before.

It was answered on the second ring. The frantic fumbling of sheets sounded in the background as my sister answered. "Yes?"

"It's me."

"Helene?"

I smiled. She almost sounded *relieved*. "Yeah," I answered, as a thrum of fear worked its way inside. "I don't have a lot of time. But something is going down. Someone is taking over The Order. Someone called Harmon."

"What?" she queried, her voice sharp as sleep was forgotten.

"Harmon," I repeated in a hurry. "The same asshole London took hostage, I think. I need you to tell him that is the man he needs to focus on. I don't have much time. But his men...his men are—"

"Stop," she pleaded. "Just stop. I need you to tell me where you are. I need...I need you to tell me you're safe."

I swallowed hard and closed my eyes. "I'm safe."

"You're lying." There was pain in her voice. The kind of pain you couldn't fake. "You're lying and you're in trouble."

I didn't answer, not because I didn't want to, but the words just wouldn't come, trapped behind the lump in my throat. "I don't want to scare you, but it almost sounds like you care, sister."

Silence followed, then, "I do care. I care very much and so does Ryth. Come back, Helene. Come back and..."

She stopped, not knowing what would follow. But I did. I saw it all. I *felt* it all.

There would be more broken women.

More ruined families.

I stared at the image in the photo frame that sat beside Riven's bed.

More sisters sold to cruel, controlling men.

"I have to go," I whispered. "I'll call as soon as I can. Remember what I said, tell London Harmon is now the one in control. He'll know what to do, and Vivienne...it was really good to hear your voice."

I didn't wait for her to respond.

I didn't think my heart could take it.

My finger stabbed the screen, ending the call. But I didn't place it back in the dresser, instead, I tucked it away in the clothes, closed the drawer, and quickly backed out of the room. I was playing with fire, not knowing the moment I'd be burned. The empty apartment waited when I closed the door, but there was still one more bedroom I hadn't searched. One last bedroom I was terrified to see.

Memories of that warehouse came rushing back. The Priest's screams haunted me as I made my way back through the apartment. Darkness, that's where I'd stood while I watched London torture him, and that's what waited for me now.

I stood in the doorway, peering into the gloom.

Steady, harsh breaths filled the space. I knew what he'd looked like then, bloody and broken, as he'd turned his head to search the space where I stood through the slit of one bloody, swollen eye.

I took a step, made my way inside, and waited for my eyes to adjust to the dim light. The shrouded outline on the bed rose and fell with every breath. I suppressed a shiver as I watched him. He was hurt...but how badly hurt? It had to have been... how long now?

I took a step and stood over him. The choked hiss told me he was still healing. Had London broken some ribs? Had he done deeper damage? I wasn't sure. But I knew one thing...The Priest wouldn't help me now. I'd turned away and taken a step toward the door when a low murmur cut though the room.

"I know you."

Cold rushed through me. I tried to keep the tremble from my voice as I turned around. "No, I don't think so."

He pushed upwards, sitting up. I couldn't help but stiffen. Maybe he wasn't as wounded as I'd thought?

"I do...I do know you." His dark eyes narrowed in on me. "I just need to remember how."

NINETEEN

Riven

Shrill, terrified, screams tore along the hallway. I winced at the piercing sound as a Daughter was wrestled through the doorway and shoved into the meeting room.

She stumbled, then fell to her hands and knees in front of me. Her hair was down, covering her face.

"There." Coulter sucked in hard breaths, his eyes blazing.

There was a red handprint blazing on his cheek. Looked like he'd picked himself a fighter...

She slowly lifted her head. Her busted lip was a damn mess and the remnant left by his fist was already swelling on her cheek. If this was what her face looked like, I'd hate to think what the rest of her was like.

Flickers of Helene pushed in. Her power. Her rage. The icy sting of wrath moved through me at the thought of her like this. If anyone raised a hand to her, they wouldn't have a goddamn hand for long.

Coulter stabbed his finger at her and fixed a deadly glare on the woman cowering in front of me. "Do your fucking job. I want that bitch...I want her *broken.*" He met my stare. "I want to see it all. Every. Fucking. Thing. I want to see all your processes. How they're trained." He looked at my brother. "And what we can expect when they're done."

Hate moved through me. I slowly bent down, brushed her filthy, greasy hair from her face, and tilted her gaze to mine. She flinched, her brown eyes shining with terror. I searched the amber of her stare. But inside, I was panicking. The Daughter's face faded until all I saw was Helene's. The thought of touching someone else made my goddamn skin crawl.

I hadn't felt that before.

But I felt it now, and as that sickening feeling took hold, I realized I was trapped.

Caught between survival and...*what was this...love?*

No.

Not love.

I let her face go and rose, facing the bastard. "No."

There was a tic in his jaw. "No?"

"That's right, no." I took a step closer, meeting his stare. "You might be used to cowering, back-alley prostitutes, Coulter, but that's not what we produce here. The Daughters of The Order are highly skilled and carefully trained. They are worth every million-dollar price tag that comes with it. Those men might fuck them within an inch of their lives, but these women will smile and pant while they're doing it. So, to expand on my answer, no, I won't *'break this bitch'*. Instead, I'll expect her wounds to be treated, and her body scrubbed. Then, I'll expect her to have food and water and when she faces me again, she won't cower like a *fucking dog*."

He stilled.

My pulse was booming, filling my head with the thrashing sound.

Take the goddamn answer.

He turned to her, watching as she curled her shoulders, desperate to get away. "Fine," he said carefully, then met my stare. "You want to bathe and feed them, then have it your way. But when that's done, I want to see a start. You have many more of these women coming and I want as many sold and shipped as possible."

He took a step closer until we almost touched. "But if you think for one minute, I'm not onto you, then you'd be wrong. You're hiding something, Cruz. You and your fucking brothers." His gaze flicked to Kane. "And I intend to find out what that is. So play your games...I love a good challenge."

He stepped away, giving a nod to the rest of his men in the room. Every single one of them left, leaving my brother and Walker behind.

It felt like someone had kicked me in the balls. My stomach tightened as I looked at Walker, giving him a nod. "Take her and get her cleaned up. I want all of them checked and processed as soon as possible."

"Will you be overseeing any?" he asked.

The last time I'd done that was with Ryth Castlemaine. And look how that had turned out. Not only did her goddamn father and stepbrothers almost destroy the place getting her out, but it had almost cost my fucking life. I shook my head. "No. I won't be."

One nod was all he gave. He stepped behind me, grasped the beaten woman's arm, and gently pulled her to a stand. "Come on. Let's get you cleaned up."

She tried to fight him, pulling away from his grasp. But it was useless, causing him to grab her roughly and haul her toward the door. "Don't make this harder than it already is," he warned.

Until they left and it was only the two of us.

I turned to my brother, watching his stony expression search mine, hating the fact the place was probably bugged and yet there was no avoiding this. He took a step closer, stopping at my side. "She's in your head, brother. Careful there."

I wrenched a glare toward him. "And she's not in yours? I see the way you look at her, *brother*." I turned on him, driving my chest against his. "How about you just focus on getting us out of this fucking mess and less about the woman in your goddamn bed?"

There was that wince. His light green eyes darkened in an instant. He didn't like the fact she was mine. Not at all. That almost made me smile...until I really thought about her.

I saw the moment he realized what had just hit me like a blow.

She was alone...with our brother.

He turned at the same moment I did. Both of us took a slow step toward the door, only he was half a step ahead, and pushed me backwards as he stepped through.

Sonofabitch.

I cast a hate-filled stare his way as he lengthened his stride. By the time we hit the locked doors, we were almost running.

His heavy steps thundered. I fixed my gaze on the connecting door to the apartment straight ahead and surged forward. But the sonofabitch wouldn't back off. Instead, he shoved me, barging me out of the way as he slammed his card against the scanner and yanked open the door.

We charged through the doorway, shoving and pushing, then stumbled inside, casting stabbing glares at each other.

"I...I know you!" the panicked growl came from in front of us.

I jerked my gaze upward to where our brother had Helene's shirt in his grip as he pinned her against the doorjamb outside his bedroom. Her back was against the frame, her eyes wide and fixed on the swollen mess that was Thomas' face.

"Don't *fucking* lie to me!" He pushed close, staring her in the eyes. "Tell me!"

Kane glanced my way, then held out his hand. "Easy, Thom...*easy*. What the hell is going on here?"

He didn't turn away from her, just pushed her harder against the doorjamb with a trembling fist.

I grabbed his fist, dragging him away. *"Thomas, stop!"*

But my brother was like a goddamn bloodhound, peering at her through the slits of his eyes. I pulled him away, forcing his gaze to mine. "What the fuck has gotten into you?"

He just shook his head, glancing her way before he inhaled. "Nothing. Nothing's gotten into me."

Something clearly had and whatever it was, it had made Helene tremble.

I narrowed in on the shuddering of her body. She turned those dark eyes my way with a soft shake of her head.

"What am I supposed to make of this, Helene?" I asked, leaving my brother behind as I took a step toward her. "First you step in front of my car, then I find out you're my brother's client." I glanced at Thomas over my shoulder. "Want to tell me the truth?"

She jerked a panicked glance toward the door that led outside.

I moved just before she did, lunged to grab her as she made a run for it, and grabbed her around the waist. "Easy now..."

She kicked and fought, slamming her head backwards. I was so fucking in tune with her, almost like I saw her every move now before it even happened. I wrenched my face out of the way, and hauled her backwards through the living room to throw her onto the brown leather sofa.

She bounced and scurried forward. Fuck, she was fast, lunging.

"You *will stay!*" I roared, grabbing her and pushing her back.

She just glared at me with that murderous stare. My body thrummed. Heat rushed through me as I stood over her. Jesus, she affected me more than any other woman I'd met before, and as Kane stepped closer, watching the two of us, I realized she affected him, too.

"You'll stay," I gasped and stabbed the air. "And this time, you'll tell us the goddamn truth. How the fuck do you know my brother?"

She jerked that glare toward Thomas. He moved closer, standing beside me. "It's her voice. Her voice...I—" He scowled, searching his memory.

"I don't know you," she spat.

Lie.

I knew it before she said a word. It was more than a tell, more than a twitch of her temple. She was under my skin and inside my head. I leaned down and placed my hands on either side of her on the sofa. "You're lying, Helene. You're lying and you're about to get caught."

"One way..." Thomas said, his voice distant. "One way to put out a fire." In an instant, he came rushing back into the present, his gaze narrowing in on her. "That's what she said, one way to put out a fire."

Her eyes widened. She shook her head. "No...no, you couldn't possibly have—"

There...she said it.

"You were in the church with that *bastard St. James.*"

Cold rushed through me as she met my gaze.

"And the warehouse," he added. "She was at the goddamn warehouse. I saw her."

"You're a l-liar," she stuttered.

I reached down and wound my hand around her throat. "I don't think so, Helene. The only one we've proven is a liar so far is you." I gripped her throat tighter, not enough to cut off her air. But enough for her to know...her life was on the line. "How about we start with the truth this time? Who the fuck *are* you?"

I felt the panicked flutter of her pulse under my hand as she held my stare and answered. "Helene King."

TWENTY

Helene

"HELENE KING."

The moment my name left my mouth I knew it was a mistake, one I could never go back from, and the impact was like a bomb.

"You're...*who?*" Riven snarled, his dark eyes glittering with rage.

But I couldn't stop. I was a runaway freight train, one fueled by terror and sheer fucking satisfaction. I pushed upward and snarled back. "That's right, *motherfucker*. My real name is Helene King. You know, the same *King* your fucking leader has been hunting for the last goddamn decade. Well," I pushed against his hold around my throat. "Here I am."

My breaths were light and fast. My body was screaming at me to fight or run. But I couldn't run, not now...not when I was so far in. That left my only option to fight, and fight I could...the only way I knew how. *Dirty*.

Riven's grip eased around my throat as he jerked a glare at Kane. "Did you know about this?"

The doctor's eyes were filled with fear. "No."

Riven released his hold, his brother now his sole focus. "Are you sure about that? Something like this would come under doctor-client privilege."

You've got to be kidding, right? I unleashed a hard bark of laughter. "Somehow I doubt any of you ruthless fucking bastards would think twice about any goddamn oath you took." I glared at The Priest. "Including one made to God. So no, Kane didn't know, because I never told him."

Riven swivelled his focus back to me. "So why tell us now?"

I jutted my chin in the air. "Because right now, you have as much to lose as I do." I jerked my head toward the connecting doors. "Those men out there are my enemy, not you, not anymore, at least. Nor am I yours. We can work together."

"Work together?" He lashed out to grasp my throat once more. "I don't *work* with my food."

Rage burned inside me and if I was honest...*desire.* How could someone so vile be so fucking hot? "Is that all I am to you?"

His lips curled as he searched my eyes. Still, I saw the truth, even if he was too gutless to admit it. I saw it in the way he looked at me, especially when his brother looked at me the same way. He was so fucking jealous he couldn't think straight.

The edge of his lip curled before he rose. "What makes you think I won't kill you?"

"I could ask the same," I murmured. "After all, I've had plenty of opportunities. *If* you remember."

The deep scowl came. Stars ignited. *There it was...that understanding*.

"You planned this?"

I smiled, for a second at least. Until he clenched his grip, cutting off my air. Panic plunged deep inside. I kicked and thrashed before he let go, and instead, gripped my mouth. I gasped, spluttering, trying to tear my head away as he shoved his thumb into my mouth, forcing my jaw to open.

He leaned down. "You think this is going to give you the upper hand? This changes nothing between us. If anything, it makes you fair game."

Movement came from behind him. Riven's cruel grip held me still. I couldn't track Thomas as he shuffled toward a cupboard.

"Are you ready for that, Helene *King?*" Riven asked.

I jerked my gaze to Riven's as he reached behind him. Steel shone as he grabbed my wrist and slapped a cuff tight.

No!

"What the fuck?" I yanked from his hold.

All three moved in like predators cornering their next kill. Riven yanked the cuff, pulling me forward. "Kane, cuff her to the heater until we decide what to do with her."

I lunged, swinging my fist, aiming right for the bastard's cock. I didn't get there. Riven grabbed my wrist, stopping my blow. "Careful with this one." He stared into my eyes. "She's trouble."

Kane grasped the cuff his brother held. "Think about what you're doing here," he started with that low, dulcet tone that lulled me. "We knock you out and you'll be helpless. You don't want that, do you?"

I fixed my focus on him.

And gave in.

They'd won...and they knew they had.

My ass slid from the sofa as I was pulled to the far wall of the apartment.

"Sit," Kane urged.

I looked at the heater.

"It's not on, don't worry. You won't be burned."

Hate filled me as I glared at him and reached out with my other hand, touching the cold steel. He dragged me toward the floor, feeding the other end of the cuff behind the pipe sticking out of the wall and grasped my free hand, cuffing it on the other side.

"You don't have to do this," I urged. "I'm on *your* side."

He gave a chilling smile as he rose. "Somehow, Helene, I doubt that."

I yanked the cuff as he rose. "Give me a chance to prove it."

He glanced at the steel as it bit against my wrist. "This *is* us giving you a chance."

Riven and The Priest stepped closer until all three stood in front of me.

"We need to keep her quiet." Riven's deadly gaze moved down my body. "Every day and all night long."

"She stays with me," Thomas muttered, that same chilling stare fixed on me. "When you leave."

My body reacted.

Tightening, warming.

"You wanted this, right, Helene?" Riven dropped his hand and unbuckled his belt. "We're about to see how much."

"Fuck you," I whispered, meeting that stare.

He just smiled. Still my pulse skipped as he unbuttoned his trousers and sank to his knees. "I think you prefer me to do the fucking." He gripped my legs and gave a yank, wrenching my ass along the floor until my arms yanked backwards and I dropped. "In fact, if I remember correctly, you fucking *loved it.*"

He ran his hands along the outside of my thighs, then reached for the button of my jeans. "Tell me, what was your plan here? Invade our lives, seduce us enough to what? *Use us?* Was that the plan?"

He licked his lips as he looked down at me helpless underneath him, my arms stretched over my head, the angle jutting my breasts hard against the fabric of my shirt. I didn't need to look to see how hard he was at the sight. He looked so fucking desperate.

Panic surged inside me, making me thrash under him.

His voice was husky when he spoke. "Was that it? You thought you were the one using us?" He flinched a second before he lunged forward and grasped my jaw with his cruel hands as he stared into my eyes. "I wonder if it was part of your plan to enjoy it?"

Fuck you!

I clenched my shackled fists, bucking as I tried to tear my gaze from his. I would not let him get under my skin...*I would* not *let him get under my skin.*

"Those sounds you made when I fucked you were too genuine to be fake." He gripped me harder and yanked my legs apart as he pushed himself between them. "And you hate yourself for it, don't you?"

"GET THE FUCK OFF ME!" Rage seethed as he grabbed the top of my jeans and stopped.

"All you have to do is say the word and this can all stop," he said carefully.

I gasped, sucking in hard breaths, and stopped fighting. He was testing me, pushing me to what? Buckle under the pressure and give them everything they wanted? They'd use me. That's what men like Riven did. They exploited and used, then hung you out to dry.

I said nothing as he waited, then slowly slid the zipper of my jeans down.

"Last chance, Helene." He gripped my ass and lifted, tugging my jeans off to mid-thigh. "Say the word and this all stops."

"So you can hang me out to dry?"

That cold smirk was callous. "Now why would we do something like that?"

I flinched. I didn't trust him. I glanced at the others. I didn't trust any of them.

Only, they'd protected me, hadn't they?

My jeans slid out from under me and my panties were pulled off. Heat rushed to my cheeks when I met The Priest's stare as Riven pulled one boot free, then the other.

In the space of a heartbeat, my jeans were gone, leaving me on the cold tiled floor. Panic filled me...the kind that made me freeze.

He saw.

Staring down at me.

He saw.

His hands stilled. That smirk faded instantly.

"Say the words, Helene." His gaze drifted over my scars. "Tell me to stop."

Come home, Helene. Vivienne's words resounded in my head. She was why I was here. Without them, I had nothing. I licked dry lips and whispered, "Not on your fucking life."

There was a quirk in the corner of his mouth. His thumb brushed along a scar on my thigh, drawing his gaze. He fixed on that scar before those dark eyes shifted higher. I swallowed hard as realization dawned in his stare. His scowl cut deeper, moving upwards to the tiny white lines I'd done to myself, then the thick, pink raised scar the bomb had left behind.

"King," he whispered, and licked his lips. "The same King that bombed the building. The same King that took out five of my men to get Ryth Castlemaine and her father free."

A cold shiver raced through me.

He lifted that dangerous stare to mine, then he slowly pulled away and pushed to stand.

I said nothing, just watched as he turned and walked toward the door.

"Where are you going?" Kane barked.

But Riven didn't answer, just zipped and buttoned his pants once more, then shoved through the connecting door and disappeared.

"What the hell just happened?" Kane turned back to me.

I wanted to answer, but that icy grip inside me clenched tight, choking the words in the back of my throat. I should've known this was dangerous. Should've known telling them the truth was placing my life in the palms of their hands.

Only, without it, my life was forfeit anyway.

And so were my sisters'.

The *thud* of the door sounded and Riven's heavy steps faded until they were gone.

Where the fuck are you going, Riven?

And what are you planning to do?

TWENTY-ONE

Riven

You planned this? My words resounded in my head.

But it was that cold, calculated smile which haunted me.

The smile that said *I won.*

Goddamn her...GODDAMN HER!

I strode toward my office, slammed the card against the scanner, and pushed in. My hands shook with anger, my jaw was clenched tight as I rounded the desk and yanked out the chair. It had been her...it had *all* been her. My knuckles ached from the tension as I unfurled them and grabbed the mouse.

Barely three clicks later and I had the video of the night the bombs had detonated on my screen. That night...that *failure,* was never far from me. It was stuck like a thorn in my fucking side, one that dug a little deeper every goddamn time I watched it. I stared at the black and white image of the corridor minutes before the explosion, watching the timer countdown.

I knew it all.

The silence. The emptiness.

Then the blur of the intruder, wearing a mask.

How many times had I stared at the thief, memorizing that dark, calculated stare the moment they'd seen the camera? A hundred? A thousand? I lifted my hand and pressed the button, playing it one more time.

The seconds counted. The hallway was empty, until it wasn't. I slowed the playback, watching in slow motion as the gunman appeared, turning to fire their gun. That bullet alone had taken out one of my most trusted men...right before they turned and lifted their gaze.

Dark eyes found the camera a second before they were gone, tearing from the frame. I pressed the button, changing the camera's view. Blinding white light exploded in the camera. I counted the seconds until there was nothing. Just emptiness... just a giant *motherfucking* hole, right where that section of the building had been.

It was almost instinct now, east camera 6 finding the intruder again. Only this time, they weren't alone. Jack Castlemaine's arms were wrapped across their shoulders as they led him out of the blown-out section of the building and through the forest to where a car was waiting.

I knew now.

It had been her.

I hit the controls, moved back again to the moment those dark, careful eyes had met the camera, and pressed pause, staring at them. They were the same eyes I'd seen the moment I'd punched the brakes and skidded my life out of control. Every glare she'd given me since that moment returned.

All her rage.

All her desire.

All her pain.

Those thick, raised scars on her side returned. Jagged and pink. Remnants from the explosion.

She'd played me.

That woman...she'd fucking played me.

My jaw popped with the strain.

My breath burned, trapped in my belly.

No. She'd played us all.

Crack!

The mouse buckled in my clenched fist, one side now split. Only it wasn't just rage that consumed me, was it?

I jerked my gaze back to those big brown eyes, and that vehement hunger roared inside me. I wanted her. *No, I fucking craved* her. I wanted to strangle her and fuck her, tear open her goddamn chest to capture her heart for my own weak fucking needs.

She'd made me feel dangerous.

More than I'd ever felt before.

"I bet that day haunts you."

I swallowed the flinch, holding still...so fucking still I barely moved, until I slowly turned my head. That same *bastard* who'd barged into me standing in Hale's office now stood in mine—right at my back—and I hadn't heard a thing.

He just looked at the screen in front of me and the still image of Helene as she looked into the camera. A nerve twitched in the corner of my eye. I didn't like him looking at her. Not. One. Fucking. Bit.

"Come with me," he demanded, and turned away, heading for the door before he stopped. "Now."

The fuck?

What was I, some kind of fucking dog they could command to heel?

Yes.

That's exactly what I was.

I gave a snarl and rose from the seat, hitting the button and ending the video. Gone was the desire, leaving behind the savage craving to tear the goddamn world apart, starting with this asshole. I followed him out of my office and along the corridor, heading toward the Daughters' rooms.

The moment I pushed through the last set of doors, I heard the screams. Guttural, terrifying roars of the new guards were met with shrill cries from the Daughters. I clenched my jaw at the sounds. We might've been fucking cold, controlling bastards, but we weren't fucking barbarians. Not like those guys.

Walker was the first one I saw when I turned into the corridor. He stood outside the communal bathroom door, his face ashen and his eyes filled with rage. The sickening *thud* of a fist echoed before the weak, pathetic whimpers turned into low, chilling moans.

They were beating them.

The fucking bastards!

They. Were. Fucking. Beating. Them.

I pushed past Walker and strode into the neon bright bathroom. Memories slammed into me, Ryth Castlemaine standing terrified in a stall while I implied we had her stepbrother hostage. I was a lying, manipulative asshole, that was for sure. I strode in, pushing past Coulter and his three leering scumbags as the guard crowding the cowering Daughter raised his fist once more.

I stared at her green eyes wide and terrified. Her face was bleeding, lip swelling where he'd already hit her. She lifted her hand, trying her best to shield herself from his blows, and for a second, all I saw was Melody.

My pulse boomed. Rage filled me as the guard's fist clenched tight.

That's my sister.

The words roared in my head.

THAT'S MY GODDAMN SISTER!

I strode forward and grabbed his fist as it arced through the air. She lifted her gaze to mine and the face of Melody faded. Still, that merciless rage was left behind as I turned to the guard. "Touch her again and I'll put a bullet in your head."

He jerked his gaze upwards, bestial fury shining in his eyes.

The Daughter kicked against the cold tiles, curling her naked body even tighter into a ball, if that was possible. He jerked that raging glare behind me to where his leader stood. But I wasn't budging.

"Malcolm," Coulter murmured.

There was a curl in the bastard's lip before he turned that sickening hunger for blood my way. In the corner of my eye, Walker slipped in and slowly lifted his gun. But it wasn't the Daughter he aimed it at, it was the asshole in front of me.

"Walker," I said clearly. "You're to shoot this asshole, and anyone else who raises a fist to these women, do you understand?"

"My fucking pleasure," he answered.

He would, even if it meant he'd take one in return. We had rules about anyone beating or hurting those we were tasked to protect and train...we had *responsibilities*.

I swung my gaze to the man responsible, the one who'd just stood there watching this all unfold.

"They have twenty-four hours," Coulter said, shifting his stare from the cowering Daughter to me. "Twenty-four hours for you to train them." He took a step closer. "Or they won't be the only ones I lead down into the basement once more."

I sucked in hard breaths as he cast that sickening fucking stare at the naked woman behind me before he turned and walked out, taking his men with him. Goosebumps raced down my arms as the piece of shit who liked to beat women stopped behind me.

I waited for a blow to come, *craving* it almost. Anything to give me a goddamn excuse. That savage hunger burned in my belly as I turned around and met his stare. "Do it," I urged.

Desperation roared in his stare.

He wanted to.

But one tiny shift from Walker and he gave a smirk before he turned around and walked out, leaving the heavy thud of his steps behind. I inhaled, my mind racing as Coulter's words hit home. *They won't be the only ones I lead down into the basement once more.*

Once more.

Once more.

I scowled, my mind racing, as the Daughter behind me still wept.

"It was them," I whispered, meeting Walker's stare. "The kill squad. The basement. It was Coulter."

He flinched before he shook his head. I saw the disgust and the anger. I saw the rage, then the fear. The fear I was sure was echoed in my stare.

"What the fuck do we do?" he murmured.

I didn't know. We were outnumbered, even with the paid guards protecting the compound. I knew that and so did he. My gut clenched. Revulsion drove the bitter tang of acid into the back of my throat.

I needed to think. Not only that, I needed to act.

I needed to do *something,*

Her whimpers called to me, resounding through my head like shards of glass. "Take care of her," I said to Walker. "See she's seen by the infirmary. I need to think."

"Will do." He took a step, then stopped. "Be careful, Riven. I have a feeling these men aren't here to play."

I nodded and left him. I had that feeling too. The same foul stench of death seemed to waft from the basement and spill down the corridor to find me. I'd had my suspicions about who'd done the killing. The moment I'd heard London and his son had found them, I'd come to find them on my own.

There were bodies.

Daughters piled on top of each other.

Some still silently screaming as they'd pleaded for their lives.

It had been them...it had been *Coulter*.

His men had been the kill squad, the ones Harmon had sent in to clean house. He was still fulfilling those orders, bringing in all the other Daughters from whichever orphanage and secret location they'd been held. But he wanted these trained and sold.

Why?

I pushed through the doors, heading for the one that'd lead me outside, when a chill raced along my spine, stopping me cold. I felt him before I turned, finding the cruel piece of shit who liked the feel of his fists on soft flesh standing on the other side of the double doors in the distance.

He watched me.

Watched me like he was dangerous.

I turned back, pressed my card against the scanner, and strode outside. There were sharks in the water. Sharks circling, desperate for one taste of blood before they attacked. I felt the current battering me against the rocks. One scrape was all it'd take. One tiny cut and I was gone for good.

They won't be the only ones I lead down into the basement once more.

Those motherfuckers.

Those *goddamn* motherfuckers.

I strode forward, sinking into the forest, desperate to get out from under their controlling grasp for a second. The moment I sank into the darkness, the door opened behind me and the screams of the cowering Daughter returned in my mind.

We might've been savage bastards who controlled them and manipulated them.

But we'd *never* beaten them.

We never hurt them.

Not physically, at least.

But these...relentless savage bastards were something else.

Thud.

The sound of the door reached me through the trees. But I was already surging forward, desperate for the darkness...and to think. I had to find a way out of this. Not only did I need a plan to find Hale's black site and our sister, I needed to figure out what to do with the woman hidden in our apartment. The one under Coulter's nose.

The one who could bring us all down.

With one...shrill...scream.

TWENTY-TWO

Helene

"We don't go anywhere, not until he returns," Kane announced, sounding pissed off. "You know that, so stop acting like a terrified child and grow the hell up."

"And what happens when this all goes to hell?" Thomas stumbled toward his brother, his eyes filled with pain and anger. "What then, we just forget about her? We forget about our Goddamn sister? We leave now and we might have half a chance with The Hunter. We find every lead...and we..."

I'd been listening to them fight for hours, sitting on the floor, my hands cuffed over my head around the damn steel pipe for the heater. Every *clang* of the steel cuffs drew their gaze, but only for a second before they were back at it, bickering and fighting like...*brothers.*

"I'm not going to even dignify *that* remark with a response." Kane glared at him, the corner of his eye twitching. "If you weren't so hurt, I'd—"

"You gonna *beat me, brother?*" Thomas sneered. "You've never raised your hands. No, you like to guilt trip, and ridicule until you get your way. You like to—"

Click.

The external door cracked open as Riven stepped inside, glancing over his shoulder to the forest before he yanked the door closed behind him.

His face was flushed, cheeks burning bright red, and his breaths were panting, just like he'd been running.

"What is it?" Kane asked, glancing at the door.

But Riven said nothing, just strode past his brothers, grabbed a bottle of Scotch, and poured himself a drink. Kane scowled and Thomas looked nervous, even more than he was before, as Riven swallowed the drink and swiped the back of his hand across his mouth.

"We train them tomorrow." He looked strange, focused on a spot on the floor between us, like it took all his strength not to meet my gaze as those words hit me like a blow to my stomach.

"Tomorrow?" I whispered.

Only then did he lift those dark eyes and meet mine.

There was something different about them, a kind of horror screaming inside him, one he refused to unleash.

I knew exactly what he meant by 'train them'. He'd break them down, force them to their knees. He'd make them...make them...he'd make them take his cock. He'd fuck them, use them. They all would.

I winced, trying my best to swallow my revulsion as I glared at Kane. He stood frozen, his skin pale. One shake of his head said it all. "We can't."

"We don't have a goddamn choice," Riven answered coldly.

"We leave." Thomas finally said the words caught in his throat. "We take our chances with the information we have."

"Thomas," Kane warned.

But it was too late. Rage coiled in Riven's stare, dangerous and hungry. He jerked his gaze toward Thomas and strode toward him. "You want to leave?" He grabbed him by the shirt, and drove him toward the door, before slamming his fist against the handle and shoving it wide. Cold night air rushed in as Thomas stumbled at the doorway.

"Get the fuck out," Riven demanded.

"Riven." Thomas tried to fight against his hold. "Stop. I don't want to go."

Riven jerked him closer, glaring into his eyes. "Say it again and you're out on your own. Get it?"

Thomas punched his hold, tearing it free before he straightened his shirt, casting me a confused and embarrassed glare. "I only meant..."

Riven turned away. "I know exactly what you meant. We're *this* fucking close to a lead on the black site." He stopped, then turned back, lifted his fingers and pinched them until they almost touched. "This close to finding Melody for good. You want to fuck it up and walk out now without knowing for sure, then by all means, go right ahead. It's taken us almost ten fucking years to find her. There's no way in hell we're walking away now."

Ten years to find their sister?

It hit me hard.

These men weren't the monsters I'd been led to believe. They were dangerous, yes. They were even damaged and cruel. But they were here for a reason. They were here for *family*.

Riven cast me a careful gaze and raked his fingers through his hair. "They fucking beat them. One guard even had a Daughter on the bathroom floor, punching into her. I thought for a second," he looked my way again. "I thought for a second it was her."

"Mel?" Thomas whispered. "You thought it was Mel?"

Riven scowled, then shook his head. "It wasn't."

"But it could've been," Kane added. "It could've been, and that scared you more than anything. All this time we've been chasing a ghost. But at that moment, she wasn't a ghost any longer. She was real." He moved closer and grabbed Riven by the arm. "She was more real than the memory we have of her."

An ache plunged through my chest. I knew what that feeling felt like. That desperation, that isolation. No wonder they were cold.

"Then we stay," Thomas croaked. "And we see this through."

Riven met his stare. "We have no choice."

"Then all of us need to sleep," Thomas added, and stumbled toward his bedroom. "I have a feeling we're going to need it."

Riven gave a nod. Thomas glanced my way. I could see he wanted to say something...or do something.

"I'll take care of her." Riven's tone sounded possessive.

Kane just gave a nod and turned away. "You know where I am if you need me."

But Riven didn't even glance his way. He didn't need him. Not when he had something else to occupy his thoughts...and his savage desperation. He took a slow step closer, moving soundlessly until he stopped at the high cupboard, sliding the key for the cuffs free. I looked up at him as he bent over and unlocked the clasp, letting my aching arms drop with small thumps.

"You're with me, Trouble."

I waited, staring up at him, trying my best to pinpoint exactly what had changed between us. There was a desperation now, a need that was far removed from the demanding, possessive, cruel way he'd been before. He lifted his hand, that vulnerable hunger burning in his eyes.

Please.

That's what it said.

I hated him.

Deep down, there was a part of me that wanted him dead, him and his brothers. Still, I found my hand rising, taking his as he helped me to stand. An ache spread throughout my back, making me wince. But there was no time to care as he tugged my hand, leading me through the apartment and to his room.

Soundless.

That's what we were as I stepped inside, leaving him to close the door behind us and switch on the light. I'd been in this room before. The thought of being in his space had scared me then, but standing here beside him now as he turned and pushed me against the wall, I was downright terrified.

He reached down and slid those bloodstained fingers between my thighs. I shook my head as he held my stare. I didn't want him. I didn't want this. *I couldn't.* Still, those fingers pushed in deeper, rubbing me through my jeans.

"Open your legs, Helene King," he murmured. "Let me see just how much you still despise me."

My body reacted on its own and my thighs trembled as they parted. I closed my eyes, hating him more now than ever before. Only now I hated myself just as much.

That slow rub along the crease of my jeans made me weak. Heat bloomed with every graze of his thumb until he pulled away and worked the button before sliding the zipper down. I opened my eyes, finding that hollowed out desperation in his stare as he slowly dropped to his knees.

No words were spoken, just the graze of denim as he tugged my jeans down. I lifted each foot, allowing him to slide them away. I shivered under that stare, the same haunting need consuming me as it did him. I slid my fingers through his hair, clenching hard enough for him to lift his gaze to mine.

"Don't," he whispered, his voice thick and husky. "You need to hate me, Helene. You *need* to recoil every fucking time I touch you. Because, if you don't..." His chest heaved with a breath. "If you don't, then I'm more dangerous to you than I was before. I don't want that."

My pulse sped and thrashed in my head.

He looked away, but his fingers trembled as they tugged my panties down. Panties he'd bought me. Panties he wanted me to wear. Because he felt something for me. I'd seen it before when he'd cooked for me. I'd seen it again tonight when he said they were training the Daughters.

I clenched my grip, fisted his hair, and jerked harder, forcing his gaze to mine once more. "Will you fuck them?" I whispered. "Those Daughters? Will you get on your knees just like you're on them now?"

Pain slashed across his face. "No. I won't get on my knees for them."

"But you will for me."

It wasn't a question. I knew by now how Riven Cruz worked. If there wasn't a direct response required, he avoided answering.

"Yes." That scowl deepened. "I will for you."

A lump grew in the back of my throat. I wanted to say more, but I couldn't. I just eased my hold around his hair, leaving him to slide my panties all the way down until they hit the floor. Warmth brushed along my skin as he leaned closer and kissed my thigh.

My pulse skipped.

Oh fuck.

Oh...fuck.

The brush of his lips moved over. Those fingers pushed in, sliding over the sensitive nub. He gripped the back of one leg, easing it over his shoulder, and moved in, then the warm slide of his tongue took over and cast me into oblivion.

It had all been for their sister.

Every cruel, terrible thing they'd ever done.

I wanted to hate them for it, but the truth was, I'd done worse for mine.

I'd killed. I'd tortured.

I'd detonated bombs and razed buildings.

I'd done a thousand things to innocent people I could never take back.

And I'd do it all again...to protect those I loved.

A moan tore free. I looked down to where his head was buried between my thighs and I did something I'd never expected to do. I caressed his cheek, drawing his desperate stare upward. Gone was the savagery. Gone was the unfeeling demeanor. Gone was the man who'd tied me to a chair and fucked me with his fingers until I'd drenched his sofa. Although, some sick part of me hoped that that man hadn't left entirely.

"Take me to bed, Riven," I urged. "And fuck the hell out of me."

He eased my leg from his shoulder and rose swiftly. Strong hands gripped my waist and lifted, letting my legs wrap around his waist. He carried me to the bed and gently laid me down before he unbuttoned his shirt and pulled it over his head.

His shoes were kicked off before he fumbled with his belt, unbuckled his trousers, and slid them down. He came to me naked, sliding his hand under my thigh to cup my asscheeks.

Heavy breaths brushed like a caress along the insides of my thighs.

With a guttural moan, he plunged his tongue deep inside me. I arched my back, releasing a cry. My toes curled as he sucked, driving his fingers deep inside. He cradled me in his palm, my body, my desire while he devoured the center of me.

"Riven," I cried.

He lifted his head, his powerful grasp wrapping around my throat, as though he knew exactly what my body needed. "Beg for me," he demanded. "Beg me to let you come."

Tears sprang to my eyes, shimmering his face. "Please," I whispered. "Please, let me come."

He rose upward, settled his body between my thighs, and plunged his cock in deep. "You look so pretty when you beg, Helene. So pretty while I choke and fuck you."

The brutal slam of his hips sent me over the edge.

I couldn't get my knees wide enough, desperate for every inch of him.

His hold clenched as I thrashed my head. Slick sounds came from between us.

"Look at you, coming while I fuck you. Look into my eyes, Helene. Look at your tormentor."

I forced my gaze to his, fisting the bedding beside me as my climax barrelled through me.

I cried out, giving myself to him. That dangerous look of pride and predator filled him.

Mine. That's what it said. *You are now mine.*

He gave a cold, calculating smile, then pulled out, unfinished, grasped me around the waist and flipped me over. He manhandled me, lifting my hips until I was on my knees, and plunged back in, thrusting so hard he lifted my body and pulled me back.

My pulsing core clenched as he stretched me. His hand in the middle of my lower back rocked me as his hard thrusts sent me over the edge again.

"Ruin me," I pleaded. "Please, just fucking ruin me."

He forced himself deeper, causing me to grasp onto the sheets as my climax surged even higher. A low, guttural moan sounded and he lifted his hips upward, driving me facefirst into the mattress. He was a beast, driving inside me with frantic thrusts until he stilled, buried to the hilt, and moaned. *"Fuck me."*

Warmth spilled. I pushed back against him, desperate for him to fill me.

"I don't want to touch them," he groaned, sucking in a hard breath. "I don't want to even look at them. But they're not giving me a choice here..." He brushed my hair to the side, desperate to see me. "All I want is you, Helene King...*all I want is you.*"

Agony ripped through me as he pulled away. I collapsed onto the bed, unable to move or think.

But I felt.

Oh, fuck, I *felt* as an unseen dagger ripped open my chest and hacked out my heart.

Tears welled as the words rose inside my head, *I want you too.*

TWENTY-THREE

Riven

YOU HAVE TWENTY-FOUR HOURS...

The words found me the moment I cracked open my eyes. The room was still dark, kissed with the promise of sunlight, but I closed my eyes once more. Twenty-four hours...until I became the monster once again.

A light snore came from behind me, drawing my attention to her, and my pulse sped, driving sleep further away. I opened my eyes and turned my head, finding the murky silhouette beside me. *Helene King.* The same King we hunted, the same King who evaded her.

She was his goddamn daughter?

I inhaled, letting my gaze drift down the sheet barely covering her naked body. A lick of my lips and my body came alive, my cock hardening instantly, until I remembered last night and the change between us.

Gone was the sadistic hunger to control and consume. A different yearning filled me now, one that was fucking terrifying. I reached for her, curling my fingers to gently brush her cheek. A memory invaded, the same touch, only last night it'd been her fingers and my cheek.

She opened her eyes at the touch and said nothing, just stared into my eyes.

All I want is you, Helene King.

Those words still gripped me, clenching tight around my heart.

Until reality took hold, forcing me to pull away.

"Riven," she whispered as I rolled away and pushed upwards.

I sat on the side of the bed, watching the soft spill of sunlight creep closer and hating every second of the things I'd have to do today. Cold gripped me as I rose, letting the sheet fall from around my body. The bed moved as she pushed upward. I knew every move she made, every catch of her breath, every stare of those dark, haunting eyes. But I couldn't meet them. Not today.

I opened my bedroom door and walked out, heading to the bathroom I shared with my brothers. I winced as the glaring lights bounced off the crisp white tiles. One glance into the mirror and I looked away.

My eyes were bloodshot and felt grainy. I looked like hell. And I felt every bit of it.

The hiss of the shower came as I hit the faucets. I stepped in, letting the hot water carry me away before I reached for the bodywash. By the time I was done, I was a different person, stony and unfeeling. I stepped out and toweled myself dry.

There were no longer bloodshot eyes and a tortured stare in the mirror. There was just *nothing*.

Gone was the man.

Now there was only The Principal.

I cast my towel aside and made my way into the bedroom, where she was waiting. I didn't look at her as she sat on the side of the bed, dressed in yesterday's clothes. Instead, I headed for the walk-in closet and grabbed boxers, navy slacks, and a black open-collared shirt before carefully selecting my belt, watch, and boots.

That was my armor.

My mask.

I dressed in silence, buttoning and zipping, then tugged on my boots. When I was dressed, I rose and stared down into her tortured eyes.

"You're really going to go through with this?" she croaked.

Tears shimmered in her eyes.

I turned away and headed for the door without saying a word. But inside I was howling in rage, beating bloody fists against the cage around my heart. Hard breaths only pushed me closer to the edge, my frantic pulse nearly out of control.

Footsteps came behind me.

I spun, to find Kane heading toward me.

Showered and dressed, the same empty stare in those green eyes which I'd seen in mine.

"Are you sure you're ready for this?" he asked.

Movement behind him drew my gaze. Helene moved closer, slipping around him.

"No," I answered, and stepped toward the cupboard to grab the cuffs. "Helene." I turned to her, hating the cold, unfeeling tone in my voice. "Can't have you sticking your nose where it doesn't belong now, can we? Not now that we know *who* you are."

She flinched at the words. Her damn lip trembled. I looked away at the sight.

"Fuck you," she hissed.

I gave a nod. *Fuck me, indeed.*

She didn't even fight, just strode to the heater and spun, glaring at me as she sank to the floor and lifted her arms. I cuffed her without meeting her gaze.

The moment my back was turned, she muttered, "Gutless bastard."

I hesitated, flinching, hating the way she could hurt me with words alone. I forced myself to move, leaving her and her hateful glare behind as I strode from the apartment alone. I slapped my card against the scanners, making my way to where the new shipment of Daughters was kept.

The closer I got, the more I felt the tension. The hairs on my arms stood on end as I rounded the corner of the corridor and stopped. Walker stood there, surrounded by almost all the permanent guards, all of them armed to the teeth, and glaring at the asshole who'd barged into me and Coulter's other men.

"Walker." I approached slowly, feeling the tension building with every second. "Everything okay here?"

"Just peachy," Walker answered, not once looking away.

They were all a Molotov cocktail, just waiting for the match. The Daughters' rooms behind Coulter's men were open, but there was no movement.

"I was just explaining to David here that we have a process for onboarding," Walker explained. "The women bathe and eat, *only* then do they start."

Coulter's men glanced my way. I was missing something here. Something that had pissed Walker off.

"The process has been this way for years," I added. "Men far smarter than you and I have carefully created it. We have proven any deviation from the program will probably have disastrous effects. Now, you don't want that."

"That's right," came the cool, dulcet tone of my brother. "When he says smarter men, he means me. I planned the programming, virtually down to the second. I know these women better than anyone else. Their needs, their hunger. I know when they will fight and when they won't. I know all of that because *I am the programmer.*" He stepped closer, facing Coulter's man. "*You* change *that* programming and you change everything. Do you want to hand over screaming and hysterical women to whoever is now in charge? Or would you prefer *we* do what we've successfully done previously and provide the very best care?"

The bastard said nothing. Kane gave a slow nod, then stepped forward, meeting his stare with an unflinching gaze. "Now, if you don't mind." He nodded to Walker and his men. "Kindly get out of our way."

Coulter's man curled his lip, shooting me a look of pure rage. One of his men reached down, pushing the tented outline of his cock to the side. I knew instantly what Walker had interrupted. Motherfuckers.

"Walker, take them to the cafeteria, make sure they're fed before you take them to the media room for the first round of programming." I said, make sure I held the bastard's gaze for a full second before I took a step and pushed past, walking into the first room.

"You heard The Principal," Walker ordered his men.

Grunts sounded, threats were mumbled. Kane headed further down the hallway as I stepped into the darkened cell, finding the young woman curled up on the cot, knees to her chest, as she stared at me.

"It's okay." I lifted my hand for her. "You're safe now."

My gut clenched with the words. It was a lie. A terrifying, sickening lie. She wasn't safe. No one was, not here. She was about to learn just how unsafe she was.

"Come," I commanded.

A battle raged in her eyes as she tried to fight the conditioning embedded inside her subconscious, pulling away even further from me. But I didn't move, didn't twitch, just held her gaze, my hand hovering in the air. Finally, she unfurled her body and slowly slid to the side of the bed.

They had bred her to obey.

Groomed her to do whatever men like me wanted.

Revulsion burned at the thought. My sister was one of them now. Groomed. Used. Bred.

The Daughter neared, letting me grip her arm and lead her from the room. Walker still stood in the hallway, supervising the rest of his men as they led each of the women from their cells.

Coulter's men remained, standing to the side as they watched... all but the bastard who'd seemed to have a hard-on for me. He was gone. That made a chilling whisper of fear rise up my spine once more.

"The asshole who was just here. Where is he now?" I searched for the rest of the Daughters as they stepped out of their rooms one by one.

"Never said," Walker answered. "He just left. Why?"

My pulse raced, filling my head. Something was wrong...*something was very wrong*.

I shook my head. "Nothing," I answered, but inside my head, instinct screamed. "Take care of them."

I glanced at Kane as he stepped out of the last room and lifted his gaze to me. He stopped, concern furrowing his brow.

I couldn't explain what I was feeling, all I could do was act. I turned away and headed for my office, with the desperate need to find that motherfucker roaring in my head. He was up to something. I just *knew it*.

TWENTY-FOUR

Helene

*T*HUMP.

I flinched when the door closed as Kane walked out, leaving me alone with The Priest. He stood there glaring at me, giving me that look that said he wanted to have it out with me.

Not now.

Pain filled me, the sting more brutal than anything I'd ever felt in my life. This was why I wouldn't get involved with men. This was why...tears threatened to blur the asshole in front of me. I fixed my gaze on the door instead. This was why I shouldn't have stepped out into that fucking street in the rain.

This was all the weather's fault.

If I'd only listened to my gut.

I wouldn't be here. I wouldn't be anywhere near here.

I'd be at home, playing them at a safe distance.

Not here, cuffed to a fucking heater with my heart...*what about your heart? Don't tell me you're in fucking love?* I closed my eyes and unleashed a moan.

Jesus Christ.

I was in love.

Maybe not in love.

But it was something.

Something that made me feel...*wounded.*

Thomas stepped closer, looming over me. I glared back at him, holding his stare. His right eye was bloody, pierced only by the dark brown pupil fixed on me. I winced at the sight, taking in the mess of his mouth, knowing what I saw was nothing compared to the rest of him.

I looked away.

"Don't," he croaked, taking another step closer. "I want you to look at me. I want you to see what that bastard did."

Another step.

"You were there, weren't you? At the church and later at the warehouse."

I fixed my gaze on the dresser.

"WEREN'T YOU!"

I jumped, jerking my gaze back to the insanity in that gruesome stare.

"You were there," he repeated.

"Yes." There. I'd said it. I'd told him what he wanted to know. "I was there."

Only he didn't leave, he dropped to his knees and grabbed my jaw, clenching tight with cruel fingers. "Did you enjoy watching him torture me?"

I jerked my face from his grasp. Anger and pain filled me. But he wasn't done, digging in his fingers as he grabbed me again.

"Well?" he barked. *"Did. You. Enjoy. It?"*

"YES!" I roared, that knot-like pain radiating through my chest. "Yes, I *enjoyed* it."

He stilled, harsh, savage breaths surging between us. Fire exploded in the middle of my chest. His grip tightened until I couldn't breathe. I thrashed, yanking my hands until the cuffs bit. But under the desperation, rage seethed.

"Fire," I wheezed.

He scowled, released his hold, and shifted his weight, moving closer. "What?"

"Fire," I gasped. "I can still smell your hair burning when he shoved you onto the flames."

That memory burst into my mind. The smell of the fire. The sound of his screams. More than that, the pure rage that had been London St. James.

A dangerous sound slithered from The Priest. My eyes watered. I stopped fighting. My heart pounded so loud it filled my head as a sickening, desperate need filled me. I craved this... this force, this demand. This was worse than the sting of the blade and worse than alcohol. This was a need that bloomed inside me like an intoxicating flower.

I looked up into that bloody eye. To be at the mercy of a man's hand made me feel powerless and empty.

Use me.

The words rose.

Please, just fucking use me.

"You like this," he hissed, searching my gaze. He licked those scabbed lips and looked down to where my pebbled nipples pushed against my shirt, then lower, between my legs. His grip eased just enough for air to rush in. "You like it when my brother chokes you?" He leaned down, his other hand reaching between my thighs, forcing them wider.

Movement came from behind him. The external door cracked open...

"You like it when Riven takes you screaming?"

I bucked as a guard stepped inside, his savage gaze fixed on The Priest, whose grip clenched tighter around my throat, cutting off my air.

"I bet he likes it too. His fucking toy...his—"

I bucked, thrashing my head as I tried to get free.

The guard behind him lifted his gun and stepped closer. I could see it all. The gunshot, the blood...and The Priest slumped dead on top of me. Until, with one desperate breath, I slammed my head forward against his and screamed, *"BEHIND YOU!"*

He fell backwards, turning at the last instant. I didn't know how he knew...but he reacted, flinging his arm backward in a perfect arc that knocked the gun out of the guard's grasp. The guard lunged, slamming into The Priest.

I wrenched against the cuffs as the guard lifted his fist, grasped hold of his black t-shirt, and unleashed, hitting Thomas in the cheek.

"NO!" I howled. *"GET THE FUCK OFF HIM!"*

But the guard didn't stop, landing another blow, one that hit The Priest square on the nose.

Crunch.

His head snapped backward and his eyes rolled in his head. All I saw were the whites as the bastard flung him to the floor with a *thud.* Then he slowly turned his gaze to me...and smiled.

"He has a toy to play with, yet he stands in our way."

I shook my head, and for the first time in my entire life, fear found me. True fear. I shook my head as he stepped over the slumped body of The Priest and slowly came toward me.

"I fucking knew it."

"No." I forced a croak as he stood over me. *"No."*

He reached for the button of his pants and unzipped his fly.

"I've heard you bitches take it all. We can do anything we want with you." He reached down and fisted a handful of my hair, yanking my head backwards. My eyes watered with the burn.

I couldn't do anything. Cuffed. Alone.

I wasn't getting out of this.

"Isn't that right?" His eyes glittered as he stared down at me. "You won't even fight when I fuck you so hard you'll see stars? I might take you back to the boys, how about that? Let's see how many of us you can take at once."

"*Fuck. You.*"

He stilled, scowled. "What did you say?"

"She said...*fuck you,*" The Priest mumbled as he staggered to his feet, then grabbed a gun from the top of the cupboard. "She's *not yours to touch!*"

The strands of my hair strained, blurring my vision. But it wasn't the gun in his hand I cared about...it was the key, the fucking key Riven had slammed down a second before he turned and walked out on me.

Fire lashed my scalp as the guard released my hair and lunged at Thomas with a roar. Fists flew. They slammed together with savage roars and sickening howls of pain...ones that came from the only man who could help me.

Bang!

I jumped at the terrifying sound, frantically jerking my gaze from the gun in The Priest's hand to his body. *Who shot who? WHO SHOT WHO?*

The guard stumbled backward, then looked down. His fingers came away bloody as he touched his side. Everything happened in slow motion. The Priest turned as the guard lifted his gun and lunged, slamming into the same dresser with the gun...*and the key.*

Bang!

Wood splintered under his hand. He swiped the surface and spun with a roar. Metal glinted as the key flipped end over end toward me. My heart lunged, slamming against my chest as I shoved my feet out, sliding as far as I could. The key hit my body, coming to rest against my stomach.

Screams came from The Priest.

Guttural and desperate.

Like a man fighting for his life.

One he was about to lose.

I fixed my gaze on that key, my breaths punching it higher. I tried to slow them, my entire body straining as I gripped the steel cuffs and pulled my weight backwards. *Come on...COME ON!*

My knees shook as I slid my feet underneath me.

The Priest and the guard still fought.

But it wouldn't last long.

Please...

PLEASE...

I pushed upwards and twisted my hand in the cuffs. But there was no way I was going to reach it. I grabbed my t-shirt instead, gripping it until the fabric pulled taut, lifting the key. It slid, tumbling toward me at speed. I did the only thing I could. I opened my mouth, snapped my head forward, and bit.

My teeth gnashed against the cold metal. I jerked my gaze toward them as The Priest stumbled and went down. The gun in the guard's hand was all I saw as I wrenched my head to the side, forcing my focus back on getting free.

I prayed, maybe harder than I'd ever prayed before, and twisted around, pushing the key in my mouth to the lock. It pushed in, letting me bite down and twist my head to the side.

Click.

The cuff snapped open.

I'd never been so frantic in my life as the guard lifted his gun and took aim. I yanked the key free, my movements automatic as I shoved the key into the lock and twisted.

I was moving before I knew it, driving myself forward until I slammed into the guard's legs, knocking him sideways.

BANG!

The gun went off.

I tried to shove myself upward, but my knees buckled. The guard swung around as I shoved up, screaming, *"Get the fuck off him!"*

He roared and swung his fist, driving his gun against the side of my head with a *crack!*

Blinding white lights detonated behind my eyelids.

Then there was only darkness as I fell.

I hit the floor hard and my head bounced. Agony ripped through my skull. I moaned and rolled, staring up as the guard stepped over me, then reached down.

Panic surged and I tried to shove backwards, desperate to get away from him...but my thoughts were slow...too slow. He clutched a fistful of my hair and dragged me up,.

Searing fire lashed my scalp. I screamed, clawing his clenched fist, until he released my hair but grabbed my wrist instead and yanked me hard against him.

"You're not supposed to fight me, remember?" His eyes blazed as he grabbed my other hand and wrenched my arms behind my back.

Agony tore along my muscles. I bucked, fighting against him. But he was strong...really strong, holding both my wrists in one hand.

I slammed my head forward, kicking and howling.

"*STOP!*" he roared, grasping my throat with his other hand.

Only he wasn't like the others. There was no slight pressure, no playing and teasing. His bruising fingers clenched around my windpipe, cutting off my air.

A hiss came, but there was no gasp.

Only blinding white...

Until he released me.

I jerked forward, slamming against him to feel the fabric of my shirt tearing. His other hand was all over my breasts, frantically mauling before he yanked the soft satin cups of the bra Riven had bought me...before he stilled. "What the fuck?"

I didn't even have the strength to look down. I knew he was looking at the thin white lines that marred my soft flesh.

"You're fucking ruined."

I gasped, flailing as he reached for my jeans.

"Don't care, pussy's still pussy," he grunted, jerking open my zipper.

"NO!" I screamed, trying to get away. *"NOOO!"*

He grabbed my mouth, grinding my cheeks against my molars. His eyes were wild with desperation and rage. *"You'll shut the fuck up. Do you hear me?"*

His fingers pushed into my mouth. I gagged at the salty taste of him.

"Fucking *bitch*. Aren't you whores supposed to just lie back and take it? You need breaking in, Daughter, and I'm gonna enjoy doing it. It's better when they fight anyway. So fight. Scream. Let me feel you kick and buck when I ram my cock all the way inside. Let's see how that bastard likes you when you're split from asshole to cunt."

I bucked, the fight in me fading, until his eyes widened.

Gray ate at the edges of the room...but Riven's face was the blinding light I needed as he wrapped his arm around the guard's neck and dragged him backwards.

Those dark eyes glanced at his brother, unconscious on the floor, before they fixed on me, taking in my ripped shirt and my torn-open jeans. But it was my mouth he fixed on, swollen lips pulsing. The taste of him was still on my tongue.

Riven said nothing, just tightened his hold around the guard's throat. His chest was heaving with brutal breaths, as though he'd been running. But there was no running now and no release.

Just.

Pure.

Icy.

Rage.

The guard slammed his hands against the floor, his eyes bulging from Riven's strain.

I was mesmerized by Riven's ruthlessness as the sick, raping bastard swung his hand up, those fat fingers still shimmering with saliva from my mouth, clawing for a hold.

Riven just ducked his blow, clenching even tighter until the corded muscles in his arms stood out and the tendons in his neck strained, but never once taking his eyes from mine.

Until, with a choked hiss, the guard in his hold slumped.

I expected Riven to release him. But he didn't. He clenched even tighter.

Until, at a sickening *crunch,* his lips curled, baring the true predator to me.

I held that stare, my heart booming in my chest.

He'd killed the guard for his brother.

But he'd fucking destroyed him for me.

Until, finally, he let go.

The guard's body tumbled sideways to the floor, the head rolling unnaturally.

"No one touches what's mine." Riven's tone was chilling. "And you, Trouble, are mine."

TWENTY-FIVE

Helene

______

You are mine.

One look into those merciless eyes and I knew it was the truth. He stepped over the splayed arms of the dead guard and held out his hand. Fear still trembled and made me hesitate for a second before I rushed forward, slamming against him.

Those murderous hands slid over my ruined shirt and tugged my bra back into place before they moved upward to grip my jaw. He tilted my head from side to side, his thumb gently brushing my throbbing lip. "Did he hurt you?"

I knew what he was asking. *Had he raped me?*

I shook my head, hating the way his face blurred. The Priest gave a sickening groan, drawing Riven's gaze at the same time the door to the apartment slammed open and Kane lunged in. He hastily scanned the apartment before his gaze landed on us.

His hard breaths stopped suddenly as he saw the body of the guard, then he quickly stepped in and closed the door, instantly locking it.

Riven moved to The Priest as Thomas coughed and wheezed.

"What the fuck happened?" Kane demanded as he headed toward us. He jerked his gaze toward The Priest before it crept back to the guard's body.

"He was going to hurt her," The Priest gasped as he pushed upward, wincing as he touched his cheek, then glanced at the guard, grimacing at the angle of his neck. "Who the fuck is he?"

"One of Coulter's men," Riven answered. "Who had a hard-on for me, it seemed."

"Fuck," Kane barked as he turned to pace the living room. "What the hell do we do now?"

I stared at the dead asshole, my pulse racing. But I didn't succumb to the fear, because all I could think of was Riven... Riven training the Daughters.

I heard you bitches take it all. You won't fight when I fuck you...

I winced at the stabbing pain and snarled. "He...he thought I was one of them—a Daughter."

"What?' Riven snapped coldly.

I turned to him, searching those dark eyes before I checked his clothes. Had he started already? Had this interrupted him?

My stomach clenched as revulsion burned. The thought of his hands on them, even under these sickening circumstances, was enough to make me spin out of control. "He..." I turned back to the dead guard. "He thought I was a Daughter."

Riven snarled, "The *hell you are.*"

Desperation filled me now. "So make me one."

"No," he said instantly, rage glinting in his eyes as they fixed on me. *"Hell no!"*

But I wasn't letting this go. "You need to find your sister, right?" I looked toward the others. "You *need* a way in...let *me* be that way."

Riven shook his head. *Goddamn stubborn man.* Didn't he see what I was doing here? Didn't he see why—

The image slammed into me. Dark. Erotic. *Desperate.*

Him and me and all the dark, depraved things he'd done.

"It's not the craziest decision," Kane offered.

"No." Riven scowled, this time with a shake of his head. "I'm not having her at the mercy of those bastards."

"But I wouldn't be," I whispered, and took a step toward him. "I would be at yours."

The scowl disappeared.

"You need to train someone, right?" I murmured, searching his eyes. "So, train me."

"Jesus," Kane whispered.

But it was Riven I focused on. Riven was the one who'd make the call. He flinched, his face paling as he shook his head. "You don't know what you're saying."

"Don't I?" I slowly sank to my knees in front of him.

In my head, I saw all the women he'd touched, their mouths, lips, breasts, his fingers deep in their pussies as he forced them to obey his every debased whim. I wanted to be that for him. I stared at that crisp black shirt, then the gleaming buckle of his trousers. I lifted my gaze, looking up at him like a god.

Because he was in that moment.

A dark, murderous god.

I leaned forward and closed my eyes, rubbing my throbbing cheek against his cock. The warmth of my breath heated the fabric. It didn't take long for him to respond, twitching, thickening.

"Helene…" he croaked, unleashing a bestial sound as I opened my mouth and rubbed my lips against the outline.

I pulled away and reached up, tugging his belt and working the buckle. "Use me. Train me. Let me be at *your* mercy."

He grabbed my chin, stopping me. Fear blazed in his stare. "You don't understand. There'll be others. *All* of them, and it's not just the ones here. It'll be streamed. Anyone could be watching."

"Then let them watch." I was past the point of caring. All I wanted was him. I opened my mouth, pressing it over the head of his cock. "You want to do this with one of them out there, or me?"

It was that simple.

He moved fast, grasped my arms and dragged me upward until I stared into his eyes. "Tell me again. Tell me you want to do this."

There we were…

Not a no.

He was thinking about it.

"If you have to touch someone, force someone...train someone. Then let it be me."

A tortured need filled those dark eyes. I reached up, brushing my thumb across his cheek. This wasn't right...but none of this was right. I shouldn't feel breathless around a man like Riven Cruz—I glanced at The Teacher, Kane, and The Priest, Thomas—or any of them.

But I did.

"And if we're forced to take over, what then?" Kane stepped closer. "Will you give us the same..." he glanced at Thomas, then turned back. "Devotion."

I swallowed hard.

"It's not just one, Trouble," Riven urged, his voice husky. "Think carefully before you commit to this. It has to be all three of us and it won't just be sex, either. There's mind control, faith control. We will take the person you think you are and bend you to our will. Are you prepared for that?"

I tried to catch my breath, meeting every gaze.

It wasn't just my sisters' lives on the line here. It was mine. My existence. My sanity. I met Riven's intense stare...my heart too. Because no matter how terrifying this was...I wanted him. "Yes," I answered. "I'm prepared for that."

In the corner of my eye, Kane's lips quirked.

"The mind control we have is hard," Riven warned.

I met that debased look of hunger in Doctor Cruz's stare. He was about to finally get what he'd wanted all along...me. "Then I guess it's lucky I have the best doctor to take care of me."

That smile grew wider.

"What do we do with him?" Thomas croaked, rubbing his cheek with one hand as he gestured at the body with the other.

The body stood in the way of all this.

"The woods," Riven answered. "We hide the body, then at the first opportunity, we get it out."

"And how do you suggest we do that?" Thomas muttered. "It's not like we can roll it up in a rug and stuff it in the trunk of the car."

Riven gave a snarl and instantly the tension between us changed. We were no longer fighting to figure out a plan. We now had one to execute. I glanced back at the body. If there was anything Riven did well, it was that.

"Let me go out and make sure it's all clear." Thomas headed for the external door.

"Wait," I said, stopping them cold. They all turned to me. "We have one slight problem."

"And what's that?" Riven asked.

"If we need me to be a Daughter, that means I have to take someone's place."

"Or we alter the books," Kane offered, turning to Riven. "Can we do that? Add another asset?"

My gut clenched with that word. *Asset.*

"If that bastard doesn't have it locked down, we could try."

"The Hunter?" Thomas offered. "He could do it."

"I haven't contacted him in days."

Kane gave a nod. "Then do so, brother. Time is running out."

Riven met my gaze, then turned away, pulled his cell from his pocket, and started typing.

"Let's do this." Thomas limped carefully toward the external door, hit the lock, and carefully pushed it open.

Daylight streamed in, along with the heady scent of the forest. I took a step closer, drawn by the allure of freedom.

"Okay," Riven muttered. "It's done."

"He's hacked it already?" I asked.

Riven just shook his head. "No. I message and we wait."

My stomach clenched. "So how do we know this *Hunter* will actually be able to do the job?"

Kane glanced at Riven. Something passed between them.

"We don't." Riven stepped toward the body. "Kane, you grab the arms."

"Why the fuck do I get the heavy end?"

"Because." Riven gave his brother a savage smirk. "That's what you get for pissing me the hell off."

I scowled, my gaze bouncing between them. The edge of Kane's lips twitched before he shot me a glance and muttered. "Fine, have the ass end, see if I care. Just make sure you're the professional when I start with Helene."

There was a flicker of anger in Riven's eyes.

Oh shit.

I hadn't thought about that. Rivalry and rage were about to go hand in hand...and I was in the middle of it all.

Riven grabbed the ankles of the dead guard. Kane struggled, heaving his torso up from the floor. I made awkward movements with my hands, wanting to help as Kane stumbled, almost dropping the sick bastard, until he righted himself.

But the truth was, it was too much fun watching them shove and snarl, glaring at each other as they staggered toward the open door. I followed them out, stepped down from the side entrance of The Order, and headed for the cover of the trees.

We made our way as far as we dared, until they dropped him with a *thud* against a large ash tree. "Remember where the hell we put him," Riven gasped, out of breath, and shot Thomas a glare. "Or you'll be the one explaining his damn broken neck when he's found."

Thomas flinched, glaring at the body. "Hopefully, the wolves will eat him, then we won't have to worry about a damn thing."

Riven gave a chuff and turned back, his gaze finding mine. "Let's go, Trouble. You need to shower and get dressed."

Dressed.

He means in clothes fit for a Daughter.

He watched my every reaction, testing me.

"You get me the clothes, Principal, and I'll wear them."

His gaze darkened at the use of his title.

But that's what he was now...to me, that was.

The Principal.

The Teacher.

The Priest.

And now, a Daughter.

We all had a role to play. The only question was, could we pull it off? I hoped we could. Because now we had more than our sisters' lives on the line...*we had ours.*

"Wait." Kane stopped us.

I turned back to him, then lifted my gaze. His stare penetrated all the way through me, driving a quiver of fear deep. He stepped closer, stopping only when he towered over me. "If we're going to do this, then we need to do it properly."

He reached out, grabbed the bottom edge of my shirt, and yanked. The need to slap his hand away was overwhelming. Instead, I grabbed his hand, stopping him. "What the hell do you think you're doing?"

His smirk pissed me off. "Looking for the perfect place."

"For what?"

He looked up to Riven, then turned back to me. "To insert a tracking device."

My blood turned cold. For a second, I couldn't breathe. *You do this and there's no escaping them.* The words gripped me.

"You want this, right, Helene?" Kane urged, taking one more step closer. His grip on my shirt twisted until he cupped my breast.

"Yes." I answered, my tone empty.

"Good." He smiled, those green eyes glinting. "I'll try to be careful."

He was careful, leading me to the kitchen counter. Riven stood by and watched as his brother lifted me. He reached around me, unhooking my bra with a single twist of his hand.

"Lie down." He commanded and a shiver raced up my spine with the tone. "I'll be back in a moment."

He disappeared into his bedroom. I did as he instructed, lowering my head to the hard surface. Faint sounds came as bathroom drawers opened and closed before the rush of running water followed. I listened to the sound of scrubbing before the rush of water once more, and when he returned his hands were cleaned, carrying items I couldn't quite see.

I craned my neck as he placed a small pack of cotton balls, a bottle of iodine, a single-use scalpel, and a small device in a tiny, clear canister at my side.

"Now, I'm sure you already know this is going to leave a small scar." Kane murmured, opening the pack of cotton balls.

I just looked up at the ceiling, my heart pounding. "Just get on with it."

There was that smirk again in the corner of my eye. He tugged up my shirt as Riven came closer.

"Hey." Riven grabbed my chin and turned my head to him. "Christ, you're beautiful." He whispered, staring at me.

My pulse stuttered as he lowered his head and carefully kissed me. My mind was so busy racing from the effect of his mouth that I barely felt the sting at first.

"Oww." I hissed and jerked away to look down.

Kane's focus was on his hands as he moved to my side and grabbed a set of tweezers to push the tiny device into the small cut he'd made.

"One...small...stitch." He murmured, working fast and carefully.

His skills would make any surgeon proud. I knew he was a doctor of the mind, but the way he worked made me realize he was so much more.

"There." He gave one tiny tug, making me wince before he lifted his head. "All done."

All done? Maybe for him...but this was only the start for me. I was not only about to be put through the most brutal of mind control...I was also tracked for the rest of my life, or at least until I could get that thing out of me.

And I wanted it out.

Almost as much as I wanted this all to be over.

TWENTY-SIX

Helene

I WORE RED. RED THAT LOOKED LIKE BLOOD SPLASHED against my skin, swallowing the reflection of the white bathroom behind me. I'd sworn to myself I'd never wear it, not after what my sisters had gone through.

Yet, here I was, dressed in the same vile lingerie—in the same place of terror—about to embark on the hell they'd endured...willingly.

The door to the bathroom opened and Riven stepped in. Those brooding eyes shifted instantly to my reflection before he scowled, then looked away.

He couldn't even look at me.

How the hell was he going to carry this through?

But then he turned back, the deep crease in his forehead matching the tortured stare. One step and he stood at my back. There were no words between us. Just the brush of his fingers under the satin strapping at my back as he caressed my skin all the way to my shoulder. I shivered with the touch.

"Forgive us," he whispered, meeting my stare. "For what we're about to do."

My pulse skipped, and my stomach sank all at once. I felt like I was going to pass out before I'd even started, until the door opened once more.

"It's time." Kane looked at me, then his brother.

There was regret in his tone, he swallowed it as he disappeared out the door.

Riven dropped his hand, exhaled, and followed, leaving me to do the same.

Thomas was there, wearing his black suit and white clerical collar. His face was still swollen and his eye bloody as he fixed that chilling stare on me. "After you." He motioned.

My bare feet made no sound as I followed the others like a ghost through the doorway of the apartment and along the hall. Riven was in front, Kane slowed, falling behind with Thomas, all three boxing me in.

The secure doors were unlocked one by one as we headed to where they kept the Daughters, until, through the section of glass, I caught sight of a guard.

Riven spun, grabbed me, and pushed me against the wall, his gaze full of rage, his voice full of fear. "They can't hear us," he murmured. "Only see us."

My eyes flicked instantly to the cameras above us.

"You know what you have to do?" Riven searched my stare.

It was the last moment he would be Riven to me.

Somehow, we both knew that.

I suppressed a shiver and gave a nod.

He swallowed, grabbed my arm in a savage grip, and shoved me toward the doors. "See you on the other side, Trouble."

I stumbled forward, barely reaching the door before the lock clicked and it opened. Heavy steps closed in. I was grabbed around the back of the neck and driven forward, past the guards and into the cafeteria, before I was shoved hard from behind.

My head snapped backward and my knees buckled, sending me crashing to the floor.

But he wasn't done. No, The Principal descended, grasping me around the jaw to jerk my gaze to his. "Try to run again, Daughter, and see what happens."

His eyes were wide. His pupils were so dark they were endless pools.

He was scared.

No.

He was terrified.

Sparks ignited in his gaze. His chest moved in shallow, panicked breaths. There was no way he was going to get through this, not without me taking the lead. I yanked my hands up. "*Please,* don't hit me again."

The heavy thud of boots rushed in. "You found her." The man I knew as Walker strode forward.

"We found her." The Principal released my jaw and straightened, glaring down at me.

"I'll keep a better watch on this one," Walker declared as he grabbed my arm and hauled me to my feet.

"We all will," Riven added coldly, watching as I was dragged to where the other Daughters sat.

They stared at me with terrified expressions. Some were dressed in red, others in white. They cared more about the guards across the room than they did about a pretender.

"Sit." Walker shoved me toward a seat and nodded at the cafeteria staff.

Revulsion rose as they slid a plate of barely yellow looking eggs in front of me along with a plastic cup filled with some kind of juice.

"Eat," Walker commanded. "You have ten minutes."

Ten minutes?

My skin crawled with all the attention in the room, every set of eyes burning into me. But this was what we needed, wasn't it? The only way any of us survived, by them believing I was someone they could use. My fingers trembled as I grabbed the plastic fork, picked up some of the rubbery mess, and slowly placed it in my mouth.

My stomach tightened as I bit down and chewed. It could be anything. I lifted my gaze to the Daughters at the table in front of me. Their downcast eyes never moved as I forced myself to swallow the vile squishy mouthful. This could be pancakes for all I knew. Hot, buttery, golden brown pancakes that were the best I'd ever tasted.

How are they?

Riven's voice invaded my head.

Not a good time for that right now. Not a good time to think about him at all.

A little dry actually.

My pulse sped as I swallowed, reliving that moment for a second before it was gone.

"Okay," Walker's voice boomed, making the Daughters flinch. He scanned them all and settled on me. *"Everyone finish up. You'll be escorted to the media room."*

No one moved, they were all terrified. Still, my mind raced. Media room? I tried to figure out what was about to happen and dropped my fork, taking a gulp of juice to wash the food down as the guards descended from across the room. It was almost like they couldn't wait to get their hands on us, dragging us to our feet.

Aren't you whores supposed to just lie there and take it?

The memory of that bastard surfaced, but it was Walker who headed for me, grabbed my arm, and pushed me forward and in line with the others. "Move."

And just like that, I was one of them.

A Daughter forced to line up and paraded like a piece of meat past Riven and the others.

"Eyes front," one of the guards barked at me, his gaze sliding down the see-through lace I wore.

I jerked my focus forward, my heart hammering, and slowly I followed the rest out of the cafeteria and along the hall.

Bare feet slapped the cold floor. Panicked stares found mine as we headed past three sets of doors and turned, stopping at an open door.

"You'll wait here." The guard lifted his arm, barring our way. He shifted his gaze. "Teacher."

Then Kane was there, stepping around me to face the rest of the line. He didn't look my way, didn't meet my stare. "You'll be escorted in and given your seats. One of the medical staff will come along and secure you. Any attempt at evasion will be met by force, am I understood?"

No one said a word.

Secure us? What the hell did that mean?

A nod to the staff behind me and nurses strode forward.

"Let's go." One nurse took a Daughter's arm and led her into a dimly lit room.

I knew this place, knew it intimately, every corridor, every diagram. I knew images and layouts, but standing here at the jaws of this gaping mouth, I realized I didn't know this place at all.

Not really.

Not like this.

"You." The next nurse grabbed the Daughter in front.

One by one they were taken inside until one came for me.

"Let's go." The older woman took me by the arm and pulled me toward the door.

I met Kane's emotionless stare as I passed. He never even flinched, not even when I stumbled into the gloom and along the outside of what looked like rows of theater seats. I glanced at the darkened screen. But this was like no theater I'd ever been to. I was gently pushed along a row and forced to shuffle toward the middle.

"Here," the nurse commanded.

The dull shine of metal caught my eye as she guided me into the seat. Another nurse stepped toward me from the other side, grabbing my arm and holding it as they strapped it down.

"Wait." I pulled against their hold, earning a glare.

My other arm was next, strapped and secured.

"Ouch," I cried out as a sting came on my arm.

Fear howled to the surface with the withdrawal of a needle.

"What...what was that?"

"Just something to help you relax," the nurse with a syringe urged.

Her face blurred as she straightened, and on the screen a recording flickered to life.

I knew others were being pushed into seats all around me and given the same drug. I shook my head, trying my best to keep my focus. But my mind wavered and my strength weakened. On the screen, flickers of words filled the view, neon white against the glare.

OBEY.

RELEASE.

OWNED.

My pulse spiked. *Boom! Boom! BOOM!* The sudden blare of music was deafening.

I'd made a mistake...

I'd made a *terrible* mistake.

BOOM!

BOOM!

BOOM!

FORBIDDEN.

CRAVE.

MINE.

I bucked, fighting the bonds around my wrists. But my movements were slow and weak...and those glaring words on the screen called me.

OBEY.

OBEY.

OBEY....

I wanted out of here. I wanted out...I wanted OUT.

I opened my mouth to scream, only no sound came.

There were only the words.

Words that filled my head.

The words...*that filled me.*

TWENTY-SEVEN

Helene

Cold ate all the way inside me. Cold like I'd never felt before. Not that I remembered anyway. My thoughts were slow. My memories are hazy, fighting against the icy blast from the air above. One that made my bones ache and my teeth chatter with every violent shudder.

I wrapped my arms around me, wincing at the sting in the crook of my arm.

Who are you?

The words floated from somewhere. I searched for an answer until fear drifted in, floating like fog around my ghostlike thoughts. I turned my head to a sea of red. Rows of women dressed in lace stared with vacant expressions. They lined up like soldiers all the way to where they blurred against the darkened backdrop at the edge of the room.

Who are you?

Those words came again. *Think...come on...you can do this. Think.* I tightened my hold as a fresh wave of icy air blasted down on me and that fresh sting in the middle of my elbow forced me to twist my arm.

There were needle marks there.

Pinpricks of red were neon against fine white scars on my arms.

There were lots of them. The sight of those dots was chilling.

Oh, shit...oh shit...

I lifted my gaze as movement came from the corner of my eye. A faint blur of darkness came closer, hovering just out of view.

"Who are you?" The deep snarl was met with a soft murmur. One I couldn't quite catch.

I fixed my gaze on those tiny red dots in my flesh as fear and panic danced inside me.

"Who are you?"

A murmur...one I could almost hear.

Thud. Thud. Thud.

I lifted my head as that darkness strode closer. Darkness that brought with it a face I knew somehow. Sparks ignited in bottomless pools.

"Who are you?" he questioned, and I opened my mouth to speak.

I knew who I was...I knew...I knew.

I'll see you on the other side, Trouble.

I gazed into that endless stare. My pulse pounded like clenched fists in my chest as I stared at the man.

"I said, *who are you?*" he demanded.

The words came on their own, cruel and hateful. "No one," I answered.

He gave a nod, desperation filling his eyes before he turned away and was gone.

No one.

That's who I was.

No one with a name.

No one important.

I tried to remember how I got here and where here was.

Was this some kind of hospital? I risked a glance at the men standing at the edges of the room. Men who didn't look like any doctors I'd ever known.

Fight.

Fight...

FIGHT.

I flinched and took a step backwards, the only one now out of line. "Let me out of here." The words barely made it to my lips. But panic was taking over, screaming and howling on the inside as I turned my head, staring at the sea of blood red and screamed, *"LET ME THE FUCK OUT OF HERE NOW!"*

The sound broke the spell.

I spun around, my teeth gnashing, and searched for the door.

"Riven!" A roar came from somewhere in the room.

But I didn't care. All I saw was that door.

Let me out.

Let me ooouutttt!

LET ME OUT OF HERE!

I ran, slammed against the woman dressed in red in front of me, and shoved her out of the way. All I saw was the doorway. All I saw was my survival and the end, the end of all this.

Until the blur of darkness came for me, barreling down on me like a hurricane.

"I've got her!" the darkness roared, slamming into me and taking me down to the floor.

That cold waited, pressing against my face as I was held down and my arms were wrenched behind me.

I screamed and kicked, unleashing panicked blows. But I moved too slowly, and my punches were weak, too weak to do anything.

"Easy!" darkness bellowed, grasping my wrists as I drove my head backwards. *"I said, easy now!"*

"Get *off* me!" I screamed, staring at the open door in the distance. *"GET OFF ME!"*

"We have a fighter," came a dangerous voice came from somewhere above.

The blur of movement came again as he descended and gripped the flesh of my arm before the sting happened once more. *"Owww!"*

"We're going to need to watch this one," the deep, smooth tone of the Devil murmured.

I jerked my gaze upward, looking at him as he towered above me.

"I agree," said the man whose heavy breath was a rush in my ear as he gripped my arms. "I think we make this one an example."

"Fu…" I tried to find the words. But the room swayed and shimmered, like an illusion. *"Fuckkk you."*

That darkness pressed closer against me, his words a whispered rush in my ear. "That's the plan, Trouble. That's the goddamn plan."

I wanted to fight them. I *tried* to fight them, but I had nothing, no strength, no will. I was nothing more than chattering teeth and an empty stare. Strong hands gripped my arms, pulling me upward.

"You fight against the programming," he shouted. "So we're here to make sure the programming wins."

He looked down at me, taking in my body. His mouth twisted into a snarl. "Who are you?"

I sucked in hard breaths.

He moved fast, grabbed my jaw and clenched tight. *"I said, WHO ARE YOU?"*

Agony roared through my jaw when he bruised my cheeks against my teeth as I cried, "No one."

His chest rose hard and fell as he jerked his gaze down. "That's right. You *are* no one. No one with a need of their own. Your need is *my* need. Do you understand me?"

I nodded through his crushing grip.

"Then you'll get on your knees," he demanded, his eyes wide. "You'll get on your knees and you'll beg for forgiveness."

I didn't want to. Every cell in my body screamed in defiance even as my knees buckled and hit the floor.

OBEY.

RELEASE.

OWNED.

The words flashed neon bright inside my head.

He didn't use words. Not anymore. One look had me eased back on my haunches and my arms sliding to my back.

You are my property.

The words resounded somewhere in the back of my mind.

Good. Now spread your legs.

His lips never moved. Still, I knew what he was thinking. What he wanted. What he *ached* for.

His chest rose with a heavy breath. His gaze moved instantly to my thighs as they slowly parted.

Wider.

The skin on my knees squealed against the floor. I couldn't look away from his eyes. Eyes that seemed so familiar. My fingers twitched, aching to touch the red lace at my thighs. *I think these are too tight.* The words resounded in my head as though somehow...somewhere I'd already said them.

No, that husky growl came. *I know it's the perfect fit.*

He wanted me. This man who looked down wanted me more than he wanted anything else in his entire life...and I wanted him. I licked my lips. I *wanted him.*

"Please," I whispered. "I'm sorry."

"What are you sorry for?" he demanded.

My jaw clenched. Still some part of me kicked inside as I answered. "I tried to escape."

"Do you want to escape?"

I slowly shook my head.

He bent down and gripped my jaw, only this time it was softer. "Then open your mouth."

My lips quivered and slowly parted. There was a dangerous look of satisfaction. One hard brush of his thumb and it dragged the soft flesh of my lip against my teeth.

"Wider."

My jaw ached, jerking and shuddering, fighting against the cold. He slid his fingers inside and along my tongue.

"Suck," he commanded.

I closed my eyes as shame filled me.

"Did I tell you to close your eyes?" he snarled.

I wrenched them open.

"I said, *suck.*"

I did, drawing his fingers deeper inside my mouth.

He looked down. "You like to cut, *Daughter*? Is that it? You like to cut and bleed and be empty?"

Tears filled my eyes as he thrust and withdrew, penetrating deeper with every motion. This was not foreplay, this was a violent assault. One that didn't fill me with pleasure...it filled me with fear.

"You are nothing but my own needs. Do you understand that?" He pushed his fingers all the way inside until my throat closed around him, until he dropped his knees to the hard floor and grabbed the back of my head in a savage grip. *"You are no one."*

My eyes teared. My throat clenched, until he let my head go and instead savagely yanked the strap of my bodysuit, tearing it down...and exposing my breasts.

"You are nothing but *my* entertainment." He gripped my breast with one hand, his fingers still shoved down my throat. "Nothing but a string to *pluck*."

I flinched as he pinched my nipple. Pain flared, the cruel, blinding rush, familiar. He pinched again, only this time harder, until a low animal sound tore free from me.

"I am your blade now, *Daughter*. I am the honed edge of the razor you crave, the prick of the needle you long for...and the drug you can never escape."

Saliva strung from his fingers as he pulled them free before he dropped his hands and rose, looking down at me.

"Now, you will go with the others. You will not fix yourself. You will not kick and scream and you will not try to run. Do you understand me?"

My shoulders trembled, threatening to curl.

Some part of me wanted to.

But this was a test.

And more than a test for me.

The...*darkness* lifted that cruel gaze.

"Walker," he called one guard at the edge of the room. In an instant, the male obeyed, striding closer. I realized every set of eyes was fixed on me. There were more men here than I expected, each one watching me with ravenous stares. "I want you or your man to watch her every move. You'll call me the second she steps out of line, or any issue at all. Am I clear?"

The guard's gaze moved to me and he nodded. "Understood." He turned his head and waved his man over.

"I do not want her out of your sight," Darkness commanded, then lifted his gaze to the sea of women behind me. "Let this be a lesson for all of you. Your bodies are no longer yours to command. They belong to someone with far more power than you."

He lowered his gaze to mine. There was something unspoken in them. A plea...a prayer. One he was desperate for me to understand before he stepped away. "Go." He turned his gaze away. "Your lessons continue tomorrow."

Then, on a dime, he turned and strode away, heading toward the men at the edge of the room.

"Sleep well, Trouble," the smooth, seductive tone of the Devil came behind me. "You're going to need it."

I wanted him to leave with the other man. My chest ached with every resounding boom.

Something was happening here. Something I didn't understand...or remember.

"Move back in line," the guard called Walker commanded.

My arms trembled as I slowly pushed upward. I didn't think my body would hold my weight, but it did as I turned and slowly made my way back into line. The woman I'd shoved aside didn't even glare at me, just stepped aside, allowing me to pass.

That wasn't right.

I knew that.

Still, I was helpless as I took my place along with the others, feeling every set of eyes from the edge of the room.

Who are you?

The words resounded.

Who the hell are you?

MINE.

OWNED.

RELEASE.

DAUGHTER.

No one. That's who I was...

I was no one.

Not anymore.

TWENTY-EIGHT

Riven

"That...what you did today was...*goddamn impressive.*"

I slowly lifted my gaze from the edge of the large command center desk in front of me and met Coulter's ugly fucking stare. His eyes sparkled, glinting with the hunger men like him come to a place like this for.

Destruction.

He waited while the room fell silent around us, a tiny scowl the only indication that I needed to speak.

"I'm glad you enjoyed it." I answered.

My tone was hollow, so fucking hollow I felt numb, like I existed in a drum of depravity. Thoughts of violence played out inside my head. My palm ached for the feel of a gun, or a knife...or anything, for that matter. I wanted to hack and claw and shoot my way through this room, killing everyone and everything.

Then I wanted to burn this entire place to the ground.

And all the fucking cruel things I'd done here.

Then me along with it.

I am your blade now, Daughter. The honed edge of the razor you crave.

...and the drug you can never escape.

Never. Escape.

I'd shattered her mind.

Broken it into a thousand tiny pieces to recreate my will.

What I'd done to her, to someone so full of rage and life and power...could never be forgiven.

My fist clenched at my side.

And it was all because of them.

These fucking vermin.

"Marks still hasn't returned." One guard looked up from his cell and spoke. "And he's not answering my calls."

Coulter scowled and shook his head. "That's not like him. I want him located, immediately."

Crunch.

The sound of a neck snapping rose in my head. The heavy weight of his body surfaced. They wouldn't find Marks...no matter how hard they looked, not unless they could commune with the dead.

"If he will not answer my goddamn messages, then I'll use the locator."

I jerked my gaze his way. "Locator? What locator?"

He didn't answer, just took a seat in front of his computer, which he'd now set up in the large conference room. He and his men were like locusts, invading and consuming every section of this goddamn place, and slowly choking us out.

"I'll find him." Coulter muttered as he typed.

I took a step closer, going as close as I dared. He pulled up a GPS screen on the monitor and, with the strokes of a few commands, brought the map of the compound to life with tiny, moving green dots.

He hovered over one and it instantly revealed the guard's name and last known location. My pulse sped, filling me with panic. I took a step backwards, turned, and headed for the door.

My fingers shook as I lengthened my strides. My mind raced with all the possible scenarios as I pulled up my messages and typed: *They have a fucking tracking system for the guards. MOVE THE BODY NOW!*

I hit send, then delete, shoving my cell back into my pocket. My damn hand shook, causing me to clench my fist as I kept on walking. This was sliding through my fingers, all in the space of a matter of days.

Days for me.

But an eternity for her.

I winced and kept on walking, slammed my card against the scanner and pushed through the doors.

You are nothing but my entertainment...

Nothing but a string to pluck.

I rounded the corner and found Walker standing sentry outside her door. He jerked his gaze toward me. The semi-automatic in his hand had nothing to do with any attempt at escape and *everything* to do with her protection.

After today, she had a target on her back...and on her body.

"Boss." Walker murmured.

I glanced at the darkened room, then turned to him. "Any problems?"

By problems, I meant with the guards.

"A few came by to check on her. They were told to kindly *fuck off.*"

I gave a nod, my focus shifting to the dark room once more. She didn't eat at dinner, nor did she drink. She'd just sat there staring with that same glazed fucking expression. *I'd told her not to do this...I'd told her...I'd fucking told her...*

"I'll take it from here." I said, my heart hurting.

"Here." Walker handed me his weapon. "Call me if you need me."

I took the gun and waited long enough for him to leave before I dared step closer. There was no movement inside, nothing more than fucking darkness.

I tried to swallow past the ache in my throat as I unlocked her door and stepped inside. Light spilled deeper into the room and fell across the curled body in the middle of her cot as she faced the wall.

The lock clicked as I closed the door behind me. I waited for a reaction. There was none.

"Helene?"

She didn't move. Was she asleep?

I stepped closer, hating the weight of the gun in my hand.

"I tried to warn you, Trouble." I murmured.

She turned her head and those empty eyes found mine. I'd done this to her. *I'd done this to her.* My fingers bucked and danced, trembling as I brushed her cheek. "But you just wouldn't listen, would you?"

She shifted on the bed, turning her body toward me.

But it wasn't her...not anymore.

It was the programming and the seeds I'd planted deep inside her brain.

Seeds that would eventually grow into vines and choke whatever might've been between us.

I didn't deserve it, anyway.

I brushed my thumb down her cheek, staring into those vacant eyes. Still, I couldn't stop myself. Not that I ever could have... where she was concerned.

I leaned down, closed my eyes, and brushed my lips across hers. Warmth met mine. In my head, I still saw her cuffed to my bed in the house in the city, spitting words full of poison and rage.

Ahh...Trouble. Agony ripped through my chest, the kind that made a man like me weak. Because I *was* weak when it came to her. I'd known she was my undoing the moment she'd stepped in front of my car. My hand drifted down and cupped her breast. She let out a soft moan that spilled out of her throat and into my mouth.

I swallowed that sound, drinking it down like a man dying of thirst. The kiss deepened. My touch grew more desperate, sliding to thumb her nipple. I pulled away from her mouth to lower my head.

"Spread." I commanded.

She obeyed instantly. There was no fight, no *'fuck you'*, just *submission.* I couldn't stop myself, couldn't slow. I gripped the soft flesh of her thighs as I sank my face between them, licking her through the lace of her lingerie.

Just a taste.

To know she was real.

My balls tightened. My cock swelled.

I ran my thumb along the crease of her pussy, pushing against her clit.

That soft moan turned louder, and I was lost in the taste of her. To the feel of her touch as her fingers slid through my hair, and the sound of that throaty hunger. My fingers didn't tremble now as I tugged the elastic aside and parted the lips of her cunt.

I needed her.

Like my life depended on it.

Like my entire existence was made *for this.*

I looked up, staring into that vacant expression as she looked down at me.

Some part of me knew this was wrong, that *this* wasn't her.

But I was a bastard.

I knew that.

A. Selfish. Savage. Monster. Not fit for anything as fucking perfect as her.

Not really.

The scales of justice had already weighed my soul...and there was no coming back from hell. I knew that...still...staring into those dark, empty eyes, part of me wished for more.

"Do you..." I croaked and swallowed, trying to wet my mouth. "Do you want me to stop?"

"Never." She whispered. "I never want you to stop."

Her fingers lazily touched me, trailing down around to the back of my head, before she pushed me back down. "Do whatever you want with me. Yours to command. Obey. Release. Owned. That's what I am...I'm owned by you."

I flinched and yanked my head away, my fingers sliding from the warmth of her pussy as I stumbled backwards.

She followed the movement, scowling and pushed upwards. The elastic cut into the soft flesh of her pussy. I stared at what I wanted and licked my lips.

"Please." She murmured. "Don't leave me."

For a second, that emptiness in her eyes flickered with life. The corners of her mouth trembled as she glanced around the darkened room like she was taking it in for the first time. "Riven?"

Desperation surged, forcing me to lunge forward. I grabbed her, pulling her close. "Trouble."

"Where...where the fuck am I?"

And just like that, she was back, roaring to life with the tang of disdain in her tone. I smiled, pulling her closer. "With me. You're safe, baby. You're safe."

She gripped my shirt, holding on and lifting her gaze to mine. I felt her body tremble. I felt every goddamn thing with her... maybe a little too much.

"Don't go." She whispered. "I need you."

My will buckled, bowing under the loneliness in those dark brown eyes. I lowered my head, pulling her upwards. "I won't leave you."

Tears shimmered in her eyes. I knew it was because of the conditioning. Still, to see her in pain was a knife hacking its way into my chest.

She lifted her head and kissed me, and that same hunger came roaring back, more dangerous than ever before. I lifted her, driving her back against the small cot. The legs squealed against the floor, but it didn't matter, none of it mattered.

"Lie back." I urged. "Let me take care of you."

She eased back onto the cot. I did the only thing I could...I became the monster she needed. The one who'd steal her from this place...if only for a moment. My fingers trailed down her body, dragging over the peak of her breast until they fell further.

Wetness met the tips as I pushed against the lace between her legs. I didn't even have to command her. Instead, her legs opened, her knees crooked to gain an extra inch. She wanted to be open for me, parted and dripping.

I broke the stare and looked down, to find my fingers disappearing into her body. I couldn't stop them trailing upwards to find the proud hood of her clit. "So swollen." I murmured, meeting her stare.

Moisture dripped from between her thighs. Fuck, she was slick. My circular motions made her shudder.

"Please," she panted, grabbing hold of my forearm. *"Please."*

"Please what, Trouble?" I moved, craning my neck to dip my head between her thighs.

Her ass clenched and tendons strained, driving her legs as far apart as they'd go. Such a needy little thing. "You ache to be fucked, don't you?"

Her fingers speared through my hair as I tugged the sodden elastic to the side.

"Wider." I commanded, reaching down to grasp under her knee and lift.

I angled my body sideways, spreading her wide with my fingers as I licked all the way along her slit.

"Oh, God. Don't stop." She moaned, driving her hips higher.

I sucked her clit, drawing it gently into my mouth. "Don't worry." I speared her with two fingers, driving all the way inside. "I don't plan to."

My cock jerked, making me desperately thrust against the cot. I pulled my fingers out and reached for my belt. Slick fingers slid against the leather as I fumbled and yanked, shoved the button open, and opened my pants.

One yank on her parted thigh and I pulled her half off the cot. One crooked leg held her in place as I shoved my boxers down and thrust, driving all the way inside.

Fuck...

FUCKK...

Sweat beaded along my brow. I couldn't slow, couldn't stop... even if I'd wanted to.

And I didn't want to.

Not anymore.

"You're mine." I grunted, holding her stare as I drove all the way inside her.

I was like a man possessed.

A man ravenous with a hunger far more powerful than money or greed.

I wanted her.

All of her.

Her body.

Her mind.

Her soul.

I wanted it all.

"Tell me." I grunted, desperately yanking out of her to drop my head. "Tell me you're mine."

I licked and sucked, my tongue stroking until she whimpered. "I'm yours. *Please, I'm yours.*"

I roared like an animal, bucking my hips until her warmth closed around me. "Come for me, Trouble...come...for...me."

Her eyes were wild, full of panic and pleasure. "Make me come." She whimpered. "Please, Principal. Make me come."

One last thrust.

She clamped tight around me.

I was too far gone, even as I registered the name.

She'd called me Principal. I moaned as I drove deep inside and stilled. *She'd called me...Principal.*

I slammed my eyes closed and spilled inside her.

It didn't matter. None of it mattered. Only this...only her...*only us.*

But what if she talked?

I opened my eyes, finding her empty stare again and her parted lips.

I unleashed a low moan. I hadn't thought about that. Hadn't even imagined she might be so conditioned now that she'd tell anyone everything. I pulled out of her and gently grabbed her chin. "You won't say anything to anyone about this. Do you understand?"

She stared at me, then slowly nodded her head.

Some part of me didn't believe her. I looked down to where my come shone against the insides of her thighs. Christ, she reeked of sex...*our kind of sex.* I tucked myself away. My mind raced, trying to figure it out. But I was a conniving bastard, and I knew there was no way I could ever leave her alone.

I wanted to fuck her.

And keep fucking her.

Until I forgot the bastard I was.

And the things I'd done to her.

"Repeat after me. I won't tell anyone about what we do."

"I won't tell anyone about what we do." She whispered.

I eased back, tugging her red lingerie back in place.

I'd need to take better care. Watch her more. Be fucking vigilant.

Beep.

My cell chimed, breaking the spell.

I reached down and grabbed it, reading the text.

All taken care of. We need to be more careful.

We did. I met that desolate stare and knew I couldn't do this on my own.

She flinched as I leaned closer and kissed her forehead. "My brothers and I will take care of you, Trouble. Do you understand? No one will hurt you here. We'll make sure of it. Do you hear me? We'll make sure of it."

TWENTY-NINE

Helene

"You are a vessel for pleasure."

I winced, trying my best to hold the spell of his words at bay. But this *Devil*, the one with the slippery tongue, had a way into the dark recesses of my thoughts. He was all around me, invading in stereo as I stood blindfolded amongst the others.

Owned. Release...Daughter.

The words flashed neon white inside my head.

I was here. But I couldn't quite remember where *here* was.

My name?

I tried to conjure the thought.

What was my name?

"You are hunger and need in the flesh."

I was fighting the allure of release, kicking against the current that pulled me under. My body trembled. My thoughts clawed,

307

desperate for a hold against the overwhelming urge to just *let go.*

"Don't fight it." The Devil murmured, his voice so smooth it was barely there. "*This* is your purpose."

A shiver raced along my spine. I clenched my fists.

"You've each been paired with the Daughter next to you. Allow them to touch you. I want you to give into the sensations, feel the warmth of their hands, lips, tongues. Let them wash through you and take you away. Forget your inhibitions. This is your purpose. You exist for this sensation and this sensation alone."

My breath caught. *Touch me?* The only people in the room this time were us...the *Daughters.* I waited for the soft touch of a woman, fighting the overwhelming urge to tear the blindfold free and make a run for it. But I knew what had happened the last time that I'd tried that.

You are nothing but my entertainment.

Those words resounded.

And the events that followed slipped in.

Repeat after me...I won't tell anyone about what we do.

"I won't tell anyone about what we do." The words seemed to spill from my lips of their own free will.

"That's right, Helene." The Devil whispered in my ear. "Nor will you have anyone else touch you. You're mine." Then loud enough for the rest of the room to hear. "Focus on the sensation of my touch, whether it's pleasure or pain. Let it move through you."

I waited...

Waited while my trapped breath burned in my chest.

"Are you ready?" He whispered, his breath warm against my ear. "You didn't think I'd let anyone else enjoy you, did you?"

His big hand cupped my breast, his fingers pinching my nipple. I flinched under the touch.

"Uh-uh," He purred in my ear. "You will forget yourself. You exist for my pleasure alone."

My breaths sped with the lull of those words.

"And everything I'd ever dreamed of doing with you." He tugged the strap of my bra down. "You want this...you crave this."

A tiny shake of my head was the only defiance I could manage.

"No?"

"N-no." I whispered. "I want...I w-want..."

His hand slipped down, cupping my sex. "Look at you so warm and wet at the mere sound of my voice. You were so bold before, now you stutter and trip over your words. Go on, fight against the allure."

I squeezed my eyes closed under the blindfold and reached up to grasp his arm, those powerful muscles I'd felt before.

"What do you want, *Daughter?*" He urged, his breath coming faster against my ear as he pushed between my legs. "Do you want to sink to your knees in front of me? I can tell you right now, you have never been more beautiful than when you are staring up at me with your eyes watering and your mouth full of my cock."

I shook my head.

Still, that voice.

That slithering, spelled serpent's words invaded, slipping into my head. My hold on his arm eased.

"That's it." He murmured. "Give all the way into me."

He pushed down, those big fingers curling as they rubbed the outside of my pussy.

You are nothing but my entertainment.

Nothing.

Nothing.

Nothing…

I jerked my hand away and reached for the blindfold until my wrist was caught. My muscles strained, pulling against him.

"You're a strong one, aren't you?" He roared. "There is always one who fights the programming. *That's enough, everyone! You can remove your blindfolds.*"

My hand trembled as I tore the covering free. I scanned the room to find Daughters kissing Daughters. One had her hand buried in another's hair, her hand moving between her legs. Heat rushed to my cheeks, making me look away.

This wasn't me.

None of this was.

But the current of this place was far too strong and as I lifted my gaze to the Devil in front of me, I felt my hold slipping. The crook of my arm stung with the mark of a fresh needle. I didn't know when it had happened, only that it had.

"Walker." The Devil called and from out of the darkness came the guard. "Take them to their rooms. Make sure they're fed, but they're to be isolated until tomorrow."

"Will do." He muttered, then took a step toward me.

"No." The Devil stopped him. "Not this one. She's with me."

I jerked my gaze to his, fighting the haze of distortion. His face blurred, then sharpened. Light green eyes shimmered as they fixed on me. There was a scowl before those eyes widened. "That's all." He murmured.

Walker turned and motioned in the air.

The guards came again.

Like they always did.

How many times? I was fighting the delirium, kicking against that dark, seedy undercurrent that was wrapped around my ankle like a stone, pulling me all the way under.

Fight.

The word roared inside me.

But I couldn't quite remember what I was fighting for.

I shook my head, watching as those wide eyes of the Devil grew wider. He jerked his gaze toward the edge of the room, then jerked his gaze back and moved fast, surging forward to grab my arm.

I stumbled forward under the force. Panic surged as I glanced toward the edge of the room where he'd looked a second ago. Something was happening. Something that made my stomach clench with fear.

"You want to ruin this completely?" He hissed, those green eyes growing darker. "Move...*I said, move.*"

My feet didn't work like they should. My knees buckled, his vise-like grip around my arm the only thing keeping me upright as I was taken away from the others and shoved across the expansive room. Only, I didn't quite remember how I got here... or where I was?

"Wait." I whispered, wrenching my gaze over my shoulder.

The rest of the Daughters were gone, ushered through the doors on the other side of the room.

"I increased your goddamn dosage and still you continue to fight me." He seethed. "You're one fucking speech away from ruining everything, you know that?"

He jerked that savage glare my way as we disappeared into the gloom. He shoved heavy black curtains out of the way and slammed his hand against the lock.

Beep.

One shove and we were through. But the moment we were out, I was yanked backwards and spun around.

"You were the one who wanted this, *remember?*" The Devil stepped forward.

There was nowhere to go but backwards until my heels hit the wall.

"You wanted this. You *begged* for this," He snarled.

I shook my head. The fog inside my head was so thick. "No." I whispered.

You were the one who wanted this.

His grip around my arm eased, leaving the throbbing marks of his fingers behind. "Your mind is shattering and remolding into someone else. We tried to warn you this would happen. But you wouldn't listen, Helene. You put your sisters above your own sanity."

Helene?

Was that my name?

I tried to remember.

"My sisters?" I whispered.

The faint sound of voices drew his focus. His jaw clenched before he stepped backwards, dragging me with him. "Come with me. I need to push you harder. I need to make sure you can withstand this."

My head snapped backwards with the sudden jerk. I staggered forward, dragged along as he turned and took me along a corridor. *"Withstand what?"* I urged, trying my best to yank my hand from his.

He didn't answer, just pulled me through one more set of doors toward a door at the end of the corridor. There were no overhead lights down here, just faint white floor lights to illuminate the way.

"Withstand *what?*" I said louder as he opened the locked door and shoved me through.

I stumbled into the darkness. The slaps of my bare feet were the only sound, until they too were gone. There was nothing but total darkness and that chilling sense of eeriness...just like the blindfold.

The *click* of the lock sounded far too loud, making me jump before that low, throaty rumble came. "No one can hear you here. But they can see you."

I spun around, searching for him in the pitch-black dark. "I can't see..."

"It's called a sensory deprivation room, designed to limit stimuli from the normal world. Everything in here is...*heightened*."

I spun around, searching for him in the dark. "Where are you?"

"Here." The whisper was in my ear.

I turned, swinging out my hand, and found nothing but air.

"I tried to program you along with the others, but you are determined to fight me every step of the way, aren't you?"

My pulse was booming. Panic surged with every whisper. "Who are you?" I searched the room. "What is this place?"

"You know where we are, Helene, and you know why you're here."

But I didn't...I didn't know—

I was grabbed from behind and pulled backwards until I slammed against his warm, hard chest. His hand wrapped around my throat. "I never understood desire until I felt my hands here." He murmured. "Every session we had, I envisioned it, and now...now, I can't seem to get it out of my head." He shifted, his other hand rising with a small remote in his grasp. "Now, you remember what I said. They can see you, but they can't hear you."

He pressed a button and a tiny red light came on in front of me.

From the washed-out blood red light, I caught sight of a camera. One that was pointed at me.

"You don't have to smile." That soothing voice murmured, his breath warm against my neck. "But you need to play along. After all, this is what you wanted, wasn't it, Helene? For your sisters. You remember your sisters, don't you? Ryth and Vivienne. You want to protect them. You want to keep them safe and far away from this place, don't you? This is why we're doing this."

Memories collided.

Faces that should be familiar.

Deep brown eyes that looked like mine, blazing with anger. That rush inside me took flight, racing and running. The *boom...boom...boom* of my pulse was a panicked thing as the familiar brown eyes were replaced by others. Only these were the sad, washed-out green eyes of a young woman who was pregnant.

A woman I called. *"Ryth."*

"Yes." He murmured, his grip tightening around my throat as we faced the camera. "You wanted this, throwing yourself to the wolves in order to keep them safe."

My body trembled. I knew this man...I knew his voice. "Kane."

"Yes, sweetheart. It's me."

I closed my eyes. "Doctor Kane Cruz...brother to The Principal, Riven Cruz. My primary target."

He stiffened, then chuckled, dragging his finger down the slope of my neck. "Yes, I suppose he is. We had to drug you like the others not to arouse suspicion. But we've kept you close." That touch carried down. "Although not as close as I'd like. Are you going to play the game now, Helene? Are you going to be our little sparrow?"

He dropped his hand from my throat and cupped my breast.

"After all...you are dressed in red." I stared into that camera as he tugged the strap of my bra lower until the lace rubbed my nipple. "Do you see your sisters, Helene?"

They were all I could see. "Yes."

"Say it, say what you'll do to protect them."

"Anything." I whispered.

"Would you let me fuck you?"

My core clenched, my breath deepened. The image of him and me was inescapable. "Yes."

He let out a low growl and cupped my breast. My nipples tightened. Desire exploded inside me.

"Would you let my brothers fuck you?"

I closed my eyes as their faces burned bright. Those dark eyes I knew so well. My spine bowed, my body warming with the memory of his savage hunger. *Tell me.* His voice filled my head. *Tell me you're mine.*

"I'm yours." I whispered, the frantic sound of my breaths filling my ears.

"We could take turns, all night and all day. Fill your pussy until you overflow. Would you let us stretch that tight cunt of yours?"

I moaned with the words.

It wasn't just what he said, but the way he said it. I parted my lips as he unhooked my bra, letting it fall to the floor.

"Now, hands behind your back, Daughter, and on your knees."

The back of my hand brushed my thigh as I obeyed instantly. My knees buckled, easing me to the floor.

"Knees apart, Helene."

I did, pushing them wide as he fisted my hair and tugged it backwards. Deep green eyes stared down at me. "You exist for me." He murmured.

That voice. Depraved and aching, slipping inside until it filled me. I stared into his eyes as he reached all the way down. His fist in my hair was the only thing holding me upright.

"Now, let's play nice for the camera. After all...my brothers are watching."

The thought of that made me tremble. His fingers skimmed the outside of my panties, pressing the lace against my flesh.

"Look how wet you are. I'm going to treat you like a possession." He rubbed my slit, working my desperation until I moaned, then he grasped the edge of the elastic and with one savage yank, tore it. "A quite valued possession."

I grasped his arm again, only this time it was in desperation.

Corded muscles flexed under my grasp. His fingers sank in, stroking, thrusting.

"That's the way." He urged. "Give them what they want."

I turned my head, finding that blinking red light.

Heat rushed to my cheeks. I looked away.

"No, don't look away." He groaned, his voice husky. "You look perfect like that. Look down. Look at where my fingers sink into your perfect pussy. Christ, I want to fuck you."

My knees inched open as that need rose inside me. His fingers came away shining.

"That's the girl. That's the good fucking girl."

I moaned and grabbed his arm tighter. That delicious hunger mingled with the allure of his voice. I drove his hand down harder, forcing his fingers all the way inside.

"Look at me, Helene." He commanded.

I jerked my gaze to his.

"You belong to me."

There was no battling those words anymore, no fighting against the current. There was only him...and this.

"I belong t-to y-you." I croaked as my pussy trembled, clenching tight around his fingers. "Oh, *God. Oh...God. I belong to you.*"

His fingers moved in a frenzy. "Come for me, Helene. That's it...*come.*"

I cried out, grasped his hand, and forced it still...

MINE.

OWNED.

RELEASE.

DAUGHTER.

And with a low, husky moan...I slipped into the undercurrent of these men and was swept away.

THIRTY

Riven

Her mouth was stretched wide, just like her legs with my brother's hand buried deep between them. Kane's fingers came away slick as he spread her pussy, dragging his fingers around her clit, before he pushed in once more.

"Fuck me." One guard croaked, staring at the live video from inside the deprivation room.

Fuck me indeed.

Her gaze was fixed on Kane's. That desperate, tortured need to climax blazing in those dark eyes. He had her hair fisted in his grip, his lips moving in words we couldn't hear.

Good fucking girl. He mouthed.

She was a good fucking girl.

So...*fucking good.*

And my brother was using her just how a Daughter should be used. Her senses dulled in there, until there was just him and what he was doing to her.

My nostrils flared and my jaw clenched as I bared my teeth at the low guttural groans in the room.

I should've kept her secret and cuffed to my bed. Leaving only the stain of my fingers on her soul and the scent of my come in her cunt. I wanted her...I *wanted her*.

Harder, she mouthed. *Please...please, use me.*

Her hair was fisted in his other hand. But it was her beautiful pussy we all stared at. The shine of her come so fucking bright on the camera as she lifted her ass, driving his fingers deeper inside. Until with a silent cry, she shuddered...and collapsed, giving in to the wave of euphoria I could almost feel clamping around my hard cock. And if I felt that, I was damn sure every other male in this room did as well.

But my brother wasn't done. No, he pulled his fingers from her cunt and worked the button of his trousers. His cock sprang out...hard as a fucking rod, and she knew just what to do.

He drove in all the way, using the fuck out of her mouth. Saliva drooled from her lips until that hunger turned into the overwhelming urge to breathe.

She bucked, jerking out of his hold, beating against his thighs until he pulled out.

Heaving breaths consumed her. She looked up at him with a mixture of fear and pleasure.

It was that look that sealed the deal.

Making the hunter in all of us rise to the surface.

He knew they were all watching.

And this was the only way we had to secure her position with the others and deliver her right where we needed her to be. In the black site where Hale waited.

Heavy breaths were the only sounds in the room. All eyes were on her...and I didn't like it one fucking bit. My fingers ached to feel the cold steel of a gun, one I'd aim at every ravenous fucking gaze in this room. I clenched my jaw, biting down on my rage as I turned my head.

One guard tried to fix himself and turned away. But it was the steely stare of Coulter fixed on the camera that pissed me more.

Turn your head, motherfucker...while you still have a head to turn.

If it had been anyone else, I would've had the bastard against the wall with cold steel pushed between his teeth. But he wasn't just anyone else, and the longer I watched Coulter, the deeper that desperation moved. His skin looked almost white in the screen's glow. He was mesmerized, never once shifting his gaze from the display.

"I want her." He said quietly.

My gut clenched.

What the fuck did he say?

I scowled.

Goddamn motherfucker.

Thoughts of violence filled my head. My body trembled, fighting against the need to launch myself across the room and tear out his goddamn eyes with my fingers. He turned his head in that moment, that stony stare fixed on mine.

"Make it happen." He commanded like I was his fucking dog.

My voice shook with rage. "It *doesn't* work like that. There are contracts and money. Only Hale signs off on—"

He turned and stepped closer, cutting me off. "In case you haven't yet caught on, Hale Order is under new management...*me*. So when I say I want something." He turned his head and stared at Helene in the camera as she sat naked and panting on the floor. "I want it."

He turned back to me, holding my stare. "So, will you make the arrangements, or do I need to do that myself?"

"I'll do it." I forced the words through clenched teeth, my mind racing. "*After* the Daughter has completed the training requirements."

His nostrils flared. Hate glinted. "Fine." He answered. "But not a second longer."

He looked once more at the screen where she waited, before he turned around and strode from the room.

This wasn't over. That I knew. Not by a long shot.

I glanced toward where Thomas watched the interaction. His bloody stare followed Coulter, watching his men leave with him, but not before two of them looked back at Helene on the screen.

"We have a problem," Thomas murmured. "A very big problem."

I needed her to pass as a Daughter, but not once had I ever thought anyone would want her contract, not like this. Still, I should've known. There was something about her, and it was more than defiance. It was power, a lethal mess that was intoxicating.

I should know.

I'd tasted it a number of times.

A nerve twitched at the corner of my eye. There was no fucking way I was having a piece of shit like Coulter anywhere near her. "So it seems." I answered my brother before I turned and strode from the room.

Motherfucker...

Goddamn. Motherfucker.

I grabbed my cell as I headed back along the hallway. My fingers raked my hair back. I felt desperate, desperate enough to swipe my fingers across the screen and type out a message:

You'd better have something for me.

Then I hit send, casting it into the black void of nothing.

It may as well be that for all the fucking response I got.

I ground my teeth and stopped walking. The urge to put my fist through the damn wall was overwhelming.

I want her.

Those words swirled inside my head until they were all I could think of. They felt like pebbles thrown into a well, and the ripples echoed in my mind until everything else was stilled.

I want her. I. Want. Her.

My pulse sped.

Her stretched mouth and silent cry of release were all I could see.

Beep.

I jerked at the sound and looked down to my cell.

They've received communication to move them.

They're moving them? Panic and fear moved in. My fingers trembled as I typed. *When?*

I waited.

And waited.

And...waited.

Still, there was no response, until.

Beep.

That's for you to find out.

"Fuck." I whispered, my mind racing.

I needed a way in. Something. I kept on walking, heading back along the corridor until I got to my office, then unlocked the door and stepped in.

They were moving them. It wasn't the time...they knew the structure of the programming. Brainwashing was a very fragile technique. One missed step, one rushed experience could have disastrous consequences.

First we broke them, then we rebuilt.

Maybe they didn't care about that?

They would when we delivered a shipment of 'assets' who were mentally shattered and prepared to kill the man who'd just paid a million dollars for his very own personal whore.

A smile tugged at the corners of my mouth. As enticing as that might be to watch, the reality was very different, especially now Helene was involved.

I want her.

The smile died.

In case you haven't yet caught on, Hale Order is under new management...*me.*

"Let's just see about that, shall we?" I murmured and started typing, finding my way into the database.

There had to be something here. Some kind of information that would help me out.

I ran my fingers through my hair as I logged into each new file listed and scanned the data of the logged shipments. Nothing.

Every Daughter was listed here, along with where they'd come from. Everything *but* where they were going. I scrolled until I found the name...Helene.

Her name, her history. Even if it was fake.

Each step, from the time she was a child to the time she'd arrived here. I stared at the details, knowing instantly what the Hunter had done.

I'd asked for her to be put in the system.

I'd asked for her to be hidden.

And he had.

I stared at the screen and the image of the woman who looked almost identical to Helene King...she should be, after all, she was her sister.

Vivienne.

Christ, this whole thing was a fucking mess.

We should never have been here...and nor should our sister.

I tore my gaze from the image of Helene superseded over her sister's details and kept on moving.

The New Order.

I stilled, scowling. What the fuck?

I hit the button.

Access denied.

My jaw clenched. I tried again.

Denied.

In case you haven't yet caught on, Hale Order is under new management...*me.*

"The fuck it is." I forced the words through clenched teeth and rose.

Rage boiled within me. No one will dare touch a single strand of her hair.

Protect her.

That same savage hunger filled me now as it had before when I'd burst into the apartment to see her at the hands of that fucking guard.

I'd killed for her before.

And I'd kill again. I'd kill them all if I had to...until she and my brothers were the last ones standing.

THIRTY-ONE

Kane

"I WANT YOU." I BREATHED HEAVILY AGAINST HER collarbone and slid my fingers out of her. "Christ, I want you."

Her clit trembled under my touch, pulsing harder as I dragged my fingers over the tiny nub. She let out a whimper as she grabbed my wrist and clamped her legs shut.

So swollen...and so goddamn sensitive.

My cock twitched. The urge to fuck her was overwhelming.

"Open your legs, Helene." I demanded.

She jerked her gaze to mine. Panic and desire ignited in her stare before those perfect thighs parted. It was just the programming, I tried to tell myself. Just the drugs and the conditioning. But the longer I held that stare, the more I knew this was more.

Her mind was strong. Probably one of the strongest I'd ever seen...she could fight this if she wanted. She could buck against the voice I'd put inside her head, the one that told her to obey. She could defy me easily, but she didn't.

Those dark eyes looked black in the wash of the tiny red blinking light as they fixed on mine. She scowled just slightly before that carnal hunger pushed through, and I knew instantly this was more than the techniques I'd used on her and the others.

This was real.

Fuck.

My pulse thundered, booming in my goddamn skull. I lowered my head and grazed her neck with my lips. I wanted to kiss her...more than that...I wanted all of *her*...and it wasn't just sex, either. I lifted my gaze to hers and could almost feel the rush of air as I fell into oblivion.

This wasn't supposed to happen.

I jerked my gaze to the blinking red light on the camera and inhaled, drawing in the seductive scent of her come. I was moving before I knew, pushing up from the floor, her once warm desire cooling on the tips of my fingers.

She sat naked on the floor, her knees bent, cunt on display. I reached up and hit the switch on the camera, ending the view. They'd seen enough...and there was no goddamn way they were going to watch what was about to happen.

"Kane." She whispered, her tone etched with fear.

"It's okay." I reached out, heading to the opposite side of the pitch-black room. "Just stay where you are."

The special insulation swallowed my footsteps in the room, one designed to absorb every sound, to leave the space completely silent. One designed to strangle the senses, leaving you disoriented and vulnerable.

It worked, even on me. I reached out, tentatively searching the air until I touched the edge of my desk. The *flick* of the light came, spilling soft light through the room. For a second, I didn't want to turn around to see her. I didn't want to meet those eyes.

Because if I did, she might see the battle that raged inside me.

I was falling for her.

For the same woman my brother was infatuated with.

The woman who held our fragile existence in the palm of her hand.

One wrong word, one wrong move, and we'd all be kneeling with a gun pointed at our heads.

There was too much at stake.

Cool air reached through my unbuttoned shirt as I took a step, making my way slowly toward her. She sat on the floor, craning toward me as I neared. I reached out and caressed the side of her face.

"This...wasn't supposed to happen." I said.

She closed her eyes, almost purring, as she rubbed her cheek against my palm. "Maybe...it was."

Maybe it was?

I thought about that, and all the times I'd barricaded myself away from her and all my patients on the other side of my massive desk. I'd seen her as a therapist for the last few months, and even though the desire to fuck her had been there, it'd been a surface feeling. An act of possession and nothing more.

But this...

This was something else.

"I feel something for you." She whispered and opened her eyes. "And it scares me."

She lifted her head, and our gazes collided. My heart clenched as panic raced through me. I'd felt more when I was with her than I had for a very long time. Memories came flooding back, all the times I'd proposed evening sessions at my apartment, ending with the moment I'd fantasized fucking her throat until she almost passed out.

My cock moved, thickening at the image of that. She shifted her gaze, then reached upwards and cupped the bulge. I moaned and closed my eyes. The warmth of her hand wrapping around the length almost made me fucking come.

She pulled away, eased the zipper lower, then reached inside. I opened my eyes at the heat of her hand and looked down as she eased my length out. The shimmering head twitched as she pushed up onto her knees, opened her mouth, and looked up at me.

My breath stopped. I wanted to see it all, every fucking second of this woman. I moved her hair aside as she closed her lips around me and sank all the way down.

"Fuck *me*." I moaned, mesmerized by the stretch of her mouth.

But I'd already had this...and I wanted more.

No.

I wanted *everything*.

I reached down, cupped her jaw, and eased out.

She waited, then slowly pushed backwards as I knelt. There was no stopping this. Her and me...*it was fate.* She parted her thighs, letting me crawl between them. A twist of my button and the rest of my trousers opened.

"You sure?" My voice was husky.

"Yes." She grabbed my arm, pulling me against her.

I looked down at the raised pink scars on her side, and her own words came flooding back. *I was the one who bombed The Order.* She wasn't just ruthless...she was also a survivor. "Never trust a survivor." I whispered and leaned over, brushing her lips with mine. "Until you find out what they did to stay alive."

She leaned back, leading me forward until I pushed in. Heavy breaths stilled as the energy crackled between us. My pulse skipped, fluttering and panicked.

"Oh, *Christ.*" I moaned, thrusting with a brutal jolt.

She whimpered, gripping my arm and splayed her knees wider. "Fuck me hard."

A twitch came at the corner of my mouth. I pulled out, then with all my strength, drove all the way inside.

Her ass skidded on the floor and it was like a switch flipped inside me. I grabbed her hips, pulling her back as I rammed in again.

"Yes...*Oh, God...yes.*"

Her cries were all the encouragement I needed. I set my jaw and went to work, driving my cock inside her. My hand went around her throat. She stared at me, her eyes wide with desperation.

"Good girl." I groaned. "Fuck, you're taking this so good. Look at us. Look how well you're taking your punishment."

Because that's what this was.

You should've let me fuck you.

You shouldn't have fallen for my brother.

I tried to push the thoughts away, concentrating on the warmth of her cunt as I pushed in. The scent of sex was so bold in the air. I sucked it down, desperate for more.

"You even fuck like him." She said, her voice vibrating against my hand. "Raw and savage."

The words only made me feel even more dangerous.

I gripped her throat, hard enough to let her know who was in charge. "You like that?" I grunted. "You like being fucked by my brother and me?"

She arched her back, never once fighting my hold as I slammed into her once more. "Yes."

I pressed my thumb against her throat as the image of that rose.

Riven.

Her.

Me.

Both using her. Both tasting her. I unleashed a groan, captured by the memory. My hunger was ignited and there was no turning back. She bit her lip and her body clenched around me. Just like that, I was done. I groaned and stilled, buried in her heat as my cock spasmed, releasing warmth deep inside.

"That's it, Teacher." She whispered. "Fill me."

I moaned, my cock jerking hard with the words. I wanted to fill her. I wanted to fill her so fucking bad. I gripped her throat and wrenched her forward. Panic filled me as I lost myself in her stare. Then, without warning, I yanked her forward and kissed her.

I was gone, falling headlong into the pit of darkness.

I closed my eyes and kissed her harder, holding her in place. She gave a moan, the sound wounded and desperate. That was exactly how I felt. I broke away, transfixed by her power. "This...changes everything."

"I agree." She answered. "Now, we both have something at stake."

What did that mean?

Did it mean...*she*...

Her stare never wavered...and in those deep brown eyes, I saw the truth.

Shit...

I released my hold and pulled away, looking down before I pushed against the floor and rose. Her thighs were damp, with come glistening around her core. The sight stopped me cold.

"I trust you." She whispered, pushing upwards. "With my body and now my heart."

Was she playing us?

A pang tore across my chest. Christ, it felt like I was going to have a heart attack.

"Get dressed." I urged, my tone a little harsh. "I want to escort you to your cell...to make sure you're...safe."

The truth was, I needed to get away from her, away from those eyes and the temptation to drop to my knees and fill her with my cock once more. Because the truth was...I didn't want to let her go.

She flinched, then moved slowly, pushing up off the floor to stand.

I felt like a bastard, hating how cold I was. But there was nothing I could say, nothing that could change what we were... and where we were. This wasn't a place of love. No matter how much that aching throb in my chest wanted it to be.

She pulled on her red lingerie and turned around. There was an emptiness in her eyes. One that hit me like a punch to the balls. *You fucking asshole.* I looked away, tucked in my cock, and headed for the door.

Coulter had wanted a show, and he'd gotten one.

We'd played pretend and now it came down to getting Helene to Hale. Everything hinged on that, regardless of my heart.

Movement drew my gaze as Helene stepped toward the door and waited. She didn't look at me anymore. Not that I blamed her. I grabbed my card and headed for the door, leaving the light on. I'd return later and check the results from the other Daughters for today.

"Let's get you back to your room." I reached out, unlocked the door, and waited for her to walk out.

She never said a word, nor did she look my way, just headed through the viewing room and out into the hallway. But she didn't need to, because my head was already spinning.

We reached the hallway to her room and turned the corner. Walker's man looked our way, armed with a sniper rifle as he stood guard. I stepped forward, unlocked her door, and waited until she stepped in before closing it.

She turned at the last minute, finding me in the glass panel of the door. Pain and confusion raged in her expression before she turned away.

"Do not leave this room." I murmured, then slowly glanced at Walker's guard. "For any reason. Do I make myself clear?"

"Crystal." He glanced toward the room. "Don't worry, my instructions are every clear."

One look my way and I knew. He was well aware of the battle that raged…and more than that, how important Helene was. That ache filled my chest, rippling out like poison, one I gladly swallowed.

"Good." My voice was husky. "Call me instantly if there's a problem."

"Will do." He answered as I turned. "Right after I call The Principal."

My step faltered before I forced myself to move. Of course, they'd call Riven first. It was always Riven. Not once had I ever cared about that—I clenched my jaw and slammed the card against the scanner—until now.

Now I cared a great deal.

That ache in my chest grew talons, puncturing all the way into my heart. I winced and slammed my fist against the crushing agony, but it wouldn't stop. If anything, it grew bolder. The lights overhead turned neon white, buzzing and brightening.

Fuck. I winced, scanning the hallway, to see movement from Coulter's guards in the distance. I needed to get out of here, I needed to *get out.*

I stumbled toward the external door and thrust my card against the scanner before I lurched out. Cold night air washed over me, plunging in deep with every gasping breath.

I headed for the safety of the trees, my boots crunching on the gravel until I met the grass. What the fuck was happening to me? *What...the...fuck—*

"I need you to keep this quiet."

The words reached me through the trees. I lifted my head, scanning the darkness as I waited for my eyes to adjust to the gloom.

"They don't know we found Marks. So we do what Coulter said and keep it quiet."

Marks?

The name resounded...until the icy grip of fear clenched tight.

The body.

They'd found it.

The ground seemed to fall out from under my feet.

"And whatever we do...we keep those Cruz bastards in our sights."

The shadowy figures shifted. One turned his head, scanning the trees near where I stood. My heart lunged as I waited for him to see me, but he didn't. Instead, he turned back to the other, said something else I couldn't quite catch before they walked away.

They'd found the body?

No fucking way.

There was no way.

I'd taken everything off the bastard who'd almost killed Helene and my brother. His clothes, his weapons...*everything*.

I turned my head, scanning the dark. I had to make sure the body was right where I'd left it...then I had to find Riven. The night grew cold...too cold. An eeriness washed through me. My gut clenched as panic rose. This was going to be bad...I just knew it.

Boots crunched on gravel, drawing my gaze. I stood in the darkness, hidden by the trees, and watched Coulter's men disappear into the building. Desperation filled me, forcing me to swivel around...find my bearings, and lunge.

THIRTY-TWO

Riven

I WANT HER.

Those words resounded in my head until they were all I could hear.

I. Want. Her.

"Riven."

I slowly lifted my head from the tumbler of Scotch. Thomas stood in front of me, that gruesome, bloody stare fixed on mine.

"You're worrying me." He said carefully.

"Don't I always?" I took a swallow, relishing the burn as it hit my belly.

Click.

My focus moved instantly to the external door of the apartment. I was already reaching behind my back for the gun tucked under my belt as it opened and Kane stepped inside. He was flushed and panicked, hastily locking the door before he turned and fixed a frantic stare on me.

My gut clenched instantly as he moved. He never even looked at Thomas, just lengthened that already long stride as he hurried my way. We'd never been what you'd call close. None of us were, but the gap between the doctor and myself stretched a little wider.

Only none of that mattered at that moment.

He headed straight for me, grabbed my arm that held the alcohol, and yanked me close...so close his words were a low hiss in my ear. *"They found the body."*

Cold plunged all the way deep inside me, snuffing out the heat I'd relished before. I turned my head slowly, meeting the light green as his eyes stared into mine. I fought to think, tried to search through all the implications. "Are you sure?"

He just gave a nod as Thomas watched.

They'd found the body.

They'd found the damn body.

The fucking locator. But how? "I thought you said you had that handled?"

"I did."

My lip curled. "Obviously not.'"

He sucked in a hard breath, flinching at the chiding remark. But I didn't give a shit about his feelings. Not anymore...not when I was...*invested.*

I drained the last of my glass and turned away.

"Hey." He stopped me.

I turned back.

"I'm deep in this too."

"I doubt that." I muttered.

But as soon as I spoke, I saw just how wrong I was. His cheeks were burning and his chest still heaved with savage breaths. He'd been running, and not just running, he'd been hauling goddamn ass. That wasn't Kane, not in all the years he'd been my brother had I seen him put himself out for anyone.

Even when our sister had been taken.

So, the mere fact he'd been running just to get back to me with this information was...life shattering.

"You're in love with her?" Thomas murmured, staring intently at our brother.

There was a tiny shake of Kane's head. I turned away as a low, bestial chuckle spilled free. "That's so fucking you, isn't it?"

"I don't—" He started.

I whipped around as rage drove to the surface. "You're really going to stand there and lie to my face?"

"Riven." Thomas murmured.

I ignored him, taking a step toward Kane. "Go on, admit it. Admit the truth, you fucking love her."

"*Riven.*" Thomas urged again, a little louder.

I jerked my blazing gaze to his. "What?!"

"You abducted her. You drugged her and you raped her. This isn't some fairytale perfect romance here. I want you to be aware of that."

I sucked in a hard breath as it all hit home, every terrifying moment of it. *So?* I wanted to snarl like a petulant child. Instead, I looked the bastard in the eyes. "Why did it have to be her?"

"You think I wanted this?" He winced, shook his head and turned away. "This isn't *me*. I don't feel so fucking..." He wrung his hands, and the movement drew my gaze. "Sickened."

I knew exactly how he was feeling. Wound so fucking tight you thought you were going to break. She made me feel desperate... teetering on the edge of insanity. Murderous. That's how I felt. *Fucking murderous.*

"None of this matters." I said. "We have a job to do and so does she. We protect her, get her on that goddamn truck. We give her every opportunity to do what we've failed at...finding Mel. What you feel about her or what I feel doesn't matter. Once this is over, we figure out if any of this is even real."

He flinched. "It is...for me."

An ache filled my chest. Just hearing the words made me feel nauseous. She was mine. She *was mine* because I'd...had... her...first.

"It's late," Thomas urged. "Now we need to be more careful than ever. They may suspect it was us, but they have no proof."

"How do you know that?" Kane cut him a glare.

"Because if they did." I started. "Then we'd be dead."

It was that simple. If they had any proof at all, we'd all be looking down the barrel of a gun. Still, we had to be careful, especially where Helene was concerned.

"Get some sleep." I made for the bedroom. "Tomorrow, the fun begins."

I left them, headed into my bedroom, grabbed clean boxers, then took the first shower. Thoughts raced through my head as the hot water hit my skin and they were all about her.

Kane.

Coulter.

And every other fucking male in a hundred-mile radius.

I lowered my head, letting the water sluice down.

Tell me. Tell me you're mine

My own desperate words filled my head.

I'm yours...please, I'm yours.

"Fuck." I muttered.

My balls ached. My cock was stiff. I reached down, grasping it hard.

I'm yours. I'm yours. I'm yours.

I fisted the length, pumping slowly. "Damn fucking right you are."

I was too far gone with this woman and I knew it. I'd kill for her...and that included my kin if it came to that. The woman was mine...and mine alone. Kane needed to remember that.

I lifted a hand and braced it against the wall, leaning into it as I pumped my length. It was a poor fucking replacement for the real thing. But right now, I was too wired to care. I needed her, even if it was the illusion of her. "Mine." I croaked as greed turned to infatuation. *"You are mine."*

My thrust grew harder, my fist squeezed tight. I wanted more...more...*her.*

Make me come, Principal. Make me come.

My cock twitched. Warmth jetted out, leaving me to groan and still clenched tight around the pulsing vein that ran underneath.

You're in love with her?

I winced at the memory and lifted my head. My heart was hurting, far more than it should have. I hit the faucet and switched off the spray, stepping out before I wound the towel around my waist and headed for the door.

But the moment I opened it, Kane was there, jerking those betraying fucking eyes to mine.

He never said a word. But the bastard didn't need to.

He stepped to the side, to the *wrong fucking side.* We stepped around, dancing like two goddamn idiots, until I grabbed his shoulders and shoved him to the side as I pushed past.

Motherfucker.

I headed into my room, toweled hard, and tossed it to the floor. Thomas was right. Tomorrow we'd need to be careful...and all of us needed to sleep.

THERE WAS no sleep and not a second of fucking peace. When I finally rose after tossing and turning all goddamn night, my eyes stung and my nerves were raw. I showered again, this time hurrying. By the time I stepped out of my bedroom, I still felt like hell...but I was ready for this day to start.

We needed to know exactly what their plans were. More than that, we needed to find out when they were sending the shipment of Daughters to Hale. If the wolves were closing in, then we needed to be prepared.

The apartment was quiet. I scowled, turning my attention to Kane's room. The bastard must be still sleeping. Figures.

I headed out and made my way along the corridors, slapping my card against scanner after scanner as I made my way to my office. But the place was silent...deathly silent. I stopped at the doorway and turned, listening.

There was no thud of boots, no deep murmur from any guards. I turned back and headed inside, but the moment I sat down, I stilled. It didn't feel...right.

My skin crawled as I stared at the mouse. I reached out and hit it, making my screen come to life. I logged in, staring at the screen. The file on Helene was gone, not filling the screen like the last time I'd left it. Someone had been here.

That chill moved deeper.

I want her.

Coulter's fucking demand resounded in my head. "Goddamn bastard."

I shoved up from the seat and shoved my chair aside. All I could think about was her. Finding her. Protecting her. *Loving her.* I lengthened my stride and pushed through the door.

Silence filled the corridors. It was early, too goddamn early. The Daughters would still be asleep and most of Walker's guards would still be patrolling the grounds.

Movement came through the glass section of the double doors up ahead, heading this way. I recognised one of them as one of Coulter's commanders. Not someone I expected out at this time of the morning...unless it was for a reason.

I stopped, then stepped to the side. Instinct drove me as I pressed the access card against the scanner and slipped into a utility closet. Darkness quickly swallowed the room. But I left a tiny crack open as the security doors in the hallway gave a *click* and swung open.

"All you have to do is make sure you're ready to move." Coulter's man ordered.

"And what if these bastards fight back?"

I flinched, gripped the handle tighter, and strained to hear.

"You let me worry about that. Two days, that's all you need to worry about. Two days, then we move."

Two days?

My heart slammed against my ribs. Two fucking days? What were they planning in two days?

The warmth washed out of me and my stomach dropped. I knew what they were planning...they were moving them.

Two days wasn't enough. The programming took two months at least. Six weeks at a push, but two days? That was barbaric.

If they took them now, they'd run the risk of undoing what we'd done, or breaking their minds. They were fragile right now. The drugs and the hypnosis make them fragile...and that alone made them dangerous.

Footsteps thudded, then faded.

I stayed in the darkness, hiding in the closet for a couple of minutes before I risked stepping out. They were long gone, but the words lingered. *Two days, that's all you need to worry about.*

My mind reeled. My movements were on autopilot as I pressed my card against the scanner and headed for the Daughters' rooms.

Two days and she would be gone. Christ, I felt sick with the thought of not being able to watch over her, but right now, we had to do what we could.

Think...

I pushed through the doors and headed for the rooms. Only, the moment I turned the corner, I found one of Coulter's men standing outside the open door of one Daughter's cell. My first instinct was to turn and search for Walker, to make sure he was protecting the only one I cared about, Helene...until movement came from inside and Kane stepped out.

"She needs more fluids and rest." He instructed the guard. "On to the next one, please."

He lifted his head, meeting my gaze.

A flicker of confusion rose until I saw the folder in his hands. He was checking them, noting down their vital signs and their mental state. He glanced toward Helene's room, but he didn't head there, not yet. He was using the other Daughters as a cover to get to her.

Two days. The words boomed in my head. Did Kane know?

As his gaze met mine, he scowled. He didn't. I'd almost bet money he didn't know a damn thing.

I glanced at the folder and the list of Daughters on the front. More than half were checked off. That meant he'd been doing this for over an hour...well before I rose and before Coulter's men started to make arrangements.

If he didn't know we were fucked already, then he soon would. His programming was about to be destroyed and there wasn't a goddamn thing we could do about it...not until Coulter made a move.

Until then we had to play along and pray to God we enticed the bastard with someone other than the woman we'd both fallen for.

For all our sakes.

THIRTY-THREE

Kane

Riven's eyes were wide with terror and his pallor was ashen. As much as that terrified me, I turned away, pretending I didn't notice, and kept walking to the next cell.

"Outside." I instructed the guard.

He knew the procedure by now, opening the door and hovering within view as I headed for the figure curled in the bed. The drugs in the Daughters' systems were waning and right now they were more susceptible than ever.

I gripped the tiny flashlight and moved through the motions, checking her vitals before starting the same questions I had before. "Who do you belong to?"

"You." She whispered, looking up at me.

"And when instructed, what do you do?"

"Obey."

I met her stare. "Who are you?"

Those dull eyes were lifeless as she answered. "Daughter."

I stayed a while, pretending I cared as much about this one as I did the next. Only the act was just that...an act. I gave a slow nod, finished my questions, and rose. The next one was the one I needed, *Helene.*

"Next." I commanded.

Doors locked. Footsteps thudded. But Riven was still standing there, with that same pale complexion and that same haunted stare, waiting for me as we neared her room. He looked like he was about to pass out. As the guard strode past him and unlocked Helene's door, he turned.

"I'll need an updated report." Riven murmured, his tone hollow.

I gave a nod. "Of course." Then I glanced at the guard and gave a jerk of my head. "You can wait out there."

He flicked his gaze to Riven and shook his head. "You want to talk, then you talk here."

What the fuck? Anger flared. Still, I swallowed it down and instead gave a careful nod. "If you insist." I turned to my brother. "Several have elevated vitals. We pushed too hard to hit the markers. They require rest."

Click.

Helene's door opened. That same darkness waited.

"I'm not sure that's an option." Riven answered carefully. "Anymore."

I cut him a glare before I turned my focus toward the room. But she wasn't curled up in the bed like all the other Daughters had been. A quick scan of the room and I found her sitting on the floor in the corner.

"Helene?" I approached and knelt down in front of her. "Can you hear me?"

She lifted her unfocused gaze to mine. *Shit.* She looked bad... worse than the others. I checked the dilation of her pupils as Riven stood next to me.

"We might need to speed up the process." He murmured.

I jerked my gaze to his, letting him see how pissed off that remark made me. "Speed it up?" I jerked my head to the woman we both cared about and hissed. *"Do you want me to break her damn mind?"*

Movement came through the doorway. The guard popped his head in, scanned us, then turned away. Riven waited until he was barely out of earshot before he moved, bending fast to grab my shirt and snarl in my ear. "They're moving them in two fucking days. Two days and we lose her. You want to make sure she's prepared."

Two days?

Instantly, the warmth drained out of me .

I turned back to her. "It's not enough time."

"Then you'd better make sure it is." Riven snarled, then jerked his gaze to her.

She turned to meet his stare and in a moment of weakness, Riven released his hold on my shirt and instead caressed her face.

"We're right here, Trouble." He murmured, his tone husky. "We're going to do everything we can to protect you."

She just stared at him, then closed her eyes and pressed her cheek against his touch. "Obey." She whispered. "I obey."

She obeyed alright. The only problem was...which one of us?

Jealousy flared, seething and corrupting. I'd wanted nothing in my entire life like the way I wanted it to be my hand she rubbed herself against.

"Then it looks like I have my work cut out for me." I said carefully. "We'd better get started."

***

THE AIR SCRAPED like a blade against my skin when I stepped into the training room. The Daughters were lined up, looking washed-out and vacant, just what I expected when we pushed them too hard. Nurses moved between them, piercing the crook of their arms with the drugs designed to make them more susceptible to the techniques we used. They didn't even flinch with the injections anymore, just stood there unmoving... even Helene.

Coulter and his guards stood in the shadows, watching with their beady, hawk-like eyes. Hale had never been so hands-on, leaving me to have complete control. But with this asshole, we were under the goddamn microscope.

Then a gap in the line of Daughters drew my focus. I headed toward it, scanning the unblinking stares as panic rose.

A scream came from the corridor, shrill, filled with terror. One that grew louder the closer it came. Riven turned instantly, then jerked his head toward Walker, who strode from the room. But he was barely out of sight before one of Coulter's men dragged the missing Daughter into the room by a fistful of her hair.

"This one." He shoved her hard, causing her to stumble toward me. "Refused to cooperate."

I grabbed her shoulders, holding her steady as I scanned the red palm print on her face. "And did you need to beat her into submission?"

Fear was the one emotion we tried not to use. It was unpredictable...and it spread like the damn plague. It was the main reason they were showered and fed as soon as possible after inserting the tracking device. These women already came conditioned to a degree, you add in additional fear stimuli and it could turn toxic *fast*.

The guard never said a word. But the hate in his eyes said it all.

I lowered my gaze to the yanked down strap of her bra, then to the stretched elastic of her panties at the crotch. It didn't take me long to understand what had happened. "You were explicitly told the Daughters were off-limits."

I jerked my gaze to his... "unless you wish to pay?"

He said nothing.

The bastard needed to be taught a lesson.

I turned to the Daughter and the wide, panicked look in her eyes before I motioned for a nurse to come forward.

"Easy now." I brushed my thumb along her shoulder as the nurse gently turned her arm, swabbed the injection site, and pushed the needle in.

Seconds, that's all it took, before the crease smoothed between her eyes and her breathing deepened.

"That's better." I murmured, keeping my thumb brushing the same spot on her shoulder over and over.

Coulter's guard might've tried to have a taste of what a million dollars could buy in The Order, but force took that taste and it wasn't at all what *could* be explored.

I fixed my gaze on her, ignoring the bright red mark on her face and instead, I murmured. "Undress."

She never hesitated, reaching up to slide the strap of the bra down, showing a level of obedience that hadn't been there a second ago. Pale, full breasts were revealed. I risked a glance toward Coulter, standing in the shadows.

Every other male's focus was on the Daughter in front of me, except for his.

His stare was directed to Helene, the one woman he couldn't have.

Desperation trembled inside me as I turned back to the woman in front of me. I didn't care about her, not about her fate or her happiness. She was a tool to me. One I'd wield to keep the woman I loved safe.

"Keep going." I urged. "Take it all off."

She did, sliding her thumbs into the waistband of her panties and dragged it all the way down. I barely saw her. Vacant eyes, perfect tits, a shaved, tight pussy.

"Kneel." I commanded.

She did, instantly sinking to the floor.

"Hands behind your back, knees wide."

The guard's gaze was riveted. But it wasn't him I watched in the corner of my eye, it was Coulter. The bastard looked our way for a second, but it didn't last before his focus moved back to Helene.

"Show him." My tone was hard and husky. "Turn over, cheek against the floor."

I swallowed the flinch as she turned onto her knees, then lowered her face to the floor, desperate to obey like the Daughter she was.

"Spread yourself." I snarled. "Show him what could be his."

The tips of her fingers dug into soft flesh as she gripped her plump ass and spread herself wide. A low, tortured groan came from the guard in front of me.

My brother was right.

It wasn't excitement I felt at the sight of this woman.

It was savagery.

I wanted to grab her by the back of her neck. To bellow and roar in her face until her eyes shimmered with tears. I wanted to cast her aside, right into the middle of the pack of these ravenous wolves. And while they tore her apart, I wanted to capture the woman I loved...and get her the hell out of here.

My body trembled with that need until it was crushing.

"You want to tie her up?" I started. "You want to fuck her until you forget your problems, you can."

He jerked a wide, startled gaze my way,

"You want to bring your buddies over to your house and have her service all of them in front of you? You can do that too. You can do anything you want with her. Every dark, debased, carnal desire you ever harbored in secret, you can finally drag into the light. She won't scream when you fuck her brutally...unless you want that. She won't ever say no, or I'm tired, or go away. How does that make you feel?"

"Like a god." He croaked.

The corner of my mouth twitched. *Exactly.*

He jerked that desperate stare my way. "How much? Whatever it is, I'll pay it."

I stepped past him, heading across the room. "You couldn't afford it." It was Coulter I made for, standing in front of the bastard who was about to cast Helene to Hale in two goddamn days. "But you can."

He never looked away from me.

Want her, you sonofabitch, want her *and not Helene.*

Coulter just looked past me, at the Daughter still spread wide for everyone to see, before he met my stare once more and smiled.

THIRTY-FOUR

Helene

THE ROOM SWAYED IN FRONT OF ME. I LOOKED DOWN AT the fading sting in my arm and tried to hold on to my senses. Rows of us stood there waiting.

OBEY.

CONTROL.

DAUGHTER.

The words resounded inside my head until I *was* the blazing neon white words. I was *obey.* I was *control.* I was *Daughter.* Sharp cries inside the room disappeared, like they'd never been there at all. Maybe they hadn't? Maybe this was all just a dream?

It felt like a dream.

The catch of a breath invaded the daze in my head. A choked whimper drew my attention. Slow, steady breaths filled me. I focused on that and forced my gaze to the Daughter two rows in front of me.

Fight.

I clung to that need as the fading room around me sharpened. The Daughter in front of me sank to the floor in front of *him*...the man I knew somehow. *Kane.* His name resounded and as it filled me, he glanced my way. I held onto that stare, finding a flicker of desperation before it was gone and he turned his attention back to the Daughter at his feet. She turned over, closed her eyes and pressed her cheek to the floor, her ass and pussy on display.

"Spread yourself." The Teacher demanded. *"Show him what could be his."*

What could be his? A flare of agony tore through my chest. With the pain came a blazing moment of clarity. *Hold on...hold on, trouble.*

But it wasn't Kane's voice that rippled through me. My gaze moved to the edge of the room where *he* stood. The man whose dark, unflinching stare was magnetic.

Don't fight it.

His voice resounded.

You don't want to tear this beautiful cunt apart now, do you?

My breaths deepened, my pulse sped. It was him...him who transfixed me with his presence...until goosebumps raced along my arms and stood the hair at the nape of my neck. Until another man drew my focus.

I slowly turned my head, tearing my gaze from the man known as The Principal to another just as dangerous.

A man who didn't fill me with the excitement The Principal did…no, it was the opposite. The warmth drained out of me, leaving me to shiver.

"You couldn't afford it." Kane muttered, heading across the room toward the man who watched me intently. *"But you can."*

The deadly male just held his stare before his lips curled into a chilling smile. He didn't answer, but he didn't need to. My shoulders curled as he directed that focus my way.

He didn't say a thing, just pushed past Kane and headed toward me.

My breath caught.

My stomach clenched.

The entire room came alive as he stepped between the rows of Daughters.

Riven was a dark blur, hot on his heels as they both headed my way.

Move!

MOVE!

Fear gripped me. The overwhelming urge to stumble backwards before I turned and ran made my knees shake. But I couldn't move. I was fixed to the spot, riveted as the dangerous man Riven hated stopped in front of me.

Coulter.

That was his name.

"No." He murmured, searching my eyes. "But I'll take her."

A fragile, wounded sound ripped free as he reached up and cupped my breast, before he pinched my nipple until agony bloomed.

"No." Riven lunged, grabbing Coulter's wrist as he lowered his hand between my legs.

Coulter never looked at him. Just pinned me to the spot as he muttered. "Don't tell me...*the programming.*"

Riven said nothing. Still, I saw the flex of his arm as he clenched Coulter's wrist, before the savage male yanked his hand away, breaking the hold.

Tension crackled as Coulter turned and strode away. Riven followed, but not before he glanced my way, his stare desperate. The air turned heavy, so heavy each breath was an effort. *Master,* the word hummed inside me as I held his stare before he looked away.

"Rise." Kane commanded the Daughter still kneeling splayed out on the floor in front of him.

She did, pushing up to stand back in line, naked.

"You must learn to be obedient." Kane glanced around the room, his gaze skimming past me. "You will enjoy *any* attention your Master gives you. His requests are to be obeyed at all times. Any type of disobedience will bring consequences."

His voice turned dark, and savage as he scanned the room, then started walking, moving between us. "Your body will react. The air will leave your lungs and won't return. An ache will fill your entire body, one so constricting you won't be able to move, giving you no choice but to comply with his demands." I felt the weight of that stare as he moved past me. "Do you feel it now? That darkness, that waiting hunger?"

I closed my eyes as that tremble of fear grew inside me. I knew now without a doubt something terrible was going to happen to me with the whisper of one word *no*.

Obey.

Control.

Release.

"Yes." I whispered and all the Daughters repeated around me.

He sauntered. The soft brush of his fingers came against my hand. "That is why you will always *obey*." He murmured.

"Obey." We repeated.

The morning seemed to blur. Countless times Kane walked amongst us, feeding that same fear inside us before he reinforced our obedience. Every time he passed, he touched me. A slight brush of my hand. His palm gently pressed against the small of my back. The touch drew me away from those murky thoughts inside my head, giving me something to hold on to.

We're here, Trouble. Riven's voice echoed. *We're right here.* We were a vessel. Something for our Master's entertainment. The word *no* wasn't the word we would use with our Master's needs.

We were owned.

We were controlled.

We were *Daughter*.

"That's enough for today." He finally said, slowly walking amongst us. "You'll be escorted to the bathroom, then the cafeteria. Sleep well. Tomorrow, we push harder."

I winced at the words *push harder*. My thoughts were already scrambled, even with the careful brush of Kane's touch. Movement came from the edge of the room as one of Walker's guards strode forward and handed Kane a red lace playsuit like the ones we wore.

Kane grabbed it and handed it to the still naked Daughter. "Get dressed."

She obeyed instantly, pulled it on, and eased the straps into place.

"Walker." Kane murmured. "They're all yours."

We drifted. My feet ached from standing in the one spot for so long. But as soon as the ache rose, it was swallowed with that foggy feeling in my head. My movements were slow as I followed the others out of the training room and into the hall.

Murmurs from the guards and the soft *thud* of our bare feet were the only sounds as we shuffled into the bathroom, each one of us using a stall. The moment I pushed the playsuit down and sat on the cold seat, I closed my eyes.

I shouldn't be here.

I winced and wrapped my arms around my middle.

I shouldn't be anywhere near here. I need to get out. I need to—

Ryth.

Vivienne.

Their names stopped me cold and the memory of their faces surfaced. They were the reason I was here. The reason for it all. *Remember your mission. Remember Hale.* I clung to them as I wiped and rose, flushing the toilet. Careful glances came my way from the guard as I stepped out and headed for the sink.

They escorted us to the cafeteria in silence. Marched like soldiers to take a seat at the rows of tables. Staff neared, pouring a plastic cup of juice for each of us before sliding on. As dry as my mouth was, I didn't reach for the fluid. Instead, I lifted my gaze to the doorway as more guards filed in.

Only they weren't the regular ones.

No.

These men were larger, more muscled, and carried brand new guns. I scanned their weapons and somewhere in the back of my head, a sense of familiarity rose. My fingers twitched, aching to feel the grip of the cold steel in my grasp.

I met the guards' stares instead as they fixed their gazes on Walker and his men.

Something was happening here.

Something that made me scared.

As the other Daughters drank and ate all around me, I found myself riveted to the play of power in front of me and prayed Riven and Kane would indeed look out for me.

Because without them...

I was vulnerable.

THIRTY-FIVE

Riven

Clunk. *Bang.*

Clunk. *Bang.*

Clunk—

I wrenched my gaze from the monitor and the warning splashing across the screen, *Access Denied.* Anger already seethed in my veins as that fucking sound resounded along the hallway.

Bang!

"That's it." I shoved up from my chair and turned toward the door.

I'd been here for three goddamn hours after the Daughters were locked away in their rooms for the night trying to access the files...any files, for that matter. Now every time I clicked on a goddamn document it came up with a warning. Something was going on. Something I didn't like.

Clunk.

Bang!

That goddamn sound pissed me off. Did they want to entice panic at every goddamn moment? I strode out of my office and into the hallway, finding the dark blur of a guard dragging something along the doors up ahead. I clenched my teeth and lengthened my stride, slammed my card against the scanner and pushed through the doors after him. Goddamn bastard, he was about to get a mouthful.

That festering rage needed an outlet and right now...that was him.

Clunk.

Bang!

"Motherfucker." I slammed the card against the door and pushed through, finding him dragging the butt of his gun along the doors, heading toward the Daughters' rooms.

"Hey!" I barked, trying to keep it under control.

But the asshole never slowed, nor did he turn at my command. Only Coulter's fucking assholes would goddamn dare ignore me like that.

I lengthened my stride again as he neared the next set of double doors, reaching out to press his card against the scanner.

"I said, *hey!*" I roared as the asshole pushed open the double doors.

"What the fuck! Stop it! PUT THAT DOWN!" Kane's roar bloomed from his office further along the hall.

I asshole with the gun turned, holding open the door. "What?" He snarled.

A twitch came in the corner of my eye as I neared him. I lunged, grabbed his gun, and wrenched it from his grasp faster than he expected, then shoved the weapon in his face. "I hear you drag this against any fucking wall again and I'll make you eat it, you understand?"

"The fuck you DO!" Kane bellowed, drawing my focus.

I didn't have time for this asshole. I drove the gun against his chest with a brutal blow and shoved through the door, leaving the guard behind. That goddamn nerve in my temple was pulsing by the time I'd hurried to the doorway to my brother's office...and saw the carnage.

My gut clenched as I scanned the dark room. Coulter stood to the side, watching as his men tore Kane's office apart.

"What the fuck is going on here?" I barked as his men yanked the cables from the back of the desktop computer, taking the entire system toward the door.

"Exactly what it looks like." Coulter murmured. "We are taking over."

Kane's eyes were wide, his hair disheveled as he stepped in the guard's way, stopping him with a hand. "Do I at least get it back?"

The guard just looked at Coulter who gave a jerk of his head. In an instant they had destroyed everything. Files and folders were strewn across the floor. Cords had been ripped from the wall...and I couldn't do a goddamn thing about it.

"Hale is going to be fucking furious." I forced the words through clenched teeth and turned my gaze to Coulter.

The bastard had the nerve to smirk as he glanced toward Kane before turning toward the door. But Thomas was there, standing in the middle of the doorway, stopping him with his sickening, bloody stare.

Coulter met my brother's stare, then lowered his gaze to his clerical collar. "You're next, Priest."

You're next?

My jaw flared, still I did nothing as Coulter pushed through, leaving his goons to follow.

"Riven." Kane snarled.

"Easy." I warned, watching them leave.

But inside, my mind was racing. The moment we were alone, I glanced around the chaos. There was no doubt the office was bugged. I doubted there was a place in this goddamn building that wasn't...unless.

I lifted my gaze to Thomas who stared at me.

"The rectory." I muttered. *"Now."*

There was nothing we could do for Kane now, or his files. No doubt any type of effort to gain access would be met with the same warning I'd been receiving for hours...*access fucking denied.*

Kane followed as I spun toward Thomas. All three of us headed back along the corridor and turned left, making for the goddamn farce of all of this...the rectory.

The moment we pushed through the wooden double doors, the choking stench of stale air hit me. But I was beyond caring as I strode through and left Kane to come in behind.

"What the fuck are we going to do?" Kane pushed past, then turned on me, stabbing his finger toward the door. "This is out of fucking hand."

It *was* out of hand. That was putting it mildly. But right now, we had a plan we couldn't blow. "Nothing." I answered. "We do nothing."

"Nothing?" Kane snarled, his eyes wild. "That's five years of my goddamn life there."

I stepped closer, keeping my voice low. "And is that more important than our plans?"

He stilled, rage turning his light green eyes dark like emeralds.

"We have to be smart about this. Every fucking step we take is calculated. As of right now, we're flying blind here. We have no direct confirmation that Hale is in control here."

"In control?" Kane muttered, looking away in disgust. "This has his goddamn stench all over it. There's *no way in hell* he's handed over the reins to that...scumbag."

Not willingly, anyway.

The words surfaced in my mind, but I kept them to myself. The last thing I needed was my brothers panicking even more.

"So what do we do from here?" Thomas glared from me to Kane.

"We have a timeline." I murmured. "So there's nothing we can do until then."

"A timeline?" Thomas scowled. "What timeline?"

Shit, he didn't know. I lifted my hand, pressing my finger to my lips. *Shh.* Then I changed them for the number two.

"Weeks?" He mouthed.

I shook my head.

He scowled fiercely. *"Days?"*

My nod floored him. He stood there, unmoving, his gaze fixed on mine. "Then what?"

"Then we pray." I answered, knowing too well we were leaving our fate in the hands of a woman who was half out of her mind with the drugs and the programming.

"This is going to work," Thomas urged. "It has to."

It did have to...there was no other choice.

"Christ, I need a goddamn drink." Thomas turned and began to pace the floor.

"I can't argue with that." Kane muttered and headed for the door.

We all seemed to feel the same. My thoughts were so consuming, I barely felt the movement as my legs carried me through the hallways. Still, I pushed through the doors to the apartment and headed for the bar.

"What the fuck?" Kane stopped cold in the middle of the apartment, staring at the living room.

A cold, eerie feeling crept along my spine as I stepped closer.

Feet.

That's what I saw first.

Bare.

Ugly.

Fucking.

Feet.

As I took a step, more of the body was revealed, naked hairy thighs, a pale, flaccid cock.

"Oh, Jesus." Thomas groaned, staring down. "It's him...the guard."

What the fuck?

I stepped closer, seeing the ugly, deep purple marks around the swollen, distorted throat. "Sonofabitch."

Fucking Coulter.

"It's him." Kane glared my way. "It has to be. It's Coulter."

"Yeah." I grabbed my cell. "I got it."

I swiped the screen and pressed the button. I was done playing. Done waiting for that lying, sneaky motherfucker to make his move. I pressed the button for Hunter.

No service.

What?

I scowled, then pressed the button again.

No service.

I checked the number of bars, then airplane mode before I tried again.

Nothing.

"Fuck." I jerked my gaze to Kane. "Try him."

He already had his cell in his hand, pressing the button once, twice. "I got nothing."

Thomas was already trying his, shaking his head as he stabbed and stabbed. "I got nothing either."

My breaths deepened. That sickening, icy feeling that was trapped inside me turned to rage. It didn't take a genius to work out what was going on. Still, I needed to find out exactly how deep in we were here. I strode to the counter and snatched up my keys. "Wait here."

"Where are you going?" Kane bit out as I headed for the external door.

I didn't answer, because my mind was screaming. Cool night air slammed into me, shocking me back into reality. If he was taking over the compound and pushing us out, then we were in trouble. My thoughts turned to Helene. It didn't matter if we were out. If anything, I was excited about the fucking prospect...as long as we got her to Hale safely.

That's all I cared about.

But as I strode along the back of the building and headed for my car, that excitement faded, leaving the taste of ash in my mouth. Shadows moved through the trees. I felt them more than saw them, blending in with the night as they closed in.

I gripped my keys and focused on the parking lot beside the building. If our cell service was blocked and our access to the mainframe was down, then we were all alone, with no way to call anyone, not just anyone, Hunter. We had no way of calling him.

I gripped the key and pressed the button the moment my car came into view. Orange lights flared as the locks disengaged, but before I could even round the trunk, a guard stepped into view, a sniper's rifle clutched in his hand. He moved to block my way, one shake of his head, and I stopped.

"You seriously going to stop me from leaving?"

"I have my orders." He answered, his grip shifting around the gun.

I glanced at the movement, then back to that hard stare. I was sure he did, and no doubt using force to stop me from leaving was one of them. I turned around, leaving the car unlocked and strode back to the apartment.

I'd wanted to know how much trouble we were in...

Looked like I knew now.

A whole fucking lot.

THIRTY-SIX

Helene

____

We should be out by now.

That nagging feeling pushed through the fog inside my head. I turned my gaze to the section of glass in the door and slowly pushed upwards. That internal clock ticked a little louder, driving me to slide from the bed.

The guards were normally here by now, ushering us to the bathroom to shower and change before we headed to the cafeteria...and then...*and then the training room.*

OBEY.

CONTROL.

RELEASE.

I winced as the words invaded.

But there were no sounds outside my door, no barking commands of the guards or the soft padding of steps from the

Daughters. Instinctive alarm filled me as I stepped closer to the door. I reached out, grasped the handle, and pulled.

Click.

It gave way, swinging inward to leave me standing in the wash of white light from the corridor. There was no guard standing outside my door. I inched my way forward, then leaned my head out. There were no guards standing outside any door, for that matter.

Nor were there any Daughters in sight. I glanced over my shoulder to the safety of my room, then turned back. The urge to be silent and obedient was overwhelming.

Fight, Trouble.

Riven's voice filled my head.

That's it...stay in control.

I wanted to stay in control. I was desperate for it. Still, that fog in my head was like wading through mud. I forced myself to move, stepping out of the room and into the hallway. *Move. Move.* I dragged my fingers along the wall as I headed to the nearest Daughter's room.

I gripped the handle, then turned it.

Click.

Darkness waited. I pushed the door open and lifted my gaze to the curled figure on the bed. "Hurry." I croaked. "We can leave."

She rolled over, staring at me, then slowly climbed from the bed. "Leave?"

"Yes, come on." I pushed the door open wider and left, moving to the next room.

Each door I opened, each Daughter inside I called, but, they didn't step out, only lingered a step inside the room. They weren't like me. They were careful, controlled...*drugged, that's what they were.* They were drugged.

The thud of heavy steps came. I shoved backwards, scurrying for the open door of my room, eased it closed and plunged into the shadows within.

"The fuck?" The guard snarled.

With my heart in my throat, I inched my door open, straining to hear.

"Did you open this?"

My pulse was booming. I eased the door a tiny bit wider.

"You want to get out of here?" The guard's voice was bolder.

I peeked around the doorjamb to see him dragging her out by her arm. He pushed her against the wall beside the door, his hand moving from her arm to around the back of her throat. I was transfixed by the sight of him and horrified by her submission. He lowered his head, curling his spine until he nuzzled her breast. Her vacant stare was pinned on the opposite wall as a low, throaty sound came from her.

"You like that?" He bit carefully at her nipple.

"Yes." She whispered. "I like it."

He nipped harder, making her wince. "I could fuck you right here and you wouldn't even fight me, would you?"

"No." I whispered, my voice growing stronger as I stepped out into the corridor. "But I would."

She didn't look my way, didn't even turn her head. She wasn't here, not her mind, at least.

The guard narrowed his cruel stare at me. "What the hell do you think you're doing?"

Fear tore through me. In an instant, my mouth was too dry for words.

"Well?" He demanded.

"I—" I started.

"I let her out."

I jerked my gaze toward Walker as he stood inside the edge of the corridor, watching.

"You?" Coulter's guard snarled. "You were told the Daughters are off limits."

Walker just stepped forward, eyeing him until they were face to face. "The day I take orders from your boss will be the day I stop taking orders."

My breath caught as both men glared, but it wasn't long before the other guard backed down.

"How about we get you to the bathroom?" Walker murmured, never once looking away from the asshole in front of me. "Helene."

The mere mention of my name shocked me into movement. I jerked my gaze toward him, my heart hammering in the back of my throat.

"Move now." Walker growled through clenched teeth. "And take her with you."

I stepped forward, grabbed the Daughter's arm, and pulled her forward.

"Daughters!" Walker called loud enough to resound along the hall.

One by one they stepped into their doorways.

"Time for showers." Walker urged as hate rippled from the other guard's stare.

The other women spilled around them, oblivious to the standoff, and with one cautious glance at Walker, I gripped the Daughter I'd pulled into the hallway and was gone.

There were no more incidents, not when we showered or left for the cafeteria. But the tension inside was palpable. Walker and his men stood on one side of the room and Coulter's guards on the other. We sat quietly at our tables, heads down as plates of eggs and toast were placed in front of us.

My stomach clenched at the sight. I grabbed a piece of toast and nibbled the edges, watching the silent battle play out in the corner of my eye. The other Daughters were oblivious. The drugs and the mind control made them almost zombies. They ate and drank in silence, eyes down, focused on every bite.

But I felt the tension rise, especially when Riven, Kane, and Thomas stepped in, scanned the guards on each side of the room, then glanced our way. Kane moved forward, his focus skimming over me as he checked the rest of us.

"There's no training today."

I shifted my attention to one of Coulter's guards, who'd stepped forward.

"Isn't there?" Kane leveled him with a dangerous stare before turning his attention back to us.

Something had changed between them. Before, there'd been a dangerous tension, now it was something else, a chilling whisper of war waiting to be unleashed.

"Finish up." Kane commanded, looking our way.

I tossed the piece of toast to the plate, grabbed the juice, and drank before rising.

"You're to follow Walker to the audio room." Kane gave a nod to the commander. *"Now."*

The Daughters moved instantly, snapping to attention at the mere sound of his voice. He was the Master here. The one man who with a simple look made each of us sink to our knees. We'd do anything for him...and anything to him with just one whisper of those perfect lips.

My teeth scraped my lower lip as I stared at him. *Kane Cruz...* I'd seen him before when I'd been a liar sitting across from his desk. But I'd never truly *seen* him. Not like this. A surge of desire swept through my senses, cutting to the center of me like a knife.

I hadn't wanted him then, but I wanted him now.

God, I wanted him.

This wasn't supposed to happen.

His voice had trembled when he said those words. What we had was real. It wasn't the programming, or the drugs. It was real enough to scare him. I clung to that as the line of Daughters filed past, heading to the door. They all smiled at him, all looked at him with desperate longing.

My cheeks burned as I stepped into line, forcing my stare to the floor and moved out the door. He didn't look my way, and he didn't call my name. I had more important things to worry about here...like staying alive. I sure as hell didn't need my heart on the line.

Still, I couldn't stop my nostrils from flaring with jealousy as one Daughter behind me called. "Teacher?"

"Yes?" He answered.

"I—" She started.

That savage feeling only grew stronger, forcing me to stop walking and jerk a glare over my shoulder. Kane looked my way instantly as the Daughter stopped in front of him. She started talking, but he wasn't listening to a word she said. All he saw was me.

Our gazes collided, and all of a sudden, I could breathe. He scowled as I stared, then his focus dipped to my mouth and that same electric need grew between us. I licked my lip, dragging my teeth across the soft flesh, until Kane stepped forward.

"Daughter." He said huskily, drawing my focus. "Is there a problem?"

Heat rose in my cheeks as I met his stare, then shook my head. "No, sorry."

I forced myself to turn back and keep walking, heading out of the cafeteria and into the hall. The others were waiting, with Walker at the helm.

"We wait." He said carefully, glancing behind us. "Okay, let's move."

I didn't need to look behind me to know they were there. That heaviness between my legs grew as they strode past. We headed along the hallway to the auditorium, stopping outside. When the doors opened, darkness waited along with the flickering screen.

"Everyone inside." Riven urged as Kane disappeared through the doors and into the gloom.

I followed the others, stepped in, and headed for the rows of seats. But before I made it, I was grabbed and yanked to the side. A hand came over my mouth.

"Quiet." Kane growled against my ear. "We don't want them to hear, do we?"

I struggled for a second, then stilled and shook my head.

"Good little whore." He breathed hot against my ear, then stepped backwards, dragging me with him.

I couldn't see, but I didn't need to. I trusted him as I held onto his arm and followed. The brush of a hand came from in front of me and as the massive screen lit up with the words *OBEY. CONTROL. RELEASE.* I was stolen away.

But not before the Daughter who'd stopped them before glanced our way, catching us sinking behind the stage and into the back area. I was spun the moment we were out of sight and pushed gently against the wall.

"I may be a gentleman, Helene. But if you look at me like that... with the Devil in your eyes while you bite your lip like that, then we are fucking against the nearest surface I find." He let go of my arm and gently gripped my throat instead. "Do you understand me?"

Even in the darkness I saw him.

I saw *all* of them.

Kane's perfect mouth.

Riven's possessive stare.

And the white clerical collar of The Priest.

"Yes." I breathed.

Kane leaned against me and lowered his head to draw in the scent of my skin. His heavy breaths pushed against me. I lifted my gaze to his, knowing this was exactly where he wanted me, pinned against the wall with his hand around my throat. Heat bloomed between my thighs. I knew the red bodysuit I wore was already damp against my core.

"Spread them." Kane growled.

"Kane, we don't have time." Riven warned.

I glanced his way and my pulse exploded in my chest. "I need you." I whispered. "Please."

A tortured look filled his stare. The clench of his jaw followed. "Fuck it." He snarled and strode forward.

His hands weren't kind as he gripped my chin and jerked my mouth to his.

The kiss was savage and consuming...filling me with panic and desire all at once. Hard lips took my mouth, bruising my lips against my teeth until he tore free, taking a hard breath.

Riven's eyes glinted in the dark as he searched mine. "I can't fucking stand not having you, Trouble." His big hand cupped the back of my neck, his thumb brushing my cheek. "But it's getting dangerous now. You understand me, right? Those drugs, they're not..."

"I can understand you."

Pain filled him. He glanced at Kane, then turned back to me. "They're taking you tomorrow. I don't know when, or how. All I know is they are coming...and you need to be ready."

"Tomorrow?" I whispered, shaking my head. It was too soon... too...*real*. I shook my head. "No."

"Listen to me," Riven growled, searching my stare. "We will come for you. The moment we can get away, we will find you."

He lowered his hand and cupped my breast, his thumb stroking the small cut Kane had made when he'd inserted the tracker.

"Do you believe me?" His tone was desperate.

"Yes." I reached up, brushing my fingers along his cheek. "I do."

A savage, hungry sound came from him as he kissed me. It was as though a dam broke between us. Strong hands tore at the straps of my bodysuit as fingers pushed between my legs. I couldn't widen them enough.

Riven pulled away, then turned his head to Kane. "You want to touch her?"

"More than I've wanted anything in my entire life." Kane answered huskily.

"Then touch her." Riven demanded, taking a small step backwards.

Kane took a massive breath. His touch was careful at first, tentative as his brother watched.

"Get on your knees," Riven demanded. "Treat her better than I would."

"What?" Kane jerked his gaze to Riven's.

"I *said*." Riven grabbed his brother by the back of his neck and pushed, forcing him to his knees. "*Get on your goddamn knees.*"

I didn't understand what was happening. But I should have. I should've expected this and more with someone so dangerous. Riven's lips curled with a savage sneer as he leaned over and snarled. "You'd better step up, *brother*. Or you can stand by and watch while I take her for my goddamn self."

That pissed Kane off.

His lips curled and the sparkle in his eyes was just as crazed as Riven's. He licked his lips as Riven forced his brother's gaze between my legs.

"So fucking take care of her." Riven urged. "Because if you don't, then I sure as hell will."

I shook my head. "No...wait."

But there was no waiting as Riven pushed his brother's head between my legs. "Lick."

The warmth of Kane's breath was instant. I met Riven's stare. The desperate need to do whatever he wanted howled and clawed inside me.

"Open your legs for him, Trouble." Riven commanded.

As much as I wanted to fight, I couldn't. My body obeyed a new master now...and it wasn't me.

My legs widened as Kane's head was pushed harder against me. Only there was no fight from Kane, no bucking against that punishing hold. Instead, he lifted his hand and slid his fingers along my slit.

"Do it." He commanded.

Riven pushed his head harder against me. Kane dipped lower and opened his mouth.

"Helene." Riven croaked as he grabbed my chin with his other hand and pulled me forward.

Kane gripped my thighs, spreading me apart with his thumbs as he tasted more. I couldn't help but lean forward to meet Riven's mouth.

Those hard lips took everything while between my legs, Kane's tongue thrust inside. I moaned against Riven's lips. This was just like him, grinding his brother's face harder against my core as he stole my breath. I lowered one hand to Kane's head and reached for Riven with the other.

The hard licks along my slit eased. Riven's focus shifted to me, letting his brother go. He moaned into my mouth as Kane sank deeper, his hand sliding down the back of my leg, lifting until he took all he wanted. This wasn't what was supposed to happen. I was supposed to serve them.

And yet, deep down, some part of me knew this was always going to be.

Riven.

Kane.

Me.

Desire exploded with a desperate, hard suck as Kane drew my clit into his mouth. I moaned, fisted his hair and rocked my hips. Riven broke the kiss, holding my mouth against his. "Come for us, Trouble. If this moment is all we can give you right now, then come."

I closed my eyes as a pang of agony tore through my chest. But under all the pain came something deeper, something that tied us together. Something born from deception...and edged with lust. I kissed Riven, gripping his neck harder as my body took over.

"Come." Riven commanded.

Soft. *Full*. Exploding.

I drove my hips forward as Kane gripped my ass and speared his tongue inside. I moaned into Riven's mouth, coming harder than I'd ever come in my life. My body quivered. Warmth flooded every cell as Kane gave one last lick and lifted his head.

I moved from Riven's mouth and looked down to where The Teacher sat on his haunches, his mouth glistening from my desire.

"That." He started, sucking in hard breaths. "Is only a taste of what's coming." He pushed upwards, rising to tower over me. "The moment we get you out of that place, you are ours, Helene. I want you to understand that."

He looked at his brother.

But he didn't need to.

Because there was no denying what this was between us.

A deadly kind of love.

"We need to get you back to the others," Thomas croaked, standing behind his brothers.

He'd watched it all. I shifted my focus as he licked his lips and turned away.

"He's right." Kane wiped the back of his hand against his mouth, then leaned in.

I wound my arm around his shoulders, kissing him deeply... holding on for one last second before the moment was gone.

I HATED the emptiness that followed. Hated watching them as I sat in that darkened theater. Hated that they hovered just out of reach as we left and headed back to our rooms. The rest of the day passed in that ache. Every brutal throb of my heart was a reminder of all the things I'd sacrificed.

I loved my family.

I'd die for them.

And yet, this...this was almost unbearable.

The lock gave a *clunk,* and the guard stepped away. I watched the movement through the glass section of the door. *They're taking you tomorrow.* Riven's words filled me as I sat back against the cot in the middle of the room. I sat there, replaying every word he'd said. He'd been scared, maybe more scared than I'd ever seen him.

That alone was terrifying.

The lights flickered overhead before they were gone, plunging me into darkness.

Fear followed, shaking me back into the present.

This didn't usually happen.

Not like this and not this early.

I pushed forward, taking a step toward the door. The sound of heavy steps followed along the hallway, *thud...thud...thud...*

They're taking you tomorrow.

My stomach clenched. Something was wrong...something was very wrong.

Bang!

I flinched at the sound of a gunshot and lunged forward, watching the guard outside my door stumble backward in the hallway. Blood bloomed in the center of his chest.

I slammed my hands against the door as movement came. Two of Coulter's guards strode forward as one lifted the gun in his hand and took aim.

Bang!

Walker's guard slumped to the floor, lying across the doorway to my room.

But it was the chilling stare of the other which found me as they both lifted their gazes to mine.

"Get her." The one with the gun commanded.

And the other moved, snatched the keys from the dead guard's belt, and reached for the door.

"No." I shook my head and stumbled backwards as the lock gave way with a *click*. "No...no...NO!"

THIRTY-SEVEN

Helene

"No...*NO!*" I screamed and scrambled backwards.

But that didn't stop them.

They spilled through the doorway, spreading out like a plague as they came for me. One had a syringe and a gun in his hands, the other had both open as he reached for me.

"No fighting now." He grunted before he lunged.

But I did fight, drawing on that desperate need to survive. He lunged for me and I clenched my fist then swung, giving it my all.

My knuckles hit warm flesh as the blow collided with his cheek. His head snapped sideways, causing him to stumble slightly before he caught himself. When he turned back, his gaze was savage.

Terror gripped me. I shook my head and scanned the room, desperately searching for a weapon. But there was nothing, just a plastic jug and a cup. I grabbed what I could and threw my pillow at him before I pitched the jug of water at his head.

He ducked, letting the jug fly past and hit the wall. Water dribbled down as I spun and raced for the doorway. But the other one was there, lunging to grab me around the waist and lift my feet from the floor.

Instinct kicked in, making me yank my feet up before I drove one back, slamming my heel against his shin. He let me go with a roar and I dropped to the floor. Only this time I didn't run. I turned on him and snapped my fist out to connect with his nose.

Crunch.

His head jerked backwards and those dark eyes were dazed as I drew my arm back again...until a sting came at my other shoulder. The plunger was fast. I shoved backwards, swinging around and slashing my hands through the air like a wounded animal. Because that's what I was at that moment.

Cornered.

Frightened.

And alone.

"Easy now." The guard with the syringe urged. "They told us you'd fight."

I shook my head as the sight of him blurred when he took a step toward me. My pulse skipped while terror howled inside me.

"No." I slurred. *"No."*

Darkness rose, stealing my movement as the guard I'd punched came closer. Still, I forced myself to lift my head as he neared.

He swiped the back of his hand under his nose, then swung his arm back, arcing through the air.

I was too weak to fight.

Or move.

Slap!

I stumbled sideways as agony ripped through my skull. My hair lashed my face, covering the movement. But it didn't matter, not as the drug they'd injected warped my mind. Warmth slid from my nose as the room swayed and I was yanked forward.

"*No!*" I bucked, trying to fight as he picked me up and hauled me over his shoulder, carrying me out of the room like a sack over his shoulder.

"*Stop.*" I clawed the doorway, but we were gone, stepping over the dead guard as we left.

Blood splatter was neon red all around me. It marred the walls and the floor as Coulter's guard left track marks in his wake.

"*No!*" I bucked as he carried me along the corridor and turned. "*NOOO!*"

I fought, kicking and thrashing until he yanked me down. Agony burst through my feet and speared up my legs as they hit the floor. There was nothing I could do as my knees buckled and I fell to the floor. His hand was in my hair in an instant, yanking me upwards.

Tears came, blurring his face along with the drug.

"Fight me again and I'll knock you out and do whatever the hell I want with you. How does that sound?"

The words chilled me all the way to the bone.

I stilled, and slowly lifted my tear-filled eyes to his.

"That's what I thought."

My searing scalp pulsed as he released his hold on my hair and lifted me over his shoulder again. I couldn't fight him anymore. Instead, I held on as the drug slammed into me and I was carried along the hallway toward the conference rooms.

The two-way crackled and Walker's roar was deafening until the guard reached down and switched it off. "No one is going to save you anymore." He muttered and turned along a small corridor.

The faint sound of voices spilled out as a door opened, and I was carried inside. But those voices soon quieted as my attacker pulled me down off his shoulder and steadied me when my feet hit the floor.

They surrounded the massive table. All the commanders...and Coulter himself.

It was that same sickening stare that had found me before as he slowly rounded the edge of the table and came toward me.

The door closed with a *thud*.

My heart sank to the floor.

"Strip her." Coulter demanded.

I didn't have one to fight or even two, four of them came for me, yanking the straps of the red bodysuit and tearing the lace until there was nothing left. I screamed, slapping their hands, clawing what I could, until I was bare.

Until there was nothing left.

I wrapped my arms over my body, covering as much as I could as Coulter lowered his gaze, taking in every inch of me. "You are a goddamn masterpiece, aren't you?"

A sickened, choked sound ripped from me.

"Do you think I'm stupid?" He murmured and stepped closer. "A fool, perhaps? Do you think I don't notice the way they are around you? The looks, the subtle touches." He met my gaze. "He's marked you as his, I know it."

I flinched from his touch as he brushed a strand of my hair, his voice so calm. "And for that alone, I want to destroy you. Get her onto the table."

I bucked as the guards grabbed my wrists and lifted me.

"NO! NOOO!" I screamed until fire lashed my throat and then punched my feet out, thrashing in their hold as I was lifted and slammed onto the hard table.

Stars danced in my eyes as I was yanked down toward the edge.

"Hold her wrists and ankles." Coulter growled as the sound of a zip came. "You can all have what's left."

Cheers filled the room. Roars of *"Fuck yes!"* drove searing acid into the back of my throat.

"No...no...nonono...NOOOOOO!" I howled, wrenching my gaze to each one, desperate to find *someone* who'd stop this. *Please...please, don't do this!*

But there was no one.

Their grins.

Their excitement.

Was everywhere.

I wasn't someone to save here. Not like their wives, or their girlfriends, or their mothers. No, I was a *thing* to be used.

And I couldn't fight them all.

Their hands were steel shackles around my wrists, forcing my fists above my head. I slammed my feet against the table as they dragged me all the way to the bottom, kicking out as much as I could. The thud of my blows warbled, turning distorted and strange.

Faces moved in and out of focus. The burn of the table against my back from where they'd dragged me. The tear of tendons as they forced my legs open.

But it was the lights overhead I felt the most.

The blinding glare buzzed and stung as shadows moved around me, brushing the insides of my thighs. Hands touched me, mauling my breasts, parting my slit.

"Oh fuck, that's what we want." One of them moaned.

But those lights above me hummed loudly, growing more insistent as their fingers pushed in. I focused on that buzzing as it became a roar.

Whoosh...whoooosh...who-o-shhh my pulse became distant.

A tug came.

Followed by a *pushhh*.

Those lights above bounced...thrusting...throbbing and that push turned brutal. Pain followed, pain and the movement of my legs, lifting, stretching as wide as they could go...but those lights above ignited, turning blinding.

Grunts followed the violent movements.

But they were faint.

So faint I barely heard them at all.

Something cool slipped down my cheek, the slick trail turned cold in its wake. I tracked the sensation as the hold around my wrists clenched tighter as the wetness raced for my ear and slipped inside.

"I'll make sure there's nothing left by the time the truck comes tomorrow." Someone said.

But I didn't care anymore.

Because I wasn't here.

Not in this room.

Or this building.

Or this body.

I was long gone.

THIRTY-EIGHT

Riven

I swallowed that first lick of heat, closing my eyes as the Scotch raced down my throat and spread through my body. Fuck Coulter. Fuck him and Harmon and Hale and every other sick motherfucker that didn't deserve to take another goddamn breath.

The moment Helene was on that goddamn truck, we were out of here. I could finally get on with my life...what was left of it, at least. My thoughts turned to the future, to the one I hadn't planned on. A flicker of jealousy flared as I glanced at my brother.

I wanted to go back to the house in the city, and to the place I'd known Helene best. Would she come back to me after this was all over? Or would I open the door to my brother's apartment and find her there?

A wince tore through me.

"All my fucking work *gone*." Kane groaned and swallowed his drink.

It was the same thing I'd heard for hours.

His work.

His data.

His years.

I came back into my body at the faint crackle of the two-way, but the volume was low and the call garbled. I ignored it.

Beep.

"What the fuck now." I muttered and grabbed my cell.

Words danced across the screen. Words I didn't quite understand. Time slowed, seconds became an eternity as I swiped my thumb across the screen and opened my messages.

Walker: THEY HAVE HELENE! GET HERE NOW!

"They have—" I started, and the glass fell from my hand.

I was already turning as the *crash* came when it hit the floor. Already lunging toward the counter to grab my gun.

"What the fuck?" Kane called. *"What is it? Riven...RIVEN!"*

My steps were too slow. My pulse too quiet as I gripped the weapon and punched through the doors. The bright corridors blurred.

They have Helene!

THEY HAVE HELENE!

My cell rang. I answered instantly, barking down the line as I headed through the first lot of doors and out into the hallway. "The trucks are supposed to come *tomorrow!*"

I slammed my access card on the scanner and pushed through before I ran.

"It's not the truck."

I slowed at the next doors, slammed my card once more and waited for the lock to release for me to punch through.

Red.

I hit the door on instinct. *Boom!* The lock didn't release, causing me to bounce off the door. *"Fuck!"* I stepped back, slamming the card against the reader once more.

Red.

Again.

Red.

"What do you mean, *it's not the trucks?*"

"There's been no trucks through the gate." Walker grunted as he panted. *"Jesus fucking Christ.* Stevens is dead. They put a fucking bullet in his brain. There's—hold on—"

The low creak of a door echoed, followed by the thud of his steps. "There's a sign of a struggle in her room."

"A struggle?" I repeated, my voice low.

The words resounded in my brain...*a struggle.*

I turned back to the scanner and drove my card against it once more.

Red.

Red.

Red.

"I can't get in." I lifted my gaze to the doors. *"I CAN'T FUCKING GET IN!"*

"What do you mean?"

I stared at those doors as the thud of steps came behind me. "They revoked my fucking access." I answered and lunged at the doors, throwing my shoulder against them. *"They FUCKING REVOKED MY ACCESS!"*

"Riven!" Kane roared. "What the fuck is going on?"

I couldn't answer, just stabbed my finger at the scanner. "Open the goddamn door!"

He looked at me, then thrust his card against the same device. Still, the scanner glowed red.

"Walker." I gasped desperately. "We can't get in."

"Hold on." He grunted, sucking in hard breaths. "I'm on my way to you."

"Riven!" Kane barked. "What the *hell* is going on?"

I didn't want to say it. Because if I did, then it'd make it real. Instead, I shook my head and gripped the gun. "When we get there, stay out of my fucking way."

Movement came through the glass in the doors up ahead. Walker was a blur, barreling through the doors to shove them open.

"Hale's office. *Now!*" I roared.

We all ran. Walker charging ahead to open the doors, leaving us to follow barely a step behind. But the moment I neared the wing of offices, I felt that emptiness. I slammed against the handles as Walker hit the locks. The door flew open, hitting with a *crash.*

But it was empty and silent.

"They're not here." I swivelled around, my mind racing.

Images flickered. Coulter and his men were around the conference table. A choked sound ripped free as I strode forward and snatched Walker's card from his hand. I knew instantly that's where they were.

Hold on, Trouble, I pleaded. *I'm coming.*

My erratic pulse slowed as an eerie calm washed over me. I ran, driving my boots against the floor, and headed for the conference room.

"*Fuck. That's it!*" A grunt billowed out.

"*I'm next.*" Another snarled as I stumbled inside the room.

My mind froze. Men stood around the table. Coulter stood off to the side. His shirt was open, his pants, too. *Why was his fucking pants open?*

A guard thrust into something at the end of the table and as he groaned, he moved...then I saw her. Splayed out, her hands pinned to the table by two of the other commanders.

Rage moved through me.

Rage like I'd never felt in my life.

There was no room for thought. Only instinct as I lifted the gun, stepped forward, and took aim.

Bang!

Blood and brains kicked out from the fucking animal inside her, and his body followed.

I was cold.

So fucking cold...when I lunged and grabbed the bastard who held one wrist. My hands didn't shake, not when I drove the butt of the gun into his nose, hard enough to stun him with a *crack*. His head snapped backwards and blood shot out, spurting over my hands as I forced his head against the table.

"YOU GET THE FUCK OFF HER!" I screamed.

I couldn't stop.

That howling need inside me was all there was.

Bang!

His body jerked and blood splattered the table and her arms.

I was already lifting my gun to the piece of shit on the other side as roars came all around me in the room.

Walker was a blur, charging forward to slam against Coulter's guard as I lifted my gun and took aim at the dead man who held her other wrist down.

"I didn't." He shook his head and lifted his hands.

Bang!

I didn't care.

Not anymore.

Because he would have...I sucked in hard breaths and spun, catching as Walker shoved the muzzle of his gun in Coulter's guard's face.

"One fucking move and I'll blow your goddamn head off." Walker promised.

"YOU get the FUCK AWAY FROM HER!" I bellowed and aimed around the room, stepping closer to the motionless form on the table.

She was naked, her legs stretched wide, and there was blood...

Revulsion burned as I forced my gaze away. Narrowing in on Coulter. He never moved, just watched this all play out as Kane came through the door.

"Jesus Christ." Walker groaned, finding her on the table, then glared around the room. *"YOU FUCKING DID THIS? YOU GODDAMN ANIMALS!"*

No.

I sucked in hard breaths, finding the glint of amusement in Coulter's stare.

He did.

He lowered his gaze to her lying naked, spread out on the table. "Looks like this one isn't worth the two million after all."

My lips curled.

Black was all I saw.

The color of his eyes.

The cold, hard obsidian of my heart.

The gaping hole of my future where I died murdering every single one of these bastards. It'd be worth it.

I lifted my gun, took a step, and aimed.

He never even looked at the weapon, transfixed instead by my pain as though it was his entertainment.

"I will kill you." Rage shook my voice. "I will kill every last one of you."

"Riven." Walker tugged my arm. "Come on, we need to get her out of here."

He was right. He was...right.

I scanned the room, etching every fucking stare into my mind before I made for the motionless figure on the table.

Kane was already talking to her, opening her eyes, finding her pupils slow. He winced as he looked down. Blood and bite marks marred her body, but I couldn't look at them.

Not yet.

Not without spilling more blood.

Come dripped between her legs. The glistening mess shimmered in the corner of my eye as I reached under her legs. "Get her a blanket or something, for Christ's sake." I snapped.

Walker spun around, but Kane was already tearing the buttons of his shirt free and wrapping it across her. I met his gaze briefly, finding his shell-shocked stare before I looked away. "She needs the infirmary."

She needed a lot more than the help of doctors and the nursing staff, but right now, that was our only option. I handed my gun to Walker before I lifted her and pulled her body against me.

She'd held on...

But I hadn't been there.

The words detonated inside me as I carried her from that room and back out into the hallway. Walker strode ahead, slapping his access card against the scanners as we went.

Coulter had set this up from the very beginning.

The files on the drive.

The locked doors.

All designed not just to drive us out...but away from her.

"Whatever happens after this, I want that motherfucker to pay." I murmured as I turned and headed for the banks of medical beds. "And I want to be the one to do it."

Two of the male nurses rose from their seats in the nursing station and headed our way. But Kane just shook his head and turned around. "Just point me toward your antiseptics and scrubs."

One lifted his hand and pointed, kicking my brother into action. He moved fast, gathering what he needed as I shifted my attention back to her.

I didn't want to lay her down, not yet. I wanted to hold her against me forever, anything so I didn't have to look into those vacant eyes anymore and see what those monsters had done to her.

Monsters like me.

I winced, holding her carefully, my voice husky as I said. "You're okay now. You hear me, Helene? You're okay."

She never responded, not even to moan as I eased her against the cold sheets. If it wasn't for the steady rise and fall of her chest, I would've thought she was dead.

Maybe right now she wanted to be.

The words stuck in the back of my throat as I eased away. She stared with that soul-crushing vacant expression, not even flinching when I brushed the hair from her face. "Trouble." I whispered. "Can you hear me?"

I'd take her fists more than this.

Her screams.

Her clawing nails.

Just not this fucking silence.

My hands curled into fists. I closed my eyes as that punishing agony ripped me apart on the inside.

"Okay." Kane urged, coming closer. "Let me tend to her."

I didn't want to let her go. Not even for him. I opened my eyes and met his stare.

"I have to see to her injuries, brother." He said quietly.

He knew. He knew what she meant to me. As I searched his agonized stare, I knew she meant the same to him. With a slow nod, I pulled away, glancing over my shoulder to Thomas and Walker.

They said nothing, just watched until Kane pulled his shirt away from her body. Then both of them turned around.

"I'll see to Stevens." Walker muttered, before he glanced over his shoulder at her. "Goddamn them to hell for this."

He left then, hanging his head low as he disappeared. The splash of liquid followed the sound of tearing plastic. It seemed like only yesterday we were doing this exact thing when we implanted the tracking device under her breast.

I'd held her then, and kissed her to take her mind off the pain.

But I couldn't kiss her now.

"Jesus." Kane moaned and hissed.

My stomach was a stone. Still, I forced myself to turn around to her. I forced myself to look.

Every bite mark was wiped with iodine. Every torn skin was cleaned and taped. Kane worked quietly, his hands gentler than I'd ever seen before.

One nurse came closer. "Can I help, Doctor?"

"No." His tone was bitter. "This one is ours."

The nurse backed away, and I moved closer, reaching for her hands.

"She has broken nails." He started. "Internal bruising from their fists." He sucked in a hard breath and moved to the bottom of the bed before he gently lifted one leg, easing it to the side. "Easy now." He murmured. "I just need to look, baby, that's all."

It was pointless to speak. She couldn't hear us. She barely existed.

"She can hear you, you know." He said carefully. "Talk to her."

"And what the fuck am I supposed to say?" I snapped.

He met my stare. "You can start with the truth. But know this, whatever you do and say will write the course of your relationship. Hell, it'll write the course of ours. She'll remember these words forever...or until they destroy her."

I jerked my gaze to hers.

Destroy her?

Rage punched all the way through me. If I could murder those bastards all over again, I would. I would murder them all. "It's too much." I croaked, shaking my head. "It's too much for her to bear."

"It is." He answered. "So, what are you going to do about it?"

What was I going to do about it? I took a step closer and reached out, carefully taking her hand in mine. "Whatever she needs me to do."

Kane said nothing, just worked quietly, checking her over as softly as he could. "There's tearing, but it's minimal, considering."

I swallowed the revulsion that rose. "At least that's something."

I gazed at her wide, staring eyes. "I'm right here, trouble. I'm right here whenever you're ready."

A tear slipped from the corner of her eye and raced down her temple. But I was there to capture it, smoothing the wetness with the brush of my thumb.

"I will make them pay for what they did to you. Every. Single. One. Of. Them." I whispered, staring into those dark brown eyes.

She turned her head. Her eyes bored into mine. "And what about what you've done? What revenge will you enact for yourself?"

I couldn't answer.

I couldn't breathe.

Because I was shattering on the inside.

Shredding my soul apart in a million little slivers.

"I will stay." I croaked. "I will look you in the eyes every step of the way. I'll hold your bruised hands. I'll tend to your wounds. I'll love you as much as you'll let me."

I waited for her to say something that'd ease the gaping hole inside me. But she didn't. Instead, she closed her eyes and her breaths slowed.

She slept.

While I waited.

Her hold eased around mine.

Still, I held on, not moving from her bedside.

When she woke screaming an hour later, I was there, smoothing her hair. Telling her how much I loved her, and after an hour of rocking her against me, she fell back to sleep...

Only to wake fighting for her life once more.

She cried.

She hit.

She bucked and thrashed in my arms.

She screamed until her voice was hoarse and there were only gasping howls of air left.

Still, I never moved.

Because I finally saw.

I saw the devastation, the ruination...and the battle I'd never seen before.

And I hated myself more than ever.

THIRTY-NINE

Helene

____

Get her on the table.

No.

No!

NOO!

GET OFF ME. GET OFF ME. GETOFFMEGETOFFMEGETOFFME!

I jerked awake, slashing and kicking with all I had.

"Easy now." The familiar hoarse voice filled my ears. "It's me. It's Riven. I got you, trouble. Hold on to me. I got you."

I did, clawing him closer until his warmth was all I knew. I buried my head against his neck and drew in the heavy scent of sweat and pain, faintly laced with the cologne he wore. My throat burned, scalding with every savage rasp of my breath... and still I felt them.

Their hands all over my body.

Their thrusts between my thighs.

I closed my eyes. "I couldn't fight them all...I tried, but I couldn't fight them all."

Silence followed, before a husky, "You survived and that's all that matters. You hear me? You fucking survived."

He softly gripped my chin and lifted my gaze to his. "If I could kill them all again, I would."

Faded memories rose up.

His wide, shell-shocked stare. His lips curled in hatred.

Bang!

The echoes of his gunshots resounded.

He'd killed...for me. Still, it wasn't enough, was it?

I held his stare and pulled away.

"Please." He held on, desperately pulling me back to him. "Hate me. Hit me. Whatever you need to unleash that pain, just whatever you need to do...just do it to me."

I shook my head as fresh tears sprang to my eyes.

Still, he held on, triggering that pain and panic and revulsion inside me. I bucked, fighting against his hold, and swung my hand, hitting his cheek with a *crack! "WHERE WERE YOU!"*

His head snapped to the side before he slowly turned back. It was those dark eyes I hated. Those dark eyes filled with so much pain. I hit him again and pummeled my fists against his chest until I had nothing left.

"Hate me." He whispered. "But know this, it's nothing compared to how much I hate myself."

I drew in heavy breaths and stared at him.

The truth raged in his stare.

I knew he meant it.

"Walker is going to take you out of here, whatever it takes. I'll have him take you back to...London...or the Banks, whatever you need."

London.

The Banks.

My sisters.

I closed my eyes as reality slammed into me. For a while, I'd forgotten who I was here. I'd forgotten everything. My family, plan...my purpose.

Riven brushed the hair from my face. "No one will touch you, Helene. Not anymore."

But if we did that, then it would all be over, all my sisters had been through...and now, all I'd endured, would mean nothing. They'd win—Coulter's dark eyes and cruel smirk rose in my head—just like they always won.

"No." The word tore free before I realized it. "No."

He scowled. "What?"

I met that stare. "I said, no. I'm not leaving."

Rage ripped across his face. This time, he was the one who pushed away from me. Kane stood at the foot of the bed, staring at me. Still, he offered his brother no support as Riven jerked a glare his way.

"No *fucking way!*" He shoved up from the bed and turned to pace the room. "I'm *not having it. I'm not allowing you to be here with THEM for another second.*"

I waited while he raged, throwing his hands in the air as he stalked the room, shooting savage glares at his silent brother. Then when he stopped and stood there.

"I'm not leaving." I repeated and the more I said the words, the stronger I became. "I'm not letting this all be for nothing. We're finishing this, once and for all."

There was confusion in his stare, anger and desperation as he searched my eyes. Then, slowly, there was a flicker of pride. "Think about this," He pleaded. "You're going to walk back in there and pretend this never happened?"

"No." I whispered, my thoughts far away. "I'm going to make him see exactly what he's done...and what he didn't do."

I came back to my senses and reached down, yanking back the sheets on the bed before I froze.

My body was a mess of betadine smears, tiny band-aid strips, and, under all that, bruising and bite marks.

"I need a shower." I whispered. "Please help me."

Riven turned to Kane.

"There's one in the back of the infirmary." Kane stepped closer, snatching the sheet from the bed.

"Can you get her something to wear?" Riven added. "And not that fucking bodysuit."

Kane gave a careful nod. His blue eyes connected with mine. After all I'd been through last night, I still remembered how gentle he had been.

She can hear you, you know. Talk to her.

Kane's voice echoed back to me.

And what the fuck am I supposed to say?

The truth.

That's what he'd said. Riven could start with the truth...and wasn't that all we'd ever wanted?

I took the sheet from Kane's outstretched hand. "Thank you."

He gave me a soft smile, one that wasn't full of sorrow or pity, before he gave me a wink, then turned around and strode from the room.

"Come on." Riven was there, sliding his hand around my waist before he helped me rise from the bed and wrap the sheet around my body.

"Shower." He snapped at the nurse.

The poor guy just lifted his hand and pointed to a small hallway at the end of the bay. The nurse watched me as I took a step and winced at the deep flare of agony that ripped through my body. I gave a moan and reeled, reaching for the railing.

"Turn your goddamn head." Riven warned as he gripped me and we tried again. "While you have a goddamn head."

The nurse turned away instantly, his cheeks reddening.

"You know, you don't have to threaten to murder everyone who looks my way." I groaned, gripping him as he helped me walk toward the hallway.

"Yes, I do."

A smile rose, alien and gruesome. Still, it was a smile.

He led me to the small block of showers, holding me while he kicked off his boots and tore off his socks. The hot water was slow to come, but eventually steamed up the stall. Riven unwound the sheet from my body and gently helped me inside.

I hissed at the sting of the water, one knee buckling until the heat worked its way through all my aches.

"Hold on to the wall." He murmured. "Let me wash you."

I did, placing my hands against the cold tiles. He was gentle, using the medicated soap on the washcloth to wash my arms and then my back, slowly working his way to the front.

It's too much for her to bear.

Riven's faint words echoed.

So, what are you going to do about it? His brother asked.

Whatever she needs me to do.

I looked into his eyes as he ran the cloth over my breasts and down my sides, gently skirting the torn skin and deep bruising. A deep pang of need rose inside me, one akin to the desperate longing I'd had for my sisters. Only this time, it was different.

My fingers trembled, aching to reach up and touch him. But that wasn't what he needed. Instead, I closed my eyes, letting the heat wash down my back.

"Trouble." He murmured. "I need to wash between your legs."

Get her on the table.

Fuck, that's it...that's exactly what we want.

I closed my eyes as my body shook uncontrollably. A low, sickened sound ripped free when he carefully eased the cloth against the sting.

"Trouble?" He froze as the shaking turned violent. "It's me. It's just me. I'm not going to hurt you. I'm not ever going to hurt you. Can you hear me, baby?"

He lifted his hand away and rose, his hand so gentle as it skimmed my shoulder, carefully pulling me against his chest. My teeth chattered, gnashing and clashing.

"I was thinking about a trip to Morocco after all this is over. Somewhere hot. Maybe even Australia? What do you think about that?"

"Th-they have s-snakes." I opened my eyes and looked up at him.

"And spiders bigger than your head," His eyes bored into mine. "As well as crocodiles and sharks that snatch you out of the water before you even realize it. But I figured after this place, Australia sounds like a walk in the fucking park."

The corner of my lips quivered. "You're r-right. Aust-ra-lia s-sounds almost a little too e-easy."

He grinned, even if was a little sad.

"Here we go." Kane called, making us jump.

I looked at his hands, and saw the oatmeal-colored sweats he had and a red t-shirt.

"It's the best I could do."

"It's fine." I rushed, meeting his stare.

I didn't care what it was, as long as it wasn't lace and see through. Riven hit the faucets to end the spray and grabbed a towel, before handing another to his brother. There was a second before Kane nodded, took the towel, and helped his brother dry my body.

"Just to let you know," Riven started. "We're all going to Australia after this."

Kane stopped wiping. "We are?"

"Yeah." Riven snapped. "We are and every other fucking place determined to kill us."

Kane's brows rose. "Whatever you need."

I think the need was more for Riven than it was for me.

I didn't need to walk through the fire...because I was already rising from the ashes.

"Okay." Kane knelt, holding open the sweats for me.

I pulled them and the t-shirt on, tugging out my damn hair. I felt almost normal. If it wasn't for the deep throbbing aches in my body and the searing fire in the back of my throat, I might've pretended last night hadn't happened.

But I couldn't.

None of us could.

Beep.

Riven grabbed his cell and looked down. "The trucks are coming through the gates." He lifted his gaze to me. "After the Daughters are finished in the cafeteria, they'll be starting the transport process."

I thought my heart was going to burst through my chest. "Then I guess we'd better head to the cafeteria."

He winced, then stopped. "Are you sure about this?"

"No." I answered truthfully, and turned around. "But I'll be fucked if I allow them the satisfaction of not looking me in the eye."

Riven stepped forward and grabbed my face in both hands. "I've known more than my fair share of killers, but you, at this moment, are by far the strongest person I've ever known. You want to go to finish this, then let's finish it. I'll be right behind you, every damn step of the way."

He might be a little slow upstairs.

But he was finally catching on.

I gave a nod, fighting the urge to flinch when he eased forward and kissed my lips gently, then dropped his hold.

I met Kane's stare and returned the small smile before I took the biggest step of my life and headed for the doorway. My legs trembled, but they held as I slowly made my way out of the infirmary and back along the hall.

The faint sound of voices spilled out as I braced my hand on the wall and turned the corner.

Heads turned toward me when I entered, from the Daughters as well as the guards. Walker was there, not bothering to hide his smirk as he watched me straighten my spine.

People speak of hope as though it's a fragile thing, one made of thoughts and fucking prayers. But there's not much talk about spite. No, spite wiped the blood from her face with the back of her hand and locked her knees in place...right before she met her attacker in the eye.

That's exactly what I did, forcing each step as I crossed the space to stop in front of Coulter as he stood with arms crossed amongst his men. Every cell in my body was screaming for me to run.

But I didn't.

I lifted my gaze and met that cold, amused stare. "You were just how I figured you would be." I murmured. A sting came as my lip freshly split with the effort. "Small and insignificant. I barely felt a thing."

There was a twitch in the corner of his eye, and that amusement died away, revealing the cold, stony rage he hid inside.

There were damaged, desperate men like Riven and his brothers...and then there were true monsters, men whose souls were snatched from their bodies by fate just before they were born to this world. Those men were a magnet for the depraved, a hunter for the weakened, an addict for sickening pleasure.

And that's who I saw then.

"Daughter." Walker called carefully, not only reminding me of his presence, but Coulter as well. "Your food is getting cold."

I glanced toward the commander, gave a slow nod, then turned.

Spite lived inside me.

She raged.

She howled.

And she survived.

FORTY

Riven

—————

Jesus Christ, she was incredible. I stood inside the door of the cafeteria as she stared the bastard down. It took all my goddamn strength not to cross the floor and drive his head into the floor in front of her...until *his* vacant stare was the one I looked into.

I wanted that...

More than I wanted anything in my life.

I fixed my focus on her, my fists clenched by my sides. One look from him...that's all it'd take. One goddamn look and I'd burn it all to the ground and him along with it. All I saw was that smirk in my head. That *vicious* fucking sneer he'd given me after I'd found her last night.

Looks like this one wasn't worth the two million after all.

His words resounded.

Revulsion spilled like acid into the back of my throat as I focused on the defiance in her eyes. She worked her mouth, then spat, unleashing a glistening wad of spittle onto his cheek. I'd stare at that fire in her eyes all goddamn day if I could, even if it burned. She turned then, not giving the bastard another second, and slowly limped to the vacant seat at one of the Daughters' tables. It hurt her. Fuck, it hurt her.

Walker stood there, staring the bastard down.

Not worth the two million?

He was so very wrong.

She was worth far more than that.

She was worth everything.

I took a step, drawing Coulter's focus. His eyes blazed with rage as he swiped the mess on his cheek and I almost wanted to laugh. He thought he'd broken her. He thought he'd won. But he hadn't come fucking close. I glanced around the room as one of the Daughters rose from her seat, her gaze fixed on Helene, before she jerked a glare to Coulter and the others.

The longer I stared, the more I saw. There wasn't just one of the Daughters affected by what they'd done to Helene. They'd all seen. Quiet, simmering anger burned in their eyes. To entice and bend with desire was one thing, but violence? That would shatter any connection we'd started.

The programming wasn't finished, nor would it stay embedded in their minds.

Coulter was about to place a fuckload of ticking timebombs on his truck and deliver those ruined 'assets' to Hale.

I. Couldn't. Fucking. Wait.

I shifted my attention to Helene as she speared a forkful of eggs into her mouth, then ravaged a piece of toast. Eggs she hated, butter she despised. Still, she ate and drank.

Beep.

I scowled and looked down. A chill crept along my spine the moment I saw the *H*.

My breath caught as I swiped the screen and stared at the message.

"Let's go, wrap it up." One of Coulter's commanders barked.

But I was fixed on the message on the screen.

H: Thanks for doing all the dirty work, Principal.

Chairs scraped and footsteps sounded under the insistent direction of the guards.

"Riven?" Walker called.

"I'll be there as soon as I can." I muttered, not really listening.

Thanks for doing all the dirty work?

What the fuck did that mean? My pulse pounded as I focused on those words until they blurred. That chill moved deeper until a splitting spear plunged deeper. Something was happening here, something I was on the verge of understanding.

The message was from Hale.

That I knew.

Or was it?

Goosebumps raced along the back of my neck. That same eerie feeling found me now as it had when the cleaners had come to my apartment. Was this really Hale? I stared at the message as instinct howled, making me swipe out of it and type a message to the only person who could help us now.

I think we're in trouble. I need help. NOW.

I hit send and waited for a second, but then a red warning light appeared.

Message failed to send.

"What the fuck?" My breaths raced as I pressed the button again...and again...and again.

Each time, the red message glowed.

"Terrible reception we're having at the moment."

I jerked my head up as Coulter just smirked and walked past. The cafeteria was empty now, the Daughters long gone. The sight of those empty seats shocked me back to reality. They were gone...*they were gone!*

I spun around, but found nothing but the fading sound of Coulter's steps. I yanked my cell upward and stared at the screen, then started walking.

They were blocking the calls and the messages.

But why?

The truck.

The Daughters.

Helene.

I lunged, tearing around the corner as the first set of double doors closed with a *click*. Coulter glanced over his shoulder, giving me that goddamn smirk as I slammed Walker's card against the scanner.

Red.

Red.

RED!

"No!" I roared, staring through the glass as that bastard turned back around and kept walking.

I lunged, slammed Walker's card against the scanner, and again it turned red.

"Fuck!" I punched the goddamn thing and spun, desperately searching for a way through.

The external doors. They were on a different circuit. Maybe they still worked?

I spun around and lunged, driving myself back to the cafeteria. The empty room was terrifying as I raced past the counter and toward the staff.

"GET OUT OF THE WAY!" I roared and shoved past.

Get to the truck.

GET TO THE GODDAMN TRUCK!

I slammed the card against the external door scanner.

Green.

Click.

I punched the handle and barged out into the glaring sun. The light was blinding. I yanked my hand up to shield my eyes as I waited for them to adjust.

"Fuck!" My steps were too goddamn slow as I ran along the length of the building.

The closer I came to the corner, the louder the truck's engine rumbled. By the time I hurled myself around the corner, the Daughters were already being loaded.

"Wait!" I roared, lifting my gaze to the guards herding them from the loading dock.

She wasn't there...she wasn't—*WHERE THE FUCK WAS SHE?*

I slammed my hand against the platform and leaped, hauling myself upwards. "You need to stop this!" I roared, fighting to be heard over the roar of the rumbling engine.

Coulter just gave a nod to the guard gripping the arm of a Daughter as he pushed her toward the truck's open loading door.

"You're making a fucking *mistake!*" I stepped in front of them and jerked my gaze over my shoulder, scanning the faces already inside, and turned back to Coulter. "They aren't ready."

"They're ready enough." He muttered as his men moved in, pushing the remaining women into the back.

I jerked my gaze to Kane and Walker, but they were too busy staring at all of Coulter's guards who seemed to come from nowhere.

Thud!

The rear door slammed closed.

"You ruined them!" I stabbed my finger at the truck, desperate to stop this. "You think Hale's men are going to pay millions for a woman with her goddamn mind broken?"

Coulter just looked my way. "Hale and his pathetic list of buddies? You think too small, Principal." He muttered and gave a nod to his man. "That won't be an issue at all."

That won't be an issue?

"Why?" I jerked my gaze to the truck. The *hiss* of the airbrakes sounded before it pulled away. That icy chill at the back of my neck screamed like a banshee.

Deep down, some part of me knew this was all wrong.

Every.

Goddamn.

Second.

Of.

It.

Bang!

I jerked as a blast came from behind me.

Bang!

Bang!

Walker roared, charging forward as another *boom* sounded and one of our guards dropped to the concrete floor in front of me. He slammed into Coulter's man, grabbed his hand, and drove his weapon upwards.

Kane lunged with a roar, slamming into the guard standing behind Thomas...pointing a gun at his head.

The ratchet of a shotgun being loaded sounded as a *crack* came. The spray of blood was instant, splattering my face as I spun to stare down the barrel of a gun. From the corner of my eye, one more guard dropped at my feet.

"On your knees," Coulter demanded, meeting my stare.

I shook my head. That screaming in my head was desperate for me to fight and kill...*and save her*.

Coulter lifted his hand and his man moved in to press the muzzle of his gun at Thomas's head. "Now."

There was nothing I could do.

No words to say.

No begging to be had.

Still, I had to know. "They aren't going to Hale, are they?"

That same ugly fucking smirk found me now. "Now he's starting to catch on."

No Hale.

No black site.

No Mel.

I closed my eyes as the loading dock swayed around me.

No Mel and now, no Helene.

"You need us," Kane croaked, pleading. "We're important to you or Hale or whoever is running The Order."

"You're mistaken." Coulter answered as the cold, hated edge of steel pressed against my skull. "You were important, but you're not anymore. We have everything we wanted."

I opened my eyes to find the desperate stares of my brothers. But it was the faint cloud of dust that demanded my last moments here on earth. Particles of dirt danced in the sun.

I'd failed her...

Again.

My knees trembled, then gave way. I threw out my hands as I hit the hard concrete, and my brothers and Walker followed, dropping beside me.

The booming of my heart muffled the steps of the guards.

Crack!

Walker slumped forward and hit the floor face-first beside me, blood spraying the concrete where he fell. I stared at the body of the man I'd known for the last ten years as that blood spread out.

He was the *only* man I trusted with my life *and with hers,* other than my brothers.

"It's done." Coulter said behind me as that gun pressed harder against my skull. "You're out. It was always going to be this way."

The dust.

That's all I stared at.

As I whispered. "I'm sorry..."

FORTY-ONE

Helene

NOOO!

I screamed the word, but the sound was muffled. Sweat and salt and savagery smashed my lips against my mouth as I was dragged from the loading dock and forced into the rear of the truck.

"Scream and I'll make this trip fucking hell for you." The guttural snarl came in my ear.

I bucked, fighting as he spun and dragged me all the way to the front of the cargo hold.

"All of you get in there." The commands were barked.

I thrashed, drove down my fists into his thighs, and tried to reach up to claw his face. But the hold over my mouth didn't move. Instead, it crushed against my face harder, covering my nose until I couldn't breathe.

RIVEN!

RIVVVEEEENNN!

The Daughters were pushed into the truck after me, filling the front as the doors to the loading dock opened and Kane, Thomas, and Walker stepped out.

"So close, right?" Coulter's guard snarled in my ear.

I screamed, but the sound was muffled under the truck's engine noise.

"That's the last of them." Someone called from outside.

"Wait!" The faint, familiar roar came as the doors swung closed. *"You're making a fucking mistake."*

I saw him then, hurling himself upwards from the side of the loading dock to stumble toward the others.

Desperation roared at the sight of him. I lunged forward, kicking and bucking, screaming his name. But the guard's hold was like a steel band wrapped around my face and my body, smothering my howls and binding me against him.

Kane and Thomas rushed toward the edge of the dock, searching the faces of the Daughters in the truck for mine. But they couldn't see me. They couldn't...see...*me.*

Darkness descended, cleaving across the heads of the Daughters in front of me until there was nothing but blackness, and the truck's doors locked with a *thud.*

"No!" I bucked, dislodging his hand from my nose. *"No!"*

"You think you have it bad now?" The bastard grunted in my ear. "Just you fucking wait."

The truck lurched forward. I stumbled with the movement, trying to keep my balance.

"Watch this." The guard shoved me forward, barging me through the others as the truck picked up pace.

I stumbled forward then sideways, careening into the others until I slammed against the rear door of the truck. Through the vented metal slats, I caught glimpses of the carnage unfolding.

Most of our guards were dead.

Riven lifted his gaze as a gun was pressed against his head.

That emptiness found me now as it had last night.

It wasn't real. None of this...*was...real.*

I waited for the blinding bright light inside my head to find me now as it had last night as I watched Riven fall to his knees.

"You think you've had the worst of us?" Those cold, sickening words breathed into my ear. "It's only just started. Harmon doesn't care if your mind's shattered. Lots of men like to hold women like you down. Men like me."

He thrust his hardening cock against me, punching my hips against the hated steel door. The bite of agony came, but I didn't care. All I saw was the loading dock growing further away.

Bang.

I flinched, almost hearing the sound as Walker slumped forward to the ground next to Riven.

There was no escaping this.

Not anymore.

Maybe there never had been?

My body shuddered as that hollow emptiness grew. Fate whispered in my ear, telling me all the sickening things he was going to do to me.

I closed my eyes.

Closed my heart.

Closed *everything*.

The truck swayed, throwing all of us sideways as we turned hard. Tires squealed and as I shoved against the door, finding my feet, I caught sight of the towering fence line of The Order.

We were out.

We were out. I clenched my fists and swallowed the scream in the back of my throat. We were out and all I wanted was to be back there. The last vision of Riven burned inside my mind. *Did I really want* to watch him as the gun kicked in Coulter's hand and his life was over?

A cry tore free as the fence line blurred amongst the crowded forest, then faded away. I stared as The Order slipped from view until there was nothing but the road stretching out behind us and the forest at our side.

The panicked cries of the other Daughters pushed in.

"Shut the fuck up." Another guard grunted and slowly I became aware there was more than one.

Three of them stood hidden in the shadows. Three wolves amongst a flock of sheep.

And I was the most vulnerable one of them all.

I lifted my gaze to the slanted metal slats, staring at the road.

There had never been any Hale.

Never any black site.

Never any revenge or sister to save.

My shoulders curled as agony throbbed, stabbing me from the inside.

Viv...

Ryth.

A quake tore free.

Oh, Ryth.

My sisters would never know what had happened to me. There'd be no body to find, no Priest to torture. There'd be nothing but the fading memory of a sister they'd never known.

You weren't there!

Vivienne's screams haunted me as the truck rolled and bounced, the engine gunning as we raced toward a brand new hell. It felt like it now. Heat radiated from the metal of the truck. Beads of sweat gathered across my brow. My breaths turned to panic.

Riven.

Kane...

Thomas.

They would be dead by now. All because of me. *I should never have stepped in front of his car. Never followed them. Never met with The Teacher, never watched London almost kill the Priest.*

Then maybe none of us would be here.

A faint dark blur caught my focus as the truck raced to its destination. The longer I stared, the sharper the blurs became. It was two vehicles, hauling ass toward us, a tan Humvee and some kind of black four-wheel drive behind it.

Sunlight glinted off the Humvee's windshield, the reflected light finding me through the slats of the door as it hurtled closer and closer...and closer.

"What the fuck?" The guard behind me muttered.

The faint sound of a roaring engine followed. The vehicles were getting closer now, so close I could see a hulking shape behind the wheel.

VRROOOM...

As the Humvee swung into the lane beside us, the top of it opened up. A man rose, dragging a massive gun with him.

BOOM!

BOOM.

BOOMBOOMBOOM!

I jumped at the deafening gunshots. Bullets pierced the side of the truck, spearing blinding light inside to fall across the faces of the terrified Daughters.

Only .50 cal bullets did that. The words raced through my head. These weren't just any guns...nor were they just any men. They moved like...*soldiers.*

BOOM!

The truck swerved violently, throwing me to the side. I slammed against something before I was thrown backwards. Tires squealed. The crack of gunshots rang all around us.

"*FUCK!*" A guard amongst us roared. "*Who the fuck ARE they?*"

I couldn't see them. I couldn't see anything at all. I grabbed the Daughter in front of me and held on.

The truck swerved once more, only this time even harder, bouncing us before I felt the tires lift from the road. But then we were slowing...and slowing...and slowing until the squeal of brakes sounded and we came to a jarring stop.

There was nothing for a second.

No sound.

No breaths, just an agonizing silence.

"Get read—" One guard started as the rear door of the truck flew open.

Daughters screamed. I screamed with them, throwing my hands over my head as shadows appeared.

Crack.

Crack.

CRACK!

I jumped with each sound. The piercing wails filled my ears.

Until there was that emptiness, that crushing heaviness of *nothing.*

"Get them out." A deep rumble came from somewhere.

I dared to lift my gaze.

"You're safe now." Another murmured as he helped one of the Daughters to stand. "You're safe."

Safe.

What did that word even mean anymore?

I scanned the towering men who stood inside the rear of the truck, unable to see their faces...until I realized why.

They wore masks.

Every single one of them.

My gaze went to the one who didn't move. To the one I was sure gave the commands and as two more of his men moved in, pulling the women all around me to their feet, he fixed those unflinching eyes on me.

The guard who held me prisoner moaned and turned his head. My eyes widened and my body froze. The soldiers snapped to attention, one leveling his gun at this guard's head.

"No." The leader murmured, watching my every reaction. "We take him with us."

They moved instantly, wrenching his gun away, and dragged him forward. I couldn't help but stare as he was shoved from the end of the truck and onto the hard pavement.

Still, the soldiers gently lifted more of us to our feet and helped us out, until one reached for my hand.

"No." The commander ordered. "She's with me."

He was a mountain cramped inside the metal box of the truck. A man who seemed to suck all the air from my lungs as he stepped closer. I stared up at him, desperately trying to map the face behind the mask. All I saw was violence. All I saw was rage...and a flicker of something deeper...something that seemed like *hunger*.

He held his massive .50 cal rifle toward the roof and reached out with his other hand for mine.

The gloves he wore were dirty and worn. Thick fingers waited.

"Who the fuck are you?" I whispered and slowly met his gaze.

Sparks detonated in his eyes as he answered. "My brothers call me Hunter...I guess you can too."

Preorder Captured here

She was a liar. A deceiver. A seductress.

And now Helene King is a Daughter of the Order.

Under the guise she was headed for the place where Halestrom Hale held our sister she is forced into a truck.

Only that wasn't where she was headed.

A new breed of evil rose. One that told us exactly what Hell waited for her.

With the cold, hard bite of steel at my head, my last hope lays in the only man who can help us now.

A loner.

A Commander.

The one we call The Hunter.

He is a ghost. A shadow. A trained, predatory killer with a team of ruthless men at his back.

Violence is all he knows.

I only hope his allegiance of blood is strong enough.

When he saves Helene and the other Daughters, he keeps her for himself.

He heals her. Protects her...

Even from us.

As my brothers and I race to find her, a new alliance forced upon us.

One we never imagined in a million years.

Tobias, Caleb and Nick Banks demand to join forces, alongside the merciless London St James and the killers he calls Sons.

Together we hunt.

We destroy.

And try to survive long enough to uncover the truth.

www.ingramcontent.com/pod-product-compliance
Lightning Source LLC
Chambersburg PA
CBHW050958180726
48291CB00006B/1877